Finding

Sue,
Home is in your
heart!
Love,
Nikki A
James

Finding Home

Home Duet #2

By Nikki A Lamers

Also by Nikki A Lamers

The Unforgettable Series

The Unforgettable Summer (#1)
Unforgettable Nights (#2)
Unforgettable Dreams (#3)
Unforgettable Memories (#4)
The Unforgettable One (#5)

Home Duet

Dreams Lost and Found (#1)

Frey Dreams an imprint of Nikki A Lamers

ISBN (paperback) 978-1-951185-01-5
ISBN (ebook) 978-1-951185-00-8

Table of Contents

Table of Contents

Chapter 1

Samantha

I place my hands flat against my belly and smooth out my faux cashmere, cream, short sleeve sweater for the tenth time, in just as many minutes. I then begin fidgeting anxiously with my peach skirt, wondering again if it's too short. I just can't sit still. My breathing picks up its pace as Brady parks his truck at the curb in front of the large, white, Victorian house. I gulp down the lump in my throat as I assess the large pillars and windows, which appear even more intimidating than the last time I was here. I glance over at the long driveway, noticing both the black Escalade and the black BMW X5 are parked in front of the garage, causing me to inhale a shaky breath. "Does that mean everyone's here?" I rasp nervously. There's still time to turn around and go home.

"Samantha," Brady calls calmly. He reaches towards me and tucks my long brown curls behind my ear. His fingers gently graze my neck and jaw. He guides my eyes to his, helping to calm the storm brewing inside me. He grips the back of my neck, giving it a light squeeze. I take a deep breath and slowly begin to relax, locked in his gaze. His blue eyes are brighter than ever with his pale blue button-down dress shirt, causing my insides to flutter for a different reason. He quietly reminds me, "Don't worry about Jackie." I flinch at the mention of her name. "If she is home, remember I'm here for *you*. Concentrate on why you're here."

I grimace, Jackie now at the center of my thoughts, the last place I ever want her to be. This is hard enough without adding her to the mix. I'm here to meet the woman who would've helped raise me if my dad had kept me instead of giving me up for adoption. His daughter, Jackie, is my half-sister and she hates me. She hates me because I'm dating her ex-boyfriend, whom she doesn't want to let go. It doesn't matter to her that they broke up over four years ago. I'll probably make everything worse with her when I walk in there with Brady, if that's even possible. I want him with me for support, though. I felt the need to meet my father by myself, but I don't have to do this alone and I don't want to. "Are you ready?" he questions gently.

I shake my head vehemently and barely squeak, "No."

His mouth curls up in a small smile, the deep dimple in his left cheek making itself known, causing my insides to flutter wildly. I sigh heavily and fall into his chest, bumping into the armrest between us. He wraps his arms around me and presses his face into my hair, inhaling deeply. "I'll stay right here all night if that's what you want to do," he concedes.

"Okay," I agree. He chuckles in response shaking us both. I groan in annoyance and lift my head, giving him a light shove. "Fine," I grumble. "Let's get this over with."

Brady reaches for my hands and holds them between us in his large ones. He wipes the small smile off his face and stares intently into my eyes. "You'll be fine. She's going to love you," he insists.

"I don't even know if I want her to love me," I whisper my admission.

He softly kisses my forehead and leans back to catch my gaze again. "If at any point you want to leave, we leave. Okay?" he questions. I nod my head in agreement, gulping over the lump in my throat. A small smile touches his lips and he tells me for the fourth time, "You are absolutely beautiful."

I smirk, "You're just trying to get me into bed."

He huffs a laugh, "I'm hoping." I giggle in response and begin pulling away. He grips my hands tighter and gives me a swift tug back into him. He covers my mouth with his and I immediately melt into him with a gasp. He releases my hands, but I leave them planted on his chest as his mouth moves smoothly over mine, setting my whole body on fire. His hands lightly trail up my arms, over my shoulders and up my neck, until he cradles my face in his hands. I moan into his kiss and his tongue slips in, quickly tangling with mine. I try to push into him, wanting more of his minty taste, but he holds me still. He backs away with a strangled groan, gasping for breath. "If we don't go now, I'm not going to be able to walk in there with you," he informs me, gesturing down to his lap with his eyes.

My head falls back in laughter, "You started it." He shrugs, making me laugh louder. "Okay, Brady. I guess we can go in now. Your windows are getting a little bit foggy," I smirk.

He shakes his head, smiling wide. He leans forward and places a soft, chaste kiss on my slightly swollen lips. He exhales harshly and jumps out of his truck. He jogs around the front to my door, quickly pulling it open. He wraps his arm around my waist and pulls me out before I have a chance to move, gently setting me on the ground. He puts his hands up in mock surrender, "I know, I know, you can do it yourself." He grins, "I just like my hands on you."

I shake my head, unsuccessfully trying to hide my smile. I open my mouth to argue anyway, when out of the corner of my eye, I notice the outside lights flicker on by the house. My smile drops, along with my stomach. I take a shaky breath in, hoping to calm my erratically beating heart and the churning in my stomach. "I can do this," I murmur.

Brady slips his hand into mine and gives it a light squeeze in encouragement, before we turn towards the house together. Every step I take feels heavier and I begin to physically struggle to lift my feet. At the same time, I feel as if I'm watching everything from close by. This can't be happening to me. This feels too surreal. The warmth of Brady's hand seems to be the only thing grounding me at the moment. I remind myself that I'm here by choice. I want to be here…I think. I push my shoulders back and bite my lip in determination before I reach up and ring the doorbell.

The door swings open almost instantly. Lincoln stands in the doorway smiling down at me, with the same caramel eyes as mine. He's wearing khaki pants, similar to Brady's. His short sleeve black polo shirt has the top button open. I glance down nervously and notice his bare feet sticking out from under the hem of his pants, making me smile to myself. "Samantha, I'm so glad you're here," he greets me. He lifts his arm as if to hug me and then extends it as if to shake my hand. He changes his mind again, obviously unsure of how to greet me. Instead, he runs his hand softly over his perfectly styled dark brown hair, greying at the temples. Then he turns towards Brady and holds out his hand for him to shake, "Good to see you, Brady."

"You too, Mr. Scott. Thank you for inviting me to join you," Brady replies as he shakes his hand firmly.

"Thank you for having us," I'm finally able to blurt out. I feel myself drifting closer to Brady, craving the safety of his arms.

Lincoln grins and holds the door open for us to enter. A beautiful woman with long, blonde hair and light blue eyes, strides elegantly up to us, a welcoming smile in place. She has high cheekbones and a petite nose that seems to fit her perfectly. She's a few inches taller than me, I assume about 5'8 and very thin, with subtle curves that remind me of Jackie. "You must be Samantha," she beams genuinely. She holds her arms out and steps towards me, hugging me awkwardly.

I'm not quite sure what to do, so I pat her on the back with my free hand, still holding Brady's hand. I'm not ready to let go of him quite yet. "Um, yeah, Hi," I mumble.

She lets go of me and takes a step back as my arm drops quickly to my side. She turns and wraps her arms around Brady. He returns her hug with his free hand, thankfully leaving the other as my anchor. "It's so good to see you Brady! We've missed you around here," she grins.

I grimace and my stomach flips at the reminder. I attempt to pull my hand away from him, but he grips my hand tighter, refusing to let me go. He steps back, mumbling, "It's good to see you too." I feel his stare burning a hole in the side of my head and I meet his worried gaze. I take a deep breath and offer him a shaky smile. He tugs me even closer and drapes his arm over my shoulders. He declares, "I wanted to be here for Sam."

The tension slowly drains away from my body and I grin appreciatively up at him. "Well, I'm glad you're here," she responds quietly. She turns away from us and suggests, "Why don't you all go sit down in the dining room while I finish up dinner."

"Thanks Ginny," Lincoln smiles at her retreating form. He gestures towards the back of the house and Brady's hand slides from my shoulders to the small of my back, guiding me in that direction. At the back of the house, there's an arched doorway on my right leading into a large modern, black, white and silver kitchen. I notice movement and my stomach drops like lead. I quickly turn in the other direction with Brady's gentle nudge.

We walk under a matching arched doorway into a large dining room. To our right, glass French doors look out into the expansive backyard. I let my eyes skim over the darkening outside and notice a smaller version of the house and what appears to be a pool, still covered for the winter. My eyes quickly circle the room. In the middle sits an oval mahogany dining room table with two thick, clawed, triangular feet on each end. Six matching chairs sit around it, but the seam through the middle of the table suggests it may expand to fit more. I walk around to the other side of the table, feeling an almost desperate need to see anyone before they enter the room. Brady pulls my chair out and helps me slide in before dropping down in the seat to my right. I clamp my fingers tightly together in my lap and begin nervously running one thumb over the other. Brady reaches over with his left hand, his fingers sliding over the skin just above my knee leaving goose bumps. He continues to slide his hand up until he finds my clasped hands and covers them with his large one. "You have a very nice home," I declare, remembering my manners.

Lincoln grins at me as he sits down at the end of the table next to me, "Thank you." He takes a deep breath and informs me, "Ginny did most of the decorating." With this new information, I take in more of my surroundings. Behind Lincoln sits an old mahogany hutch with cabinets on the bottom and open shelves on the top. On the shelves lay various statues of hand painted people, as well as several picture frames. I quickly slide my gaze over them and notice most are of Frankie and Jackie. My heart unexpectedly stutters at the family picture in the middle. I quickly tear my eyes away as my heart nearly pounds out of my chest. I bite my lower lip, confused as to why I suddenly have such a strong feeling of loss when I have a family. I flip my hand over and tightly grip Brady's, my fingernails digging in as the pain of losing my mom and dad takes hold of my heart.

"Sam?" Brady questions. I look up into his pale blue eyes, his eyebrows drawn together in concern.

"The family picture over there made me think about my mom and dad," I whisper my explanation, blinking back tears. "I'm okay," I insist.

He gives a slight nod of his head in understanding and offers me a comforting smile, showing off his dimple. I take a deep breath and smile back at him in response. I turn towards Lincoln and blush, realizing he's watching me closely. He shakes his head, "I'm sorry Samantha. It's unreal to have you sitting here in my home. I can't help but watch you and take it all in."

I blush a deeper shade of red, not sure how to respond. Brady's hand gives mine another encouraging squeeze, just before he changes the subject, realizing I need a minute. "So where are Frankie and Jackie tonight?" he asks.

Lincoln fidgets anxiously as he answers, "Well, we thought it would be better if they weren't around tonight. We want Samantha to feel comfortable. We don't want to ambush her with a lot at once. So Frankie is sleeping over at a friend's house and Jackie," he hesitates.

My whole body stiffens at the sight of Jackie approaching. Her long blonde hair falls loosely over her shoulders as she rounds the corner. She's wearing a short black miniskirt with tall black leather boots and a cherry red V-neck sweater, quite possibly without a bra, by the looks of things. "Bragging about me already Daddy?" Jackie teases, as she floats into the room. Lincoln's shoulders tense as he turns towards his daughter, giving her a look of warning. She giggles and wraps her arms around his neck, her sweater hanging loosely. I grimace, noticing Brady could see down her shirt if he wanted to. I chance a glance at him and feel slightly relieved to find his eyes on me. I glance back over to Jackie, just as she gives her dad a kiss on the cheek and I watch the tension leave his body.

She suddenly bounces up, as if she just noticed Brady. With her eyes focused on him she happily squeals, "Brady!" She rounds the table and throws her arms around his neck. He has to turn his back to me to greet her, so she doesn't slam into his side. "How are you? What are you doing here?" she innocently inquires.

I tug my hand free of his. I watch red slowly creep up his neck and into his face, although I'm honestly not sure if it's in anger or embarrassment. "Hi, Jackie," he grumbles. He grips her waist firmly and sets her back a step. He clears his throat and informs her, "I'm here with Sam."

She grimaces before pasting on a fake smile. She appears to take a deep breath before she looks at me. "Hello Samantha," she says, speaking through her teeth, with forced politeness.

I give her a fake smile in return. She moves slowly, dragging her hand lightly over Brady's arm as she goes. "Daddy, I'm headed to Melanie's for the night. I'll be back early. I don't want to miss the family weekend we have planned," she says pointedly. She spins on her heel and strides towards the door. "I'll see you later Brady," she calls over her shoulder. I can't help but watch as she struts out the door, wiggling her ass with every step.

Lincoln clears his throat to get my attention, "What are your plans for Easter this weekend Samantha?"

I blush and glance over at Brady. "I'm not exactly sure," I answer, uncomfortably.

Brady clears his throat and speaks up. "Actually, Sam and I have plans. My parents and sister will be at the restaurant working, so I told Sam we could do that, or something else if she'd like."

"Oh, that's good, that's good," he murmurs awkwardly.

The tension in the air feels thick, making it hard to stay calm. I look around, searching for something to say, when Ginny walks into the room with a huge white platter filled with grilled citrus and basil chicken. She sets it down in the middle of the table and smiles over at me. "Would you mind helping me bring the rest of the food to the table?" she requests.

"Of course," I reply. I push my chair back, thankful for the small reprieve.

"I can help too," Brady offers.

He moves to stand, but she waves him off. "That's okay, we got it this time," she grins.

I shrug towards him and follow her into the kitchen. She turns and faces me before I have a chance to reach for anything. "Samantha, I want you to know you're welcome here any time."

I nod and smile politely, "Thank you."

She pinches her lips together and takes a step towards me, looking unsure of herself. She meets my eyes and informs me, "I realize this isn't easy for you, or for any of us really. I need you to know, we thought we were doing the right thing for you at the time."

I swallow the growing lump in my throat and nod my head stiffly, not really wanting to have this conversation right now, or maybe ever. "I know," I rasp, "Lincoln told me. I love my parents more than anything," I add.

She nods her head slowly, offering me a sad smile. "I'm really sorry about your mom and dad," she tells me sincerely.

"Thank you," I choke out the words. I tear my eyes from her and stare at the food. I fight the ache inside my chest, struggling to keep the tears at bay.

She clears her throat and walks over to the serving dishes. She hands me a bowl of mashed potatoes and salad. "Thank you," she says softly. I begin walking towards the dining room when she stops me, "Samantha?"

I peak at her over my shoulder and she smiles encouragingly at me. "I'm really glad you're here," she informs me honestly.

I take a deep breath and nod my head before turning back towards the dining room. I set the dishes on the table and sit back down next to Brady. I reach for his hand, ignoring his conversation with Lincoln about baseball and focus on getting my body to relax instead. Ginny sets down a dish of green beans and another filled with rolls on the table. Then she takes the seat opposite Lincoln and at Brady's side. I watch as she quietly says a dinner prayer before her eyes rise. She reaches for the bowl in front of her. She serves herself before handing it to Brady. I reach for the potatoes in front of me and do the same. "So Samantha," Ginny begins, "I heard you grew up in Illinois. How do you like it here in Wisconsin so far?"

I glance at Brady who focuses his attention on me. I smile gratefully up at him. I exhale slowly and turn back towards her to reply, "I like it. Everyone has been really nice and welcoming so far." I smirk, thinking of Jackie and add, "Well, mostly."

"That's good," she grins. "We have some close friends down in the Chicago area and go down to visit them about once a year in the summer," she informs me. "We love the area!"

"Really?" I question, wondering if I'd ever run into them without realizing it. Then again, that would be like looking for a needle in a barn full of haystacks.

"I don't know why I didn't even think about that," Lincoln murmurs.

Ginny laughs and comments, "Probably because all you and Ken do is hit the baseball games, especially if the Brewers are playing any of the Chicago teams."

He shrugs and grins, "Of course!"

She laughs and I can't help but giggle along with them, feeling a little more relaxed, listening to their light banter. I slide my hand from Brady's and reach for my fork, finally calm enough to eat. "So do you have a favorite food or a favorite meal?" Ginny asks, focusing on me.

I nod my head as I chew the bite of chicken nearly melting in my mouth. I respond without answering her question, "This chicken is delicious!" Ginny smiles appreciatively over at me. I realize, with her easy-going manner and Jackie gone, I finally feel like I'm able to relax and enjoy the evening. I still don't know what I want from all of this, but at least she seems to be accepting me. Maybe everything will be okay, as long as we don't talk too much about their daughter. I grimace and refocus my attention on getting to know Lincoln and Ginny.

Chapter 2

"Thank you again for having us," I tell them sincerely. "Goodbye," I repeat, giving a small wave of my hand. I spin on my heel and walk towards Brady's truck. Brady's hand moves to the small of my back, assisting with the quick release of tension in my body. Every step away from the house, I feel more at ease. He pulls my door open and places his hands on my sides. This time I don't argue as he lifts me into his truck. My whole body relaxes into the soft comfort of the black leather seat as I breathe a heavy sigh of relief.

Brady strides around the front of the truck and slips behind the wheel, pulling his door closed behind him. He turns towards me with a cocky grin, "Feeling better?" My only answer is a quiet chuckle. He leans over and softly pecks the corner of my mouth, then leans back, still smiling. He turns towards the wheel and starts the car, shifting his focus to the road in front of him before he pulls away from the curb. "That wasn't so bad, was it?" he asks curiously.

I shake my head and agree, "Not too bad." I grimace, "Although I could've done without seeing Jackie."

I watch his Adam's apple bob up and down as he gulps, "Yeah, I'm sorry you had to deal with her shit."

I shrug, "When I saw her, I kind of expected it."

"That doesn't make it easy or okay," he insists. He reaches across the truck and places his hand just above my knee and gives it an encouraging squeeze. My body heats with his soft touch on my bare skin and I can't do anything but nod in agreement. "So what do you think of them?" he asks.

I shrug, not really knowing how to answer that yet. After a few minutes of quiet, I finally settle for, "They seem nice." His fingers lightly trace a figure eight on my skin over and over again, quickening my heartbeat. Brady parks behind our building and rapidly jumps out of his truck. I move to slip out as well, but I'm caught in Brady's arms before I hit the ground.

He smirks, "Aw, I like helping you in and out of my truck. You should know that by now."

I laugh and playfully push him away from me. He grasps my hand, entwining our fingers together as we walk towards our building in silence. I can feel his eyes on me as we ride the elevator up to our floor, but I can't do anything but stare blankly at the doors waiting to get out of this steel box, as I go over every minute from tonight in my head. I quietly walk to the front door of my apartment, swiftly unlocking the door and stepping inside. I slip off my shoes with a sigh as I glance around the quiet space. I turn around to find Brady standing in the doorway with his hands above his head, grasping the doorframe above him, causing his biceps to bulge. He leans in towards me with a question in his eyes. I feel my whole body heat with just one glance from him. I open my mouth to speak, but snap it closed and softly clear my throat before I try again. "Do you want to come in, Brady?"

He pauses for a moment, staring quizzically at me before he gives me a quick nod in acceptance. He drops his arms and steps inside, shutting the door softly behind him. He closes the distance between us and holds my gaze before asking, "Are you alright?"

I chuckle humorlessly and say, "That's the question of the year." He just arches his eyebrows in response and waits for an answer. I take a deep breath and begin talking as I exhale. "It's just a lot to process, I guess. The whole thing is kind of overwhelming," I admit.

"Just kind of?" he smirks. I giggle and he continues, "I can only imagine, but I'm here if you want to talk about it."

I purse my lips, "Actually would you mind if we didn't talk about it right now? I don't want to even think about it for a little while. Maybe we could do something else to keep my mind occupied?"

He grins as he slips his hands onto my waist. "What did you have in mind?" he asks, his voice husky.

My tongue slips out to moisten my lips. I gently place my hands on his chest and slowly slide them up, over his shoulders and clasp my hands around his neck. I meet his eyes and shrug, "Maybe..." I trail off. I push up on my toes and brush my lips along the scruff on his jawline. I end with a light lick and soft kiss just under his ear, causing him to groan softly. "A movie?" I tease, knowing it's the last thing I want right now. His throaty chuckle sends chills down my spine. I slowly move my lips to the base of his throat. I again lightly lick him and follow it with a kiss before suggesting, "Or maybe a little bit of this?"

"Now that can be arranged," he grumbles. His lips possessively crash down on mine in a searing kiss, taking my breath away. Just as my tongue slips out, he suddenly pushes back breathless, his forehead resting on mine. "Where's Cory?" he asks.

"She's working, but not for much longer," I answer. He slides his arms down, just underneath my butt and lifts me into his arms. I shriek in surprise. "Brady!" I laugh.

He grins, "Wrap your legs around me. We're going to your room."

"Demanding aren't we?" I tease, just before doing exactly as he asked.

He chuckles, "It's better than having Cory walk in on me doing things to your body that I'm sure you definitely don't want her to see!"

He walks me backwards, into my room and then kicks the door shut with his foot. He walks around to the side of my bed and kisses me as he sits me down on the side of the bed. He tugs at the back of my knees, encouraging me to disengage from around his back. I slowly release my legs from the tight grip around his body and let them fall to the bed. He tears his lips from mine and I whine in protest, making his head drop back in laughter. My heart skips a beat at the beautiful sight. He kicks his shoes off and puts one hand on each side of me on the bed. He leans his forehead against mine, but keeps his lips just out of reach of mine, yet close enough to feel the heat of his breath. He slowly lowers me to the bed and covers his body with mine. I groan in satisfaction as our mouths meet. I slip my hands into his hair and pull him closer, turning my head to deepen our heated kiss. I push my tongue inside, searching for his. We lick and twist our tongues together as we let them fight for dominance. He easily wins me over and my head falls all the way back to the bed, as I gasp for a breath. His mouth changes direction, moving to my jaw, to behind my ear and then trailing down my neck. "Brady," I whimper.

"I love kissing you, Samantha," he whispers. He continues to kiss me, moving across my neck, leaving goose bumps in his wake. I slide my hands down his back and tug at his shirt, making him chuckle. He leans away from me enough to remind me, this particular shirt won't work like that. I grimace at the buttons, causing him to laugh louder. He presses his lips firmly to mine, still smiling. "In a minute," he pleads cradling my face with his left hand.

He slides his other hand down to my side and slips his fingers underneath the hem of my sweater. His fingertips skim across my skin from my hip to my belly button and back again. He lightly presses his lips to mine and traces my mouth with his tongue before slipping inside. He kisses me in a slow sensuous rhythm and I groan into his mouth, wanting more. His hand slides down over my hip and back up between my legs, causing a breathy moan to escape through my lips and break our kiss. I tug at his shirt again, wanting to touch his skin. He ignores me and continues his trail up my inner thigh. He lightly sweeps his fingers over my underwear, making me gasp, "Brady."

His breath comes in quick bursts and he rasps, "I like you in this skirt." I laugh breathily and he grins down at me, heating me even more. His hand continues to tease near my thigh, lightly running over my core, while he pushes my sweater up and presses soft kisses along my belly, working his way up. When he reaches my breasts, he pulls my sweater over my head before I have a chance to react, my hands falling back to his head. With one hand he unhooks the front clasp of my bra and then runs his hand gently over my breast, followed by his lips. His tongue flicks out and licks my nipple, before swirling around it. He finally takes it into his mouth and sucks it tenderly. I bite my bottom lip, attempting to hold back my appreciative moans as I arch into him. He licks his way to the other side and repeats the wonderful torture.

He starts to move down my body and I reach for his shirt again. I'm only able to get the top button undone before his mouth easily finds my inner thigh. He pushes my skirt all the way to my waist and kisses me higher. I helplessly fall back on the bed with a high-pitched gasp. He twists his fingers in the sides of my matching peach underwear. He pauses and looks up at me for consent before he tugs them all the way down my legs. He kneels on the floor and tugs me to the edge of the bed, before he licks the seam of my folds. I struggle to catch my breath as he does it again, my body already so close to the edge. Both of his strong hands grip my thighs tightly, as his thumbs gently skim back and forth, while he licks me. He covers me with his mouth and swirls his tongue around my clit, making me whimper. I curl my fingers into his hair and hold on. He sucks gently and my body arches into him. I feel my body already beginning to pulse as I desperately try to catch my breath. His fingers tighten, holding me where he wants me. My orgasm slows and my body finally collapses, completely spent. I look down at him and whisper his name in awe, "Brady."

He wipes his mouth and grins in satisfaction, "You needed that."

I laugh, "I still want your shirt off." He chuckles and starts unbuttoning his shirt before slipping it off. "The t-shirt too," I grin. He reaches down and pulls it off with one hand. My eyes widen at the man in front of me. I know I've seen it before, but I could get used to the sight of him very easily. His toned abs form a slight V down towards his pants. Looking at him causes my heart to pound and my whole body to charge with excitement. I watch as he unzips his khakis and steps out of them, before crawling over me in his black boxer briefs. He cups my cheek and caresses back and forth with his thumb as he stares into my eyes. "What?" I ask, suddenly self-conscious.

The corners of his lips tug upwards, showing off his dimple and making me melt inside. "I can't really describe what's going on in my head right now, but let's just say, I feel very lucky." I blush and avert my eyes down towards his chest. He coaxes me to meet his eyes again and informs me, "It's really good to see you relax. It feels like it's been quite a while since I saw you like this."

"I haven't known you that long," I mumble.

His jaw tightens and his Adam's apple bobs up and down as he gulps. "You know what I mean." I rest my head on his chest. He sighs and gives me a light squeeze. "It feels like I've known you for a lot longer than I have. I almost don't remember what my life was like before you were here and I don't want to."

My heart skips a beat. I press my lips to his chest, not ready to look at him. I don't want to think about the past or the future right now. I just want to feel. I slide my hands down his stomach and rub him over his underwear from base to tip. "Sam," he groans, " we don't have to do anything else. I just want to be near you and help you relax."

I ignore his comment and slip my hand underneath his Calvin Klein's. I rub him again with a little more pressure. "I want to Brady. I want you," I insist breathlessly as I continue to kiss his chest and neck, until I find my way back to his lips. I cover his mouth with my own, immediately forcing my tongue inside to explore. I arch my body up and against him as I kiss him with abandon. "Please, Brady," I ask again. I gasp for breath, nearly begging for him to let us continue. My fingers snag the sides of his underwear and I tug. He leans up to finish the job, kicking them the rest of the way to the floor.

He lies next to me, his fingers lightly trailing a path up to my breasts. I pull away and reach for a condom in my nightstand drawer. I straddle his legs and open the packet. "Are you going to let me do anything?" he teases. He takes it out of my hands and easily slips it on.

He leans up to kiss me and I gently push his shoulder back down on the bed. I break the kiss and lean back with a sassy grin, "Maybe."

He begins to chuckle, but stops abruptly as I lower myself onto him without warning. "Sam," he groans. I gasp as he fills me up, his fingers digging into my hips. I slowly begin moving up and down, my eyes closing as I get used to the feel of him, deeper with every little movement. I attempt to speed up the pace, wanting more. I need to reach the point where nothing matters and I don't have to think. He suddenly grabs me and flips me over onto my back. My eyes pop open, drawn to his intense blue ones. "Stay with me Samantha," he rasps desperately.

"I'm here," I whisper. I hold his gaze and wrap my legs around his back, knowing I'm already close. At this angle, he hits a spot deep inside me, causing a white heat to shoot through me as the release I'm searching for hits me hard. My body pulses around him, as I fight to keep my eyes on his, watching him fall over his own edge. He drops down on his side next to me. Then he rolls me towards him with his arm around my waist. I collapse on top of him and bury my face in his slick muscled chest, as we both catch our breath.

He presses his lips to my forehead and slips out from underneath me. He mumbles, "I'll be right back." He pushes up and ties off the condom before tossing it in the garbage. He then pulls his pants back on before opening my door. I roll onto my side and pull my comforter over me, just as he strides back in with a wet towel. He holds it up and walks towards me, but I quickly snatch it out of his hands and clean between my legs before tossing it towards my laundry basket.

I feel awkward and I'm not sure why. I curl up into a ball and avert his questioning gaze. He sighs and lifts my comforter, slipping in behind me and wrapping me up in his arms. I gulp over the lump in my throat. I concentrate on my breathing, trying to calm the tingling creeping up from my chest, as an attempt to hold back my tears. "Are you okay?" he asks. I nod and an unwanted tear slips out. "Are you sure? Cause it almost felt like I lost you there for a minute. Almost like you were using me for sex or something," he jokes, only half teasing. "And now you're pulling away?" he questions, hesitantly.

No longer able to hold back, my tears begin to flow freely at his words. "I'm sorry Brady," I whisper hoarsely. "I wasn't...I'm not," I hiccup a sob and shove my face into my pillow.

"Fuck," he mumbles and twists my body so I'm facing him. He releases a harsh breath as he pulls me into his chest. I let him wrap me in his arms and cry harder. He brushes my tears away, his jaw ticking with tension. "Sam, please talk to me," he begs.

I take a couple deep breaths to try to calm myself down. Then I repeat, "I'm sorry Brady." I feel him take his own deep breath, which makes me feel even worse. I gulp and attempt to speak over my growing tension. "I wasn't trying to…I was just trying to…it's just a lot and…" I stammer, struggling to explain my thoughts and feelings.

"Just take a deep breath for me and talk to me. That's all I'm asking," he insists.

I do as he says and try again, finally slowing myself way down. "Today was a lot. Everything has been a lot lately. I was just trying not to think about any of it. I wanted to be with you, but I guess," I grimace. "I wanted to forget everything for a moment and I thought I could do that with you," I explain. I shake my head in frustration, "but…" I trail off.

He sighs in defeat, "But you weren't completely with me. I had to pull you back," he grumbles. He hesitates and then he demands, "Listen to me for a minute." I nod my head in acknowledgement. "I understand needing a distraction. I'm more than happy to oblige with orgasms or anything else you want," he says with a slight smirk. "But I can't have it be when I'm inside you. I'll tell you again and again until you understand; you're not just any girl. I need to know, to see," he emphasizes, "that you're with me. Do you understand?" he asks anxiously. I nod my head as a few more tears slip out. "I need to hear you this time, Sam."

"I get it. That's what I want too. I didn't mean to, I'm sorry," I apologize again. He shakes his head as if to argue, but I stop him with my fingertips on his lips. "Please let me say I'm sorry. I didn't…when you insisted I look at you…" I gulp again, "I want that connection with you. You're not just a distraction to me. I promise."

"Okay," he concedes. He reaches for his undershirt and pulls it over my head with a grin, showing off his deep dimple. "I need you covered," he chuckles. "No distractions," he teases, as he readjusts me in his arms, my head falling lightly on his chest.

I giggle lightly, "Bad joke."

"Sorry," he apologizes with humor lacing his voice.

"Will you please stay tonight?" I ask, trying to keep the desperation out of my voice. He leans down and kisses me lightly on the lips and smiles tenderly in response. I relax into him and focus on the figure eight pattern he's tracing on my back, hoping to fall asleep easily.

Chapter 3

I take a deep breath and exhale slowly, attempting to tamp down my anxiety. "What am I so nervous about?" I grumble. I glance out the windshield of my car at Brady's family's restaurant. I've watched family after family walk in with little girls in pale pink, yellow and blue dresses and little boys dressed in mini suits or khaki pants with a button down. Every single one of the kids hold an Easter basket in their hand. Some kids skip giddily across the parking lot, only to have their enthusiasm held back by the protective hands of their mom or dad.

Brady left early this morning to help set up the breakfast buffet. I told him I wanted to meet him here, but now I'm wondering if that was the right decision. I bite my lower lip, second-guessing myself, pondering if I should've gone down to Uncle Tim's. Out of the corner of my eye, I notice an adorable little boy. He reminds me a little bit of Brady, his dark brown hair an adorable mess. I grin at the pale blue bowtie he's wearing and the huge smile lighting up his face, with matching dimples on each side. He tugs on his mom's hand, urging her forward. I chuckle at the sight. A strange feeling comes over me, as if I'm the one the little boy is tugging forward toward the building. I grip my keys and take a deep breath. I step out of my car before something else makes me change my mind. "Here it goes," I mumble under my breath.

I walk carefully across the gravel parking lot in my white strappy sandals with two-inch heels, which is more than I'm used to. I admire the spring decorations covering the sprawling porch as I approach. Hand-painted pots are placed on both the ground and on small tables near the handmade benches and Adirondack chairs. They're all filled with different color tulips including red, yellow, orange, purple and white. A large porcelain Easter bunny, holding a basket filled with wooden eggs, stands near the entrance. On the opposite side of the door sits a small pine tree decorated with wooden Easter Eggs. A wreath with the same wooden eggs hangs from the large Oak front door, standing ajar. The maître-d steps outside, holding the screen door open for me. He greets me, wearing a light tan suit, with a pastel green tie, "Good morning! Happy Easter!"

"Thank you, Lou," I smile at him appreciatively before stepping inside. "Happy Easter," I force out the holiday greeting. I quickly scan the crowded rooms looking for Brady and grimace when I come back empty. A waiter, coming from the bar, steps in front of me with a tray full of mimosas in champagne flutes, causing my mouth to water. I peer into the room to my left with the large round wooden tables, each currently covered with a different pastel colored tablecloth. The carved wooden chairs only accented with a mismatch of pastel colored cushions. A small hand-painted pot, filled with tulips, sits as the centerpiece on each table. A huge buffet is set up at the far end of the large room, making my stomach grumble, even without being able to see what it entails.

I reach for my phone to text Brady to ask him where I can find him. I find his name just as a tall, thin, redhead steps in front of me. She offers me a beautiful smile, "Happy Easter! Do you have a reservation?"

I shake my head and respond, "No, I'm just looking for someone."

"Could I help you?" she offers politely.

I shake my head, "No, thank you."

Just then, Brady steps up next to her. He places his hand on her forearm to get her attention, giving me a slight pang of jealousy. "I've got this one Ashley," he informs her.

She nods at him and gives him a flirtatious smile, but his eyes instantly focus on me. His eyes slowly trail down my body as I wait for him to speak. I bite my lip nervously, hoping he likes my pale yellow dress with spaghetti straps. It fits my curves on top, before flaring out at the bottom and resting lightly on my thighs. He finally meets my gaze and gives me a crooked grin, causing me to flush. "You look absolutely beautiful," he rasps.

I feel my body turn a deeper shade of red as I mumble, "Thank you."

He steps towards me and lightly brushes his lips over mine. My breath hitches with his touch. He pulls back and grins widely, his dimple on full display. He proudly takes my hand in his, helping the tiny bit of jealousy left to tumble away. "Follow me," he murmurs.

I do as he says, admiring his firm backside in his khaki pants. I raise my eyes to his broad shoulders, which appear huge in his pale pink button-down shirt, causing my lips to twitch. He pushes through a set of glass double doors and we step out onto a gray stone patio, empty except for a few overflowing black garbage bags tied off at the top. He suddenly stops and spins around, facing me. His hands find my waist as he backs me into a large white pillar. "I'm glad you're here," he whispers just before his mouth comes crashing down on mine. I gasp in surprise, but my body instantly relaxes into his kiss. I grasp his forearms and push towards him, slipping my tongue in to taste him. He pushes me back against the pillar with both his mouth and his body. Our lips move together in a perfect rhythm, teasing, tasting and wanting. A loud bang startles me away from him, making him chuckle. We both glance over to find his sister Becca, smirking at us. My whole body instantly heats with embarrassment. "You may think you're hidden, but not that well," she teases, my face flaming even hotter.

"Becca," Brady scolds, at the same time holding me in place.

She crosses her arms over her chest, "Figured it was better me than Mom. She's now on this side of the dining room." Brady shrugs like it's not a big deal either way. "Don't say I didn't warn you," she says nonchalantly. "It's good to see you, Samantha!" she grins, before she turns and walks back inside.

"We should go," I declare anxiously.

He gives me another crooked smile and my body heats for a completely different reason. He lightly brushes his lips over mine, before he pulls away, resting his forehead against mine. "You good?" he rasps.

"Hmm?" I murmur.

"I want to make sure we are on the same page at all times today," he declares. "Are you okay?" he repeats making my stomach flip from the sweet gesture.

I offer him a small, almost timid smile, "I really do appreciate that Brady, but I'm okay." His eyebrows rise with doubt and I put more effort into my smile. "I really am doing okay right now. I'm actually pretty hungry too," I inform him. I don't want to talk about my parents, or missing them, or even my birth father, or his family. I just want to try to enjoy the day. It's been a while since I enjoyed any holiday and talking about them right now will make it worse. It doesn't mean I'm not thinking about them, I almost always am.

Brady holds my gaze, trying to decide if I'm telling the truth. He eventually concedes and places another soft, chaste kiss to my lips. "I'm going to take your word for it. But I need you to tell me if anything changes."

"I will," I agree.

"You know, Sam, I know you said this is what you want to do, but if you want to change your mind at any time, I'm good with that," he insists.

I nod, "That's really sweet."

"It's the truth," he proclaims. My stomach picks that moment to speak up, rumbling loudly. Brady laughs, "Ok, ok, I get it. We need some food for my girl!" I blush and push away from the pillar. This time instead of stopping me, he snags my hand, as we stride towards the door. "After we eat, do you want to help hide the next batch of Easter eggs?" he questions, gesturing towards the large black garbage bags.

"That's what's in those?" I question surprised.

"Yeah, all stuffed and ready to go," he grins as we walk through the door. "The first round was at 9:30 and the next one isn't until noon, so we have some time," he informs me.

"Okay, that sounds like fun," I agree.

We walk across the room and right up to the buffet tables. He hands me a plate before grabbing one for himself. "Help yourself to anything you want," he instructs.

I do exactly that, piling my plate with a blueberry muffin, scrambled eggs, grilled asparagus, pancakes, sausage, bacon and fresh fruit before I decide I don't have any room left. "Where do we sit?" I turn and ask Brady.

He looks up from filling his own plate and chuckles at the sight of mine. "I really don't feed you enough do I?" he jokes.

I shake my head, "It's not your job to feed me."

He shrugs and nods with his head towards the back left corner. "There's a table at the back that we always keep reserved for family during these things so we can eat."

I walk towards the back corner with him right behind me until we find a table with a small reserved sign on it. I look at him for confirmation, only to watch him set his plate down. I do the same with my back to most of the room. He pulls my chair out for me and pushes me in before dropping down in the seat next to me. "Such a gentleman," I tease.

He smirks, "I can be, especially for you." I giggle before I quietly begin devouring the food in front of me.

It only feels like a few minutes later, when Brady is finishing his second plate and I'm so full I can't eat another bite. I groan, "I can't believe I ate that much."

"What about dessert?" I look at him like he's crazy, but he just laughs. "Maybe after the egg hunt," he suggests.

I shake my head and state, "I don't think I'll ever eat again."

He chuckles, "Yeah, it's so much better when someone else makes it for you right? Especially Marco, his cooking is fantastic," he raves.

"It sounds like you grew up eating more of his cooking than your parents," I grin.

He laughs, "I definitely did!" He leans forward, placing his elbows on the table and his eyes sparkling with mischief. "Do you want to go hide some eggs?" he asks.

I narrow my eyes, "Why does it sound like you have something else in mind?"

His whole face lights up when he answers, "Guess you'll have to come with me to find out." He stands and reaches for my hand to help me up. Just as I get to my feet, Brady's gaze settles just over my shoulder. "Hi Mom."

My body tenses slightly and I pull my hand back from his as I slowly turn around to face her. As she steps up to Brady and pushes up on her tiptoes, placing a kiss on his cheek, I can't help but admire her beauty. She's a few inches taller than me with smooth, dark blonde hair, curled out on the bottom near her shoulders. She's wearing a white dress with colorful tulips adorning the hem. She turns to greet me with warm hazel eyes and a welcoming smile. "Hi Samantha! It's so nice to see you again."

"You too," I force my reply. Brady's hands fall to my shoulders and he gives them a comforting squeeze. I breathe in slowly through my nose, trying to take a deep breath without her noticing. I can't help my anxiety though.

"Samantha," she begins, "I never had a chance to apologize for my behavior the first time I met you. I am sorry. I know it's no excuse, but I misunderstood the situation and I just wanted my son to find someone who would be good for him," she explains. She reaches and gives my hand a light squeeze in appreciation. "I'm really glad he found you."

I open my mouth to speak, but barely make a sound over the lump in my throat. I close my mouth and clear my throat before I try again. "Thank you," I rasp, taken aback.

Brady's dad suddenly steps in front of me, enveloping me in a quick hug. "Samantha, we're so glad you came today!" He steps back with a broad smile that looks identical to Brady's with just a few more lines. He pats his son's back and asks, "Are you two helping with the eggs?"

Brady and I both nod in agreement, but with a quick glance at him, I notice he's not smiling anymore. "We'll meet you outside," Brady informs them.

"Right behind you," his mom warns.

As soon as we're a few steps away from them I ask, "Is everything okay?"

He grimaces, "Yeah, I just want a few minutes with you alone before anyone else comes out there with us." I burst out laughing at his admission and he shrugs shamelessly.

We step outside with Becca and a few of the staff right behind us. Becca hands out maps to show where the property is broken into each age group. "That way you know where you can make the eggs more difficult to find," she informs me. I nod my head in understanding.

Brady picks up one of the black garbage bags and tosses it over his shoulder like Santa Clause. He slings his other arm around my neck and claims me. "You're with me."

"But I partnered her up with Glen," Becca whines. I sneak a glance at her teasing smile.

Brady immediately argues, "Not a chance!"

I hear laughter as we saunter away together. "So what's in the eggs anyway?" I ask curiously.

"Candy, quarters, tickets for a few big prizes," he lists.

Brady and I begin hiding the eggs all around. We start in the 2-4 year old section hiding them in plain site. When we only have a few eggs left I admit, "I've never done this before."

"Done what?" he questions.

"Hidden Easter eggs. It's fun," I smile.

He stops and stares at me with amazement, "Really?"

"Yeah, even when I didn't believe in the Easter Bunny anymore, my mom refused to give in. My dad and I thought my mom was a lot happier if I just pretended and searched for the eggs. So we decided we would do that for her." I smile at the memory. I look up to find Brady standing right in front of me. He cradles my face in his hands and lowers his head, gently kissing my lips. He pulls back and looks into my eyes, his own full of emotion. As my throat begins to clog I tear my gaze away. "Anyway," I trail off.

Brady entwines my fingers with his and we saunter towards the back patio hand in hand. "What took you guys so long?" Becca calls. Brady opens his mouth to respond, but she puts her hand up and she shakes her head vehemently, interrupting him. "Forget it! I don't want to know."

I open my mouth to defend myself, but Brady stops me with a kiss to my forehead. "Ignore her. She doesn't mean it. She's just trying to irritate me," he tells me.

I tilt my head to look up at him curiously. I can't really imagine what it would've been like to have a sibling. I wince and glance down towards my toes. I have two now. One that despises me and one I don't know at all.

Brady interrupts my thoughts, informing me, "I have to go help with traffic control. That basically means make sure big kids don't take eggs from the little kids," he smirks. "Wanna' come?" he asks.

"Um, I'll watch the beginning from here and then I think I'll run to the bathroom. Hopefully it will be empty by then," I say.

He puts two fingers underneath my chin and tilts my head up until I meet his eyes. After a moment he leans down and lightly presses a kiss to my lips. He leans back and nods his head, "Okay. Come find me when you're done."

I nod and wave before he turns and walks away. I'm not standing there long, when I suddenly hear a whistle, followed by utter chaos. Parents are pointing out eggs to the little kids, while a couple bigger kids practically bulldoze through the other screaming children to get to the eggs. As I watch the families, the smiling faces, the playfulness and even the crying children, an ache builds in my chest and my gut, reminding me again of what I lost. I take a deep breath and turn towards the back doors leading into the dining area. I have to get away for a moment and pull myself together.

I bolt towards the bathroom, but I slam into someone on the way. I gasp as I'm instantly covered with a wet, sticky Mimosa. I look up to meet laughing golden eyes and a satisfied smirk. "Oops," Jackie grins wickedly.

My body heats in both anger and embarrassment. My hands fist at my sides, trying to stop myself from screaming like one of the kids throwing a tantrum outside. "Samantha," a deep voice questions as he steps up next to Jackie, a hand on the small of her back. "What are you doing here?" my birth father, Lincoln, questions.

"I'm…" I rasp and trail off.

"Oh," he says, most likely recalling what my Easter plans were, without me saying any more.

"Are you here with your family like us?" Jackie questions cunningly. She glances back to the expansive table behind her, with places for so many more than just the four of them.

"Jacqueline," Lincoln reprimands.

"Yes, Daddy?" she questions innocently. He gives her a hard look of what looks to be a warning, but doesn't continue speaking.

"Would you like to join us?" Lincoln offers uncomfortably.

My face heats with embarrassment and I shake my head, "Um, no thank you. I was actually just leaving."

He looks at me with uncertainty, but responds, "Oh, okay. Happy Easter, Samantha."

I force a smile and spin on my heel, determined to find Brady and get out of here without losing it. "Happy Easter," I mumble over my shoulder.

"Daddy I'm going to go talk to Brady. He should be outside with the kids about now," she informs him.

I change direction again, this time towards the front door of the restaurant. I barely make it to my car before the tears begin to fall. "So much for having a good holiday," I mumble. I ignore the painful ache in the pit of my stomach and try to turn my focus to the short drive home.

Chapter 4

Brady

I bounce on my feet, impatiently. I glance back at the last few texts from Sam, wanting to get to her.

"I don't feel well. I'm going to go home. I'll see you later," she claims.

"I'll come with you," I offer immediately.

"No! Stay with your family. I'm just going to sleep for a little while," she tells me.

"Do you need anything?" I ask.

"Just sleep," she maintains.

"Are you sure that's it?" I ask, anxiously.

"I'm fine, Brady," she insists. I can almost hear the impatience in her voice when her texted reply comes through.

"You still didn't answer my question," I mutter under my breath. I grit my teeth in frustration. Of course I'm going to wonder what the hell just happened for her to do a complete 180. I thought she was doing okay. Did I just not read her right?

Two small, cold, hands, with the familiar scent of lavender lotion suddenly covers my eyes. The simple touch causes my body to freeze and my fists to clench. "Guess who?" Jackie purrs into my ear, dripping with sweetness.

I tense even more, knowing she must have something to do with Samantha's sudden disappearance. I take a step away, her hands running down my arms as they fall from my face. "What are you doing here Jackie?" I question, accusingly. Her family hasn't come here for Easter in a really long time.

She grimaces and crosses her arms over her chest. "That's not a very nice way to say Happy Easter," she complains.

I sigh, feeling slightly chastised and completely annoyed at the same time. "I'm sorry," I apologize and paste on a fake smile. "Happy Easter, Jackie." She grins, satisfied with my response. She throws her arms around me and my hands reflexively fall to her waist. After a brief moment, not wanting to appear rude, I gently push her away from me. "Now, what are you doing here?" I repeat.

She gestures behind her towards her family. "I'm here with my whole family for your delicious Holiday brunch," she announces proudly.

My thoughts again go to Sam. I have a strong feeling in my gut that all of them being here, had everything to do with her quick departure. "Did you happen to see Samantha?" I ask, anxiously.

She shakes her head, "No. Who is she here with?"

"Me," I mumble irritably. I spot my mom near the front entrance and glance back towards Jackie. "I'm sorry, but I have to go take care of something," I tell her. I slip past her and jog towards my mom, before Jackie has a chance to respond.

"Hey Mom. I need to take off. Are you guys good for the rest of the day?" I ask in a rush. I don't really care too much what her answer is, but she is my mother, so I ask anyway. I just need to get out of here, no matter what. Besides, I wasn't supposed to be working today anyway.

"Where's Samantha?" she asks, instead of answering.

"She wasn't feeling well. I want to go check on her," I inform her. There's no need to tell her I think it might be more.

She nods sympathetically, "Of course, go ahead. We'll be fine."

"Thanks Mom," I tell her appreciatively. I lean down and give her a quick hug and a kiss on the cheek. I run out the door and get in my truck before I even register her goodbye. I could tell there were a few moments when Sam was having a hard time today. I don't blame her. I just thought if I showed her I was there for her, it would be enough. I didn't plan on the Scott family showing up today, though. The only time I remember them ever coming to our Easter brunch was when I was dating Jackie back in high school. I have no idea why they were there today, but I'm almost positive they're the reason Sam took off without even coming to find me first.

I park my truck in the small gravel lot behind our apartment building and quickly make my way inside. I bypass the elevator and take the stairs two at a time. I stalk past my front door and immediately knock softly on hers. When she doesn't respond instantly, I knock harder, giving me the answer I'm looking for. "I'm coming," she snaps. I chuckle in relief as she groans heavily and trudges towards the door. She pulls the door slowly open and gasps in surprise the instant her red-rimmed eyes meet mine. "What are you doing here?" she questions in shock.

"Sure, I'd love to come in," I reply with a cocky grin. I step past her into her apartment and stride over to the couch, flopping down in the middle. Her eyes narrow and she crosses her arms over her chest, pushing her cleavage up in her already close-fitting, mint green tank top. I take a deep breath and bite my lip hard to keep myself from looking down. This isn't the time for a distraction.

She sighs, feigning annoyance and repeats, "What are you doing here Brady?"

I tilt my head to the side, trying to read her. The only thing I'm sure about is something isn't right. Her eyes are slightly puffy and red, indicating she was probably crying. Instead of answering her question, I remind her, "We were supposed to spend Easter together. If you're not feeling well, I want to be here taking care of you." She grimaces and looks towards the kitchen. I pat the couch next to me, "Since you know I'm not leaving, why don't you have a seat next to me."

She lumbers towards me and cautiously settles down next to me, leaving a couple inches of space between us. I place my arms around her and pull her towards me, giving her a light squeeze. I bury my face in her hair and inhale her beautiful scent of vanilla and coconut. I begin tracing figure eights lightly on her arm, relishing the feel of her relaxing into me. "You're parents were okay with you leaving?" she whispers, interrupting my thoughts.

"When I told them we were coming today, I told them not to depend on me for anything. I said my schedule revolves around you today," I inform her. "Although, they appreciate the extra help, they had staff to cover everything I would normally do today."

"Only today," she jokes, making me laugh.

She exhales harshly, “Sorry, I just had to get out of there.”

“Does that mean you’re ready to tell me what’s really going on in that head of yours?” I ask calmly. I feel her whole body tense in my arms, before she sinks back into me and rests her head on my chest. “Does this have anything to do with the Scotts’ showing up?” I ask anxiously.

She sighs in resignation, but instead of answering me, she asks, “Why didn’t you tell me they were going to be there?”

I wince at the sound of pain in her voice, wishing I could make it go away. “I didn’t know they were going to be there,” I tell her honestly. She pushes off me to look into my eyes. I feel a slight pang in my chest from the obvious doubt in her gaze. “I didn’t, Sam,” I insist, unflinching. “They haven’t been there on Easter for at least five years.”

She visibly cringes and softly grumbles, “When you two were dating.”

I nod warily, “Yeah, I don’t know why they were there today. Maybe Mr. Scott thought you might be there?” I suggest.

She laughs humorlessly, “No, he was definitely surprised to see me.” I grind my jaw in irritation, knowing they were probably there because of Jackie, but not wanting to say it. “I’m sure it was something Jackie set-up to either torture me or to see you,” she purses her lips in disgust, reading my mind.

I exhale harshly in frustration, “I don’t know what to do or say to her that I haven’t already. Not long after you left, she came out to talk to me, but I told her I had something important to do. I just *knew* when I saw her,” I grimace and trail off.

“Don’t worry about it Brady. There’s nothing else you can do,” she insists. She sags further into me, slightly defeated.

“Well, we have to figure something out. This is a damn small town. I’m not going to let you run away every time we see her!” I declare.

“I wasn’t running away,” she asserts, pushing away from me.

“That’s not what I meant,” I defend. I reach out for her, but she slides to the back corner of the couch. “Sam,” I beg, my voice full of anguish. “I just meant we have to come up with a way to deal with her. You can’t turn the other way whenever you see her because you don't want another confrontation with her."

Sam fists her hands at her sides and her face turns red, a tear slipping out of the corner of her eye. I want to reach out for her, but I'm afraid she'll push me away again. She presses her lips tightly together and turns her head towards me. Her hard gaze crashes with mine and I flinch at the storm brewing in them. Her voice comes out eerily quiet, yet hard, when she speaks. "How bad is your opinion of me Brady?"

"What?" I shake my head, not understanding what she means. "What are you talking about?" I ask in confusion.

I feel her controlled anger even before she speaks and I know I said something stupid. "I realize I don't get along with Jackie. I would probably even be a lot happier if I didn't have to see her ever again. But I did not leave because I saw her or even because I knew she was there. I left because I was already struggling seeing all the families celebrating a holiday together, all the moms and dads with their kids and missing mine. When I go inside to take a breather from all of that, Jackie spills her mimosa all over me." She pauses and glares at me before continuing snidely, "In case you're wondering, it wasn't an accident."

"She said she didn't see you," I say, suddenly unsure.

She shakes her head in disgust, but doesn't even bother to respond to my comment. I run my hand through my hair feeling unsettled as she continues, her voice frazzled. "Then Lincoln comes over and puts his arm around his *real* daughter and asks what I'm doing there. The bitch has the audacity to ask if I was there with my family like them," she forces a hollow laugh and shakes her head. "Then Lincoln asks if I want to join them, even though it was obvious he didn't want me to. Then again, I didn't want to either. They aren't my family. My family is gone." She gulps as more tears escape. "I miss them every day and today it was thrown in my face a few too many times. I was going to tell you, but when I turned to go find you, I overheard Jackie say she was going to talk to you. I wasn't about to follow her outside after the uncomfortable conversation we just had inside. I can only take so much," she expresses, sounding lost. She pulls her knees up to her chest and wraps her arms around her legs, as her whole body sags in defeat.

"I'm so sorry Sam," I begin.

She shakes her head, "Don't! I don't want you feeling sorry for me."

"That's not what this is! I care about you. I knew today would be tough for you and I just wanted to be there for you. I thought you were doing okay. I thought we were maybe even having a little fun. Then when I saw the Scotts," I shake my head thinking about Jackie showing up. "I knew seeing the Scotts would affect you, but I didn't think..." I try to explain.

She interrupts, "You're right. You didn't think. You just assume the worst of me when it comes to Jackie."

I shake my head, "That's not true."

"I expect the worst from her, so when it inevitably comes, I can take it. But I don't expect that from you Brady," she murmurs, painfully.

I gasp, as if I were punched in the chest. She's right. My heart feels like its been ripped out and being stomped on and I feel every painful kick. I did this. "I'm sorry Sam. I'm so fucking sorry. I was worried about you all morning. Then when I saw her right after you left, I panicked because I know she's a bitch, especially to you," I emphasize.

She ignores my comment. She sits a little taller and takes a determined breath as she stares into my eyes with defiance. "I'm not weak, but lately around you Brady, I feel weak," she whimpers, crushing my heart.

I take a deep breath, hoping to calm the ache in my chest. "It's not weak because you lean on someone you care about and who cares about you. It's not weak when someone who loves you tries to support you and what you're going through. You're one of the strongest people I know," I insist. She pinches her lips together and looks down at her hands, still wrapped around her knees. I watch her and I can't help but think about everything this beautiful girl has gone through. I know if I were in her position, I don't think I would survive and come out a better person, but that's exactly what she's doing. I just need her to believe it. I need her to believe me.

She glances up at me, uncertainty clear on her face. My heart clenches so tightly, I'm struggling to breathe. I run my teeth over my bottom lip and try to put all my emotions into this one look. I want to open myself up and hopefully show her my sincerity. She sniffles and wipes her eyes with her fingertips. She pinches her lips together again and breaks my gaze. She drops her head and rests it on her knees. "Maybe I just wasn't ready for today like I thought," she whispers, her voice catching.

I close my eyes, feeling her agony and hating how small she sounds. "I get it Sam, I do." I hesitate before I continue, "But your parents wouldn't want you to stop living," I remind her, hoping it's the right thing to say in this moment.

She nods jerkily, "I know, but that doesn't make it any easier."

I swear a piece of my heart breaks off with her words, to find its place within her. I don't want her to be alone anymore. I don't want her to do any of this alone. I cautiously slide closer to her on the couch and reach out, letting my hand glide lightly over her arm. When she doesn't flinch away from me I breathe a sigh of relief and plead, "Can you come here? Please?"

She loosens her hands from around her legs and pulls them in towards her stomach before she falls towards my chest. I immediately wrap my arms around her, putting her head right underneath my chin. I give her a light squeeze, grateful to have her there. "I'm sorry I'm such a mess," she whimpers.

I grimace, "Please don't apologize Samantha or I'm going to feel like even more of an asshole."

"Maybe that's because you kind of are," she murmurs.

I chuckle lightly knowing she's right and thankful she forgives me. "You did nothing wrong," I insist. "I'm so sorry Samantha. I just want to be there for you and I don't always know how, but I fucking swear I'm trying to do right by you."

She exhales slowly, "I know Brady."

I wrap one of her curls around my finger, searching my thoughts for how to help her. "Do you want to watch a movie or something to take your mind off everything?" I suggest.

"I think I really do need to get some sleep," she says, referring to our earlier conversation. "I feel completely drained," she admits.

I nod in understanding. "Would you like me to stay with you?" I ask anxiously.

She hesitates before she opens her mouth to answer. "Actually I think I just need some time by myself tonight," she informs me.

My heart sinks to my stomach, hating her answer. I gulp down the lump in my throat and ask greedily, "Are we okay?"

"We're fine," she tells me, quietly. That doesn't make me feel any better. I hate that fucking word.

"Fine," I grumble inaudibly. I quickly remind myself, this isn't supposed to be about me. Don't be an asshole, again. "I'll go and let you get some rest then," I tell her reluctantly. I close my eyes and kiss her lightly on her forehead. "Please call me, or better yet, come over if you need anything from me, anything at all," I emphasize.

She giggles and the light sound sends tingles down my spine, giving me a small amount of comfort. "I will," she says confidently.

I cradle her face in my hands and look into her eyes. "I'm sorry," I repeat remorsefully. I softly brush my lips across hers. I slip my tongue out, tasting the salt of her dried tears on my lips, breaking my heart a little more. I tip my head back, taking in the sight of her, relaxed in my arms. Her eyes are closed and her lips are slightly parted. I lean in and kiss the corner of her mouth. I move up to place a kiss near the corner of her eye where her tears escaped. My lips move to the other side, placing a kiss near her other eye and then the corner of her mouth. I press my lips to hers as I exhale, a small gasp escaping through her lips. I groan, needing the connection with her. Our lips move together in a perfect rhythm of give and take. I hold her firmly to me, wanting more, but knowing I can't take any more than this right now. I give one more push of my lips against hers before I grudgingly break away, resting my forehead against hers. "I love you Samantha," I whisper, needing her to know the truth in those words. I brush my lips over hers one more time before I let go.

I stand and unwillingly walk to the door. I need to do what she wants right now, even though it feels so wrong to walk away. "Goodnight Brady. Thank you for today." My eyebrows rise in surprise and she shrugs. "It was good, until it wasn't," she concedes.

I grimace, but nod in acknowledgement. "Get some rest," I quietly encourage. She lifts her hand and waves, a reluctant smile tugging at her lips.

I walk out her door and into mine, dropping back against it as soon as it closes. I rub my hands over my face, feeling like an even bigger asshole because I'm worried about the fact she didn't say she loved me back. She has a lot on her mind, I remind myself, feeling like a pussy. I push off the door and walk to the kitchen. I pull the refrigerator door open and grab a beer before slamming it shut. I swiftly pop the top and toss it in the garbage, before I return to the living room. I drop down on the couch and kick my shoes off. "I'm such a fucking asshole," I berate myself again and take a swig of my beer. I should know better than to believe anything that comes out of Jackie's mouth. "Of course she saw her and treated her like shit," I grumble in annoyance.

My phone beeps with a text. I reach for it, hoping its Sam. At the sight of Jackie's name, I drop my phone back on the table without reading it. I take another long pull of my beer, knowing it's going to be a long night.

Chapter 5

Samantha

I stare up at the white ceiling, enjoying the warmth and comfort of my bed for a little bit longer. I glance at my small nightstand drawer, wondering if I should pull out one of the letters from my birth mom to reread. I grimace knowing that would only lead me to thinking more about my birth father. I really don't know how to handle any of this with him. Of course, Jackie has to be his daughter, the girl who hates me. How am I supposed to get to know him or learn more about who I am when I have her as an obstacle? I can't depend on Brady to be there for me all the time. I already depend on him way too much.

My phone begins ringing loudly and I quickly reach for it, hoping it doesn't wake my roommate. I press answer without looking at the caller. "Hello?" I rasp.

"Sam? Did I wake you?" my cousin, Ryan, asks through the line.

I groan his name in annoyance, "Ryan." He chuckles. I sigh and push myself up to lean against the wall. "No, you didn't wake me. I just haven't had the energy to get up yet."

He laughs, "Well, since you didn't call me back last night, I decided you needed to hear from me right away this morning."

"Gee thanks. I'm so honored," I grumble.

He chuckles and follows it with a long sigh. "So how was your day yesterday?" he asks cautiously.

"It was fine," I tell him, attempting to keep my voice neutral.

"Hmm," he murmurs.

"What's that mean?" I ask, defensively.

"That means I should be asking you what fine means. Did something happen?" he asks, knowing me all too well.

I sigh, "Not really. It really did start off fine, but I guess it didn't really end okay. Brady and his family were great, but it was a lot seeing so many families celebrating," I tell him, knowing he'll understand what I'm not saying.

He sighs and tries to comfort me, "I'm sorry Sam. I miss them too." He pauses and then adds, "We missed your grumpy self here, too."

"Gee thanks," I mumble sarcastically.

"So, why do I get the feeling something else happened? That it's more than that?" he asks curiously.

I huff in exasperation. "I guess the only thing that really happened is Jackie..." I trail off.

"Shit," he grumbles. "They were there? Why didn't Brady tell you?" he questions, immediately going on the defensive for me.

"He said they haven't come in years and he didn't know they would be there," I inform him. "Anyway, it's no big deal. I'm done with this conversation. How was everyone yesterday?" I question.

He hesitates before answering, "It was good. We really did miss you, though. Just don't tell anyone I said that," he warns. I laugh and listen to Ryan drone on for a few minutes about their day. It's comforting listening to the sound of his familiar voice. "Samantha!" Ryan calls through the line, startling me.

"Oh, sorry Ryan. I guess you were putting me back to sleep," I joke.

"Ha! You're trying to be funny," he taunts.

"Oh, but I am funny," I state.

He chuckles, softly. Then he asks, "Seriously, are you good?"

I sigh and admit, "Yeah, I'm fine. I promise. I just think I'm feeling a little guilty for leaving Brady when we had plans."

"He'll get over it. You should feel guilty for ditching us," he declares. I chuckle, but don't respond. "Anyway, I wanted to check in, but I have to get to class now. I'll talk to you later?"

"Yeah. Later Ry!" I tell him.

"Say Hi to your roommate for me," he requests, just before I hit end.

I groan and drop back onto my bed, intending to curl up under the covers again. I close my eyes and take a deep breath. A whiff of fresh brewed coffee suddenly hits my senses and instantly perks me up. I toss off the rest of my covers and push out of bed. I trudge into the kitchen, my nose leading the way. "Mm," I inhale deeply. "That smells incredible. Is there enough for me?" I turn hopeful eyes towards my roommate, Cory. She's sitting in our corner booth, cradling a cup of coffee in her hands.

She shrugs and offers me a small smile, "Have at it."

"Thanks," I grin, appreciatively. I quickly reach for a blue, ceramic mug and fill it before adding a touch of creamer. I wrap my hands around the warm cup and cautiously make my way over to the seat across from Cory, without spilling. I take a sip and sigh in satisfaction as the warm liquid coats my throat, down into my stomach.

Cory giggles. I blush slightly, but offer only a shrug in response. "How was yesterday?" she asks, innocently.

My body tenses. "It was okay," I answer stiffly.

She raises her eyebrows in question, "That good, huh?"

I grimace and scrunch my nose up with distaste just thinking about Jackie again. Cory continues to stare at me, waiting for me to respond. I sigh in resignation and set my coffee cup down on the table in front of me. "The place was beautiful, the food was good, Brady and his family were nice to me," I tell her, trying to keep everything general.

She huffs out a laugh, "Well I should hope so!"

I shrug and quietly admit, "It was hard though." Cory's face softens with kindness and understanding. "Please don't look at me like that," I plead. She opens her mouth to argue, but I interrupt before she can say anything else. "The Scotts were there."

Her eyes widen in shock, "What?"

I nod my head and grimace. "Yeah, Brady was surprised too. But that was too much for me. I had to leave after that whole..." I pause not quite sure how to explain it, "debauchery."

"What happened?" she asks her voice rising.

I shake my head, "Nothing really. It was just incredibly awkward." I shrug like it was no big deal. "Jackie was not so nice, but that's really no surprise."

"What did Brady do?" she asks.

My face heats with embarrassment and I stumble over my words. "Um, I didn't really give him a chance to do anything." Her eyebrows draw together in confusion. "We took two cars," I explain. "I texted him that I didn't feel well and I was leaving." Her eyes fill with understanding and compassion, two emotions I don't know if I want at the moment. I take another sip of my coffee and watch the motion of the light brown liquid swish around in the light blue mug, as I set it back on the table. "Jackie was going to talk to him and I didn't want to deal with her anymore," I justify weakly.

"It's okay, I'm sure he gets it," she says with encouragement.

I nod with a sad smile. I know he does, but that doesn't make me feel any better for ditching him yesterday. Then I go and accuse him of being an asshole, even though he was just trying to look out for me. That's a great way to isolate myself. He doesn't deserve that. I take a deep breath and try to pull myself out of the depressing direction my thoughts are heading. "Anyway, how was your Easter?"

Cory smiles genuinely, "It was good. Cody and I ate so much. I should never try to keep up with him," she complains, patting her stomach. "We may be twins but he is almost twice my size." I chuckle in response. "Anyway, we also have a few little cousins who still believe in the Easter Bunny, so we did an Easter egg hunt for them." She glances down at her coffee cup, her cheeks suddenly flushed. She finally comments, "Ryan called last night. He was having trouble getting in touch with you. I told him you were sleeping when I got home."

I smirk, understanding her blush. "Yeah, I talked to him just a little while ago," I admit, nodding. "Thanks."

She takes a sip of her coffee and then clears her throat. She swiftly changes the subject asking, "So what are you doing today?"

I shrug, "I'm not sure. I should probably start looking for a job if I'm going to stay," I tell her honestly, knowing it's the last thing I want to do today.

She waves her hand in dismissal and shakes her head, "Not today. You can start that tomorrow," she informs me. I raise my eyebrows in question and she adds, "You and I are going to do something today."

I laugh and arch my eyebrows in challenge, "Oh yeah?" She nods with confidence and I ask, "So what are we doing?"

The smile drops from her face and she crinkles her nose up in confusion. She finally shrugs and admits, "I have no idea, but go get dressed."

I laugh harder and ask, "Can I finish my coffee first?"

She rolls her eyes and says with false annoyance, "I guess we have time." We both burst out laughing. I already feel slightly better. Brady's right, I can't let Jackie get to me or I might as well go back to Illinois now. I grimace thinking of how I kicked Brady out last night. He didn't do anything to deserve that from me, especially with how good he is to me. "Sam?" Cory questions loudly.

I shake my head and meet her curious gaze. "What?"

She chuckles, "You just disappeared on me. Where'd you go?"

"Nowhere," I reply. "I guess I just still feel bad about kicking Brady out last night."

"You kicked him out?" she asks in surprise. I flinch and slowly nod. She shrugs like it's no big deal and asks, "Why don't you text him?"

I scrunch my nose up with uncertainty, "I don't know what to say." She raises her eyebrows in disbelief. "I know I need to say something and I know he'll text back," I say, feeling unsettled. I hesitate, not quite sure how to explain myself. "I feel like I'm making everything too complicated. I'm just having trouble processing everything with Lincoln and then the fact that Jackie is his daughter," I groan. "It's just a lot to take in," I admit. "I don't want to depend on Brady too much and sometimes I feel like I do. I just think I need to be able to deal with all of them on my own, even Jackie," I grimace. "I just think I was kind of hard on him last night when I kicked him out. I think I might've twisted what he was trying to say because I was having a hard time yesterday," I concede.

Cory pinches her lips together and remains quiet for a moment before she responds. "Just text him. Then when he has time, talk to him about how you feel," she advises.

I sigh in consent and pick up my phone, pulling up Brady's name. I skim over his texts from last night and this morning, all without a response from me. A wave of guilt hits me in the chest, spreading nervous tingles throughout my body. I bite my lower lip and quickly type. "Sorry I didn't text last night. I was exhausted. Hope classes go well today. If you don't have too much homework, maybe I can see you?" I want him to feel like I'm in this too because I am, even if I'm not sure if it's what's best for either of us yet.

His response comes through, just before I set my phone down. "Sleep well?" Followed immediately by, "I'll have time tonight. I have a test to study for, but I want to see you."

"Yes, I slept good. You?" Followed by a smiley emoji and, "Ok." I reply with a satisfied smile on my face.

"Great – I dreamt about you!" he answers.

I laugh and blush at the same time. I send a quick blushing emoji and press send before pocketing my phone.

"All good?" Cory questions, trying to hide her smirk.

I nod in satisfaction, "Yeah."

"Great! Go get dressed. Your coffee is probably cold anyway," she declares.

I laugh, but stand, intending to do as she requested. "I'm going!" I grin playfully as she tosses a napkin at me. I laugh when it lands in the middle of the table. I add, "But I'm also showering, so you'll have to wait!"

"Good, I wasn't going to tell you, but you stink!" she jokes. I chuckle as I walk to my room to grab some clothes for today.

Chapter 6

I pull the front door open, with a smile on my face. The sight of Brady leaning against my doorjamb with tired eyes, his body sagging and a grin tugging at his lips, when his eyes meet mine, takes my breath away. "Hi," he greets me. His smile widens, showing off his dimple.

I clear my throat, before I attempt to open my mouth to speak. "Hi. Want to come in?" I offer. I take a step back and hold the door open.

He pushes off and takes two long strides towards me, purposely crowding me. He smirks and closes in on me, until I feel his warm breath on my lips. My breathing picks up as I stare into his eyes, just waiting to see what he's going to do. He finally murmurs, "Hell, yes," just as his lips cover mine. I relax into his kiss, just as he pulls away. I sigh in disappointment, making him chuckle. He grips my waist and tugs me away from the door before shutting it behind him. "I don't want to share you with the neighbors," he jokes, making me blush.

I step away and offer, "Do you want anything to eat or drink?"

"No thanks," he replies. He reaches for my hand and pulls me with him towards the couch.

I plant my feet and pull my hand back. "Not out here. Let's go talk in my room. Cory is home," I inform him.

He nods, "Okay." He turns and follows me to my room. "Hey Cory," he yells through her closed door as we turn into my room. I hear her muffled return greeting just as I push the door shut behind us. I sit down on my bed and scoot back, resting my back against the wall. Brady follows my lead and sits down next to me. He kicks his shoes off and pulls his knees up, propping his arms on his knees. "So, what did you do today?" he asks, bumping me lightly with his shoulder.

I shrug, but answer, "Cory and I hung out today. We went to the mall and did a little shopping, got something to eat." I look over at him sitting on my bed, twisting his fingers together anxiously. "It was fun," I murmur. I reach out and grab his hands to stop the fidgeting, causing him to freeze. "I'm sorry, Brady," I whisper.

He twists towards me, eyes wide. He forcefully asks, "What the hell do you have to be sorry for, Samantha?"

My eyes scrunch together in confusion and I quickly explain. "I'm sorry for kicking you out last night. I'm sorry for treating you like you were the asshole, yesterday."

"I shouldn't have acted like Jackie would be your reason for leaving, when I knew yesterday would be hard," he interrupts.

I admit, "Well, she was part of the reason, just not the whole reason. I just seemed to take it all out on you when you just wanted to be here for me."

"Sam," he whispers my name in understanding.

"I'm sorry for this whole situation, but I'm not sorry for you and me, if that's what you're thinking." His body physically relaxes and I take a deep breath needing my body to do the same. "I just need to do some things on my own. I feel like since I moved here, you're always there for me."

He interrupts me again, sounding shocked, "And that's a bad thing?"

I shake my head, "No!" I grind my teeth, frustrated with myself. I don't know how to explain myself, without sounding like I'm pushing him away. I take a deep breath and steel myself ready to try anyway. "Lincoln is my birth father and I don't even know exactly what I want from him, but I do know I need to figure it out for myself. I also have to add in his family. I want to figure that out for myself too, even Jackie," I grumble, scrunching up my nose in disgust. I take a slow breath and hope he understands what I'm trying to say. "I'm a lot stronger than I've been around you lately. I love that you're there for me, as long as that's where you want to be."

"I want to be here with you, for you, whatever you need," he declares without hesitation.

"Okay," I smile softly. "Then you also have to understand, I'm just trying to figure out who I am and what I need from any of the Scotts, but everything about them is completely overwhelming to me. The fact that Jackie is your ex-girlfriend and you guys have a dramatic history makes it ten times more difficult," I admit. He flinches and my stomach flips at the thought of them together, yet again. I force myself to continue, "I want you to be there for me, just like I want to be there for you, but I don't want you to save me from everything and try to make it better or fix it. Sometimes I may even walk away, until I can get my head straight. The thing is, I need to figure it out by myself, no matter what the outcome. Does that make sense?" I question, nervously.

Brady slowly turns towards me, biting his bottom lip. He stares into my eyes like he's trying to read my mind, before he nods. He releases his lip, sticking his tongue out to lick his lips, before taking a deep breath of his own. "I get it Sam. I really do. You want to do this on your own and I have to go along with what you want because this is about you. The thing that annoys the fuck out of me is Jackie. She can be a bitch when she wants to be. I hate to think you're in a bad situation with her because of me and you won't let me do a damn thing about it," he announces.

"It's not just because of you," I remind him.

He nods, "True, but dating me does the opposite of helping you with her crazy." He reaches for my hand and gives it a light squeeze. "Don't let that change your mind about me," he begs.

"I won't," I tell him sincerely.

"I mean it Sam," he pleads, causing me to roll my eyes. He slips his free hand over the top of my left knee and stops between my legs. "Don't give her any power over us." He gives the inside of my thigh a light squeeze to punctuate his request.

I jump and squeal in response, "Brady! That tickles!"

The corners of his lips twitch upwards and a playful spark lights up his eyes, making them almost electric. "Really?" he asks, feigning doubt. He reaches over me with the same hand and grips me firmly at my hip. His free hand moves to my right knee and slides up, making me gasp. His grin widens, deepening his dimple. He squeezes my right thigh, pinning me at my hip. I squeal again and try to wiggle away. He removes the hand from my hip and wraps his arm tightly around my legs. "So you don't kick me," he explains.

"Brady..." I screech as his hand moves from my thigh to my waist, digging friskily into my sides. I burst into a fit of giggles and unsuccessfully try to wiggle and push my way out of his strong grasp. "Stop," I laugh uncontrollably.

"You want me to stop?" he questions, innocently.

"Please!" I beg.

He uses his arm wrapped around my legs to tug me hard, easily sliding me down the bed onto my back. He slides his warm body up until it lightly covers mine. He cages me in with his arms on both sides of my head. He props himself up on his elbows and pushes my hair out of my face. He grins broadly down at me, his eyes sparkling with mischief, as I catch my breath. "I'll stop, for now," he chuckles. "I love hearing you laugh," he admits fondly.

"You don't have to tickle me to death for me to laugh," I remind him.

He smirks, "No, but that was a lot of fun."

I giggle lightly and reach up to rest my hands on his hard chest. He leans towards me, quickly closing the space between us. He pauses as his lips barely brush mine. He whispers reverently, "How did I get so lucky?" My breath rushes out of my lungs just as his lips meet mine in an all-consuming kiss. I push back slightly to catch my breath, but he doesn't stop. He takes his time tasting, licking, nipping and sucking my mouth. His fingers lightly trace my jawline as he kisses me. He pulls back, gently rubbing his thumb over my now plump lips. "You're so beautiful Samantha," he murmurs, causing my rapidly beating heart to stutter.

"Brady," I whimper, my heart aching for him. I pull him towards me and meld our mouths together. I open, thrusting my tongue inside his mouth, in search of its mate. My whole body hums, heated by his kisses and words alone. "I want you Brady," I whisper.

His hand drops to my waist and slips underneath my shirt, tickling my bare skin over my belly. His hand slips up my sides and stops just below my bra. He caresses the bottom of my breast with his thumb, his kisses devouring me. His phone suddenly rings loudly, startling us both apart. He grips my side and drops his forehead to mine, our breathing ragged, as we wait for his phone to stop. He sighs in relief and lightly presses his swollen lips to mine. The ringing starts right back up again, giving us no reprieve. "Fuck," he grumbles. He pushes off my bed and away from me, leaving me cold.

I sigh in disappointment and roll over onto my side. I watch his muscles ripple underneath his shirt as he reaches for his phone. "Hi Mom," he greets, making me flinch. His eyes light up and he smirks at my reaction. "I'm just talking to Sam," he fibs as his hand falls back to my side. "That's tonight?" he questions. He groans and lifts his hand, running it through his hair. "Yeah, okay," he agrees, sounding defeated. "I'll be there," he confirms. I can hear his mom talking when he's quiet, but not enough to hear what she's saying. He finally responds, "I don't know, but I'll figure it out." He sighs and adds, "I love you too, Mom. I'll see you in a little while." He hits end and drops his phone next to him on the bed. He flops down next to me and groans in annoyance.

"Everything okay?" I ask, hesitantly.

He grimaces, "Yeah, everything's fine. I just completely forgot about a meeting I have tonight at the restaurant," he explains.

"What kind of meeting?" I ask curiously.

"I'm meeting with a bride and groom about possibly doing their wedding. They live in Madison, but they don't want to get married there. They want something more casual, more small town, even a little bit country. My friend Owen, from class, recommended me to them. We're definitely small town, but I don't really know how to give them the rest. I honestly have no idea what to even tell them, besides showing them our property and what we've done in the past," he grumbles.

I pinch my lips together as an idea forms in my head. "What if?" I question, stopping short.

He turns his head towards me, his eyes hopeful and asks, "What?"

I scrape my teeth nervously across my bottom lip, before I release it. I suggest, "Why not use your old barn?"

His eyes flash, full of curiosity, "What? How?"

"It's so peaceful out there, there's plenty of room, but definitely a lot more casual than the main restaurant. You could decorate the poles, doorways and even along the edge of the loft with toile, ribbons and flowers. You could probably even make it a little bigger if you took out a few of the old horse stalls. You just need to put in a dance floor and get one of those fancy outhouses."

"That's a great idea!" he exclaims. "I have to check with my parents and get the proper permits in place, but I'm sure it won't be a problem! It would just be like we're catering food to an outside venue, except it's on our property, so that should work too," he talks out some of the details. I don't think I've seen him this animated about work since I met him. I can't stop the smile that encompasses my face.

"Don't you think you should talk to your parents first before you figure out all the logistics?" I ask, chuckling. "Or how about asking the bride and groom what they think?" I question, smirking.

He laughs and sits up grinning. He leans forward and places a chaste kiss on my lips. "Yeah, but now I actually have an idea to run by them. He kisses me again. "Thank you!"

I giggle, "You're welcome."

He kisses me again, before sitting back and looking down at me. "Do you remember when I said you should do events at our restaurant?" I nod my head slowly, wondering where he's going with this. "I may have been kind of joking at the time, but I think you would be really good at it." My body heats in embarrassment and I look down at my lap. His fingers slip under my chin and he tips my head up until I meet his gaze. "I'm serious Sam. This is a fantastic idea and it could bring in a ton more clients and revenue. Even your ideas on decorating the barn sound perfect," he raves.

I blush and shrug my shoulders, "It's no big deal."

"It is to me, or else I would've thought of it myself," he insists. "Thank you," he repeats. "I want to hire you," he tells me. My mouth drops open in response. He chuckles and taps my mouth shut, kissing me on the corner of my lips. "I'm serious Sam, just think about it."

"I don't know Brady," I admit, feeling uneasy. I don't know if I can handle something like this. I don't even have connections around here like I would in Illinois.

"How about this," he proposes, "I'll talk to my parents and if they like the idea, I'll work on getting all the logistics and paperwork done. In the meantime, if the bride and groom like the idea and decide to go with us, I'll hire you to be the event planner for this event. If you like it and you're happy and it works for us as well, you will consider doing it full time." I open my mouth to respond and he presses his lips to mine to keep me from talking. He pulls back with a crooked smile, making my heart skip a beat. "Don't answer right now. Just think about it," he requests.

I chuckle and shake my head at him in disbelief. "You're crazy," I grin. He stares down at me, hopeful and I know I can't say, no. "Fine, I'll think about it," I agree.

His smile widens and he presses another kiss to my lips. He pulls back with a grimace, "I'm sorry, but I have to go. Since I forgot about this meeting, I have some studying to do before I take off for the restaurant."

"Okay," I nod in understanding.

He kisses me again, still smiling broadly. "Think about it!" he repeats, before he stands to leave. He leans over me, pressing his lips firmly to mine one more time. He pulls away with a light smacking sound, making me laugh. "I love you beautiful," he declares, just before he turns and walks out of my room.

I sit on my bed feeling stunned. At the sound of the front door closing, I release the breath I didn't know I was holding. I've always loved planning parties, but is this really something I could do? I don't want to screw up someone's wedding because I don't know what I'm doing. I heave a sigh and mumble to myself, "I guess it won't matter if things don't fall into place on his end." Maybe I'll just wait and see. If Brady and his parents are for it, I'll go for it and if not, it won't matter anyway. "I guess I already made my decision," I murmur the realization aloud. "It would be fun."

"What would be fun?" I startle. I whip my head around to my bedroom doorway and find Cory staring at me with curiosity.

I shake my head, "Nothing. Just something Brady wants me to do."

She eyes me with interest, before finally shrugging her shoulders, like it doesn't matter. "Come watch a movie with me," she demands. She turns and walks away without waiting for a response.

I laugh and push off my bed. "Okay," I answer my empty room. I follow her out to our living room, my head still on Brady's proposal.

Chapter 7

Brady

I walk into my apartment and drop my backpack just inside the front door. "Hey man," Cody calls, barely looking away from his computer. "You look like shit. What's up with you?" he asks.

I chuckle humorlessly at his blunt comment. Cody knows me better than anyone. Besides sharing this apartment for nearly three years, he's also been my best friend since I can remember. He's one of the few people who can say something like that without me taking him seriously. I slip my lightweight, black coat off as I walk towards him and hang it over the back of the couch. I sigh and flop down next to him, feeling completely exhausted. "Nothing really. I just can't wait for classes to be over. Today is just day one back from spring break and every teacher is slamming us with work," I complain. "I know I have less than six weeks left, but I have no idea how I'm supposed to get this done, help at the restaurant, and have time for Sam, or sleep for that matter," I grumble.

"Well, if you're debating between Sam and class or Sam and sleep, that's a tough one, but I'd go with Sam. I'm sure she's much better in bed," he jokes.

"Asshole," I mumble. He chuckles in response. "I'm going to head over there before I go to work," I inform him.

"Okay. I just ordered a pizza," he informs me. "I ordered enough for you if you're hungry," he offers.

I arch my eyebrows in surprise, "Thanks Cody. Are you going soft on me?" I smirk.

He stops what he's doing and looks up at me like I've lost my mind. "You bought the last five, I owe you. I'm paying you back. It's not that complicated," he teases. "I have a shitload of work to do on this program and don't have time for anything else," he adds, sounding exasperated.

I grumble and accuse, "Glad to see you're in as good a mood as me." Cody grimaces. "Everything ok?" I question.

"I'm working," he declares. "Now leave and go talk to your girl, so I can do what I need to do," he instructs, dismissing me.

I pinch my lips together in confusion. He doesn't act like this, even if he has a ton work. There's definitely something going on with him and he doesn't want to talk about it.

I run my hands over my face and back up through my hair, in attempt to wake myself up. Then I stand and stride back towards the front door. "Whatever you say," I mumble. "I'll be back for pizza soon," I tell him. Cody barely grunts in acknowledgement as I walk out the door, pulling it shut behind me.

I take the three long strides to Samantha's place and immediately knock. I lean back on my heels and wait for someone to answer. The door swings open and Cody's twin sister (and Sam's roommate), Cory, greets me. She smiles up at me, "Hi Brady. Trying to get away from the beast or are you here to see Samantha?" she asks sweetly.

"Can't it be both?" I force a grin.

She giggles and steps back to let me in, "You look exhausted."

I step inside and close the door behind me. "That seems to be the consensus," I grumble. "At least you're nicer about it," I grimace. "What's going on with your brother anyway?" I ask tipping my head in the direction of my apartment.

She frowns, "Olive isn't talking to him. I don't know exactly what happened, but whatever it was, she hasn't talked to him for a couple days." I nod in understanding, knowing how crazy he is about her and yet they are rarely in sync. "He's made the last couple days so much fun and I don't even live with him," she adds, sarcastically.

"I can imagine," I murmur. "Guess it's a good thing I've been too busy to be home." She laughs. "Is Samantha in her room?" I ask.

"Yeah. We're going to go out to dinner tonight. She should be in there getting ready," she informs me.

I nod and stride for her door, "Thanks, Cory."

I knock on Sam's bedroom door, "Samantha? It's me."

"Come in," she calls.

I push the door open and take one step into the room, before my breath catches in my throat. Sam is standing in front of her dresser, looking into her mirror and applying make-up under her eyes. She's dressed in dark blue skinny jeans and a pale yellow tank top with spaghetti straps and a triangle of lace in the front. "Hi Brady," she says. She catches my eyes in the mirror and smiles, making my heart skip a beat.

I clear my throat and rasp, "Hi. You're going out in that?" I ask.

She tilts her head to the side and narrows her eyes on me. She challenges, "What's wrong with this?"

I gulp down the growing lump in my throat and murmur, "Absolutely nothing. You look really fucking sexy," I practically growl.

She instantly blushes, causing my heart to beat even faster than a moment ago. She shakes her head and answers my first question. "It's not warm enough for that yet."

I step up behind her and place my right hand gently on her waist. I tip my head down and take a deep breath, inhaling the scent of vanilla and coconut. "Mm," I murmur. I kiss her on the top of the head and then rest my chin on her head, making her giggle.

"It's kind of hard to finish getting ready when you're resting on my head," she teases. She tips her head back and pushes up on her toes, placing a chaste kiss on my lips, before falling back on her heels. "How were classes today?" she asks.

I sigh and step back, sitting down on the end of her bed. "It was a long day and I have a ton of work tonight," I tell her honestly.

She nods, "I thought that might be the case, just coming off break."

"Don't you want to know about my meeting last night? The one with the engaged couple?" I ask her curiously.

She scrunches her nose up adorably and focuses on brushing her hair. She insists, "Only if you want to tell me."

I laugh as she attempts to avoid my gaze and relax back onto my elbows. "I planned on telling you, no matter what happened and you know it."

I watch for her reaction. She tilts her head, assessing her hair and make-up in the mirror. She finally sets her brush down on her dresser, before she suddenly spins to face me. She exhales harshly and then finally meets my eyes. "Okay, how'd it go?" she asks, nervously.

I lean up towards her and give her a crooked smile. I reach for her and request, "Come here." I grab her hand and pull her between my legs. I wrap my arms around her waist and mumble, "Much better." She offers me a small smile and sighs as she places her hands on my shoulders. "They met me at the restaurant, but then I brought them over to the barn and explained what we were working on. They love your idea Sam," I announce, proudly.

"They do?" she asks, surprised.

I nod, grinning fondly up at her. "Yeah, I told them your ideas for decorating and everything too. They said they would book with us if we can guarantee the barn will be ready in time. I asked them to give me a few days to make sure all of the permits go through, then we'll be all set." She nods slowly, processing my words. "I already looked into it earlier today and the permits aren't going to be an issue. I just want to make sure you're in," I clarify. "They want to meet with you after they book," I inform her.

"Why me?" she asks perplexed.

I chuckle lightly, "Because this whole thing was your idea. You saw more than I could imagine and I told them that. I can't do this without you," I insist.

She blushes and shakes her head in denial, "That's not true."

"Sam please," I beg. "This will give you a chance to see if event planning is something you'd like to do full-time. I'm not saying you have to do it at the restaurant, even if you decide that's what you want to do, but the option is there. You'll have me to help. Plus, I can answer questions about what businesses we've always worked well with or about menu options and other things like that. You were going to look for a job anyway," I remind her, trying to persuade her to try it.

She smiles stiffly and meets my eyes. I see the anxiety in them and my heart skips a beat, wanting to help ease it away. "What if it doesn't work?" she asks so quietly, I almost can't decipher the words.

I shake my head and my eyes soften. I run the back of my fingers gently down the side of her face, adoringly. I insist, "Then it doesn't work, but I think the only reason it wouldn't work would be because you don't enjoy doing it, or some unforeseen circumstances, like the weather."

She bites her lower lip nervously and slowly releases it. I bite my tongue to hold back my groan at the movement and continue watching her, as she makes a decision. She finally blurts out, "Okay Brady, I'll do it."

I grin in satisfaction. "Thank you," I whisper appreciatively. She smiles and I lean backwards, pulling her down with me. We fall onto her mattress, her body instantly aligning with mine. I press my lips to hers before she has a chance to say anything else, or maybe even take it back. I pull back just enough to look into her eyes. I repeat, "Thank you."

She smiles shyly, causing my heart to skip a beat. "I have a lot of research to do before I meet with them. I want to be prepared," she declares. "Is it okay if I start on it tomorrow?" she asks, hesitantly. "Cory and I were going to go out for dinner tonight," she clarifies.

I quickly reply, "Of course. You don't need to explain yourself. I'm not your boss, you know." I smirk, "Although, I could be, if you want me to."

"Brady," she scolds, narrowing her eyes on me and making me chuckle. She releases a breathy sigh and lightly drops her head to my chest, just underneath my chin. "Thank you for giving me this opportunity," she whispers.

My heart clenches tightly and I rasp, "You deserve it, Samantha. It was your idea. You're the reason they're booking with us in the first place," I remind her. "I honestly think you'll be really good at this," I tell her sincerely, "but I want you to do what you love. If this isn't it, I'll be there to help you figure out what it is."

She sighs with content and holds me a little tighter, causing my body to heat. I tighten my arms around her, loving the feel of her against me. I begin making figure eights lightly on her back and remain quiet, knowing she's trying to process everything.

"Samantha!" Cory calls down the hallway. "Are you almost done in there? I'm getting hungry," she complains.

She grins up at me before she calls back to Cory, "I'm almost ready. I'll be right there and then we can go."

I groan and give her a light squeeze, "I guess that means I have to let you go."

She chuckles and softly presses her lips to mine. "You have homework to do anyway," she reminds me, making me grimace.

"Less than six weeks," I mumble.

"Then you're done," she nods. "Is that strange?"

I shrug, "I guess. After everything happened and I transferred to Madison and moved back here, college felt different."

"What do you mean?" she asks.

"I guess I mean college became more like a job. I did what I had to do, to find what I wanted to do for the rest of my life. Then I worked hard to make it happen. It didn't matter which direction I decided to go. Only the outcome was important. It still is. My parents assume I'm taking over the restaurant." I shrug, "The only problem is, I'm still not positive that's the right thing for me," I admit.

"You'll figure it out," she murmurs. "You have to do what makes you happy," she repeats my sentiment to her from last night.

A loud knock at the door startles us both, making Sam giggle. "Come on Samantha! Let's go eat," Cory pleads, through the closed door.

"I'm coming right now, Cory," she replies.

She gives me a chaste kiss, not nearly enough for me. She attempts to push up off the bed. I tighten my arm around her and cradle her face with my other hand, guiding her back to my lips for a soft kiss. I push in closer because I cant' help myself. I just need a little more. I barely flick my tongue out tasting her lip-gloss before I pull away with a reluctant sigh. "I guess that will have to tide me over," I frown.

She laughs and pushes up off her bed. "I guess it will," she grins mischievously.

I grudgingly stand and follow her out of her room. I laugh at the sight of Cory standing impatiently in the hallway, with her arms crossed over her chest. "Took you guys long enough," she grumbles.

"Not long enough," I complain. Cory laughs and I revel in Samantha's beautiful blush. "And you're starting to sound like your brother," I accuse Cory.

She immediately schools her expression and apologizes. "Sorry. I have no idea what's gotten into me."

I laugh and lean down, giving Samantha one more kiss on the corner of her mouth. "Have fun," I murmur.

She smiles and grabs a thin, white coat. I help her slip it on and we all walk out the front door together. I watch them step onto the elevator and wait until the doors close, before I retreat back to my own apartment, with a sigh.

Chapter 8

Samantha

"Excuse me, do you mind if I sit in the other chair?" a man asks, his voice a low grumble.

I look up and my gaze locks on a guy in his early twenties. He has dark hair, hazel eyes, a strong jaw and a crooked smile. "Um, what?" I ask confused.

He has a coffee in one hand and his phone in the other and gestures around the coffee shop. "There are no free tables. If I'm going to ask to sit with anyone, I knew it should be you," he grins, playfully. He pockets his phone and holds his hand out for me to shake. "I'm Logan," he says, introducing himself.

"Have we met? You look familiar and I recognize your name," I tell him.

He laughs, "This is a small town, but I would've remembered meeting you. What's your name?" he asks.

"I have a boyfriend," I reply, causing him to laugh again.

"Glad you're honest," he says. He takes off his black leather coat and hangs it over the back of the chair across from me. He sits down, without my consent and makes himself comfortable. He grins, "I'm not going to sit with the mommy and me group, or the old women's group, or the guys in the suits," he fakes a shiver, like he can't imagine wearing something like that every day. I assess him warily and notice the ends of a tattoo on his right arm underneath his fitted black t-shirt.

"What about the guy over there?" I ask. I nod to a guy about the same age as us, sitting at the table behind him.

He turns and glances at the guy behind him, with his dark hair sticking up in all directions, as if he were pulling on it in frustration. He's using every available space, including the chair next to him to spread out papers. He's staring intently and typing furiously on his laptop, as if whatever he's doing might be life or death. "Definitely not going near whatever he's working on," he grimaces.

"And the pretty redhead behind him on her phone?" I ask.

He grins, not even glancing in her direction. "I'm not really a redheaded kind of guy. Besides, she seems a little too busy talking on her phone."

I laugh in response, knowing he already noticed her and shake my head. "I'm working," I inform him. "I'm busy," I add.

He glances down at my things on the table and shrugs. I laugh again and nod my head, "Oh, I see how it is."

He chuckles and narrows his eyes slightly. He tilts his head to the side and acknowledges, "You know, you do look a little familiar. Maybe we have met. Do you ever go to Mae's? I bartend there," he informs me.

I nod my head in realization. "No, but I know who you are. You're my neighbor!" I announce. His eyes widen in surprise. I clarify, "I'm Cory's new roommate. Well, newish," I shrug.

He grins and nods as everything clicks into place. "You live across the hall," he acknowledges. "Now that makes sense. You said you have a boyfriend?" I nod my head in affirmation. "You wouldn't happen to be dating Brady Williams, would you? He had a lot to say about you last time I saw him. Samantha right?" he asks.

My eyes widen in surprise. "He did? What did he say?" I ask.

He chuckles, "I'll take that as a yes."

"Oh, I'm sorry. Yes, Brady is my boyfriend and my name is Samantha or Sam," I clarify. "So what did he say about me?" I repeat.

He grins, "Let's just say he was right about you." My eyebrows draw together in confusion, but he changes the subject before I have a chance to ask anything else. "So what are you working on?" he questions.

I pinch my lips tightly together and try to read his expression, without much success. I finally sigh in defeat. I gesture towards my red accordion folder and reply, "I'm trying to get as much information as I can about local businesses that could be essential with planning events." I put my hand on my laptop and add, "Then I'm also making lists of the best websites for my research, as well as for each of the different areas necessary or possible for an event. Just in case someone doesn't find what they're looking for locally," I add.

He nods in understanding and asks, "So, events like parties? Is that what you do?"

I shrug, "Sort of. Brady and I are meeting with a couple that is planning their wedding. I've planned parties before, but this is a first for me," I admit.

He laughs. "How did that happen?"

I scrunch my nose up in thought. I can't help but wonder if Brady is just doing this for me. Instead I tell him, "Well, do you know that Brady's family has an old barn on their property?" He shakes his head and I continue. "Well, they do and this couple wants something a little bit more country, but close to Madison for their wedding reception. I suggested he use the barn and kind of told him what he would have to do to make it a beautiful venue. Then I had ideas for design and decoration and he loved them and I guess so did the couple. Now that they definitely booked with Brady, they want to meet with me to help plan their wedding reception," I blush at the reality.

"Wow, that's huge," he praises. I shake my head in denial. He leans forward and places his elbows on the table, setting his coffee cup between his hands. "It is big. You shouldn't brush it off as nothing," he insists. I take a deep breath to calm my anxiety. "Are wedding receptions the only kind of events you're planning?" he asks curiously.

I shrug, "I don't know. I don't even know if this is what I want to do with my life. I do know it's a great opportunity and I love planning things like this. It will be fun," I insist. I feel a little as if I'm trying to talk myself into it, even though what I'm saying is true. I glance up at Logan. He smirks at my response and arches his eyebrows in challenge. "I do like planning things like this and if it goes well, that's great, but I think I would also like to do other kinds of events."

He nods and smirks, "Like birthday parties?"

I laugh, "That's not really what I was thinking, but I can do that."

"I work on a lot of fundraisers with volunteer organizations. Would you be interested in something like that?" he asks.

My eyes widen in surprise, "I thought you just said you were a bartender."

He chuckles, "Well, technically I said I'm a bartender at Mae's and that's true, but I also do fundraisers."

"And career counseling," I murmur.

He laughs harder and leans back in his chair. He grins and crosses his arms over his chest. "This weekend we are having a fundraiser at the bar for Sexual Assault Awareness and Prevention Month. Why don't you come down on Saturday and check it out," he suggests.

"I'd love to, but I'm only 20, well almost," I murmur.

"Huh," he mumbles. Then he shakes his head, "That's okay. Saturday from 12-3 the bar will be open to everyone for the event and no alcohol will be served. Ironically it's also alcohol awareness month, so it's a great opportunity to remind people to be responsible when drinking."

"Wow," I mumble. "How did you get involved in all of that?" I ask curiously.

He grimaces and admits, "Well, the easy answer is I have a father who's an alcoholic. I've also seen a lot of shit happen with owning a bar."

"You own the bar?" I interrupt. "You said you were a bartender there."

He smirks and continues, "Some things I've been able to control and other things I couldn't. This is my way of doing what I can to help."

"That's the easy answer?" I question. He frowns and nods solemnly. I sigh and concede, "I can't even imagine what the tough answer would be."

He takes a deep breath and exhales slowly before he continues, ignoring my comment. "Each month I pick a different focus and do a fundraiser. Then I donate to the local volunteer organization that works to make a difference in that area. For this one, the Madison campus has a few student groups I'll be donating to, depending on how much we raise."

"That's incredible," I insist.

"So come down and see what it's all about. There's National Health Awareness days for everything," he emphasizes. "Next month I'm debating between Skin Cancer Awareness, Cystic Fibrosis Awareness or Lupus Awareness," he informs me.

I gasp and place my hands flat on the table to steady myself. "Did you say Cystic Fibrosis?" I ask for clarification.

He nods in confirmation, "Yes. Is that something that interests you?"

I gulp down the sudden lump in my throat and nod my head. "Yeah," I rasp.

He purses his lips, assessing me with indecision. He finally gives his head a light shake and maintains, "Then you should definitely come down on Saturday. If you like what I do, I'll do Cystic Fibrosis Awareness for May and I'll pay you to help me work on the event." I shake my head and open my mouth to argue, but he interrupts me. "I have the money to pay you. I always pay someone to help. I don't have all the information for all these different awareness days," he swears. "I'm no health expert. Besides, I can't do everything by myself," he reminds me.

I look down at the colorful brochures and business cards spread out on the table in front of me. I have almost everything I would need to help with a fundraiser like this, except more information on cystic fibrosis. I researched it when I first found out about my birth mom, but I haven't done anything since. I bet the local chapter would have information like that for me. I wonder if there's one in Madison.

"Samantha?" Logan calls, waving a hand in front of my face.

I shake my head and focus back on him. "I'm sorry. I was just thinking about what you said," I admit.

"And?" he asks with an arch of his eyebrow.

I sigh and concede, "I really like that idea."

He grins and takes another sip of his coffee. "Excellent," he declares. "I have to get going, but I'll see you Saturday?" he asks.

I nod in agreement, "Yes, I'll be there."

He stands and slips his leather jacket on before he grabs his coffee cup. "I'm really glad I finally met you Sam."

I smile, "I'm glad I met you too."

"Thanks for having coffee with me," he grins and winks, before turning and striding quickly out the door.

I chuckle to myself and return my attention to organizing the rest of the colorful brochures and business cards of all the local businesses into my red expanding folder. I have all of them separated into different areas such as flowers, bakery, dresses, tuxedos, costumes, hair, make-up, nails, spa, music, rentals, decorations, photographer, videographer, ceremony options outside of a church, travel agents, gifts, and catering. On my laptop I have lists of different websites I think could be useful if someone doesn't find what they're looking for. I make a note to research National Health Awareness Days and non-profit organizations that might be able to help with each. I feel like I'm missing something, but Brady insists I'm not. Then again, Brady has been so busy with school and work lately that I'm surprised he can think about anything else.

I close my laptop with a sigh and reach for my coffee cup. I put it to my lips, grimacing as I realize it's empty. "Oh well," I mumble to myself. I pick up my laptop and folder and slip them both back into my bag. I stand and raise my arms above my head, stretching my stiff body. I drop my arms to my sides and grab my things along with my empty coffee cup. I toss the cup in the garbage before I stride out the door.

I take two steps down the sidewalk, before I abruptly stop, gasping in surprise. Lincoln's wife, Ginny is walking towards me with a huge smile on her face. A young teen boy walks next to her, dressed in a blue and gray baseball uniform. I'm frozen as I watch Ginny lean down towards Frankie and whisper something to him. His head snaps up and he looks at me with wide eyes. He offers me a welcoming grin, causing my heart to stutter.

"Samantha," Ginny greets me first, "It's so good to see you!"

"Hi Ginny," I rasp.

She steps towards me and embraces me in an awkward, one-armed hug. Then she steps back and looks down proudly at Frankie. "This is your brother, Frankie." She looks quickly back at me before bringing her focus back to him, "Frankie, this is Samantha."

"Hi!" he practically shouts with excitement.

I can't fight my smile at his reaction. "Hi, Frankie. I'm so happy to meet you," I declare, my voice shaking.

He smiles happily. "I'm really happy to meet you too Samantha. I've been asking my mom and dad when I could meet you," he enlightens me.

"Really?" I ask surprised.

He nods, "Yeah, I wanted to know if you want to come to one of my baseball games. If you don't like baseball, I play soccer and basketball too," he tells me making me laugh.

"I'd love to come to one of your games," I insist. "Just tell me when and where and I'll be there. The sport you're playing doesn't matter," I add, grinning.

"Awesome!" he declares gleefully. "My mom will send you my schedule."

I look back at Ginny, who's discretely wiping a tear from the corner of her eye. "Thank you. I'd really like that," I contend.

She smiles in satisfaction and gives a slight nod of her head. "We have to get going or we're going to be late, but I'll send you his schedule when I get home. Let me know when you will be coming, so I can save you a seat," she requests.

I nod in agreement, "I will. I'll see you both soon."

"Bye Samantha!" Frankie calls as they rush away.

The moment they turn the corner, I take a deep breath and begin walking back to my car. Frankie seemed so excited to have me come to one of his games. I'm going to make sure to go as soon as I can. Hopefully, I won't have to see Jackie when I'm there. I don't even want to think about what that would be like. I shake my head and attempt to force her out of my mind. Thoughts of her still cause me so much anxiety. It's just not worth it.

Chapter 9

I finish organizing the last of my papers, brochures and ideas on the smooth, wooden tabletop. I sigh as I slide into the booth and sit down. Brady quickly slips in next to me, leaving the other side open for the couple that's coming to meet with us. He lays his arm over the back of the booth behind me and turns towards me. He slowly assesses me, as I squirm in my seat. His eyes narrow slightly and he asks, "Are you alright?"

I take a deep breath and nod stiffly. "I'm fine. I've just never done something like this before. I guess I'm a little nervous. I don't want to mess up," I admit, with a harsh exhale.

"You'll be fine, Samantha. You're more than ready," he encourages. He tucks a lock of my wavy hair behind my ear so he can see me better and smiles warmly. "You probably know more than I do about all the businesses in this town with how hard you've been working on all of this," he teases.

I roll my eyes, making him chuckle. "Sure I do," I mumble.

He leans in and kisses the corner of my mouth, causing me to exhale breathily. He grins and gives my knee a light squeeze under the table, sending chills of a different kind down my spine. "You're going to be great. You've got this," he insists. "Thank you for doing this," he repeats.

I smile tightly and nod my head in acknowledgement. "I really do want to do this," I declare. "I'm just nervous."

He gives my knee another light squeeze, just as a man and woman, probably in their upper 20's, step up to the table. "Hi Brady!" the blonde woman greets him, exuberantly.

He stands and shakes her hand, "Hi Heather. Hi Dave," he greets, with a firm handshake. I can't help but notice what a beautiful couple the two of them appear to be. She's tall and thin with light blonde hair, round blue eyes and pale skin, while he seems to be almost her opposite in appearance. He's tall, but broad, like a football player with black hair, dark brown almond-shaped eyes and dark skin. Brady turns towards me with a proud smile and introduces me, "This is Samantha."

"Hi, I'm Heather," she grins and holds her hand out for me to shake.

I hope they don't notice my clammy hands and square my shoulders. I shake her hand, followed by his firm one with a quick nod. "It's nice to meet both of you and congratulations on your engagement," I smile and remind myself to breathe.

"Thank you. We're so excited!" Heather exclaims and grins giddily up at Dave. She looks back at me and tells me, "It's so nice to meet you Samantha. Last time we met with Brady, he gave us an idea of what you were thinking and we both absolutely love it! In fact, when he showed us the barn after telling us about your idea, I could picture everything in my head. It's absolutely perfect!"

I grin, "Good. I'm glad to hear it. Do you want to sit down and we can go over some of those ideas in more detail?"

They both slide into the booth, Heather across from me and Brady sits back down next to me as Dave takes the seat opposite him. We talk about the construction and what we can do for decorations and set-up in that type of venue, as well as how the food will be handled by the restaurant. Then I make suggestions on the local businesses that I believe will be of benefit to her, followed by ones in Madison, as well as websites for what we don't offer here in Chance. It's not long before we finish and they're thanking us both. We all slide out of the booth and stand to say goodbye. Heather grins and wraps her arms around me in appreciation, startling me. "Thank you so much!" she exclaims.

I smile politely and nod in acknowledgement. I quietly breathe a sigh of relief; grateful I can finally feel myself relax. "You're welcome. We'll see you both soon. Call me if you have any questions and I'll do my best to answer them for you," I remind her.

"I will definitely be calling you. Thank you," she repeats as they turn and walk towards the front door.

Brady faces me and wraps his arms around me, pulling me close. "You were fantastic, just like I knew you would be," he declares.

Instead of looking up at him, I return his embrace and hold him tighter. I speak into his chest and hesitantly ask, "Do you really think so?"

He takes one hand from around my back and slips two fingers underneath my chin and tilts it up until I meet his gaze. He smiles giving me comfort. "I know so. You're not just creative, you're organized and you did a lot of work to make sure you had everything. I'm really impressed. I knew you would be good at this. I couldn't do that," he insists.

I arch my eyebrow with apparent skepticism as he drops his hand on my chin back down to rest on my waist. "Really?" I ask doubtfully.

He laughs and shakes his head. He declares, "No, I really couldn't. When you mentioned the barn, I honestly didn't get it. When I looked at the barn, all I saw was a barn, until you showed me your vision. I'm better at numbers. You're creative. You see things so differently than I ever could," he smirks.

I pinch my lips tightly together, considering his words. I open my mouth and murmur, "Imagining what the barn could be was the easy part for me."

He chuckles and repeats, "And that's truly amazing." He reminds me, "And now that you've researched the area, you would have all of that information for next time. Which makes that part much easier on you too." I nod slowly in agreement. "I know we've just barely gotten started, but are you having fun planning this?" he asks.

I pause momentarily as I think about what I want to say. "Yes, but I guess it will be better when I see the finished product. I want to know what it's like to do something like this from start to finish," I explain. "Plus I still want to do more than regular parties," I inform him.

He nods, his lips twitching up at the corners, "A wedding reception isn't exactly a regular party, but I think I know what you're saying."

"True," I admit sheepishly. I drop my arms and take a step away from him so I can see him better. He lets his hands slide away and he reaches for my hand, entwining our fingers together. "Did you hear about the fundraiser at Mae's this weekend?" I ask, as we begin walking slowly towards the front of the restaurant.

He nods, "Yeah, but I have to work on Saturday afternoon. I'm going to meet with the contractor and go over what we have planned for the barn. We have to get to work as soon as possible if we want to get everything done and get some use out of it this summer. Plus, that way we can pay it off as quickly as possible."

My heart sinks. I can't help but feel slightly disappointed, but I quickly push the feeling away. I tell him, "I'm sorry you're working, but that's good news."

He nods in agreement, "Yeah."

"I know Cory works Saturday afternoon too, but I'd really like to go check it out. I think I would love to get involved in planning events like that," I inform him.

He nods, a small smile on his face. "I could definitely see you doing something like that," he agrees. "Did Cory tell you about the fundraiser?" he asks curiously.

I shake my head and admit, "No, Logan did."

He suddenly halts and tugs my hand, pulling me to a stop. His eyes widen in surprise and he asks, "You know Logan?"

I nod in affirmation, "Yeah, I've seen him around the apartment, but I actually met him at the coffee shop the other day. I was there doing some research for this. When he came in the tables were all full and he asked to sit with me." I shrug like it's no big deal.

Brady clenches his jaw and grumbles, "Hmm. He's a huge player." I arch my eyebrows in challenge and attempt to hide my smirk. "Does he know you have a boyfriend?" he asks.

My smirk turns into a genuine smile and I nod, "Yes. I told him I have a boyfriend and when he found out who I was, he seemed to assume it was you." Brady visibly relaxes and chuckles. "Any idea why that might be?" I ask, laughter in my voice.

He shrugs and grins, showing off his dimple, making my stomach flip. "Well, let's just say I knew there was something special about you from the very first day I met you," he whispers. I feel my face heat as my heartbeat speeds up. He tilts his head down and softly presses his lips to mine. He pulls away with a defeated sigh.

"What?" I ask, my eyebrows drawn together in confusion. "What's wrong?"

He huffs a laugh and shakes his head. "Nothing really. I just want to go home and hang out with you tonight," he admits. He presses another slow kiss to my lips, making my breath hitch. He pulls back slightly and licks his lips. He continues with the low rumble of his voice sending shivers down my spine, "I would kiss you," he softly kisses me again, "and maybe we could do some other stuff." He leans back, his eyes sparkling with mischief. "I'd tell you what I want to do, but not only would that spoil the surprise, but my parents are around here somewhere," he grumbles.

I giggle, my whole body feeling heated. I whisper, "That sounds nice."

"Nice?" he questions playfully. I smile innocently up at him and he chuckles and kisses me again. He pulls back and looks down at me, the corners of his mouth twitching up. "I'll show you nice," he grumbles.

He leans towards me, but I step back with a nervous laugh. "Aren't there other people here getting ready for dinner too?" I ask, quickly surveying our immediate surroundings.

He gulps and nods regretfully, "Yeah."

"So what's stopping you from doing what you want? It's certainly not me," I taunt and smile wickedly.

He glances up at the ceiling and groans, "Samantha." After a moment he drops his head and meets my gaze. I smile innocently up at him causing him to chuckle softly. He takes a deep breath and exhales slowly before he concedes and explains. "Anyway, you win." I laugh and he continues, "I can't hang out tonight because I have a paper I have to finish for one of my classes that's due tomorrow. If I didn't need it to graduate, I would probably come over to your place and procrastinate with you all night."

"Oh," I murmur. I quickly push the feeling of disappointment away and insist, "That's okay, I have some things I have to get done anyway."

He nods just as his dad steps out of his office and walks towards us. "Hi Brady. Hi Samantha. It's so good to see you again."

"It's good to see you too, Mr. Williams," I reply, forcing a smile. I feel my face flush in embarrassment, hoping he didn't see us kissing.

"Brady told me about your ideas for the barn and I want to say thank you!" I breathe a sigh of relief and at the same time blush at his compliment. He continues to praise me, "I think it's an absolutely brilliant idea."

I shrug like it's no big deal. "I'm happy to help," I murmur.

He nods in acknowledgement before bringing his focus back to Brady. "Are you two headed out?" he asks.

"Yeah, I have a paper I have to work on," he tells his dad.

"Okay, I'll talk to you later this week then," he nods. "When you have time, I want to go over everything for your meeting on Saturday," he informs him.

"I know, Dad," Brady says quickly.

His dad purses his lips and reminds him, "I'm not retired yet, Brady. I want to be involved in this project too. You're running with it, but I plan on helping."

Brady nods and smiles, "I know. I promise I'll let you know when I have time before Saturday. I'll come in to meet with you. We can go over everything then."

"Excellent," he nods and grins in satisfaction. "I'll see you kids later," he waves goodbye and strides back towards the kitchen.

"Bye," I call.

"Bye, Dad. Let's go home," he announces. He grasps my hand tighter and strides quickly for the door with me in tow.

Chapter 10

I read Brady's last text with a frown, "Can I come by tonight after work?"

I sigh and pocket my phone without responding. He's been so busy with work and school the last few days, I feel like I haven't seen much of him except at the meeting last night. I do want to see him, but I'm not sure what time I'm going to get home tonight. Plus, I don't want to feel like I have to rush home from Frankie's baseball game. I should probably text something though, so he doesn't think I'm ignoring him. I reach for my phone and reply. I tap out a reply, "Not sure when I'll be home. I'll text later." I flip my phone over to do not disturb and slip it into my small black wristlet to keep myself from looking at it every few minutes.

I glance down at my outfit one more time, even though I'm not about to turn around and go home to change. Hopefully this fundraiser isn't a really dressy occasion. I have on simple black pants, a soft, fitted, pale pink short-sleeve sweater with short black boots and my white lightweight jacket draped over top. I take a deep breath and walk with feigned confidence towards Mae's.

I pull the glass door open and step inside a room full of people of all ages, but I don't recognize anyone. I immediately notice the casual atmosphere and smile. The pale, tan wood floors are worn-down and the wood paneled bar has a wood top, covered in different bottle tops from beer companies all over the world and then sealed over to make a smooth surface. "Do you have a ticket?" a woman asks, pulling my gaze away from the bar. I turn towards her and look up to meet her dark brown eyes. I can't help, but notice how beautiful she is. She's probably a couple years older than me with straight, black hair, high cheekbones and flawless, olive skin.

I realize she's waiting for an answer and quickly mumble, "No, sorry. How much?" Then I reach for my wallet.

"It's $15 to get in and another $25 if you want a wristband for food and non-alcoholic drinks," she informs me, with a fake smile plastered on her face.

"Samantha!" Logan calls. I spin around, grateful to meet his familiar gaze. I feel the nervous tension drain out of me, replaced only with my excitement.

"Hi, Logan," I greet him with a relieved smile.

"You made it!" he grins back as he embraces me, eliciting a squeal from me. "You look fucking hot," he declares loudly. I feel my body heat as he sets me back on my feet. He leans towards me and quietly pleads, "Please, just go with it. I need to get her off my back," he explains. He gestures towards the girl at the door with a bouncer behind her I didn't notice before. The girl crosses her arms over her chest and glares at me. I gulp and give a slight nod, watching as he visibly relaxes. He turns towards her with a huge smile and declares, "She's with me." He puts his arm around me and gives a nod to the bouncer. He calls what I assume is his name, "Seth!" Seth is about 6'2" with broad shoulders and obviously defined muscles in his tight black shirt. He has short brown hair and friendly emerald green eyes as he takes us in. "This is Sam," he introduces us. "Sam, this is my roommate, Seth."

"Oh!" I grin up at him. "It's so nice to finally meet you!" I declare.

He smirks, "So you're the Samantha I've heard so much about."

"Um," I mumble nervously, making him laugh.

"Don't worry, it's all good. I almost feel like I already know you," he jokes.

"Thanks?" I say as more of a question than a statement.

"We're going towards the back for a few," he informs Seth. I feel him kiss the top of my head before walking us towards the back corner, where we find a couple pool tables and dartboards.

The minute we reach the back, I slip out from under his arm and tell him, "I don't mind helping you, but please don't put me in an awkward situation. I'm with Brady," I remind him.

He nods, and smirks, "I'm aware. I promise I don't want to make you uncomfortable, Samantha," he insists. "You just saved me, that's it," he repeats.

I watch him for a moment, assessing his sincerity before responding, "Okay." I look around the room one more time, trying to take everything in, "This is really something. Are those gift baskets over there?"

"Yeah, we collect donations for the baskets and then people can buy raffle tickets to win them. We add the money we earn from the raffles to the total for the donations. The only thing we really pay for is the staff and food and drinks, but the cost of the wristband pays for that and usually still has a good amount leftover. The door price goes straight to the cause," he explains.

I nod in understanding and ask, "So not that this place isn't fantastic, but with a different venue, do you think you could increase the cost of the ticket at the door?"

"Absolutely," he answers confidently, "but this place is free," he reminds me. I huff a laugh and nod. He gestures towards the pool table and asks, "Do you play?"

I smirk, "A little."

He grins, "Why do I feel like you're downplaying your abilities?"

I laugh, "You'll have to ask Brady about that."

He chuckles, "I think I'll like that story."

"Do you ever do tournaments at these events?" I ask.

"Tournaments?" he questions.

"For pool or darts?" He shakes his head and I continue, "There could be an entrant's fee and a cash prize for first through third place, it doesn't have to be much. Then you could have a permanent plaque displayed on the wall in here, one for pool and one for darts with the name of the first place winner each year. It doesn't take much to have a new nameplate engraved each year."

He nods slowly, agreeing, a smile spreading across his face. "That's a really good idea," he praises me. "Need a job?" I laugh and he adds, "Seriously, you can waitress or bartend and then help me with my fundraising events."

I bite my lip nervously, "I don't know. I'm helping Brady with planning a wedding right now, but I really like the idea of helping with fundraising events. Didn't you say next month is cystic fibrosis?" I ask.

He nods, "I believe that's one of the options for next month. Why? What are you thinking?" he asks curiously.

"I'd really like to help with you with a fundraiser for that and if we work well together, maybe we can go from there," I suggest.

"I know we'll work well together," he teases, quickly raising and lowering his eyebrows. I blush and roll my eyes making him laugh. "I have to look at our numbers to see what I can pay you," he informs me.

I nod, "That's fine. We can work that out later. I want to make sure enough would go to cystic fibrosis."

"We usually do pretty well on our fundraisers," he informs me. "Plus everyone that comes leaves with information and sometimes giveaways."

"Giveaways?" I question.

"Yeah," he grins. "Today everyone leaves with a whistle keychain. Plus the local gym is offering one free self-defense class for women next weekend. They have a limit on how many they can take, but if you show up and the class is full, they'll give you a voucher to come back on another day."

"That's fantastic," I declare.

"What kind of information are you giving out?" I ask.

"We have a brochure from one of the organizations on campus and a flyer from another," he explains, pointing towards the end of the bar.

"There are a lot of organizations that provide you with that kind of stuff for free," I tell him. "You could fill a table with free information, especially for something like sexual assault prevention." He grins broadly making me blush. "What?" I ask.

"You and I are going to be great together," he announces.

"Or she'll be great with her boyfriend, Brady," he emphasizes, "and you can go find some other woman to hit on," Cody declares as he steps between us.

Logan laughs and pats Cody lightly on the arm, "Stand down man. We're going to work together on a project. I know she's with Brady."

Cody relaxes slightly and nods his head in understanding. "So those girls I heard complaining about you bringing someone tonight, they think you're with her?"

He shakes his head and grins, "Sam may be with Brady, but she's a fantastic beard." Cody chuckles and Logan adds, "What they don't know, won't hurt 'em." He shrugs, "Besides, she's fun to look at."

"Hey," Cody warns as I feel my whole body heat from head to toe. He turns towards me with a smile. "Hi Sam," he finally greets me.

"Oh, you do know I'm here," I joke. "I was beginning to wonder."

"Ha-ha," he states in monotone. "You're hard to miss," he informs me.

Logan laughs, "And that's not flirting?"

Cody shrugs nonchalantly, "Brady is my best friend. I'm allowed. Are you guys playing pool?" he asks, changing the subject.

Logan grins, "We were talking about it."

"I'm on Sam's team!" Cody declares.

Logan laughs and announces, "I knew it! You're a pool shark," he accuses. I pinch my lips tightly together and pretend that I'm really interested in my surroundings. Both Cody and Logan laugh at my antics.

"Logan," Seth calls from near the door.

He holds his hand up to signify he's on his way before he turns back towards me. "I have to go take care of something, but stick around, take it all in and come up with more great ideas for next time," he grins.

I nod in agreement, "I have to go in a few minutes, but I'll talk to you soon."

"How about we get together one day next week to go over some things?" he suggests. "I already have the date on the calendar, so it's easier if we can stick with that since it's already out there," he informs me.

I nod in understanding, "That sounds good. I really can't wait to get started!" I declare feeling my excitement building. "Thanks Logan!" I tell him appreciatively. I quickly give him a one-armed hug that he returns, before turning away.

"Later Cody," Logan waves and strides away.

Cody purses his lips and looks down at me before asking, "You're working on a project with Logan?"

I shrug, "What's wrong with that?"

He shakes his head, "Nothing. He's just a huge player."

I arch my eyebrow and ask, "Really?"

"You're telling me he hasn't hit on you?" he asks incredulously.

I shake my head, "No, he has, but you've hit on me," I point out. Cody narrows his eyes at me and I add, "Besides, he's been really respectful since he found out I'm dating Brady. Plus, I'm just working with him. I can hold my own. If Brady doesn't trust me, than we're not good for each other anyway," I proclaim.

Cody holds his hands up defensively, "Whoa, I was just saying, if you were my girlfriend, I wouldn't want you working so closely with someone like Logan."

I cross my arms over my chest and glare at him. "But I'm not dating you and I'm pretty sure Olive wouldn't want to hear you say something like that either," I accuse.

Cody visibly cringes. "You're right. I'm sorry." I nod in acceptance, still feeling tense. He sighs and changes the subject, "Where are you going anyway?"

"Frankie invited me to come watch him play today. He has a baseball game," I inform him proudly.

He grins, "That's great!"

I glance at my phone and notice the time. "I actually should probably get going. I don't want to be late."

He nods and smiles back at me. "Are you okay on your own?"

I nod, as a hollow feeling rushes over me, suddenly missing my parents. I force a smile and answer, "I have my phone and I'll grab a whistle on my way out." He arches his eyebrows indicating he either doesn't believe me or that's not what he meant. Either way I don't want to continue this conversation with him. "I'll see you later, Cody."

"Bye, Sam," he offers a small wave. I hear a girl screech his name from the other side of the bar, garnering his attention. I roll my eyes and quickly turn for the door. I wave to Logan as I rush away, feeling the sudden need to escape.

Chapter 11

I saunter towards the baseball fields, the smell of dirt and freshly cut grass apparent in the air. When I'm a close enough to see the field, I put my hand on my forehead to block the sun and squint out at the players, trying to identify Frankie. After a few minutes, I sigh and give up. I turn towards the small set of bleachers mumbling to myself, "They all look the same out there."

A woman chuckles and my head snaps towards the sound. I audibly gasp at the sight of the woman in front of me. The sun shines at her back and I have to squint to see her, making her appear to look like my mom. I freeze, feeling as if I'm seeing her ghost. My breath stops and I feel myself pale. I give myself a slight shake and look into her eyes, realizing I'm just seeing things that aren't there. She tilts her head up, assessing me from her spot on a set of long silver bleachers, consisting of only a few rows. "I'm sorry. I'm just laughing, honey because if it weren't for the numbers on the back of the uniforms, I probably wouldn't be able to pick out my own son," she says with a slight accent. I exhale slowly, willing myself to calm down. She sounds nothing like my mother.

I force myself to take a breath and nod my head slowly, still not quite able to speak. "Samantha," a woman calls my name. I search for the owner and see Lincoln's wife, Ginny. She smiles down at me, two rows up. "Come sit with me," she offers. I give her a small, grateful wave back as I turn towards her.

"Oh," the woman who looks like my mother says, sounding surprised. "You're Samantha, Lincoln's *other* daughter," she states matter-of-fact.

I flinch and fight the urge to make a rude comment. Instead, I offer her a fake smile and grumble, "Nice to meet you." I quickly leap up the last two rows and flop down near Ginny before the woman can say anything else. At least I no longer feel a weird connection to her. Looking down at her from this angle, I don't think she looks anything like my mother.

"Frankie will be so happy you made it!" Ginny exclaims, ignorant to my anxiety. She points out towards the field where Frankie is covering 3rd base. "He's right over there on 3rd. He usually plays third base, but sometimes they move him to second," she informs me.

I nod and mumble my earlier thoughts, "They all look a lot alike out there in those blue and grey uniforms."

She giggles, "They do, but there's little things that help us notice Frankie. He takes his hat on and off a lot to run his fingers through his hair. Plus, when they are turned around, you can look at the numbers on their back. Frankie is number 11," she explains.

Just then the batter hits the ball right down the first base line. Frankie's teammate catches the ball and tags the base to end the inning. Frankie glances up as he jogs towards his team dugout, immediately spotting me. He grins and waves with a sudden little jump in his step. I wave back with a genuine smile of my own. "I'm sorry I didn't get here sooner. I had to stop by the fundraiser at Mae's, but I got here as quickly as I could," I tell her.

"Oh, Jackie was going to be there today for the event. Did you see her?" she asks sounding hopeful.

My stomach drops, feeling as if it's suddenly filling with acid. I clench my jaw and force myself to keep my face neutral as I respond. I shake my head and murmur, "No. I guess I missed her." I can only hope she didn't see me either. I can just imagine how she would twist around my interaction with Logan, probably running to tell Brady.

I watch as Ginny's face fills with obvious disappointment. She softly mumbles, "Oh, that's too bad."

I look down towards my lap, not able to hold back my grimace. I take a deep breath and lift my head, focusing back on the game, just in time to watch Frankie approach the plate, with bat in hand. I watch as the pitcher throws a fastball over the plate and Frankie swings with everything he has. The loud crack indicates his connection with the ball. I stand up, clap and cheer loudly for him as the ball goes over the top of the third baseman's glove. The outfielder runs in, attempting to catch it, but the ball falls to the grass. Frankie makes it to second base before he stops, his whole team cheering him on. "Alright Frankie!" I yell. He grins proudly in the direction of the bleachers, before he focuses back on the game.

It takes three more players at bat before Frankie runs across home plate, giving his coach and all his teammates high-fives. I squint down at the coach and gasp at the familiarity. I ask, "Lincoln is Frankie's coach?"

Ginny looks over at me in confusion, "Yes, I thought one of us told you. Lincoln and another one of the player's dad's coach the team together."

I shake my head and mumble, "I didn't know."

She smiles softly and apologizes, "I'm sorry. I don't know how we forgot. Lincoln loves coaching Frankie. It gives them lots of father-son time."

I gulp over the growing lump in my throat and nod my head in understanding. I stare out at the field as another overwhelming feeling of loss rushes over me. I can't help but miss my own parents in this moment. Whatever I tried, they were always there for me, just like Lincoln is for Frankie. I continue to watch the game and cheer at the appropriate times, but I'm lost in my own head with memories of growing up. In this moment, I realize it's not about Lincoln or Catherine not being there for me, or him being there for Frankie now. The ache in my chest feels like a hole in my heart that I can't completely mend. It's a direct result of missing my mom and dad and knowing I won't have any more moments like that with either of them.

I notice Ginny assessing me out of the corner of my eye, but thankfully she doesn't say anything. I'm grateful she just continues to watch the game. It's not long before it's the bottom of the 9th inning and Frankie's team is up by one run. They only need one more out to win the game. The player up to bat swings at a fastball. It bounces and goes right to third. Frankie catches the grounder and throws the ball to first before he gets to base, ending the game. Cheers erupt all around me. I stand and clap along with them, pasting on a smile. "Come on," Ginny encourages me, with a nod towards the dugout. When I don't move for a minute, she stares intently and reminds me, "I know Frankie is happy you came. He will be excited to see you."

"Okay," I agree. I force myself to move and follow her to the dugout. Frankie takes a step towards us when he sees us approaching. He bounces back and forth on his toes, grinning as he greets me. "Hi Samantha!"

"Hi, Frankie. That was a great game! You're really good," I praise him.

"Thank you," he pauses before launching himself at me, startling me. He quickly hugs me and releases me before I have a chance to process what just happened. "Thank you for coming," he says, back to bouncing on his toes.

"I'm really glad you invited me," I respond earnestly.

He flushes slightly. I can't help but wonder if it's from the exertion and excitement of the game, or if it has something to do with me. "Would you like to go out for pizza with us?" he asks, looking hopeful.

I glance at Ginny who gives me a nearly imperceptible nod. Then I glance over to where Lincoln is still talking to one of the other player's parents, before my eyes land back on Frankie's expectant gaze. I make an instant decision and reply, "Sure, I'd like that."

His grin grows before he quickly masks his happiness. He mumbles, "Cool. I just have to get my stuff."

He turns towards the dugout and immediately goes back to joking with his friends, while he packs up his things. "Who's that?" I hear one of his friends ask. He glances at me before focusing on his friend and answering him, but I don't hear his response.

"Thank you," Ginny whispers, bringing my attention back to her.

I tilt my head towards her, slightly confused. "What are you thanking me for?" I ask.

"Thank you for coming to the game today and thank you for coming with us for pizza. It really means a lot to Frankie, and me," she emphasizes.

"I wanted to be here," I insist.

I glance over at Lincoln, my stomach instantly churning with nerves. "You know, this all means a lot to Lincoln too. He's just not very good at this. He's not quite sure how to handle everything," she attempts to defend him.

I laugh humorlessly and mumble, "Neither do I."

She grimaces and exhales harshly. "He's never been too good at handling serious issues. Sometimes he holds off on saying or doing anything until he's sure that it's the exact right thing to say or do. One of the problems with that is, sometimes he waits too long." I can't help but think that's why he's so lenient on Jackie, but I quickly steer myself away from thoughts of her. "With you I don't think there will ever be the perfect thing for him to say or do, especially if he doesn't even know if you're on the same page," she emphasizes. "I've given him a few pushes, but I think he may need another little push from you," she informs me.

I wince, suddenly feeling the pressure of initiating more with Lincoln. "I'm not supposed to be the adult here," I remind her.

She agrees, "No, you're not, but it's obvious you're a strong independent woman. Maybe just let him know what you want from this, what you're looking for."

"I don't really know," I admit, quietly.

She pauses and looks around the now empty baseball field. She states, "I think you might know more than you're willing to admit, even to yourself."

My eyebrows draw together in confusion and I ask almost accusatory, "What do you mean by that?"

She shakes her head and explains, "I don't mean to offend you, Samantha. I just mean, I don't think you'd be here at Frankie's game and coming with us for pizza, if you didn't at least know a little bit of what you want from this." I sigh and bite my bottom lip in thought. "I'm just saying, that I really think you should talk to Lincoln. Maybe you can even figure it out together, but talk to him," she declares.

I remain quiet for a moment, staring at the ground, as an unsettled feeling closes in on me. Ginny steps a little closer to me and places her hand on my back. She gives me a gentle, reassuring pat. She drops her head, just as Frankie strides up to us with a backpack and a baseball bag that appears to hold his bat and glove. "I'm ready to go," he announces. "I'm starving!"

"Okay," she smiles fondly at her son. "Would you like to meet us there?" she asks, peering over at me in question.

I force a smile and nod my head, "Yeah, that would be great, if that's okay. I have my car with me."

She nods politely, "Okay, we're just going to the pizza place right on Main Street in town," she informs me.

"I know where that is," I confirm.

She waves and encourages Frankie, "Come on, let's go."

Frankie smiles and waves, "See you there, Sam!"

"Bye," I state. I wave, remaining frozen as I watch them walk towards the parking lot, stopping to grab Lincoln on the way. He turns around and spots me. He holds his hand up in greeting, offering me a friendly smile. I'm not able to do anything, except smile back. I groan in frustration and drop my head towards the ground. "I can do this," I mumble to myself. I lift my head high and square my shoulders. Then I stride to my car, feigning confidence.

Chapter 12

Brady

I glance at my phone and run my hands through my hair in frustration. I still don't have a text from Sam, since this morning when she said she didn't know when she would be home and it's getting late. I know she doesn't have to check in with me, but I can't help the need I feel to look out for her. That's what you do for someone you love.

"Thanks for helping out tonight, Brady," my dad tells me as he stops in the doorway of his office. "I can take it from here," he informs me.

I nod, "Thanks Dad."

"Are you heading right home?" he asks as he steps into the room. I nod my head and drop the pen in my hand on the desk and let it rattle before it settles. "Alright, Goodnight then."

I should've been out of here hours ago, but after the meeting with the contractors, I ended up dealing with an issue for my dad. I drop the reports back in the top of my dad's desk drawer and slam it shut. I stand and quickly pull my black coat on. "Goodnight," I grumble, as I stride past him and out of his office. I hear him chuckling, while I continue to stare at my phone, as I walk quickly down the hallway. I crash into someone and drop my phone. "Shit," I gripe. I try to steady both of us by gripping her elbows tightly. I mumble, "Sorry." I look up and meet Jackie's startled golden gaze.

"Brady, I was just looking for you," she smiles happily.

I sigh and quickly disentangle myself from her. "Hi Jackie," I murmur. "What are you doing here?" I question, feeling apprehensive.

She grimaces at my tone and asks, "Bad day?"

"Yeah, I guess," I blurt out honestly. I shake my head dismissively. "What do you want Jackie?" I ask in exasperation.

She purses her lips and takes a step back. She crosses her arms over her chest, defensively and narrows her eyes on me. Although, I expect her to do that, so she can push her chest up and flirt with me like she usually does, I can tell that's not what this is, which makes me even more wary. "What do I want?" she asks, like I'm crazy. She huffs in annoyance, glaring at me. "I guess you forgot about today," she accuses me, her voice thick with disappointment.

I shake my head cautiously, not able to remember anything special about today. "Forgot what?" I ask warily.

"The fundraiser for sexual assault and sexual harassment prevention was today at Mae's. I thought you were going to help me give away all the raffles," she states. "You always come to these things with me."

I sigh in defeat and drop my head. I knew I should've said something about not going, but I thought it would be better not to bring attention to it at all. I remind her, "I told you I couldn't be the one to do that stuff for you anymore, Jackie."

She winces and tears form in her eyes, but she doesn't let them fall. "I didn't know you meant for things like this too," she rasps painfully, causing my chest to ache for her. "Didn't this mean anything to you at all?"

"Shit," I mumble. "I'm sorry, Jackie," I apologize, feeling like an asshole. I take in her faded blue jeans, black boots and her teal off the shoulder sweater, the color that represents sexual assault and harassment prevention.

She blinks her tears away and mumbles, "You could've been more clear. I thought this was different. I thought you would at least be there today, even if we weren't going together. To me, this is different," she emphasizes.

I sigh and run my fingers through my hair again, not sure of how to respond. She's right. This is different, but I don't want her to twist my words around if I were to admit it to her. I should've at least gone to the fundraiser with Samantha for a little while, even if I had to change my meeting with the contractor. "I really am sorry," I repeat. Guilt begins weighing down on my chest as her tears spill over onto her cheeks. I step towards her and wrap her in my arms with a heavy sigh. She willingly curls into me and holds on tightly. I attempt to comfort her, even though I feel incredibly uncomfortable with this whole situation. Cody's right. Sometimes I don't know how to get out of situations with her. "It's okay Jackie," I tell her, as I gently pat her on the back. I glance around, ironically grateful to be alone with her in the hallway.

She takes a deep breath and exhales slowly, before wiping away her tears with her hands. "Thank you," she mumbles. I don't respond and she continues with a long, drawn-out sigh. "Well, I guess I have to forgive you" she mumbles into my chest, "but it was really hard to be there without you, Brady."

I ignore the last part of her comment and chuckle, uncomfortably. I give her one last pat on the back and drop my hands to my sides, not wanting to hold her longer than necessary. I lean my shoulder against the wall and cross my arms over my chest to keep my distance. Then I ask, "So, the fundraiser seemed to go well?"

She shrugs, "I guess. I just handed baskets to people. It's not like Logan ever really tells me anything." She grimaces, "He probably wishes I wasn't there. He doesn't seem to like me very much." I bite the inside of my cheek to hold back my laughter, knowing that's a gross understatement. "He seemed to have a lot to say to your girlfriend though," she states, obviously trying to cause some kind of trouble.

My eyes narrow and I nod slowly, assessing her. I want to do what I can to anticipate the direction she's going with this conversation, but I know that's never easy with her. "That's good to hear. I'm sure she had a lot of questions," I respond vaguely.

I notice the flick of her head and the surprise in her eyes, before she swiftly wipes it away. "So you knew she was going to be there to see Logan and you still didn't come?" she asks. "Trouble in paradise?" she asks snidely.

"Jackie," I caution, glowering at her. She rolls her eyes and doesn't let my warning bother her. "Sam and I are good. Everything else about our relationship is none of your business," I blurt out angrily. "If you think," I begin.

She puts her hand up to interrupt me and shakes her head, "It's fine, Brady. I don't want to know about your relationship with her," she says with complete disgust. "Anyway," she gives herself a physical shake before she continues, “I’m just surprised you’re okay with Logan, the player, of all people,” she emphasizes, “being all over your girlfriend.”

“Jackie, stop!” I demand, pushing off the wall, but keeping my arms crossed.

“Stop what?” she questions innocently. She shakes her head, “I’m not doing anything, Brady. I’m just stating a fact. He was all over your girlfriend and I’m not making it up,” she declares. “I know they aren’t related like that other guy,” she reminds me of when she saw Samantha at the Pit Stop with her cousin Ryan and thought Sam was cheating on me. “You don’t have to believe me, but pictures don’t lie. Look” she insists. She shoves her phone in my face.

I begin pushing it away, but I freeze at the sight on her screen. I feel my face pale and my heart drop into the pit of my stomach, as I unknowingly grip her phone tightly. The bottom of Logan’s fire tattoo is peaking out from underneath the sleeve of his black t-shirt as he drapes his arm over Samantha’s shoulders. It appears as if he’s pulling her towards him as he leans down towards her, his lips brushing the top of her head. Her hands are nowhere in sight. I can’t tell if she’s pushing him away or not, but Seth’s smirk and Vanessa’s glare, focused on my girl, tell a story I’m not sure if I want to know. “There’s another one,” she says. She quickly flicks her finger over her phone and it slides to another picture of them, before I have a chance to react. This time, Logan’s face is close to hers, but from the angle of the picture I can’t see her face. I know it’s her, by both her outfit and the soft wave of her hair down her back. If it were anyone but Samantha, I would swear he was making out with the girl in front of him.

I take a deep breath and exhale slowly, repeating the process a few times to calm my anxiety. I remind myself I trust her and she’ll be able to explain this. I force myself to place Jackie’s phone back in her hand before I lean back against the wall again, attempting to look at ease. “I knew she was going to talk to him,” I finally inform her, defensively.

She snorts a laugh, “Maybe you did, but your reaction tells me you weren’t expecting that, no matter how hard you’re trying to hide it from me. I know you very well Brady," she adds, turning on the charm.

I grind my jaw at her response and repeat my apology, "I'm sorry I wasn't there today. If you ask me next time, I might consider going, but Samantha is not a topic of discussion I'm willing to have with you, no matter what you think you saw. In fact, especially then," I emphasize. I remind myself I can't trust anything Jackie tells me about Sam.

She purses her lips like she's considering her options. Then she shrugs and declares, "That's fine. It's not like I want to get involved in anything with the two of you," she declares ironically. I'd be laughing if I didn't feel so sick right now. "I'll send you the pictures though, just in case you want to ask her about them," she shrugs like it's no big deal. I flinch when my phone beeps with her message. I just want to block the pictures from my memory, not have them on my fucking phone.

She stands tall and squares her shoulders, as if she needs the strength before she speaks. She reminds me, "MADD is having their awareness dinner at the end of the month. I will be there for Max and his family," she informs me.

I feel a slight pang in my chest at the mention of his name. "I will be too. I wouldn't miss it," I insist.

She nods in acceptance and smiles appearing relieved, "Good." She smooths down her sweater with her palms and focuses back on me. "So…what are you doing tonight?" she asks, attempting to change the subject.

I glance at my phone, noticing I still have no missed calls or text messages from Sam. My only new message is the pictures Jackie just sent. I grind my teeth and push up from the wall, feeling as if I'm about to explode. If I don't get out of here and away from Jackie, I might lose it on her. "I really gotta' go," I inform her, without answering her question.

"Oh, okay," she responds dejectedly. "I have to go too. I just wanted to see where you were today and make sure you're going to be at the event later this month," she rambles. "I guess I'll see you later, Brady," she tells me, with a sad smile.

I force a reassuring smile of my own. “Goodbye,” I say. I step around her and stride for the front of the restaurant. I walk out the door without looking back.

I slide behind the wheel in my truck and drop my phone into the cup holder. I glare down at it, like it might be poisonous, but than again, it sure as hell feels that way at the moment. “I need to talk to Sam,” I mumble to myself.

Chapter 13

Samantha

I slip out of my apartment in my fuzzy purple socks, pink flannel pajama pants and gray tank top. I knock on Brady's door and it swings open almost immediately. His eyes meet mine and his body deflates, as he breathes a visible sigh of relief. He reaches for my hand and gives me a gentle tug, causing me to fall into his arms. I face plant into his chest and squeal, "Hi" as he wraps his arms tightly around me.

"Why didn't you text me?" he asks. Then he kisses the top of my head. "I was worried about you. You didn't answer me all day."

I wince, "I'm sorry. I haven't really thought that way since my parents." I gulp and change the direction of my response. "I was just really busy. I didn't want you to wait around for me and then I don't get there in time. I figured I'd text you when I knew what was going on." He pinches his lips tightly together and gives me a slight nod. "I went to the fundraiser for a little while and then I went to Frankie's baseball game," I explain.

He leans back to assess my expression and smiles down at me. The appearance of his deep dimple causes butterflies to nearly take over my stomach. I can't help but smile back. "It went well," he states.

I nod and barely rasp my confirmation, "It did."

I hear the elevator doors open, but before I have a chance to look to see who is stepping off it, Brady's lips come crashing down on mine. I sigh and kiss him back, noticing the faint sound of a low chuckle behind me. Without removing his lips from mine, he lifts me up and spins me out of the way of the door. He closes it by pushing me up against it. He sweeps his tongue inside my mouth and I wrap my legs around his waist for support. He groans and tries to push the kiss deeper, but I tear my lips away and drop my head to his shoulder, already desperate to catch my breath. "What was that for?" I'm finally able to mutter.

He chuckles, "I'm happy things went well for you today. I'm happy you're okay and I'm really fucking happy you're here in my arms."

I smirk, "Okay."

"You taste like pizza," he informs me. He presses his lips to mine again and flicks his tongue out, licking my lips and making me laugh. "Mm," he murmurs. I let my feet fall to the ground, but he doesn't let me go. He walks us both to the couch and lies down on his back, flipping me on top of him.

I lift my head slightly, so I can look at him. I tell him, "Frankie invited me to go to pizza with them after his game."

Brady's eyes light up and he encourages me, "That's fantastic Sam!"

I nod in agreement, "Yeah, He's a really good baseball player."

"I believe it," Brady concedes. "I haven't seen him play in a long time though."

"You should come with me sometime," I tell him. I open my mouth and begin rambling about Frankie's game, but falter when a vision of the woman I thought was my mother crosses my mind. I gulp over the lump in my throat and tell him, "I thought I saw my mom today."

"What?" he asks, perplexed.

I shake my head, trying to shake off the strange feeling and explain. "It hasn't happened in a long time, but I use to see my mom and dad everywhere. There was this mom there with the sun behind her and I had to squint to look at her." I shake my head again, "Anyway, as soon as she started talking, it was fine, but…is that weird?" I ask, nervous as to what he might think.

He shakes his head, "No. I think it sounds pretty normal for someone who lost her mom and dad."

His words comfort me and I smile down at him. I quickly change the subject back to going out for pizza with Frankie, Ginny and Lincoln. "Anyway, going out for pizza with them went pretty well. It still feels pretty awkward around Lincoln, but he tried. I think it was actually a little easier to talk to him when I first met him. I was thinking that maybe it's because he wasn't around his family then. It's seems to me that when he's around them, he's constantly worried about how they might react to anything that comes out of his mouth. He doesn't want to do, or say anything to upset them, but Frankie is such an easy kid. I can't imagine what it would've been like if Jackie were there," I grimace. "I do really like Ginny though. She's really nice. It feels like she's the one doing everything she can to make me feel comfortable. Yet, at the same time, she doesn't want to step on my toes," I tell him. He just nods in understanding. "Do you know what Frankie told me?" I ask grinning.

"Tell me," he urges.

"Well, he told me he's excited to have another sister," I admit. I feel my face flush, as I say the words out loud. A lump forms in my throat and I try to explain what I think, "He's so sweet and innocent." I shrug, knowing those weren't the best words to describe a teenage boy. "He even hugged me…twice," I grin.

Brady lightly runs the back of his fingers down the side of my face and slips his hand into my hair, holding me still. He stares into my eyes and insists, "I love seeing you so happy."

His comment gives me the urge to tell him what I'm thinking. "I am, but I feel more like they're all distant relatives that I just met. Kind of like an Aunt and Uncle and even a cousin." I bite my lower lip, as I try to organize my thoughts. He lifts his fingers to my lips and tugs it free. He lightly kisses my lips, making me smile. "I want to know more about my history, but I can't imagine going to family events," I grimace. "I want to spend time getting to know them, but I don't want them to replace my family."

"That would never happen," he declares.

I nod, "You're right, it wouldn't. I love my mom and dad so much." My voice cracks with emotion. Brady caresses my cheek with his other hand before weaving it into my hair on the other side of my head. He moves his thumbs back and forth in a soothing motion.

"They would be very proud of you," he insists.

I smirk, "Even though I want to accept Frankie, but not Jackie, as part of any kind of family of mine?"

He chuckles and confirms, "Yes." He lightly kisses my lips and lets his head fall back to the couch with a sigh.

I lean up further and his hands fall away from my face. "Are you okay?" I ask, peering at him a little closer.

He nods and tucks a lock of my hair behind my ear with another sigh. "Yeah," he whispers. My eyebrows draw together in confusion, but he stops my inquiry. "Just keep going. Tell me about the rest of your day," he prompts.

My eyes flick back and forth assessing him, but I have no idea what's going on in his head. I finally concede and remind him, "You know I went to the fundraiser earlier, at Mae's."

He gulps and nods in agreement, "Yeah."

"Well, it was really pretty cool, but I had a few ideas that could make it even more. I know I promised to work on the wedding and I still will. I want to," I emphasize, "but May is Cystic Fibrosis Awareness Month. I'd really like to work on a fundraiser with Logan for that," I inform him. "Especially since my birth mom died from complications, due to her cystic fibrosis," I tell him.

He nods and barely mumbles, "Yeah, makes sense."

"That's all you have to say?" I ask.

He sighs again and my heart leaps into my throat. I feel the anxiety beginning to crawl all over my skin. "If that's what you want to do, I can see if the banquet room at the restaurant is available. You can utilize the space, tables, linens and other things like that for free. The only cost would be for all the extras like food, decorations, music, and staff. Plus it's a bigger space."

"That would be wonderful! Are you sure that would be okay with your parents?" I ask. He nods slowly. Thank you!" I exclaim. I press my lips to his in appreciation.

He barely accepts my kiss, before he pulls back and smiles stiffly. "No problem," he grumbles.

My eyebrows arch in challenge. "Are you sure about that?" After waiting a moment and getting no verbal response from him, my stomach sours and twists into knots. "What's wrong?" I ask anxiously.

"Nothing is wrong," he insists. He looks at me with his jaw clenched, like he's holding something back. "I'm just happy your day went so well," he states flatly.

I plant my hands on his chest and push myself up and away from him, sitting on the other end of the couch. "What the hell is wrong with you?" I question irritably.

He sighs and sits up facing me. He pinches his lips tightly together and runs his hand through his hair, before dropping both hands back on his lap. He tilts his head and holds my gaze. "I saw Jackie tonight. She came by the restaurant," he informs me.

I grind my teeth and narrow my eyes on him, waiting for him to continue. Just hearing her name causes my whole body to tense. I know no good can come from this conversation, but I also know it would be worse, if we didn't talk about it at all. When he doesn't say anything else, I prompt, "She came to see you?"

He nods and mumbles, "Yeah."

"You're going to have to keep talking, if you want this conversation to go anywhere, Brady," I remark irritably.

He visibly winces at my tone. "Remember when I told you the story about what happened to Max?" he asks quietly.

My eyebrows draw together in confusion at the change in subject. "Yeah," I reply hesitantly.

He gulps, "And do you remember the part about Jackie?" he questions. I nod. "Well, Jackie has tried to do something, no matter how small to support sexual harassment and assault prevention and awareness every year. Well that and a drunk driving prevention event. Since she doesn't really do much volunteering, she didn't know what she could do. So, she latched on to Logan's event. They don't exactly get along. He doesn't let her do much, but he respects that she wants to help. So he gives her the job of handing out raffle baskets to all the winners." He grimaces, "In fact, that's partly why she came to see me. In the past, I've always gone with her to these things. When I wasn't there..." he trails off.

I cross my arms over my chest, my whole body practically shaking in anger. I refrain from rolling my eyes, as I imagine what she said to him. "And?" I ask. I need to hear him tell me what she said about me.

He sighs and mumbles, "I was hoping you might want to finish the story for me." I glare at him. He attempts to reach for me, but I pull back into the couch cushion. He flinches and concedes, "Sam, I need you to know, I don't believe what she said, but I do need you to explain the pictures to me."

"Pictures?" I ask in confusion.

He nods in defeat, "Yeah, pictures." He reluctantly holds his phone out to me.

I cautiously reach for it and gasp at the picture of Logan and me. "We weren't kissing!" I blurt out, vehemently. "I wouldn't do that to you!"

He slowly closes his eyes and opens them back up, focusing on me. "I didn't think you would. I just don't understand what I'm seeing," he says, his voice cracking.

I shake my head, "Honestly I don't either. The girl behind us was hitting on Logan and he begged me to play along. All he said was, 'She's with me.' He did put his arm around me, but as soon as we were back by the pool tables, I moved away. I also told him, he couldn't put me in a situation like that again. I told him it made me uncomfortable and it wasn't fair to you or me," I emphasize. "This must've been when he was asking me for help. It was loud and he obviously didn't want the girl to hear him," I explain.

Brady nods his head slowly and stares at the black screen of the television. "Okay," he mumbles.

"Can you please say something else? I shouldn't have to deal with her trying to sabotage our relationship every chance she gets," I complain.

He turns back towards me and reminds me, "Even though Jackie's view was distorted, I shouldn't have to hear, or see anything like this from her…or anyone else, for that matter," he emphasizes.

"I would've told you," I insist. He gives me a look, indicating he doesn't know if he should believe me. I clench my jaw and practically spit words out through my teeth, "I would've, if I had the chance!" I stand and turn towards the door, suddenly ready to leave.

He sighs and runs his hand through his hair, "Sam, wait. Please," he begs. He catches up to me in one long stride and wraps his arm around my waist to stop me. "I'm sorry," he whispers into my ear. My body relaxes, slightly. He sets me on my feet and steps around in front of me. He stares into my eyes, his own searching for understanding. "I know not to take anything she says too seriously. I also didn't think you would do anything like that to me, especially with what happened with your ex." He pauses and a flash of pain runs over his face before he quickly covers it up again. "It doesn't mean it didn't suck seeing a picture like that," he states.

My heart clenches at the memory of seeing a picture of him in a similar position with Jackie. "Like the pictures I had seen of the two of you," I remind him quietly. Hopefully, that will also help him understand I didn't do anything.

He grimaces and nods. "Yeah," he croaks.

"I get it. I hated seeing something like that, but after what happened last time, why didn't you want to talk to me?" I question.

He winces, "It's not that I didn't want to talk to you about it. I just didn't want to ruin your night. You were so happy when you got here. You obviously had a great day. I just wanted to listen to you talk about everything and watch you smile."

I grin and mumble, "That's sweet."

"Only because it's you," he smirks. He leans down and kisses me lightly on the lips.

The motion makes me gasp in realization. "Is that what all of that was about?" I ask gesturing wildly towards the front door with my hands.

Brady's eyes widen in surprise and he stumbles over what to say, "Ah, what?"

My eyes narrow, but his arm remains around my waist, holding me to him. "The way you kissed me in your doorway when I got here. Was that a whole possessive thing with you? Who got off the elevator?" I ask.

He flinches and concedes, "I'm not exactly sure, but whoever it was went into Logan and Seth's apartment." I wiggle away and he drops his arms. "I'm sorry, it was a stupid reaction. I really was relieved to see you, though. The only text I had gotten from you all day, was you telling me you didn't know when you would be home. School has gotten intense and work has now gotten so crazy with this construction project. I just miss you," he insists. "I want to see you, Sam! I'll admit I was jealous Logan got to spend time with you, when I've barely seen you at all this week, except for that damn meeting."

I sigh and reluctantly agree, "I guess you're right. I did want to see you. I just wasn't sure what time I would be home. Plus, I was just walking into the fundraiser when you texted this morning," I begin rambling.

He nods, "I'm sorry, it made me a little crazy."

"A little?" I smirk.

He chuckles, "Anyway…can we not talk about this anymore? I'm completely exhausted. Will you just stay here with me for a little while?"

I nod my head in agreement, "Okay." He smiles in satisfaction. I push up on my tiptoes and kiss his left cheek right on his dimple, before it disappears.

He links his hand with mine and leads me back to the couch. He lies down on his back and I curl up next to him on the backside of the couch. His arm goes around me holding me close as I rest my hand across his hard stomach. I curl my leg up slightly and rest it on his. He kisses the top of my head and whispers, "Thank you. I needed this." He gives me a light squeeze, warming me from head to toe.

I look up at him and admit, "I think I did too." He lifts his head and I push up towards him, meeting him halfway. His kiss is soft, tender and slow. We move together in a slow rhythm. It's perfect. I moan into the kiss, but just as I'm about to push for more, his head falls back to the couch, with a content smile on his face.

He reaches for the remote and turns the TV on, before handing it to me. "Watch whatever you want," he instructs.

My eyes widen in surprise, but then I notice the dark circles under his eyes and the exhaustion in them. I nod and flip through the channels before finally stopping on an old episode of One Tree Hill. I glance down at him just as he loses the fight to keep his eyes open. I turn the TV on mute and watch him sleep for a little while, looking both peaceful and vulnerable. I know I'm in love with him. He's been there for me through so much already and I want to be there for him the same way. I just can't help but wonder if I depend on him too much. Maybe that's what I was trying to do today, by turning my phone on silent, be independent. Can I figure out who I am and who I want to be with him by my side?

I give myself a mental shake as exhaustion begins settling into my body. I carefully push myself over Brady and off the couch, trying not to wake him. I lean down and kiss him lightly. I smile at the soft sigh that escapes through his lips. I reach for the blue fleece blanket thrown over the back of the couch and cover him with it the best I can. I cover my mouth, giggling at how much of his body hangs over the end of the couch. I kiss him lightly one more time. Then I lean down and whisper, "Goodnight Brady." I quietly slip out the front door and return to my apartment and my own bed.

Chapter 14

I grab my mail out of my mailbox, then close and lock the small door. I spin around, just as Jackie walks in through the front door of our apartment building. She smirks when she sees me. She stops in front of me and sticks her hip out, placing her hand on her hip. I attempt to keep my face neutral, but I don't really know how successful I am. Just seeing her ignites a fire inside of me, giving me the desire to do something about it, but I'm not about to start a fight with anyone, let alone my half-sister.

"I heard you went to *my* brother's game and then went out for pizza with *my* family," she states icily. She glares at me and declares, "You're not stealing my family away from me, like you stole Brady."

I sigh in annoyance at her accusation. "That's not what I'm trying to do. I'm just trying to figure out where I fit in," I explain, ignoring the part about Brady. It's just not worth going at it with her again about him.

"You don't," she announces, matter of fact. I attempt to gulp down the lump in my throat and remind myself, this is hard for her too. "I saw you getting pretty cozy with Logan at Mae's the other day," she informs me. My phone rings, flashing Paul's name. I grimace and silence it, wondering why he's even bothering anymore. "Who's Paul?" she asks, curiously.

"Why is that any of your business?" I snap and immediately regret it. Jackie grins devilishly at my reaction, causing me to sigh in defeat. "What are you even doing here, Jackie?" I question, out of patience.

She smiles, "I came to see Brady and thank him for comforting me the other day." My stomach bubbles up with acid, as I fight to control my reaction. I cannot give her more than I already have today. I pinch my lips tightly together as she continues. "We've been through a lot together and you showing up here, doesn't change that. He was there for me, when I needed him. Plus, I wanted to make sure he was okay. You know, after the whole thing with you and Logan," she taunts, looking completely satisfied with herself.

I grind my teeth in annoyance, no longer able to sit there and keep my mouth shut. "There is no Logan and me," I insist.

Brady walks in the door with his backpack slung over one arm and freezes at the sight of Jackie and me standing in the lobby. His eyes widen and he moves his gaze back and forth between us. He clears his throat and confidently strides up to me, smiling reassuringly. "Hi Sam," he says and kisses me lightly on the lips. He clasps my hand and turns to face Jackie. "What are you doing here, Jackie?" he asks, trying to break up any conversation we were having before he walked in.

"Your *girlfriend* and I were just talking," she claims, her eyes narrowing on me. "I actually came over to see you," she adds, focusing on him.

"I've got it Brady," I tell him.

He shakes his head and announces, "Well, now you see me."

She purses her lips and laughs uncomfortably. "Yes, I just wanted to say thank you for the other day."

He nods abruptly, "You're welcome."

"Then I was lucky enough to run into Sam and we were talking," she informs him.

"I've got it Brady," I repeat.

"Talking about what?" he questions.

I tug on his hand to get his attention and he turns towards me, perplexed. I repeat, "I've got it. We were just talking about her family."

Jackie grins, "That's right. We were just talking about *my* family."

"Jackie," Brady warns.

I huff in annoyance and pull my hand away from his. I turn towards the elevator, but think better of it, not wanting to stand in the lobby with either of them for another second. I stomp for the stairs to the left and begin climbing. "What's her problem?" Jackie asks, disapprovingly. I grind my teeth and keep walking.

"Sam, wait," Brady calls after me. I climb faster, instead of listening to his plea. "Why don't you leave her alone?" Brady asks, just before the sound of their voices begins to fade.

I reach the fourth floor and sigh with relief, my legs feeling as if they're on fire from the exertion. "I should really do that more often," I mumble to myself.

I push the door open for my apartment and stride for the kitchen. Cory sits in the back corner of the nook, eating a bowl of cereal. She finishes chewing and asks, "What took you so long? I thought you were just grabbing our mail? Did you have a quickie with Brady in the elevator or something?" she jokes.

I drop the mail on the counter with an exaggerated huff, startling her. "Or something," I grumble. "I ran into Jackie," I inform her and scrunch up my nose with distaste.

She grimaces, "It went that well, huh?" I laugh humorlessly. I open my mouth to rant, but she interrupts, "Speaking of people you don't want to talk to, I got a DM on my Instagram from your ex. At least that's who I assume it is, since his name is Paul."

My mouth drops open in shock. I ask, "What did he want?"

She shrugs and replies, "He was asking how he could get in touch with you."

"Did you respond?" I question.

She shakes her head, "No. I wanted to see what you wanted me to say."

I grimace, "Nothing, I guess."

"Got it," she agrees.

Brady pounds on the front door, interrupting our conversation. "Samantha?" he calls through the door.

I remain quiet, clenching my jaw. Cory eyes me and arches her eyebrows in question. When he pounds again, she yells, "Come in!"

I lean against the counter and cross my arms in front of my chest, defensively. "Sam?" he says my name cautiously, as he steps into the kitchen.

I glare at him and ask, "Did you think I couldn't handle myself with her?"

"No," he shakes his head and takes a step towards me.

"I'm very capable," I insist.

He sighs and emphasizes, "I know you are. I just got anxious when I saw the two of you together and tried to diffuse the situation."

"But you didn't even know what we were talking about," I argue.

He shakes his head, "No, but it didn't look good." He pauses and takes another cautious step closer to me. "What were you talking about anyway?" he asks.

I huff in annoyance, "You ask now?" he flinches and I admit, "It wasn't anything good, but it doesn't matter. I need to be able to handle Jackie, without you always trying to step in to rescue me. I already told you that, Brady."

He nods, "I know. I get it. I'm sorry. It's just so hard to stay out of it, when I know I can help you."

"But you won't always be there. I need to be able to deal with her myself," I insist.

"I'm sorry, Sam," he repeats. I pinch my lips tightly together and nod in acceptance. I just can't stay mad at him. He breathes a sigh of relief and closes the space between us. He places his hand on my hip and kisses the corner of my mouth in apology, before turning towards Cory. "Hey Cory."

She grins and shakes her head. "You never learn," she teases.

"Apparently not," he agrees with a low chuckle. The sound rumbles through my bones, giving me shivers from the inside, out.

"I have to go make a phone call," Cory states. She stands and places her bowl in the sink. "I'll do my dishes later," she informs me. "Be good you two," she teases, as she walks out of the kitchen.

Brady looks at me and repeats his apology, seeming sincere. "I'm really sorry, Sam." He lightly brushes his lips over mine.

I nod and smile, knowing he was just trying to help. I look up into his eyes and my chest aches. I don't want to argue with him anymore. "Why does it feel like we're fighting a lot lately?" I ask sadly.

He sighs and drops his forehead down to mine. "We're not fighting. We just didn't look at things the same way this time."

I giggle and shake my head at his explanation. His lips twitch up, as he fights a smile. I grin and try to change the subject. "What are you doing tonight?" I ask, hoping we can spend some time together.

He grimaces and pulls his head slightly away, "I have to put together a rough business plan for one of my classes. Plus, I have a test tomorrow in finance."

"Sounds like fun," I respond sarcastically.

He chuckles and informs me, "I do have some good news, though."

"You do?" I ask.

He nods, "Yeah. I have the restaurant confirmed for the date you wanted for the Cystic Fibrosis fundraiser."

I throw my arms around his neck and squeal, "Thank you! This is going to be fantastic! I release him and plant my hands on his chest. "I have to tell Logan," I announce excitedly.

He flinches, holding me a little tighter. "Can you wait just a little while?"

"Sorry," I murmur. I wrap my arms around his waist and push up, pressing my lips to his to ease his tension. "You know you have nothing to worry about with Logan."

He chuckles and slides his hands down to my ass. He reminds me, "You don't know Logan that well."

"True, but you know me," I stress.

"You're right and I'm crazy about you," he insists.

"Good," I grin.

He chuckles and tilts his head down, brushing his lips along my jawline towards my ear. Then he kisses my neck in just the right spot, making me gasp and hold him tighter. He pats my butt with his right hand and slides it up my side slowly. He traces over my breast and up my neck, until he holds my face carefully in his hands. He kisses me, soft and slow, for only a moment. Then he tilts my head up and our mouths fuse together, instantly moving as one. His tongue sweeps in to meet mine in a playful dance, causing me to groan with need for him. I slip my hand under his white t-shirt, wanting to feel his skin on my fingertips. His stomach rumbles under the palm of my hand and I pull away from his kiss laughing. “Hungry?” I tease him.

He pats his stomach proudly and states, “I’m a very active, growing boy.” His words only make me laugh harder. “Want to order pizza?” he asks, as I slowly begin controlling my laughter. I nod as I catch my breath and follow him out to the living room.

“Cory,” he calls, “We’re ordering pizza!”

“Again?” she yells. “I’m in!”

The front door swings open, just as we flop down on the couch together and Cody waltzes in. “Did I hear you say we’re ordering pizza?” he grins.

I laugh, “Where did you come from?”

“The hallway,” he states, like it’s obvious. He pushes the door shut behind him. He walks over and drops down into the armchair next to the couch, kicking his feet up onto the coffee table.

“You can’t just walk in here whenever you feel like it anymore,” Brady reminds Cody. “What if she was naked?” Brady asks, accusingly.

Cody grins, “Thanks for that image. He immediately gets hit in the face with a pillow, making him laugh. “I heard you talking to my sister, so if your girlfriend was out here naked, you have a lot more things to worry about, than me walking in.” Brady glares at Cody, but he just brushes it off. “Actually, you just got a phone call and I thought you might be here, so I thought I’d pass on the message while I can still remember it,” he states.

“What’s the message?” Brady asks.

“That marketing company in Minneapolis called our landline to confirm you received all of the paperwork for the internship. They want to make sure you’re up and running now, so if you take their offer, you’ll be ready to jump right in after graduation,” Cody explains.

Brady looks at me with wide eyes and quickly explains, “I was planning to tell you about that tonight.”

"Don't they have your cell phone?" Cody asks perplexed. "I almost forgot we even have a landline, until I couldn't get it to stop ringing."

Brady ignores his question and instead requests, "Can you go order pizza for all of us? I want to fill Sam in on all of this?"

Cody nods and stands with an exaggerated sigh, "Fine." He grumbles, "Why do I have to do everything around here?" He stalks out of the apartment and shuts the door.

I look up at Brady and ask, "What's this all about?"

Brady shrugs and explains, "It's not a big deal, but I got an offer for an internship after graduation. It's with a Marketing company in Minneapolis."

"That's great!" I exclaim. "That would be a great experience. It would be so different from what you've been doing with the restaurant."

He nods slowly, "Yeah, but I don't know if I want to take it. There will be others."

"You can't give up an opportunity like that," I insist.

"But it's in Minneapolis. That's over a four hour drive," he informs me.

"So?" I ask. His mouth drops slightly open in surprise. "You can't make a decision like this because of me," I tell him, feeling slightly panicked.

"I can't make a decision like this and leave you out of the equation, Sam," he declares.

"If you're talking to me about it, it's not leaving me out of the equation," I insist. "Besides, I don't even know what I'm doing yet," I remind him. "What if I end up going back down to Illinois?" I argue.

He shakes his head and complains, "If that's the case, then you'd be even further away from me."

I grimace and try to think reasonably. After a moment of quiet I ask, "How long is the internship?"

"It's six months to start," he declares.

"That's not forever. Please don't make a decision like that, based on where I am," I plead. "I don't want you to resent me," I add, looking down at my lap.

He tilts his head down by my lowered one, encouraging me to look up at him. He waits until I look into his eyes, before he claims, "I could never resent you, Samantha." My face scrunches up with doubt. He flinches at my reaction and emphasizes, "I promise, okay?" I nod sadly and he elaborates on his promise, "I promise I will make the decision that's best for me. The one I know I'll be happy with the outcome."

"Thank you," I tell him. He leans down and kisses me, immediately pulling away when Cody reenters. He puts his arm around me and I curl into his side as we wait for the pizza. They begin talking about a new app and I zone out, thinking about what Brady might do. I can't let him give up an opportunity like this, especially when I don't even know if I'm staying.

Chapter 15

Brady

I walk into The Pit and smile as my gaze lands on Samantha. Her soft brown waves are pulled up in a high ponytail, exposing her neck, causing my heartbeat to quicken. I want to press my lips to her exposed skin and inhale her intoxicating scent, but I'd probably scare the crap out of her. She's staring down at her phone and doesn't see me approaching. I slide into the booth across from her instead, making her jump as her head snaps up. I chuckle, imagining an elbow to my face if I would've done what I wanted. Her body instantly relaxes the moment she meets my eyes. I grin, loving her response to seeing me. "Hi beautiful," I greet her.

She smirks and arches her eyebrows in question at my greeting. I shrug, like it's something I do every day, but it's not something I would've thought I'd be saying before I met her. She giggles softly under her breath, "Hi Brady."

The sound of her voice saying my name, like I'm a treasure, gives me chills, like it does every time. I take a deep breath and exhale slowly to calm my now racing heart. "Thanks for coming to meet me," I tell her appreciatively. She gives me a strange look for thanking her, but I don't care. I'd thank her for every minute she spends with me if that wouldn't make me look crazy. Everything just seems better when I'm with her. I fold my arms on the table and lean towards her. "I have to head back to Madison to meet with some people on a group project, but I wanted to come back and see you first. Unfortunately, I have no idea how long I'll have to be there," I grimace.

She frowns slightly and her eyes glance back down towards her phone. "That's okay. I get it. I have some things I want to do anyway," she adds. She glances back up at me from underneath her eyelashes, looking sexy as hell and also a little bit unsure.

I reach my hand across the table and cover her hand with mine, just needing to touch her. I feel better the moment she flips her hand over and weaves our fingers together. I don't really know what's bothering me, besides the look on her face, but I have an unsettled feeling in the pit of my stomach I can't explain. "Are you okay?" I ask.

She nods, "Yeah, I'm good."

Our friend, Olive, one of the waitresses here, steps over to our table. She smiles at both of us in greeting. "Hi guys. I haven't seen you in a while," she announces.

I nod, "Hey Olive. It's been a little crazy lately," I admit.

She gives me a tight smile and nods, "I get it."

Samantha talks quickly, adding, "Yeah, all of us have had a lot going on. Cody has been really busy working on a project for work."

I grin over at Sam, realizing Olive's anxiety is probably about Cody. Cody has liked Olive since we were in 3rd grade, but he never did more than flirt and hang out with her. He finally asked her out recently and they went on a couple dates, but I don't really know how things are between them right now. "He's been driving me crazy," I contribute. She arches her eyebrows in question. I elaborate, hoping she'll drop it and take our order, so I can spend the little time I have with Sam. "He needs to take a break and get out of the apartment. You should call him," I tell her.

"Really?" she questions.

I nod in confirmation, "He'd love to hear from you."

"Maybe," she murmurs, biting the end of the pen as she stares out the window on the other side of the booth.

I clear my throat, "So…"

She gives herself a light shake and clears her throat, "Sorry." She asks, "Are you guys ready to order?"

I glance over at Samantha before I nod in agreement. She orders a turkey wrap and a Diet Cola, while I order a double cheeseburger, fries and Cola. The moment Olive walks away, Samantha states, "I think Olive and Cody are great together. I don't understand what's been taking them so long."

I shrug and try to explain simply, "Cody really likes her."

"So what does that mean?" she asks, even more confused.

"He doesn't want to mess up when it comes to her," I explain. "He's been taking it slow. Like about 15 years slow," I smirk.

Samantha smiles in understanding and shakes her head in disbelief at the same time. "Idiot," she mumbles.

I chuckle and try to change the subject, "I don't want to waste our time talking about Cody. What do you want to work on tonight?" I ask.

"I actually just want to make a to do list of things I want to get done for the cystic fibrosis fundraiser and brainstorm some ideas," she informs me.

"Brainstorm?" I question, wondering if she'll be alone.

She nods, "Yeah. I want to write down any ideas I can think of before I meet with Logan tomorrow. I want to actually have things to bring to the table you know?" she asks, not really looking for an answer.

I can't help the jealous flip of my stomach at the mention of her doing anything with Logan. I attempt to push it aside and ask, "Tomorrow?"

She nods, "Yeah, he has tomorrow night off, so I asked if he wanted to work on the event. I also texted him earlier about being able to use the restaurant and I think he's happy about it." I gulp over the growing lump in my throat. She asks, "We didn't have plans, did we?"

I shake my head and grumble my response. "Nope," I say, popping the p. Her lips purse in irritation, as Olive places our drinks in front of us. I force a smile and look up at her in appreciation. "Thank you," I murmur.

She smiles and spins back towards the kitchen. "I'll be back soon with your food," she informs us, over her shoulder.

Samantha narrows her eyes and opens her mouth, I'm sure to call me on my jealous bullshit, but I don't want to talk about Logan anymore. Instead, I let out an exaggerated sigh and mumble, "I can't wait until this weekend is over."

"What?" she asks. "What's this weekend?"

I flinch and my face flushes, as it sinks in that I didn't tell her. "I'm sorry. I thought I told you," I justify, before explaining. She shakes her head and I quickly clarify. "So I have this thing for Max this weekend. Well it's actually a MADD event, Mothers Against Drunk Driving. Have you ever heard of it?" I ask.

"Yeah," she nods. "Our SADD group in high school worked with them to plan things for the students," she adds. "What do you mean by a thing?" she asks curiously.

I run my fingers through my hair and grip the back of my neck with my hand nervously. I should've already told her. "It's a semi-formal dinner and dancing fundraising event in Madison," I tell her, trying to assess her reaction. "It's not for Max, but his family goes and they always make some kind of substantial donation, or they pick something specific to support the organization in remembrance of Max. There's a few of us who always go in honor of him," I ramble anxiously. "I'm sorry I didn't' mention it before. I should've asked you sooner, but apparently I'm not thinking straight."

"It's okay," she begins.

I shake my head, wishing I would've already had this conversation with her, but at the same time, I don't want to tell her about it at all. I heave a sigh. I guess, all I can do is fix it. "Not really because I want to know if you will go with me?" I request.

"Of course I will," she smiles. Her whole face lights up, taking my breath away. "Why would you think I wouldn't go with you?" she asks, perplexed.

I wince, knowing I have to admit why I've put off telling her in the first place. "Well, I don't know if you have a dress for something like this," I hesitate, putting off the inevitable.

"I can find something," she insists, "and if I can't find anything in my closet, I can go buy something."

I smile, but I still feel anxious. I know I will continue to feel this way, until I get out the real reason I've put off telling her about it. I take a deep breath and exhale slowly, hoping my tension will go with it. With no success, I finally blurt out, "Jackie is one of them who always goes and sometimes her parents attend too."

She scrunches up her nose adorably, making me want to kiss her, but I hold myself back and wait for her response. "It's fine," she grumbles without looking at me. "I'm not going to stay home because I'm nervous about seeing Lincoln or because I don't want to see Jackie. In fact, she's a reason to go," she tells me. I give her a look of worry. She amends, "Don't worry. It's not because I'm jealous. I promise I won't cause any trouble."

I chuckle under my breath at her retort, my body relaxing. I breathe a sigh of relief, knowing she'll be by my side on such a tough night. Of course I hope it will be an easy night for both of us, but I will have to keep my guard up with Jackie around. She's the one I worry about causing trouble for Sam, not the other way around. I just hope she remembers we're there for Max. I reach across the table with my free hand and cover our clasped ones. I give her hand a light squeeze between both of mine in appreciation. "Thank you, Samantha. This event really means a lot to me," I choke up, barely able to get the words out. An overwhelming feeling of loss unexpectedly hits me hard in the chest, knocking the wind out of me.

"Are you alright?" she asks, softly.

I give myself a light shake, before taking a deep breath. I slowly exhale and stare into her caramel colored eyes, filled with concern for me. I nod and offer her an easy smile to ease her worry. "Yeah," I rasp. "I just really fucking miss him sometimes," I admit.

She nods sadly, reminding me of her own loss. "I get it," she mumbles.

I close my eyes and take another deep relaxing breath, trying to rein my emotions in. I feel selfish for complaining to her. She doesn't need to hear that from me. "I'm sorry Samantha. I shouldn't..."

"Brady don't," she firmly interrupts. "I don't ever want you to hold back with me. Definitely not about Max, not about anything," she emphasizes, with a firm shake of her head. "Just because I lost my mom and dad, doesn't mean what you went through was easy. I know it wasn't, so please don't pretend with me. I want to be there for you, just like you've been there for me, since the day we met," she insists. "Please, just let me do that for you," she pleads.

A lump forms in my throat and my chest swells, this time overwhelming me. My emotions are high and pulling me towards her. I have no idea how she does it with a look and a few words, but my love for her seems to constantly grow. I feel it so much sometimes, my whole body aches for her. I reach up and caress my hand lightly down her jawline, feeling a nearly electrical current between us through her soft, smooth skin. I let my thumb run over her full lips. I lean as close as I can to her, without climbing over the table. "Okay," I rasp. My fingers trail back behind her neck and I grip her firmly. I gaze into her eyes and muster as much feeling as I can put into my simple words. "I love you so much, Samantha," I whisper, my voice full of emotion.

"I love you too, Brady," she declares, causing my heart to swell even more.

I stand up slightly and lean over the table to close the distance between us. I brush my lips across hers, before pressing a little more firmly. I lean back slightly to see her face. Then I kiss her one more time, before falling back on my ass in the booth. "This sucks," I declare, miserably.

She smirks at me, appearing a bit breathless. She straightens slightly and asks, "What does?" even though I'm sure she knows the answer.

I grin and tease her, "I'm pretty sure you know, but just in case, I'll tell you." I pause and stare at her, my breathing erratic, "I'm really struggling to keep my hands to myself right now. I don't think I would be able to stop if I were to start anything, even right here." Her breath hitches and my own catches at her beauty. "See," I rasp, "this is why I met you here instead of meeting you back at one of our apartments. I need to eat and I'd want to do a lot more than that with you in private." At the same time, I question my own sanity. Under my breath, I ask myself, "Why the hell did I want to bring you here again?"

She blushes beautifully and quickly glances down at her lap. She murmurs my name softly, without looking at me, "Brady."

I chuckle, unsure if she heard the second part. I reluctantly bring both of my hands back to my side of the booth, so I don't do something I shouldn't be doing in public. I lean back and drop my hands into my lap. I stare at the beautiful curve of her neck and her soft skin I crave to touch and kiss. I take it all in as I wait for her attention. She finally looks back up at me, just as Olive sets our meals down in front of us, "Enjoy."

"Thank you," we both say, without taking our eyes off one another. Olive laughs as she strides towards another one of her tables.

I take a bite of my burger and Samantha breaks our eye contact again. She sighs and asks, "So how formal is this event?"

I grin at the thought of her in a sexy red dress and readjust in my seat to make myself more comfortable. I swallow the food in my mouth; my body feeling heated as I look across the table at her. "You'll look gorgeous in anything," I rasp.

She blushes, understanding my look. She asks, "Are you sure you have to go back to Madison tonight?"

I groan as if in pain and narrow my eyes at her. I grumble, "If I want to graduate in a few weeks I do." Then I tear off a huge bite of my burger and chew, as I glower across the table at her. She bursts out laughing, warming me to my soul. How the hell does she do this to me? My emotions are like a roller coaster, that I hope I never have to get off when it comes to her.

Chapter 16

Samantha

I set my notebook, pen and laptop on my desk. Then I fall back on my bed with a groan, feeling completely exhausted. I reach for my phone and send a quick text to Brady, "Are you home yet?"

"Leaving now," he replies. "How was your meeting with Logan?"

"Good," I respond, too tired to text anything else.

He sends me a question mark sticker. I giggle and drop my phone behind my head without responding. I sigh and close my eyes. Minutes later, my bed bounces and my eyes fly open to find Brady's warm, hard body hovering over me. I smile up at him sleepily and mumble, "That was fast."

He grins and rasps, "I'm home."

My heartbeat picks up on cue. I grin and point in the direction of his apartment. I remind him, "Your home is over there."

He chuckles, "Nah. My home is wherever you are."

My heart jumps up into my throat, momentarily blocking my airway. I blink, feeling overwhelmed and I gasp for air, as my body overheats. I push up and scoot back against the wall, needing both space and a subject change. "Um, how did you get in here anyway? Did I forget to lock the door or something?" I ask.

He shakes his head, "No. I actually got back here the same time as Cory and I walked in with her. Is that okay?" he asks curiously.

"Of course," I declare. I wave my hand towards him, brushing it off. "Why wouldn't it be?" I ask.

He shrugs and responds, "I'm not sure."

I shake my head and ignore his comment. I exhale harshly and quickly change the subject. "How did everything go at school today?"

He sighs and stretches out on his side. He props himself up on his elbow, facing me. "Fine," he grumbles. "It's almost over," he says, as more of a reminder to himself than anything.

"You have a lot you have to do again tonight?" I ask.

He nods and runs his hand through his hair in frustration. "I think I'm going to have a lot of work and studying to do until the semester is over at this point," he grumbles.

"That sucks," I grimace.

He nods and reiterates, "Yeah, but not for long." He reaches up and tucks a lock of my hair behind my ear and drops his hand back to the bed. "So what does good mean?" he asks. "How did your meeting go with Logan?" he repeats.

I smile, feeling great about the project. "It went really well. I told him about my birth mother and why I want to do this event specifically. He thinks it's a great idea. He loved all my ideas for the event too!"

"I'm sure he did," he mumbles.

"I have to talk to you about the menu and set-up," I inform him.

"Whenever you want," he states.

"Thanks. Logan is pretty excited to do a bigger event for this. He said he's always just used Mae's to do these things. He gave me the name of a woman I can talk to at the closest Cystic Fibrosis chapter. Unfortunately it's not in Madison, but that's okay. Anyway, he said she could help us with information, giveaways, some of the marketing and who knows what else. Hopefully I'll be able to get in touch with her tomorrow," I inform him.

He nods slowly, "That's great Sam."

I nod happily and mumble, "Yeah."

Brady bites his bottom lip anxiously. "So where did you guys meet anyway?" he mumbles as he brushes off invisible lint on the arm of his navy Henley. "I assume you didn't meet him at the bar, since you can't get in and I assume you didn't go to the restaurant…" he trails off.

My eyes narrow and I wait until he meets my gaze before responding. "Is there something you want to ask me, Brady?"

He shakes his head, "Don't get any ideas. I was just curious."

I arch my eyebrows in disbelief, but he doesn't say anything else. Finally, I admit, "He came over here since Cory was working anyway. We worked in the living room," I inform him, expecting him to drop it. He grimaces and nods his head. "Are you becoming one of those overprotective boyfriends?" I ask him.

"No!" he denies my accusation.

"I don't do well with that kind of thing Brady. If I can trust you around Jackie," I grit her name through my teeth, "you can definitely trust me around Logan," I insist.

"I do trust you Samantha! I swear, my reaction has everything to do with Logan. But either way, that's not a fair comparison," he claims.

"What would be fair?" I ask, crossing my arms over my chest. "Should I go visit my ex-boyfriend? Would that be a fair comparison?" I demand. I instantly feel guilty for my words, as he flinches and pain flits briefly across his face.

I sigh, "I'm sorry Brady. That was uncalled for." He smiles stiffly. "Maybe I should be asking you if there's something I should be worried about or aware of with him?" I question. "It's just you seem more focused on my time with him, than on the event. You know how important this is to me, so is there something?" I ask.

Brady shakes his head, "No, I'm sorry Sam." He sighs in defeat and runs his hand through his hair. He moves closer to me and stops right in front of me. He loosens my hold around my legs and I let him. He pulls my legs down with one hand and wraps the other hand around my back before he puts his head in my lap and looks up at me. "I'm sorry," he repeats. "I think this is more about me not being able to spend enough time with you. I see you for a few minutes, if at all lately. I just want more time with you and Logan is getting exactly what I want, more time with you," he emphasizes.

"But it's nothing to worry about," I reiterate. "I promise."

He nods sadly and asks, "What would happen if I end up with the internship in Minneapolis?" he asks.

"Brady," I warn, not wanting to go there until we have to.

"I'm sorry. I have all these scenarios in my head, but with every one, I'm trying to figure out a way that I can be with you. It's almost all I can think about, but I have all this other shit to deal with first and I fucking hate it!" he announces.

I sigh and run my hands through his hair. He moans in satisfaction at the motion, so I repeat it over and over again. When I finally open my mouth, I speak softly, "Like I said before, I think we both need to make a decision about what we want for our futures. I want you to make the decision based on what you really want. I love you. I want you to be happy. It would kill me if you resented me some day because you based a decision about your future on me."

He sighs and reaches up, slipping one hand behind me and curving it around my neck. He leans up, puckers his lips and kisses me. He slips his tongue out and licks the outline of my lips. He presses his lips to mine once again, before falling back to my lap. He pushes the edge of my light blue t-shirt up as he rolls towards me and brushes his lips across the skin of my stomach, making me whimper. He gives my waist a quick tug, pulling me away from the wall and plants the palm of his hand on the bare skin of my stomach, pushing me all the way back. "Lie down," he whispers. "I want to show you how much you mean to me, Samantha."

I lie back and immediately feel his warm breath over my center. "Brady," I rasp, already breathless.

He loops his fingers into my black skinny jeans and slowly pulls them down my body. He traces his fingers over my curves as he goes, revealing a lacy black thong. He tugs my jeans all the way off and tosses them on the floor. He stops and looks me up and down. His breathing becomes heavier and he quietly mumbles, "Fuck." He climbs over me and swiftly pulls my shirt over my head, leaving me in a matching lacy black bra with my nipples nearly poking through to greet him. He groans as if in pain, then declares breathlessly, "You're so beautiful Samantha."

He reaches towards my breast and my back arches into his hand, craving his touch. His teeth graze my nipple through the lace, making me whimper. He pushes the straps off my shoulders and slips his hand between my breasts. "This one is back hook," I force the words out and push up on my elbows. He slips his hands behind me, unhooks it and pulls it off, quickly dropping it to the bed. He immediately covers one with his hand and the other with his mouth. I gasp and curve my body into him. I grasp his firm biceps tightly, finding cotton instead of skin. "Take this off," I rasp and tug at his shirt. He releases my breast with a light pop. He reaches up and behind him with one hand. He quickly pulls his shirt over his head and tosses it to the floor.

He looks down at me with hooded eyes and adoration, causing my skin to tingle. He hovers over me and gently presses his lips to mine. He tilts his head and molds his mouth to mine with a soft groan. My hands trail up his arms, feeling the hard ripple of his muscles. I slowly continue a trail over his shoulders, urging him closer. He collapses onto me and I gasp for breath at the feel of his heated skin on mine. He moves his weight a little to my side, so he doesn't crush me. Then he traces his finger down my side, over my nipple and just above my core. I whimper, bowing my body into his delicate caress. His thumb runs over the edge of my panties all the way to the back. He tears his lips away from mine and drops his forehead to mine. "Are these new?" he rasps.

I nod and whisper breathlessly, "Cory and I went shopping."

"Are there more?" he croaks. I nod in answer, not able to talk as his fingers skate over my core. "Good, I fucking love them," he says. Then he slips a finger underneath and through my wet folds. "Sam," he groans my name, as he curls a finger in and out.

"Brady," I beg, feeling as if I'm already about to explode.

"I've got you," he encourages. He finds my lips and pushes his tongue in to lick and play, as he continues to push his fingers in and out. Then he gently sucks my tongue and lips, before nipping at my lower lip. His tongue slides back into my mouth, his groan vibrating my whole body. His kisses become more demanding, as mine become more desperate, as his fingers continue slipping in and out of me. He presses his thumb against my clit, slowly circling it, while his fingers push inside, then curl, hitting just the right spot inside of me. I grip his shoulders tightly, as my head drops back, ripping my mouth away from his. I gasp for breath and my whole body begins to vibrate. My insides forcefully pulse around his fingers as he curls them in, helping me ride out my orgasm. My grip on him loosens as I relax into the bed. I look up at him grinning down at me and feel myself blush. "Hey," he says, to get my attention, "That was one of the most beautiful things I've ever seen. You're gorgeous, Samantha," he insists.

I gulp over the sudden lump in my throat and lift my lips to kiss him. "Your jeans aren't supposed to be on," I tell him. He arches his eyebrows in challenge. I giggle and demand, "Take them off."

He grins, showing off his deep dimple, as he stands and steps out of his jeans. He grabs a condom out of the back pocket and drops them back to the floor. He lies back down on the bed next to me in navy blue boxer briefs. His hand reaches across, grips my hip and firmly pulls me towards him. "Is that better?" he asks playfully.

I gasp, at the feel of him pressing into me. "Almost," I rasp and snap the waistband of his underwear.

He chuckles and kicks off his underwear before pulling me close. He grins and I lean up and lick his dimple with it so close to my lips. He groans and buries his face in my neck. He inhales deeply and then begins kissing my neck, sending shivers down my spine. "Your skin is so soft, it's like silk," he whispers reverently as he brushes his lips up my neck. He braces himself on his elbows and kisses me slowly. Every lick and every kiss, feels like he's savoring every taste of me, only making me want him more. His hips push into me and I arch right back into him. He lifts his head and meets my gaze, making sure I'm ready, as he lines himself up at my entrance.

"I want you Brady," I whisper.

He pulls back, "Wait, I need the condom." He quickly picks it up off the mattress and tears it open. I watch as he easily rolls it over his full, thick length, wondering how he fits me so well.

"I love you, Samantha," he affirms, with eyes full of love. Then he pushes inside with one thrust, making me gasp. "Are you okay?" he immediately asks.

I nod, "Just give me a second." I grip his shoulders and take a deep breath. I exhale slowly, relaxing my muscles as my body adjusts to him. I smile up at him and insist, "I'm good." He doesn't move, so I arch into him. He groans in response and begins moving slowly. He molds his mouth to mine and kisses me breathless. Our hands begin exploring as we move together, finding our rhythm. His hand grazes my breast and then he moves to the other one, rolling my nipple between his fingers. He pinches my nipple as he tips his head down and licks the other one. Then he sucks it into his mouth and lets his tongue twirl around it. "Brady," I gasp.

He releases my breast and lifts up, holding himself over me. His hips push into me faster, while the angle he holds begins to make my toes curl. I move my hands down his chest and cup his ass, trying to pull him to me harder and faster as I arch into him. The intensity in his eyes and the movement of his body against mine has my heart pounding and my body overheating. I struggle to catch my breath. "I can't hold on this time. It's too much," he groans. "But I want you to come with me. Do you think you can?" he asks desperately.

I nod, unable to use my voice. I wrap my arms around him and hold him as tight as I'm able. He pushes into me harder, still attempting to keep his weight off of me. He reaches between us, barely touching my clit and I release a gasp. His gaze immediately falls back to mine as I feel my body clenching him. He groans and pushes in hard, then again and again, filling me. He stills and my body continues to milk him as he falls over the edge and we both come down from our high. He collapses next to me and drapes his arm over my stomach with a groan.

When we both catch our breath, he pushes up off the bed. He removes the condom and ties it off before throwing it in the garbage. He pulls on his underwear and jeans. "Don't move. I'll be right back," he instructs. I grunt in response, making him chuckle.

I barely turn my head, before he's back over me with a damp washcloth. He kisses me tenderly, before he cleans me up. "Thank you," I whisper.

He smiles at me and tosses the washcloth towards the laundry basket. He settles in next to me, wrapping his arm around. With his free hand he caresses my cheek, then places another soft kiss on my lips. "I don't know how I got so lucky," he states reverently. I feel myself blush. "I'm sorry I'm such an ass lately," he sighs in annoyance with himself. "I'm working on it. I know you can stand on your own. Believe it or not, with everything you've been through, I think you're the strongest woman I've ever known. I just can't help, but try to protect you, whether you want me to or not," he tells me.

I nod, "I know."

"It's because I love you, Sam," he claims. "I really fucking love you," he repeats.

"I love you too," I tell him honestly. I kiss him lightly as confirmation of my love. I sigh, wanting to say more.

He chuckles and then concedes, "but…you still need to do it on your own."

I giggle and let my hand fall to his chest. I wrap my leg around his and settle further into his arms. "You know me so well," I tell him and smile to myself.

Chapter 17

I bite my lower lip nervously, as I send a quick text to Lincoln. "I'm working on a new project I thought you might be interested in. Do you have time for coffee sometime?" I don't want to tell him everything and I don't want him to feel like he has to meet me for a meal or invite me over with his family. In fact I still don't want to be around Jackie. I grimace just thinking about her. Although I really did enjoy going to Frankie's game and getting to know him when we all went for pizza. I'd love to spend more time with him. I sigh in frustration and flop back down on my bed.

My cell phone rings in my hand, startling me. I glance at my cousin Ryan's face and quickly tap answer. "Hi Ry! What are you doing?" I ask.

"Hey Sam. I just wanted to see how your week is going?" he asks.

"Really? Personally, I think I'm getting a lot more phone calls from you since I moved in with Cory," I tease him. "Why do you think that is?" I ask, innocently.

"Hey now, that's not fair. You know you've always been my favorite cousin," he insists. I chuckle and he jokes right back, "But moving in with a hot roommate definitely helps."

"Hey!" I exclaim and we both laugh.

"Seriously though," he pauses before asking, "how is your hot roommate?"

He chuckles and I laugh along with him. I shake my head at him even though he can't see me. "You probably know better than I do. I haven't seen much of her this week," I admit.

"Why not?" he asks. "Is everything okay?"

"It's fine. I promise. I've just been working on a new project," I tell him, happily.

"What kind of project?" he asks curiously. "Something for your new job or something?"

I shake my head again, like he's standing in front of me. I reply, "Not exactly. I am working with Brady for some of it though because we're holding it at his family's restaurant."

I hear the confusion in his voice when he asks, "What the hell are you doing? And what do you mean we? Who's we?"

I giggle and respond, "I'm actually working on a fundraiser for cystic fibrosis."

"Huh, that's not what I expected you to say," he murmurs.

"What did you expect?" I ask, perplexed.

"I don't know," he concedes. "Maybe something else that's more like the wedding you're helping plan. But a fundraiser," he contemplates, "that's pretty cool. Especially with what happened with your birth mom and everything," he agrees.

"Yeah," I murmur, suddenly uncomfortable with the praise. I take a deep breath and then I begin to ramble, "It's kind of a quick turnaround to get it done, but there's this guy Logan who lives across the hall. He's a bartender at Mae's. You know, that bar you went to?" I ask, but I continue without giving him a chance to answer. "Anyway, he's always doing different fundraisers. I'm working with him on the project. I think he already had something in the works for this date, so technically we're just changing the location to Brady's restaurant. With more space, hopefully we can bring in more money for the cause. Then we were talking about some new ideas. He seems to like my ideas, so that's good. Plus, I'm helping him with everything from the marketing, gathering some of the information or educational brochures and giveaways. Then I'll do what I can to get other things donated for things like the decorating, food and music."

"Logan?" he questions.

I sigh, "He's a nice guy. I think he might actually own Mae's, or at least he's a manager or something. I'm not really sure though."

"And Brady is okay with you working so closely with Logan?" he asks.

I grimace and answer defensively, "He doesn't have a choice."

Ryan chuckles and confirms, "But he's jealous as hell and trying not to take it out on you." I grunt in acknowledgement making him laugh harder. He reminds me, "Just be careful. If he's the guy I think I met when I went there with Cory, then he's a player."

"Yeah, I've heard that. But I was honest with him. He knows I'm dating Brady and I'm not interested. I can handle myself," I insist.

He sighs, "Okay, if you say so. Sooo…" he pauses, "Have you seen or talked to Lincoln since Frankie's baseball game?"

"I actually just texted him when you called," I admit. "I asked if he had time for coffee. I want to tell him about the cystic fibrosis project since he knew my mom," I explain.

"Obviously," he states, followed by a long drawn out sigh.

My body tenses, preparing for whatever he might say. "What does that mean Ry?" I ask cautiously.

"It's just," he hesitates, "they didn't exactly keep in touch or anything. I don't want you to think this will matter that much to him. It matters to me, but I guess I don't want you to get your hopes up," he blurts out. "You've been through enough," he reminds me.

I visibly wince, again making me grateful he can't actually see me. My chest feels tight and I force myself to respond. "I know," I whisper. "Maybe, I just want him to know because it feels like it's one of the few connections I have to him," I admit.

"That's what I'm worried about, Sam!" he declares.

I sigh and inform him, "Look Ry, I appreciate you looking out for me, but I don't have any big dreams about a close relationship with him. I just want to know more about him so I can know more about me. I think this is something I need to tell him, even if it's only for me and he doesn't care." Even as I speak the words, I have my own doubts swirling around in my head trying to take root. I look around the room looking for some kind of distraction from this conversation, before I push myself over the edge. I spot the black dress I want to dry clean for this weekend and quickly change the subject. "So, Brady asked me to a MADD event this weekend."

"A MADD event?" he asks.

"Yeah, Mothers Against Drunk Driving," I remind him.

"Oh yeah, but he's not a mother," he states the obvious.

I smirk, "That thought never crossed my mind."

He chuckles, "Sure it didn't."

My heart aches even before I say the words. "Anyway, Brady's friend, Max, was drinking and driving a few years ago and died in a car accident. He and Brady were really close," I explain vaguely.

"Shit," I hear him murmur softly in understanding.

"Yeah," I agree. "Well, Max's family always donates something to recognize him at the event every year and Brady, as well as some other friends and family go in honor of him," I tell him.

"There it is," he mumbles.

"There what is?" I asked confused.

"The reason you don't seem thrilled to be going. I can hear it in your voice," he insists. "Who's going to be there?" he asks.

I laugh and ask, "What are you talking about?" Although, if he saw my face, he would without a doubt know he's right. "Is it Jackie?" he questions.

My mouth drops open in shock, "What...How did you...I didn't..." I stumble over my words before I finally admit, slightly dumbfounded, "Yeah." He chuckles at my response and I ask, "So what do I do about Jackie?" I ask.

"Want me to come?" he offers. "I could ask Cory if she wants to go on a date with me?" he suggests.

"I don't know if she's even coming. You never know with her," I declare.

"Well I'd be happy to come for the weekend for you, with or without Cory. It's up to you," he insists.

I sigh and shake my head at myself. "No, that's okay Ryan. I'll be with Brady. Besides, I really have to learn to be around her without freaking out. I'm a big girl," I joke.

"I think you know exactly what to do. You've handled her pretty well," he reminds me. "Besides, you have a reason to be uncomfortable around her. She's a bitch," he reminds me flippantly.

I chuckle and agree. A small smile slips onto my lips, "True." He laughs and I try to change the subject again. "So how are things going for you?" I ask.

He groans, "Fine! I just can't wait until this semester is over. Although I might take a class this summer, so I don't have the maximum amount of credits next year."

I hear some banging and muffled yelling in the background through the phone. I ask, "Are you guys having a party or something?"

Ryan laughs, "Or something. That's just my roommates. They want me to go to a bar downtown that has quarter taps for happy hour on Thursdays."

"Oh, I'm sorry. I can let you go," I tell him.

"Like most cell phones, my phone does travel if I want to leave," he jokes. "Either way, their sorry asses can wait."

"Well, I'm going to go anyway. I have to do some laundry," I inform him.

"Too bad you're too far away to do mine too," he says.

"Yeah, too bad," I respond flatly. "We have to make a plan for me to come home and visit you," I tell him.

"Why don't you just come down and stay with me here," he suggests. "We'd have a blast."

"I know we would, but we can figure it out when we decide on dates. Text me your free weekends," I request.

"I'll talk a look at finals dates and text you back later. That's really all I have to worry about at this point," he admits.

"That's enough," I comment. "And that sounds good. Have fun tonight, but be good," I encourage.

He laughs, "I'm single, I'll have fun. As for being good, it depends what you mean by that," he taunts.

"Ryan," I scold. "What about my roommate?" I ask.

"Like I said before, your roommate is hot, but I'm definitely single. Just ask her," he emphasizes, sounding slightly annoyed.

I sigh and whisper, "I love you, Ry."

"Love you too," he states and ends the call.

My phone beeps in my hand before I have a chance to set it down. I glance at the screen, thinking it might be Lincoln, but smile at the sight of Brady's name. I open the text and grin at his sweet message. "Wish I was home with you."

"What are you doing?" I ask.

"I'm at the library on campus working on a project with a few friends from class," he reveals. The dancing bubbles reappear and I stare at them, waiting to see what else he's going to say. "My mind keeps wandering to vanilla and coconut," he adds.

"What?" I mumble to myself. I respond with a giant question mark.

"It's what your hair smells like," he enlightens me.

Instead of acknowledging his comment, I reply sarcastically, "Sounds like you're getting a lot done."

"I wish. Looks like I'm going to be very late tonight," he informs me.

"That's ok, I'll just see you tomorrow," I tell him.

"I have to work tomorrow night at the restaurant," he reminds me.

I reply with a sad face emoji. Then I tell him, "Then I guess you'll be very excited to see me on Saturday. I have my dress and everything ready."

"Everything?" he questions with a winking emoji.

I roll my eyes and smile to myself before responding playfully, "Guess you'll have to wait and see."

"Killing me," he replies. "I have to get back to work."

"Ok, I'll text you tomorrow." I set my phone down on my nightstand. I stand and wander towards the kitchen, my stomach rumbling hungrily.

A loud knock at the door has me changing direction. I swing the door open to find Logan leaning against the doorframe in a black t-shirt and jeans. "Hi," he grins.

"What are you doing here?" I question.

He laughs in response and looks me up and down. I suddenly remember I'm wearing yoga pants and a sports bra and feel myself blush. I only dress like this when I'm cleaning my apartment or working out alone. "I'm headed to Mae's, but I wanted to see if you would be around tomorrow," he informs me. "So, are you?" he asks.

"Um, yeah. Why?" I stammer. I cross my arms over my bare stomach, self-consciously.

He cocks his head to the side and smirks, "To work on the fundraiser." I feel my whole body heat in embarrassment and I quickly glance down at my feet. "I just want to break up some of the work so we're not duplicating anything. Plus, I figured we can work on some of the marketing stuff together, if you want. I can show you what I've done in the past and we can go from there," he suggests.

"Sure, that's a good idea," I admit, feeling myself calm at the mention of the fundraiser. "Do you want to come over here?" I ask.

He grins, "Yeah, I'll grab us some lunch and bring it over with my laptop. Text me if there's anything particular you want," he instructs. "I'll be here around noon," he says. Then he turns and walks towards the stairs, quickly disappearing down them.

"I'm such an idiot," I grumble to myself.

Chapter 18

Brady

I run my hand through my hair and drop my forehead to the steering wheel of my truck, completely exhausted. I close my eyes and all I see is Samantha smiling back at me. I take a deep breath and feel my body start to relax. "I can't wait until this shit is finally done," I grumble to the empty cab. I turn the key and start my truck. Then I sit back and reach for my phone, tapping on Samantha's number. I drop the phone in one of the cup holders as the call connects to my truck's blue tooth, before I back out of my parking spot.

"Hi, Brady!" Samantha answers cheerfully.

I smile at the sound of her voice, "Hey, Sam. How's your day?"

"Good. You sound tired. Are you okay?" she asks.

I yawn before answering, "I'm okay. I'm just leaving campus and heading back towards the restaurant now. I thought I'd call you while I have a few minutes to talk." I yawn again and turn onto North Lake Street.

"It sounds like you need me to keep you awake," she says, sounding slightly anxious.

"I'm tired, but I'm okay. I promise," I reiterate. The sound of a guy's voice in the background prompts me to ask, "Where are you?"

"I'm at home. Why?" she asks.

"I thought I heard someone in the background," I tell her honestly.

"Oh, you did. That's Logan. He's just leaving to go to work. Just a second," she tells me. I grind my jaw in irritation. She told me she was going to be working with him, but I hate the sick feeling in my gut. I don't want him hanging out at my girl's apartment, but what the hell am I supposed to say without looking like a total asshole? This sucks. "Okay, thanks Logan. See you later," she tells him sweetly, causing my stomach to churn even more. "Okay, I'm back," she informs me happily. I bite down hard on my tongue, forcing myself to leave it alone. I don't want to say something stupid. "Are you there?" she asks, sounding confused.

I clear my throat, "Yeah, I'm here. You were working with Logan?" I ask simply.

"Yeah," she concedes. "We broke up a lot of the tasks so we're not doing the same thing and then we worked on some new marketing things for the event. He shared what he's done in the past and we came up with something pretty cool for this year. He's a really good artist," she enlightens me.

I wince at the compliment and grunt my own reply, "That's good."

She pauses, but continues after a moment of silence, probably reading my mood. "Anyway, the closest Wisconsin chapter for Cystic Fibrosis is this side of Milwaukee. I talked to a woman there today and she's going to have someone call me Monday morning to let us know what they can provide for us in regards to brochures and giveaways," she informs me. "There's also a local Great Strides Walk for Cystic Fibrosis the first weekend in May. So we're going to connect our event to the walk to hopefully pull in more people to us for the following weekend. We were also talking about putting a team together to walk. What do you think?" she asks excitedly.

"Um, yeah, I'll walk on your team if I'm not swamped with school. That's right before graduation," I remind her.

"Oh, yeah," she sighs. "I'm sorry, I wasn't thinking."

"No worries. I know how excited you are about this. I hear it in your voice," I concede.

"Still, your graduation is really important. I'm sorry Brady," she repeats.

"Sam, I know you didn't mean anything by it, just forget it. Okay?" I request.

"Okay," she agrees.

I hear her moving around and shuffling papers, suddenly quiet. I attempt to encourage her, "I do think it's a great idea. It could bring in people from the walk that have never been to any of Logan's fundraisers."

"I hope so," she admits quietly.

"You know I could come by with some heroes or something for us for dinner. I don't have a lot of time, but I can always make some time for you," I tell her.

"Um, I'm not really hungry. I've kinda' been nibbling on the lunch that Logan brought over for us all afternoon," she admits.

My heart clenches and I ask, "Logan brought you lunch?"

"It was a working lunch, so he figured it was the least he could do," she explains.

My shoulders tense and my hands tighten around the steering wheel, my knuckles turning white. "I bet he did," I grumble through gritted teeth, jealousy practically overwhelming me.

"What?" she asks.

I take a deep breath and exhale slowly before answering. "Nothing, just that was really nice of him," I force out the words.

"It was..." she says hesitantly, before she pauses. "I thought you two were friends?" she questions.

"We are," I acknowledge.

"Then why do you sound like you want to go kick his ass for being here and bringing me lunch?" she accuses.

I flinch and admit, "I'm trying not to be jealous, but I can't help it. To me you're every man's dream and I know Logan isn't blind. He sees who you are inside and out and all of it's fucking spectacular. I'm not planning on going to kick anyone's ass. Yes, Logan and I are friends, but most importantly, I trust you. But that doesn't mean it's easy on me Sam. It sounds like you spent a lot of time with him today and he brought you lunch," he emphasizes. "It sounds more like a date that I haven't been able to have with you this week, no matter how much I fucking want it," I tell her honestly.

"I'm sorry, Brady," she apologizes with a sigh. "If it makes you feel any better, I can't wait until tomorrow night. I'm excited about dressing up for you and going out," she declares.

"Yeah, I can't think about that right now," I tell her with a low chuckle. "I have to admit, this is the first time I've ever looked forward to this event. Thank you for going with me. It really means a lot to me," I maintain.

"You're welcome," she whispers, sending chills down my spine. How the hell does she do that? "Hey Cory," I hear Samantha greet her roommate. "You're home early."

I don't hear Cory's response, but with Sam's acknowledgement I ask, "Is she okay?"

"She says she doesn't feel well, so she switched around some of her appointments tonight to come home early," Samantha informs me.

I groan inwardly. "I guess I should let you go then, so you can check on your roommate," I offer.

"Maybe I should," she mumbles. "She looked a little bit green and it sounds like she's moaning in pain in her room."

I chuckle, "Yeah, that's Cory. Ironically Cody is the same way. With so many things they are complete opposites, but when it comes to being sick, neither of them handle it well."

"Huh," she murmurs. "Hope she's okay. Maybe you should just go to work," she suggests. "I will see you tomorrow," she reminds me.

I grunt with frustration, but agree. "Okay. I'll text you when I get home in case you're awake," I tell her.

"Sounds good. Bye Brady," she says. She ends the call before I have a chance to say anything else.

I click the voice command on my truck and instruct, "Call Cody."

He picks up before it even rings on my end. "What's up?" he asks.

"Want to meet me down at Mae's for a beer and a burger before I head to the restaurant?" I suggest.

"Hell yes," he nearly shouts into the phone. "I'm on my way," he says. Then he immediately disconnects the call.

I chuckle and park on Main Street right near Mae's. I climb out of my truck and amble towards the bar. I pull the front door open and walk in, the familiar scent of beer and grease overwhelming my senses. I quickly scan over the nearly empty room before I walk up to the bar and plant myself on a stool. I rest my elbows on the bottle-top bar in front of me and wait for Logan to notice me.

He swings his gaze to me almost immediately and smirks. "Brady," he calls and saunters over to me as he wipes his hands on a towel. "Haven't seen you around lately," he says observantly.

I nod slowly, "Yeah, been a little busy."

"Yeah, me too," he agrees, his eyes alight with mischief.

I grind my teeth and quietly comment, "So I've heard."

He chuckles, "Is that why you're here?" I arch my eyebrows in challenge and he continues, "To warn me away from Samantha again?" I shake my head and pinch my lips shut. I knew he'd harass me if I came here, but I did it anyway. "You're a lucky son of a bitch. Sam's a really amazing woman," he grins.

I nod stiffly, "Yes, I am. Are you going to do your job and get me a fucking beer?" I ask irritably.

"Make that two," Cody says as he slides onto the stool next to me.

I exhale slowly and Logan gives a nod to Cody, "You got it."

"I see you need me to get things done," Cody jokes making both Logan and I laugh. Logan sets both beers down in front of us and I reach for mine, quickly downing half before setting it back down. "Thirsty?" Cody asks. I don't bother responding. He turns towards Logan and asks, "Can we get a couple burgers and fries from the kitchen too?"

"No problem," Logan says and turns towards the bar computer. I feel Cody's eyes on me as I take another gulp of beer. Logan types something in and then turns back to us. He places his palms on the bar and leans slightly forward on them. "Brady, are we good?" he asks.

I look up at him and nod, "Yeah. It just sucks that I feel like you spend more time with my girlfriend lately than I do," I admit.

"She has a lot of great ideas," he compliments her. "I'm really glad she wants to get involved in this. Hopefully after this one is done, she'll be willing to do another one with me," he tells me.

"I'm not surprised. She secured a wedding reception for me at the restaurant with all her ideas. Well, actually at our barn," I inform him.

"Barn?" Logan questions. "I think Sam said something about that, but what barn?"

"We have an old barn on our property between my parents house and the restaurant. It hasn't been used in years. I was showing Sam around our property one day and when this wedding came along, I was talking to her about what they were looking for. She came up with this great idea on how I can redesign the barn to use it as a venue. Then she came up with some really great ideas on how to decorate it for them too. Not only is it good for this couple, but it will also expand everything we're able to do. I asked her to work with me on it to see if it's something she'd like to do." I shake my head with awe, "I couldn't figure out how to fit the couples requests and I started thinking they wouldn't use us as a venue, then Sam comes along and tells me how I can. She's really fucking smart," I praise her proudly.

I suddenly realize Logan is looking at me with an arched eyebrow, while Cody is smirking at me. "What?" I ask.

Logan shakes his head and says, "Nothing." Then he turns and walks towards the other side of the bar and begins wiping it down.

Cody chuckles, "I've just never seen you so obvious. It's hilarious."

I heave a sigh and reach for my beer. I admit, "It may be funny to you, but to me I hate feeling like I do." His brows draw together in confusion. I tilt my beer towards Logan and inform him, "She's been spending more time with that asshole, than me lately."

"For that fundraiser thing, right?" he clarifies.

"Yeah," I concede.

"So that shouldn't matter if you trust her," he reminds me.

"I do, but I've never felt so jealous in my life and I fucking hate it. I'm trying to figure out how to handle it. Even with you, when I know nothing would happen, I feel on edge," I admit.

"If I would've met her first, that would've been me," he jokes. I give him a deadly look, making him chuckle. He holds his hands up in surrender, "Ok, ok. You know I'm just giving you shit."

I nod, "Yeah, I do, but that doesn't seem to matter." I down the rest of my beer and set it back on the bar. "I guess the whole thing with Lincoln and then with her and Jackie doesn't help. I feel like I need to protect her and she wants to handle everything on her own. I know she's strong, but that's a lot of shit to deal with for anyone."

"Yeah, it's definitely fucked up. Your ex, who can sometimes be a little bit like fatal attraction," he smirks, "and your girlfriend, are sisters," he reminds me.

I run my hand through my hair in defeat, hearing the words out loud. "Shit," I mumble.

Cody laughs and slaps me on the back just as Logan sets down a plate of a burger and fries on the bar in front of each of us. "Another beer?" he offers

I nod in affirmation, "One more."

Chapter 19

Samantha

I run my hands over the sides of my silky, black, fitted dress, as I assess myself one last time in the mirror. The straps are slightly bigger than spaghetti straps, it dips down tastefully in the front, and I really like the length, short, but not too short. I twist and look over my shoulder to try to see the back. It hollows out in the middle, so I'm not able to wear a bra with this dress. I press my chest one more time to make sure my pasties stay in place. I slip on a simple one-inch, black heel, with a small, round, crystal pendant centered at the toe. I have my hair styled in a fancy up-do, with a few crystal bobby pins helping to hold all my dark curls in place, minus a couple curls hanging loose near my ears. I grab a small, black clutch with my ID, some cash, lipstick and my phone. Then I walk out into the living room, knowing Brady will be here any minute.

"Wow!" Cory exclaims. "You look fantastic."

I feel myself blush and I murmur, "Thank you."

"I love your hair. Who did it for you?" she jokes.

I roll my eyes and repeat my appreciation. "Thank you for coming home from work early to do my hair. I have very few styles when I do it. I really love it."

She grins, satisfied, "You're welcome. Seriously though, you'll be lucky if you can drag Brady out of here without jumping you. You look sexy as hell."

I smile in appreciation, but startle at the sudden knock on our front door. "Well, here it goes," I mumble. I take a step towards the door before asking her, "Why am I so nervous?"

She laughs. "He's the one who should be nervous. Look at you!"

I feel my face heat and shake my head slightly. He knocks again and I take a deep breath to relax my body. I reach for the handle and pull it open with a broad smile. "Hi," I say simply.

He looks at me, his mouth hanging slightly open. He lets his eyes slowly roam over my body. I take the opportunity to take him in. He's wearing a simple black suit with a white shirt and a silvery blue tie, making his eyes sparkle. He snaps his mouth shut and I watch as he swallows, his Adam's apple bobbing up and down. "You look absolutely gorgeous," he croaks.

"Thank you," I reply appreciatively. "You look pretty handsome yourself," I insist. He grins, his deep dimple completely taking my breath away.

"Spin for him," Cory encourages.

I glare at her. My lips tug up at the corners, ruining my intent and I start laughing. "Fine," I agree, humoring her.

I hold my hands out and spin around slowly. When my back is to him, I think I hear a mumbled, "Fuck."

My body feels like it's on fire when I stop and face him. I meet his gaze and smile up at him. "What do you think?" I ask.

"I think I'm in a lot of trouble tonight," he admits, his voice a low, gravelly murmur.

I giggle at his response, while Cory laughs outright. "I tried to tell her," she jokes.

"You're absolutely stunning Samantha," he states as he takes a step towards me. He slips his hand to the small of my back. A bolt of electricity goes through me as his fingertips skate across my bare skin. He unintentionally releases a small groan, as he leans down and softly presses his lips to mine. He takes a deep breath as he quickly drops his hand and steps away from me. He chuckles and rubs his jaw in near disbelief. "I think you're trying to kill me," he mumbles. "Are you ready to go?" he asks.

"Wait!" Cory stops us. "Let me take a picture. You need more than a selfie with you two all dressed up," she insists.

"Thanks," I tell her appreciatively. I wrap my arm around his back and press into his side. He slips his hand behind my back and lets it rest on the curve of my hip.

We smile and Cory snaps a couple pictures before she drops her phone to her side with a smile of her own. "Okay, be good guys!" she instructs. "I'll send you the pictures."

"Thank you, Cory," I tell her again. "Bye!"

"Bye," Cory waves.

"No coat?" he asks. I shake my head. "Bye, Cory" Brady waves over his shoulder. We walk out the door and he pulls it closed behind us.

I quietly walk towards the elevator, with him following. I push the button and the doors open instantly. I step in, with Brady right behind me. I move to the back of the elevator and I can feel the heat of him closing in on me, even before I turn around. The moment I do, I feel like I'm on fire. His palms are flat on the wall behind me, his body as close as he can get without touching me and his head tilts down to mine. I gasp, inhaling his scent of soap and light, musky cologne. His breathing is ragged and he rasps, "You shouldn't have worn this dress."

"I'll wear what I want," I respond defiantly.

He chuckles, "That's not what I mean. It's just that I'm not going to want anyone near you and the only thing I want to do right now is tear this dress off." I gasp as he nips at my bottom lip. "Are you even wearing a bra?" he rasps.

I take a deep breath and grin mischievously. I slip under his arm, as the doors slide open. "Not exactly," I reply. I laugh to myself as I stride confidently out the door.

I hear the sound of his footsteps jogging towards me just as I walk out the front door. He grabs my hand and tugs me towards his truck. He opens the door and lifts me into the seat before I have a chance to attempt it. "I don't want you to even try to climb up in that dress," he tells me. He shuts the door and jogs around, slipping in behind the wheel. He starts the truck and backs out, turning it towards Madison.

He glances at me out of the corner of his eye, before focusing back on the road, his hands tightening and loosening on the wheel. "It's going to be a long night," he grumbles, "Especially after not seeing you for a few days."

I giggle and roll my eyes. "So who will be here tonight that you know?" I ask changing the subject.

He chuckles and relaxes back into the driver's seat. "I'll introduce you to Max's parents and his brother, Will and his sister, Valerie. Then a couple of our old teammates might be there," he adds, "but I'm not sure if any of them are planning on coming."

"And Jackie," I grumble.

He winces and agrees with a sigh, "Yeah, and Jackie." He pauses. "You know Cody is going, right?" he asks.

My eyes widen in surprise and I admit, "No, I guess I should've known, but I didn't. Is he bringing a date?"

"I think so, but if he's not bringing Olive, I have no idea who would be coming with him," he concedes.

"You do live with him," I remind him of the obvious. "Don't you guys even talk?"

"We talk all the time, but usually it's about work or school or food or a game or you," he grins. "I honestly didn't even ask when he left our apartment earlier. I just said I'd see him there," he admits. "He's been in a weird mood when it comes to Olive lately, so I don't bring her up unless he says something. It's safer that way," he jokes.

I sigh and look out the window. "Whatever you say," I mumble.

He chuckles and turns up the radio as the soft beat of an old Coldplay song begins playing through the speakers. I relax into the seat and continue staring out the window as I listen to the music and get lost in thought. I can't help but pray that everything will go okay tonight. I don't want to get into it with Jackie again, no matter what *it* is for her at the moment. I hate not knowing what I'm walking into.

The light touch of Brady's hand on my knee startles me, bringing my attention back to him. He grins, "Sorry to make you jump. You were pretty deep in thought," he informs me. I nod and he adds, "We're here."

"Oh," I say and attempt to gulp down the lump in my throat. He jumps out of the truck and I whisper to myself, "Mom, Dad, please give me strength to deal with her."

Brady opens my door and lifts me out of the truck. He sets me on my feet and steadies me before he turns and hands his keys to a valet. "Thank you," he nods as the guy hands over a ticket to get his truck back later. He holds out his arm and asks with his panty-melting smile, "Ready?"

As I look into his eyes, I feel his comfort blanketing me and I nod my head in agreement. I link my arm through his and latch onto his firm bicep. He opens one of the thick wooden doors and steps inside behind me. We walk into a mostly white and gold lobby. I look up at the intricate golden chandelier, with 24 lights, hanging in the entryway. Solid oak doors are propped open in front of us, with a table to both the right and the left. I watch as people hand in their tickets at either table. I peek through the open doors, as Brady waits to do the same for us. I'm flooded with an array of colors, scents, music and chatter.

Brady steps in behind me and places his hand on the small of my back. The small gesture gives me comfort, as we step through the doors and into the ballroom. An older gentleman in a black tuxedo greets us, "Good evening." Brady nods and I smile in acknowledgement. He instructs, "The silent auction is to your right and the dinner tables each have a number that matches your ticket to help you find your seat. In the meantime, feel free to grab a complimentary drink. Staff will be roaming with appetizers for you to enjoy as well."

"Thank you," Brady and I both say, appreciatively. He leans down to my ear and whispers, "There's no alcohol at this event."

I nod in understanding. His hand slips around my back as we walk further into the room and I try to take everything in. Large round tables are set-up throughout the room in a scoop pattern in front of a small stage. Each table is covered in a red draping tablecloth with white tableware and red and white flowers as the centerpiece. Some of the white chairs have a red ribbon dressing the back, while others remain untouched.

I turn to Brady and ask, "Why are the red ribbons only on some of the chairs?"

He offers me a sad smile before he informs me, "MADD statistics say two out of three people will be impacted by a drunk driving crash in their lifetime." My eyes widen and my lips form an O, immediately thinking about how it has affected Brady.

He leans down and kisses me on my temple, before he begins introducing me to several people. I stick to his side as I meet some of Brady's friends, old neighbors, classmates, and of course Max's family. Cody walks in alone and gives me a quick hug, "You look beautiful, Sam."

"Thank you Cody," I tell him appreciatively. He easily joins Brady and a few of their friends from high school in a conversation, making me feel a little more like a third wheel. I want them to have an opportunity to talk without me standing here awkwardly. I tilt my head up towards Brady and wait for an opportunity to interrupt. "I think I'm going to go use the restroom," I inform him.

"I'll go with you," he offers.

I shake my head, "No, that's okay. You should take the time to catch up with your friends. I'll be back soon," I promise.

"Okay," he reluctantly agrees. He kisses me on the corner of my mouth before he lets me go.

I blush and nod towards their friends, "It was great meeting all of you." They murmur their reply, but I'm already walking away.

I cross the room and walk out into the hallway, where I was told I could find the bathrooms. I quickly slip inside the door marked, "Women". I breathe a sigh of relief, just being momentarily away from the crowd. I take my time using the bathroom, washing my hands and touching up my lipstick amongst the different ages of women gossiping. I chuckle to myself, thinking how some things never change.

I step out of the bathroom and right into a broad male chest. "Oh, I'm sorry," I mumble as I step back. I attempt to step around the man, without looking up at him.

"Samantha," Paul rasps. He grasps my arm to stop me, making me gasp in shock.

I look up into familiar brown eyes. I question in shock, "What are you doing here?"

"I came to find you," he admits.

"What? How? Why?" I question irritably.

"I talked to a friend of yours who told me where to find you. She invited me here tonight because she said you'd be here," he admits.

"A friend of mine? What friend?" I ask confused.

He ignores my question and compliments me, "You look absolutely beautiful, Sam."

I feel myself blush, despite my irritation. "Thank you, but I don't understand why you're here," I tell him.

"We never finished our conversation. I just came to talk to you," he insists.

I shake my head, feeling trapped and confused. "This isn't the time or place to deal with this, Paul."

"I realize that, but you're not answering my texts or calls," he reminds me.

I shake my head, "It doesn't matter. Either way, we're done. We've been done for a long time and you know it," I declare. "I'm doing great on my own!"

"On your own?" he asks, making me flinch. "Did you take him back?" he glares accusingly.

"That's not your business, Paul!" I grit through my teeth.

"We have history. You don't have that with him. I deserve a second chance, not him," he pleads. "He cheated on you."

"You cheated on me," I emphasize. "He didn't cheat on me. That was a misunderstanding," I shake my head in denial. I scrunch up my nose, annoyed with myself, "Why am I explaining myself to you?" I pull away and take two steps back towards the ballroom before his hand clamps lightly around my bicep again.

"Wait," he begs. "I'm just trying to show you how much I'm willing to fight for you," he claims.

"Fight for me? I don't want you to fight for me. I told you, I'm doing just fine by myself!" I exclaim.

"But you're not by yourself, Samantha. You're with that asshole," he states, as if I need a reminder.

"I am with Brady," I admit, "but I can handle myself on my own," I insist.

His eyes narrow and he questions, "Are you sure about that? When was the last time you were really on your own? First it was your parents, then me for years and when we hit a rocky road, instead of working through it with me, you jump into a relationship with some asshole you barely know," he spits out with disgust. "When have you done anything on your own?"

I gasp in shock. Each word he utters feels like a punch to my heart. A lump forms in my throat. I clench my hands into fists, as I attempt to fight the tears welling in my eyes. "I don't have to defend myself to you," I grit through my teeth.

His face softens and his eyes fill with apology. "Sam, I'm sorry. I didn't mean that," he claims reaching for me.

Brady steps between us and crosses his arms over his broad chest. He glares at Paul and asks, "Is there a problem here?"

I put my hand on his arm and gently try to push him out of the way, "It's fine Brady. We were just talking. I can handle it."

He looks down at me and clenches his jaw before he glares at Paul again. "I think you two are done talking," he declares.

Paul laughs and looks over Brady's shoulder at me with a smirk, "Really Samantha?" He shakes his head in disappointment and repeats, "When?" My stomach twists and he announces, "You're stronger than this."

I open my mouth to respond, but nothing comes out. Jackie glides up to us on her father's arm and steps between Paul and Brady with a huge smile on her face. "Oh, you found her!" she exclaims.

I turn my glare on her, my voice returning. "You were the one who invited him here?" I accuse.

Her smile falters and she admits, "Yes. He contacted me through Insta because he was looking for you. He said he was worried and wanted to make sure you were okay. I thought I'd help," she grins devilishly.

"You thought it was a good idea to invite my ex-boyfriend here?" I question, my voice rising.

Her eyes widen innocently, "Oh, I didn't realize."

I huff and reply sarcastically, "Sure you didn't."

"Why would you do that?" Brady asks Jackie in exasperation. I ignore him as my gaze falls on Lincoln. He shifts uncomfortably back and forth from one foot to the other, as his eyes flick back and forth between Jackie and me. "I'm sure it was an accident," he finally murmurs.

I grimace and nod my head stiffly, as tears begin to burn my eyes. "Sure," I grumble. "I have to go," I rasp. I spin towards the front door of the building and stride away quickly. I hear noise in the background, but I ignore it, needing to get away from all of them as quickly as possible. I push out the front door and pause, closing my eyes to take a deep breath. I hear quickly approaching footsteps behind me and open my eyes, moving towards the sidewalk.

"Samantha," Brady calls, as he catches up to me. "Please wait." I slow down, but keep walking. His hand gently wraps around my wrist and he repeats, "Please."

I stop, but don't look at him, "I have to go home, Brady. I don't expect you to leave. You can stay. I'll call an Uber."

"You're not going home without me," he insists. "I'll take you home now." I finally look at him ready to argue, but something in his eyes stops me. I snap my mouth closed, giving him a stiff nod. He takes my hand and entwines his fingers with mine. He guides me towards his parked truck and I quietly follow behind.

Chapter 20

I pull my soft blush colored sweatshirt over my head and pull it into place with a sigh. I walk out of my room and back into the living room, grateful to be out of that dress. I sit down on the couch next to Brady, leaving a little space between us. I pull my feet up underneath me before I finally look up at him, his eyes full of concern. He holds his arms out for me and encourages me, "Come here." I open my mouth to argue, but I quickly snap it closed. I awkwardly scoot an inch or two closer. He sighs in defeat and drops one arm to the back of the couch behind me and his other hand to the top of my knee. Then he moves himself slightly closer. "Are you okay?" he asks, tucking a lock of my hair behind my ear.

I sigh, feeling completely worn down, "I'm fine. You can go back to the dinner if you want. I feel bad for taking you away."

I hear the tension in his voice, as he speaks, "You didn't take me away from anything. I *wanted* to go with you." I look down at my lap, anxiously. I hear him open his mouth to speak, as I hold my breath in anticipation. "Are you going to tell me what happened with you and Paul before I found you two in the entry?"

"Nothing happened," I mumble.

"It sure didn't seem like nothing," he insists.

I shake my head in irritation, just thinking about my conversation with Paul. "We were just talking. I was handling it. I was fine. I *am* fine," I emphasize.

"You don't seem fine," he asserts.

"I am," I vow. Brady sighs in frustration and lifts his hand off the back of the couch and runs it through his hair before dropping it behind me again. I grit my teeth as Paul's words about never doing anything on my own eat away at my insides. I already feel like I've been depending too much on Brady. Hearing Paul's words only confirmed what I was already feeling, even if I shouldn't believe him. "Brady, you can't always be my savior," I declare, needing to feel my own strength.

"You've said that before, but that's not what I'm trying to do here. I just want to be here for you and I'm pretty sure you know that," he states. He pauses and shakes his head, his jaw grinding in irritation. "But honestly, why not?" he asks perplexed. "I don't want you to have to deal with your ex or mine. You're my girlfriend. I know I can't always be there when things go wrong, but I want to make things easy for you when I can," he informs me.

I attempt to gulp down the lump in my throat and explain how I'm feeling. "I get it, but I need to be able to stand on my own too," I tell him.

"Who says you can't?" he accuses. I shake my head, dismissing him. He huffs a breath in frustration. "You can stand on your own and you do all the time. I just want to be here for you. Why won't you let me? What the hell is so wrong with me wanting to help you if I can?" he demands.

I shrug, "Nothing, but that's just it, Brady, all you do is take care of me, worry about me and try to make sure I'm okay. I need to be strong and deal with my life on my own. I'm way too dependent on you. You even gave me a job!" I remind him.

"You deserve that job! You got that booking with the couple, not me," he reminds me. "Your ideas on the barn and how to handle the whole thing are not something I could've come up with. And it won't just bring money in for this wedding; it will increase the value of everything because it will bring in business that we didn't have before. It's a market we never even touched in the past, but you came up with an idea to do exactly that. Honestly, I think you can do anything you put your mind to. That's one of the things I love about you," he proclaims. I arch my eyebrows in doubt, causing him to grind his teeth in exasperation. He gently slides his fingers down my jaw to my chin, holding me still. He stares intently into my eyes and rasps, "I do love you, Samantha."

I gulp over the lump in my throat and ask, "Do you? Or do you just like taking care of me?" His eyes widen and he gasps in shock. My stomach lurches repentantly. I regret saying the words the instant they leave my mouth, but it's already too late. They're out there and I'm suddenly unsure of what I believe.

"Are you fucking kidding me?" he asks vehemently. His stunned expression is filled with hurt and disbelief. He shakes his head as if to pull himself together. "I've been trying to be there for you and you fucking question me? That's bullshit, Samantha" he firmly declares.

I wince, "That's not what I meant." I take a deep breath and square my shoulders. I may not be saying the right words, but I know I need to do something to help myself feel more confident again. I take a deep breath and rid myself of the prickling throughout my body and whisper, "Maybe if you give me a chance to prove myself, we can make it work."

"You don't need to prove yourself to me. You already have," he states.

I gulp again and shake my head, knowing he doesn't understand what I'm trying to say. I don't even know if I understand what I'm trying to say. "I need to do this for me Brady. I need to know that I can stand on my own two feet; whether I'm dealing with Jackie or someone else or I'm trying to figure out what I want to do with my life and I need to do it without a safety net."

He pauses and his eyes narrow. I watch his Adam's apple bob up and down before he prods, "What are you saying?"

I sigh and look at him anxiously from underneath my lashes. I finally admit, "I'm saying I think we need a break."

"You're breaking up with me?" he asks incredulously. He huffs a humorless laugh and shakes his head in denial. "You're letting Jackie and Paul and whatever else get between us?"

"No, this isn't about them. This is about me. I need to be able to stand on my own," I explain. I suddenly feel as if a heavy weight is lying on my chest and I struggle to catch my breath. I think I just made the biggest mistake of my life, but I'm not sure what else to do. He continues to shake his head, without speaking. I shrug and add, "Maybe the time apart will help you figure out what you really want too. You're graduating next month. You don't even know if you want to stay here or follow a career across the country," I remind him.

"Stop acting like you're doing me a fucking favor!" he yells at me, making me flinch. He sighs in defeat at my reaction and mumbles an apology, "Sorry." He groans in frustration and quietly grumbles, "Minneapolis isn't across the country." He looks at me in both confusion and apprehension. Then he asks, "Is this just an excuse?"

"No," I shake my head fervently. I pinch my lips tightly together to gather my thoughts. I look up at him, wondering if I'm doing the right thing. I hate that I'm the one filling his body with all that tension. I want to lean over and kiss it out of him, but that will either put us right back where we started or he won't want me to kiss him. Ironically, I don't think I could handle his rejection right now. "You asked me once what I want. Right now, I'm going to answer and say I want to succeed on my own. I need to succeed on my own," I emphasize. "Not with everything, but I'm just trying to figure out who I am and who I want to be without standing in anyone's shadow."

"You're never in anyone's shadow," he mumbles. I feel myself blush. My heart clenches so tight, I feel like I can barely breathe.

I smile sadly, "I need to feel as confident as you seem to be." He grimaces and begins picking imaginary lint off the back of the couch. "I also want you to figure out where your life is leading you after you graduate. I need you to make a choice that's right for you," I emphasize. "I don't want you to have any regrets. Life is too short. I know that better than I want to," I admit.

He winces then crosses his arms defensively over his chest. He asks, challenging me, "And what if my life leads me in a direction where we end up apart?"

I gulp painfully. This time, I can't stop the flood of tears from falling from my lashes when I answer him. "Then it's not meant to be," I barely croak.

"That's bullshit, Samantha!" he yells, his fists clenching reflexively. He grunts as he pounds the back of the couch once and then closes his eyes. He slowly takes in a deep breath and exhales, before repeating the process three more times. He cautiously opens his eyes and meets my gaze. He grits through his teeth, "I'll give you your time Samantha, but I'm not turning away from this, from us." He pauses and takes another calming breath, as my own breath catches in my throat at the sudden look of determination in his eyes. "I don't know what you're trying to do here, but you have to stop with the fucking 180's. I was worried about you. I'm allowed to be worried about you. That's what people who care about you do. That's what boyfriends do. Hell, that's what friends do," he announces. "If you need to do some things on your own, then go ahead and do it, but I'm *not* going to let you tell me you love me one minute and then push me away the next. I understand why you want to do some of this alone with the Scotts. Honestly, I probably understand it more because of my history with Jackie. But don't use all that bullshit as an excuse to push me away. We've both been through too much loss already to end this with excuses. If you want time or space to figure shit out with them, I'll still be here because you matter to me," he emphasizes. "But if you want to just be friends and date other people," he shakes his head in refusal, "Well, I'm sorry, but I can't fucking do that. I'm already so deep in love with you. Just being friends with you and having to watch you with any other guy would absolutely fucking kill me," he states honestly.

Silent tears stream down my face faster and faster with every word he utters. My heart feels like it's breaking, making my whole body ache, but I'm unsure what else I could possibly say. I want to take it back, but I need this. "I'm sorry, Brady, that's not what I want," I whimper. "I don't want anyone but you. I don't know what to do and I don't really know how to explain everything to you," I tell him, feeling desperate.

"You don't have to know how to explain anything. Just tell me what you're thinking and how you're feeling. It's that simple," he maintains, urgently.

"It's not that simple for me. I'm sorry," I plead, hoping he understands. "I just know I can't have you saving me anymore. Not when it comes to Jackie or Lincoln or Paul or my future or anything else. I have to figure everything out on my own," I insist. "I need to be able to stand on my own two feet. I need to know who I am without you or I will never be stronger with you."

He physically flinches at my words, causing my heart to clench and my stomach to churn painfully.

He shakes his head in disbelief. "This is not supposed to be how tonight ends," he mumbles. He runs his fingers through his hair, before dropping his elbows to his knees.

"I'm sorry," I repeat, my voice catching. "I do love you Brady," I whimper.

He shakes his head and warns me, "Don't. I can't hear those words from you right now. Do what you need to do and we'll figure the rest out later, if we can."

My heart clenches agonizingly, as tears stream down my face. I attempt to wipe them away, but they fall faster than I can catch them. Brady plants his palms on his knees and pushes to stand. He walks down the hall to the bathroom and comes back with a light blue box of Kleenex, setting it in front of me. "Thanks," I rasp.

He nods, "I gotta' go. I can't be here right now."

I gulp down the lump in my throat and watch his tall lean form stride towards my front door. He pulls the door open and pauses, looking back at me. I open my mouth to stop him from leaving, but no words come. He clenches his jaw and walks away, pulling the door shut behind him. Seconds later I hear the slam of his front door. I fall onto my side and pull my knees to my chest letting the tears fall. My whole body aches painfully, like I just gave away a huge piece of myself. I don't want to lose him, but I don't know how else to do this.

A few minutes later Brady's front door slams again, rattling my walls followed by the sound of two sets of retreating footsteps. I reach for my phone and search for Ryan's number, distracting myself from where he might be going at this time of night. "Hey Sam! I was just thinking about you," Ryan answers on the first ring.

My only reply is a whispered sob, "Ry…"

"What the fuck did he do to you?" he demands.

"N…nothing. It's my fault," I cry.

"What?" he asks. I hear some noise in the background and he says, "Just a second." I hear him talking to someone, followed by a door closing. Then he asks, "What happened?"

“I broke up with him,” I whimper.

“What? Why?” he asks perplexed. “I thought you really liked this guy. Did he do something?”

“No, it’s me,” I insist.

“Talk to me Sam. You’re scaring me,” he claims.

I take a deep breath and attempt to calm myself down. I push myself off the couch and walk towards my room. I don’t want Cory to come home and see me like this. I push my door shut and flop down on my bed. “I don’t even know what happened Ry. Paul showed up at the event tonight,” I admit quietly and curl my legs up to my chest.

“Your ex showed up at the event you went to for Brady’s friend?” he asks, sounding confused.

“Yeah,” I concede. “I guess Jackie invited him because he was worried about me. She thought she was being nice,” I respond sarcastically.

He huffs a laugh, “You know I’m not buying that bullshit, but Brady did?”

I shake my head, even though he can’t see me. “No, he was really pissed at her, but I think Lincoln did,” I admit.

He sighs, “I don’t understand, Sam.”

I attempt to explain what’s going through my head. “Brady is always there sticking up for me, trying to be my hero, I guess. I need to be able to deal with Jackie, Lincoln, Paul, or whoever on my own.”

Ryan laughs humorlessly. “You do realize anyone who cares about you is going to do exactly what Brady does. In fact, I fucking expect him to be sticking up for you, especially since I can’t be there to do it.”

I sigh and add, “I appreciate you being the overprotective big brother, Ry, but I don’t even know who I am without someone there guiding me.”

“What the fuck are you talking about? What the hell did Paul say to you?” he asks accusingly. “I know it was him.”

I grimace, “He was just trying to get me back. He wants another chance.”

“That’s not anything new. I’m asking, what did he say?” he questions, punctuating each word.

I sigh and wipe the last of my tears away with my focus on Paul. "He didn't say anything that I wasn't already thinking," I explain, blowing off his question again.

"Sam," Ryan sighs. "I'm coming up."

"No! You have school," I remind him.

"And family is always more important," he insists.

"Yeah, but I'm okay. I just needed to talk to someone. You may be my cousin, but you're also my best friend," I acknowledge. "Besides it's not like I can talk to Cory about it. Her and Brady are too close. I'm afraid she'll hate me."

He sighs, "She won't hate you. Just tell me what Paul said to you. I don't care if it's something you were already thinking. I want to know what he said."

I heave a sigh and give in, "Fine." I explain, "He was saying he deserved a second chance and got mad I was giving Brady one. Then when he knew he didn't have a chance, he basically said I went from being dependent on my parents, to him, to Brady and I don't know how to do anything by myself."

"Sam," he attempts to interrupt me.

"He's right though. I need to be me again if I want to be in a healthy relationship. I need to be able to give more to Brady, not always take," I tell him.

"I don't agree with you. Paul's playing on your insecurities," he insists.

I shrug, "Maybe, but I still think he's right."

"He's wrong!" Ryan declares. When were you ever dependent on that asshole? You were always too good for him and he knows it."

"I don't know Ryan," I murmur.

He interrupts me, "And when we were kids, you were the one leading me around on all different adventures. In fact, you got in trouble more than once because of your independence. Hell, look at what you did in the past six months!" he exclaims. "Don't let him skew your point of view," he begs.

I pause, trying to soak in what he's telling me, but still struggling to believe it. "Maybe you're right, but I'm not sure yet. I want to stand on my own two feet before I go any further with Brady."

"So you're going to sabotage what you have?" he accuses.

"No," I deny.

"Are you sure about that Sam? Life is short. No one waits around forever. Especially guys," he states.

"I don't want him to wait around forever," I insist, knowing I'm lying before the words even pass my lips. Ryan huffs a humorless laugh, instead of calling me on it. "I don't know what else to do. Maybe I am letting Paul's words get into my head, but I can't get it out now."

I hear someone in the background and Ryan says, "I'll be right there." Then his focus is back on me. He tells me, "Sam, Paul is the last person you should be listening to. As far as I'm concerned, Brady was doing what I would expect him to do as your boyfriend or anyone else who cares about you. Don't let fear of losing him hold you back because your fear could become your reality."

I gasp in shock. "That's not what I'm doing," I instantly deny.

"After losing your parents, your best friend, your ex and life as you knew it, you've been holding back with everyone. I hate to say it, but you've been really coming around after meeting Brady. I love being able to see you again," he emphasizes. "I don't want you to retreat again," he insists.

"Ryan," I try to interrupt.

"Please Sam, just think about it. I don't want you to regret this," he insists.

I close my eyes and whisper, "I know."

"I'm coming!" he yells to someone. He sighs into the phone and says, "I'm sorry Sam, but I've gotta' go. Are you sure you don't need me to come up?"

"I'm sure. I'm okay," I claim. "I love you Ry!"

"Love you too," he calls. "Alright already," he calls irritably, before hitting end.

I sigh into my pillow and sadly admit to myself, "It's too late. I already regret it." I just think it's the right thing to do, right now.

Chapter 21

Brady

"So she broke up with you, after you stepped in between her and her ex and your ex?" Cody asks for clarification.

"No...well, yes...sort of," I grumble. I drop my elbows on the bar and run my hand through my hair in frustration. "She also insinuated she was doing me a fucking favor," I add bitterly.

"So you can date other chicks?" he grins mischievously.

I shake my head and grumble, "Not even close." I glance over at him and tell him, "You mentioning my possible internship in Minneapolis didn't help me."

He flinches regrettably, "Sorry, man."

I sigh and lower my head. "I think that was just an excuse anyway. She said she wanted to be able to stand on her own two feet. I guess I was standing in the way of that by trying to be there for her," I tell him grumpily. "But honestly, every time I learn something new about her, I can't help but think she's been standing on her own for way too long, without anyone in her corner. I think it's about damn time someone step up and support her. She's been through enough and deserves for things to go her way. I swear that asshole ex of hers pushed all of her insecurities at her and got her to break up with me."

"Do you really think that's what happened?" he asks.

I shrug without looking up at him. "Maybe. I don't know," I rasp.

The tap of two beer mugs being placed on the bar in front of me has me lifting my head. "What the hell happened to you? I thought you had that fundraiser in Madison tonight," Logan comments, as he assesses my disheveled appearance.

I glare at him in response, not wanting to tell him a damn thing. I take a large gulp of my beer before setting my mug back on the bar. "I dress like this all the time," I answer sarcastically. He glances down at my unbuttoned white dress shirt, showing off my white t-shirt underneath and black suit pants. My jacket and tie are the only things I took off and left at our apartment. I was in too much of a hurry to get out of my apartment and further away from Samantha, before I lost my shit, to do anything more than that.

Cody chuckles lightly and answers for me, "They ended up leaving early and then Samantha broke up with him."

Logan's eyebrows rise nearly to his hairline in surprise. I turn my glare on Cody, "Shut the fuck up."

Both of them smirk at my response. Logan tosses a white bar towel over his shoulder and leans down, folding his arms on the bar. "What did you do?" he asks. I narrow my eyes further at him and he chuckles, "You must've done something stupid."

"I didn't do anything except watch out for her," I tell him defensively. "Stay the fuck out of it!" I demand.

Logan straightens and puts his hands up warily, "Whoa, relax. I get why you're pissed, but I didn't steal your girl. Don't take it out on me."

My whole body pulls tight as an image of her on his arm suddenly pops into my head. "Stay away from her Logan," I warn.

He sighs and pushes up from the bar. "Kind of hard when we're working on an event together," he reminds me.

I wince and grumble, "Shit." I down the rest of my beer and set the mug down in front of me. "Sorry I'm being an asshole. I need to fix this, but I have no idea how. She's not making this easy," I ramble as I exhale.

"Break-ups are rarely easy," Logan reminds me. My eyes automatically narrow and he shakes his head as he backs away. "I'm out," he mutters. He turns and approaches a couple at the other end of the bar.

"You really are being an asshole," Cody mumbles.

"Gee, thanks," I grumble. "Haven't you ever seen the way he looks at her?" I ask, shaking my head in annoyance.

Cody shrugs, "She's gorgeous. A lot of guys look at her that way."

I wince and grit through my teeth, "That doesn't help." He attempts to hide his chuckle and takes a gulp of his beer. I take a deep breath to calm myself down, "He looks at her like he would eat her for breakfast if she'd let him. I don't want him trying to take advantage of her."

He reminds me, "You have no control over any of that right now." I scowl at him, only succeeding in making him laugh. "Listen, she lives with Cory, so you'll at least know how she's doing and maybe a little of what she's up to. Wait a few days. Let her cool off and then try talking to her again," he encourages.

"You're right," I admit.

He grins. "In the meantime, you're single again. Why not enjoy it?" he asks. He quickly sweeps the room, his gaze pausing on a group of co-eds, obviously dressed up for a night out. "We can start easy," he jokes.

"I don't want to enjoy being single. There's no one here to enjoy being single with," I mumble, without looking around.

"You mean Samantha's not here," he clarifies.

I shrug like its no big deal either way, but he's right. If Sam's not here, I'm not interested. "You know how I feel about her, Cody. This is not the time to give me shit."

He sighs and concedes, "You're right. I'll back off."

"In fact, can we not talk about her at all? I just want to drink a few beers and hang out with my best friend."

Cody nods briefly and smirks, "Got it."

Two girls, slip into the small space between Cody and me. "Excuse us. We're just trying to order a couple drinks."

Cody grins at them and leans against the bar, openly staring at both of them. "We can help with that," Cody responds. He raises his arm to get Logan's attention, barely taking his eyes off either woman. Logan nods and saunters towards us.

"What can I get you ladies?" he questions.

"Can we have 4 shots of tequila with lemon and two Amaretto Sours?" the redhead requests. Logan nods his head and quickly grabs the shots with salt and lemon wedges, followed by their two drinks. They place money on the bar and the redhead turns to Cody and me. "Would you guys like to join us for a shot?" she asks.

Cody grins and asks, "Do I get to lick the salt off one of you?"

They both giggle and I can't help but roll my eyes. The blonde licks her wrist and pours salt on it, holding her arm out for Cody. He wraps his hand around her wrist and makes a show out of licking it off, before downing the shot and sucking on the lemon. The redhead turns to me and asks, "How about you?"

"I'm good," I reply, without looking at her.

She looks at Cody and asks, "Is your friend shy or something?"

Cody chuckles, "Or something." He grins mischievously, "Go easy on him. His girlfriend just dumped him."

I turn my glare on him and then down the rest of my beer. The redhead purses her lips and sidles up even closer to me. "I know what that's like. I can help make you feel better," she offers, huskily.

I force myself to look her in the eyes and paste a smile on my face. "Thanks, but I'm doing just fine on my own."

She pouts and rubs against me, causing my whole body to tense. She leans into my ear and whispers breathily, "Are you sure I can't do anything to change your mind?"

I grab the shot and down it without salt or lemon. "Thanks," I tell her. "That helps," I grin. Her eyebrows furrow and two thin arms wrap around me from behind. My heartbeat speeds up, even though I know it's not her. I turn my head to find Jackie grinning up at me, causing me to wince. "Hey, Jackie," I greet her sadly. I nod and turn back towards the bar. I hold up my empty mug towards Logan, as he looks in our direction.

"You're in my spot," Jackie tells the girl next to me. I don't bother correcting her. I want this girl to leave and I know Jackie will get her to go.

"I thought you said his girlfriend broke up with him," I hear her tell Cody. I visibly flinch at her words. "Come on," she tells her friend and pulls her away from Cody.

Cody gulps down his beer as he watches them walk away. "Thanks for ruining that for me," Cody complains immediately.

I just shake my head, instead of responding to him. Jackie releases me and steps in between us with wide sparkling eyes. She questions with obvious surprise, "She broke up with you?"

I sigh in defeat knowing this is the last thing Sam would want. "Not exactly. We're just taking a sort of break," I tell her, as Logan slides another beer in front of me.

"That's the same thing," she declares, not able to hide her smile.

I shake my head, "No, it's not."

"That means you can go to the other event for Max with me!" she announces gleefully, her hand landing on my knee.

I remove her hand and insist, "That's definitely not what it means."

She grins, "Yes, it does." I glare at her and she grimaces. "You're no fun tonight. I'm not going to let you ruin my good mood. This is reason to celebrate!" she exclaims bouncing on her toes. "I'll talk to you this week and we can make plans."

"Jackie, I'm not..." I try to interrupt.

She ignores me and leans down, kissing me on the cheek. She squeals and skips gleefully away before I have a chance to argue. I sigh in frustration, "That's the last thing I need. No matter what Sam and I are going through, she's not going to like that Jackie knows anything."

Cody mumbles, "True, but for once Jackie's right." I arch my eyebrows in challenge and he explains, "You're no fun tonight."

"I need a new best friend," I murmur.

"I need a new wingman," he throws back at me.

I nod, "I see where I rank." I heave a sigh and apologize, "I'm sorry Cody. I know you're just trying to help, but I'm just not in the right headspace to be here. Beers at home might be a smarter move right now."

"Yeah, if the redhead with the see-through shirt wasn't getting your attention off of Sam, nothing will," he comments.

"She had a see-through shirt on?" I ask.

He chuckles, "Damn. If you didn't notice that when she was in your face, maybe I should just help you get your girl back."

"I'll get her back on my own," I declare confidently. "There's no other option for me." I tip my glass up and quickly drink my beer before I slam the mug on the bar. "I'm heading back to our apartment."

"Walking?" he questions.

I nod, "Yeah. I need it. You staying?" I ask.

He assesses me and drops money on the bar to cover our bill. "Nah, I can play pool anytime," he grins.

I huff a laugh and point at the group of women, "That's not pool."

He flashes me one of his charming smiles and shrugs, "Let's go."

"Thanks for the beers," I mumble. He waves at Logan as I stride for the door. I need to get out of here. This is the last place I want to be right now. Then again, I'm afraid anywhere without Sam is the last place I want to be. I'll have to keep myself busy to stay sane until we figure this shit out because we will figure this out. We have to.

Chapter 22

Samantha

I pull my teal and white tie-dye sweatshirt over my head and brush my hair up into a ponytail. I wander back out to the living room, grateful Cory is already at work. It's barely been two days since I broke up with Brady, but she keeps asking me questions. I don't know how to answer her. Plus, my whole body hurts every time I try to talk about him. It almost feels like I'm constantly fighting gravity. I'm rounding the couch just as there's a knock at the door. I turn around and reach for the handle, pulling it open. Logan stands with his hands jammed in his jeans pockets and a black fitted t-shirt, looking down at me. "That was fast. Were you staring through the peephole or something?" he grins crookedly.

I roll my eyes and smirk at him, "I do that all the time, don't you?" He chuckles and I tell him, "I was just walking by when you knocked. I didn't even look before I answered."

He shakes his head, "You shouldn't do that."

I sigh and nod my head, "Yeah, you're definitely not the first person to tell me that. I'm working on it."

He rocks back on his heels and tilts his head to the side, giving me an expectant look. He finally asks, "Are you going to let me in?"

I blush and move back, "Oops, sorry."

He chuckles and steps inside, closing the door behind him. "I've been wanting to come by to see you, but weekends usually get really busy at the bar," he tells me.

"And it's not like that on a Monday?" I ask.

He shrugs, "Not really in the spring. But I also have someone covering the bar," he admits. I nod my head in understanding. "I wanted to see if you were doing alright?" he asks cautiously, his eyes full of concern.

I sigh and spin away from him, walking to the couch and dropping down in the corner. I curl my legs up under me. Then I finally look up at him, while he slowly lowers himself next to me.

"Why do you want to know?" I ask, not looking at him. Maybe he doesn't know.

"He came in the night of the dinner you went to in Madison," he replies simply.

I purse my lips and nod my head. "Oh," I murmur. "Who was he with?" I ask. Then I shake my head, "Forget it, I don't want to know."

"I think he just came with Cody. I saw them talking to a few other people, but the two of them came together," he informs me.

"Other people?" I question. "You mean girls?" I ask. I flinch the second the words are out of my mouth. I glance up at him and notice his grimace before he has a chance to hide his reaction. My heart jumps up to my throat and my chest clenches tightly at the thought of him even talking to another girl. I shake my head again and mumble, "Forget it."

"Are you okay Sam?" he repeats. I look down at my hands and try to focus, but my eyes start to well up. I take a shaky breath and nod jerkily. I hear his soft sigh just before he folds me into his arms, protectively.

I close my eyes and lean into his warm embrace. After barely a minute, my body tenses. I can't let him comfort me. I wanted to do this on my own, so that's what I need to do. I plant my hands on his chest and push back with a groan of frustration, "I'm sorry. I did this to myself, so I can handle it by myself."

He draws back and narrows his eyes slightly as he looks at me with confusion. "That's not really how friendships work, Sam," he insists. "I fuck up and you help me fix it. You fuck up and I make you feel better."

He grins, completely satisfied with himself. I burst out laughing. "Well, you did make me feel a little bit better," I concede.

"I like seeing you smile," he acknowledges. I blush and look away. "Seriously though, I don't know what happened with you and Brady, but nobody should have to deal with anything alone. It doesn't matter who did what. I'm here if you need anything," he comforts me.

"Thank you, Logan," I respond and force a smile. I sigh and try to change the subject, "That can't be the only reason you're here."

He chuckles, "Guess you're ready to talk about something else." I just wait for him to continue, instead of responding. "Well, I did want to talk to you about the fundraiser. Like I said before, I do a lot of these things, but this is a bigger project than I'm used to doing," he admits.

"That's why you have me," I declare. I sit up straight and grin proudly.

He laughs and mumbles, "Yeah, that's the reason. It's definitely not that you pushed your way into this project."

I narrow my eyes at him and cross my arms over my chest, "Seriously? If you don't want my help," I begin.

He places his hand on my knee and cuts me off, "I definitely want your help." I open my mouth to respond, my whole body heating with embarrassment from his gentle teasing. He continues before I have a chance to say anything, "Anyway, we don't really have much time, so I wanted to see where you're at with everything and give you an update on what I've been working on as well. Then we can take it from there," he proposes, with an easy shrug.

I agree with a nod, "Okay, sounds good." I take a deep breath and launch into what I've been working on. My body slowly relaxes as I speak. "I actually talked to the woman from the Cystic Fibrosis Foundation near Milwaukee today and they can provide us with a few different brochures on Cystic Fibrosis. Plus they have a bracelet, a key chain and a small stress ball in the purple for anyone who attends the event. We could put one of everything in small gift bags for everyone or we can set up a table near the doors, but then we would need someone to man it," I explain.

"I like the gift bag idea as long as we can get them either free or cheap," he agrees.

"They also said they would send out an email to all the walk participants as long as we provide the information or a digital flyer or however we want to advertise for it," I inform him. "I think you should scan in one of your artwork posters with all the information and we can use that. Those are amazing," I tell him honestly.

He blushes slightly and mumbles, "Okay, I'll do that. And thanks," he adds.

I nod and continue, "They will also be giving out water bottles to all walk participants at the event down the road. They asked if we could have a flyer printed to go with it for last minute tickets as well," I inform him.

"That's incredible. My events usually do okay, but this is sounding like a pretty big thing all of a sudden. Is Brady going to be able to handle all of this at the restaurant?" he questions.

I flinch hearing his name and try to gulp down the sudden lump in my throat. "Um, yeah. I'll meet with him and try to go over everything. The barn would be better, but there's no way it will be ready for this."

"Do you want me to meet with Brady instead?" he offers, his eyes full of both curiosity and concern.

I shake my head, "No. I've got it. You keep working on the marketing. The posters and emails and flyers and whatever else you're doing to advertise. I'll work on the venue details. You have a bar to run too," I remind him.

He nods and grins, "Yeah, but that's easy."

"Easy?" I ask, arching my eyebrow in question.

He ignores my question and adds. "We can both work on donations for the silent auction too. The more we have, the better it will go. I have a list of things I've been able to get a hold of so far," he tells me. "How about I email you that list and I'll also email you all the marketing stuff so you can see it and share it on social media?" he suggests.

I smile halfheartedly, "That would be great. Thank you."

He nods and grins back. "Okay, now that we have that covered, do you want to tell me how you're really doing?" he repeats.

I grimace and heave a sigh. "Not really," I murmur.

"Okay, then how about we order a pizza and watch a movie," he suggests. "It's not very often I have any free time. I don't want to use it working right now. I need a break. Even if it's only for a couple hours," he admits.

My stomach flips anxiously. I don't know if I should be doing this. I know I broke up with Brady, but I don't want to date anyone else either. Not even someone as great as Logan. "Um, I'm not sure," I stammer, awkwardly.

He offers me a soft smile, "Sam, I don't want to make you uncomfortable. I just want to hang out with a friend. I'm really hungry and I just need a night to relax with a friend for once," he explains. "I promise I'm not going to try anything," he smirks.

"Why not?" I ask slightly offended.

He laughs, "Not because I don't want to," he declares. "You're sexy as fuck," he states. I instantly blush a deep shade of red and pull my knees back up to my chest. "I would make every move I could think of if I thought you wanted it, but you're obviously not ready for anything." I grimace and he adds, "But that's okay. I genuinely like you and respect you."

"Thank you. I like you too," I murmur.

He grins cheekily and I roll my eyes at him, making him laugh. "Seth is working tonight too, so my apartment is too fucking quiet."

"Why not go out?" I ask.

He widens his eyes and reminds me, "I work at a bar."

"True, but it's not the same thing," I say.

"Yeah, but close enough. I don't want to be in that atmosphere. I honestly just want to hang out with you tonight. Nothing will happen," he insists.

I nod my head, "You're right it won't." The corner of his mouth twitches up and I giggle, "Okay. I'll trust you."

He laughs, "Gee, thanks. You sound so convincing." I shrug and he asks, "Do you like pepperoni or sausage?"

"Both," I suggest.

He nods, "My kind of woman." I narrow my eyes at him. He laughs and picks up his cell phone. "I'm going to order the pizza."

I sigh and pick up my own phone. I pull up Brady's name and my fingers hover over the number before I finally hit message instead of call. "Can we meet in the next few days to talk about the fundraiser?" I hit send and wait anxiously. My stomach churns as the dancing dots appear and I await his response.

"Of course. Do you want to meet me at the restaurant so we can talk about the set-up?" he suggests.

"Sure, what works for you?" I ask knowing he's the one with the busier schedule.

"Tonight?" he asks.

My heart drops to my stomach and I reply, "What about tomorrow?"

"Fine. 6pm?" he suggests.

"I'll be there," I respond.

"Do you want me to pick you up?" he asks. Tingles prickle my whole body at the thought of being alone in his truck with him. "I'm coming from school, but I'm happy to come and get you," he offers.

I breathe a sigh of relief knowing he won't be leaving from here. I don't want to make anything awkward, but I don't know if I can be alone with him, without desperately wanting to kiss him. "That's okay. I may be out searching for raffle donations. I'll just meet you there," I say.

"Ok," he replies.

I grimace and set my phone down on the coffee table. "Everything okay?" Logan asks as he sits back down on the couch.

I nod, "Yeah. I'm meeting with Brady tomorrow night. I'll get the specifics on numbers and we'll do set-up and hopefully talk a little about food for the night.

He assesses me momentarily before nodding, "Okay. Pizza should be here soon. Should we pick out a movie?" he asks.

I nod in agreement. Then I relax into my corner of the couch, with the remote in my hand.

Chapter 23

Brady

I park my truck and stare up at the apartment building with an exhausted sigh. It's crazy that I grew up here and lived here most of my life, yet everything around here now reminds me of Samantha. I see her everywhere, especially here. I picture her standing on the sidewalk in front of her car the day she moved in. She looked incredibly beautiful, as well as both determined and unsure. Even then, I felt a pull towards her, like we already had a strong connection. I think about holding her hand on the walkway and kissing her everywhere, every chance I got, once she was finally mine. Every single one of my memories with her is seared into my mind. This apartment building is not only where I met her, but also where I fell in love with her. Now it's also the place where she broke us apart. I clench my fist as my heart clenches painfully. I can only keep myself busy studying on campus or working at the restaurant for so long. I need to get some sleep. I briefly wonder if I should drive to my parents and sleep in my old room, but I quickly shove that thought away. I don't want to answer any of their questions about my mood. I take a deep breath and grit my teeth as I climb out of my truck. I reach for my backpack and throw it over my shoulder.

I walk inside the building and glance at the elevator and grimace. I even see visions of her there, looking at her, kissing her, or just holding her hand. I can't do that right now. I turn towards the stairs instead and slowly trudge up to my floor, feeling defeated. I step onto the top landing, ready to escape through my door, but my gaze is immediately drawn a little further down the hall. Logan is taking up Samantha's doorway, embracing her. "Thanks for tonight. I needed that and it was a good movie too," he adds, smirking.

She grins, causing my heart to leap up my throat. "You sound surprised," she says.

He smiles and shrugs, "Just about the movie," he explains.

She giggles and I hold my breath, refusing to bring any attention to myself. She adds sweetly, "I had fun."

I grit my teeth, my blood boiling as I remain frozen, still hoping they don't notice me in the shadows of the stairwell. "Me too," he grins. He winks at her, before kissing her on the cheek. I hold my breath and my hands clench involuntarily into fists at my sides. He takes a step backwards, pizza box in hand and spins on his heel towards his apartment as she closes the door.

"You're already making fucking moves on her?" I rasp accusingly, as I step woodenly into the hallway.

He stops and looks over at me. I take a few steps closer to him, waiting for him to answer. He sighs sadly and insists, "I'm not making any moves on her."

I glare at him and he tilts his head to the side and laughs humorlessly. "You didn't just have dinner with her?" I ask, gesturing to the pizza box. He arches his eyebrows in challenge. "And watch a movie with her?" I question. My heart clenches painfully, as I picture them cuddling on the couch together.

He purses his lips and nods his head in affirmation, "No, I did." I gasp, even though I knew it to be true. "But maybe you should focus on you and not what she's doing when she's hanging out with her friends."

"Friends?" I grit through my teeth.

He nods, "Yeah, friends. She needs a few of those right now. Don't you think?" I wince as he gives me a pointed look. "Since she moved here she basically has you, Cory and even Cody, but since you two are on a break, she doesn't really have anyone here," he reminds me. "You definitely can't count Mr. Scott and his family," he adds.

My stomach churns at the realization. She doesn't have anyone here and I want her to have a support system. "You're right," I murmur.

He takes a step towards me and informs me, "Look Brady, I wouldn't take advantage of someone like Samantha, especially when she's so vulnerable. Yeah, Sam's gorgeous and smart as hell, but she has too much going on right now. I would never push her when she's dealing with so much shit," he insists.

I cross my arms over my chest defensively. "And what about when she has everything all figured out?" I ask.

"I won't make any promises for then," he smirks. I clench my fists at my sides, wanting to punch that smirk right off his face. He chuckles at my reaction. "Look Brady, from what she's said, you need to make your own decisions, without regrets, if you want a chance to get her back. I'd focus on that and what she needs right now, instead of worrying about some asshole she's working with."

"I have to ask Logan, what's with the advice?" I ask.

"I like Sam," he admits. "She deserves to have things go her way, whatever that may be. But if you don't want my advice, don't take it," he retorts. "It may work out more in my favor that way anyway."

I shake my head, "That's not what I'm saying. We've been friends for a long time, but we've never really been close. I've seen your reaction to Sam. Why are you giving me advice that actually sounds like the good kind?" I ask, my lips twitching up slightly.

"You're right," he states. "We've never been close, but we have always been friends. You were always around when all that shit went down with my family and Nat," he grimaces. "You may not even realize some of the shit you did for me, but you were there and I've never fucking forgotten." He looks away at the painful reminder, his Adam's apple bobbing up and down as he gulps.

I shrug like its no big deal, "That's what friends do."

He shakes his head and turns back to me. He insists, "Not all friends. That's what you do Brady." He sighs and tries to shake everything off like it doesn't matter. "Look, I'm just telling you how I see things. I'll be honest though, I'm not going to wait forever to make a move on her. She's too fucking perfect. You can take my advice or leave it. No skin off my back," he mumbles. He turns back towards his apartment, dismissing the conversation.

I call his name to stop him, "Logan?"

He stops and turns his head towards me. "Yeah?" he asks.

"Thanks," I tell him simply.

He gives me a firm nod, before quickly disappearing into his apartment.

I glance over at Sam's door, but hastily turn back to mine and push through. I walk in and immediately drop my backpack behind the door as I kick the door closed.

Cody looks up from the couch with a beer in his hand. He greets me, "Hey, man. You coming from the restaurant?"

I shake my head, as I drop down onto the opposite end of the couch. I drop my head back and stare at the ceiling. I inform him, "No, campus."

"Project or something?" he asks.

"Just studying," I admit.

"Huh," he mumbles.

I can feel his eyes on me. I finally lift my head with a sigh and ask, "Yeah?"

He shakes his head dismissively, "Nothing. Brewers are playing," he informs me, pointing to the television.

I look over at the TV and stare at the screen, even though I'm not able to focus on the game. I can't help but run my conversation with Logan over and over in my head. I hate that I'm not the one who's there with her, but he's right. I need to get out of my own way and focus on what she needs from me. She's been through too much and if I were stupid enough to push her now, I'd probably never get her back.

"Yes!" Cody cheers. He looks over at me and furrows his brow. "You okay man? That was a Brewers homerun you're scowling over," he informs me.

I shake my head and answer, "I'm just exhausted. I think I just need to get some sleep." I run my hand over my face and back up through my hair.

Cody nods in agreement, "If you don't know what's happening in a baseball game, you definitely need some sleep, if it's not Samantha," he adds.

I flinch and push off the couch. "Goodnight, Cody" I grumble, without responding to his comment.

He sighs, "Night, Brady."

I plod towards my room, every limb feeling like dead weight. I walk in and push the door closed behind me. I fall back on my bed and kick off my sneakers. Then I pull my feet up on my black and white pinstriped comforter. I prop my head on top of my slate gray pillows and glance at the newest decoration I added to my room, the picture of Samantha and me from the other night in a small black wooden frame. It may have ended badly, but she looks so fucking beautiful, I couldn't help myself. Besides, the night started out perfect. I pick the frame up off my nightstand with a sigh. "So you want me to help you by giving you space and making sure I have no regrets?" I ask her image. "I guess I can do that."

I reach for my phone and find the last text I sent her. She needs to work on the wedding and the fundraiser with me too. They are using my family's restaurant. I bite my lower lip, while I quickly type a message out to her. "Can you meet a little earlier tomorrow? I want to show you where we are on the barn renovation and maybe talk about some plans to propose to the bride and groom? Then we can go over your plans for the fundraiser at the restaurant?" I propose.

The dancing dots appear and like a fucking idiot I stare at them until a message comes through from her, grateful for any morsel she sends my way. "Sure," she agrees and my body sags with relief. "How early?"

"Is 4 okay?" I ask.

"Ok," she agrees. "I'll still meet you at the restaurant."

I release the breath I didn't know I was holding. I can't help but be grateful she'll at least spend time with me to work on this, for now anyway. I just hope she doesn't decide to bring Logan. I grimace at the thought. I text, "Sounds good."

She replies, "Great."

With nothing left she wants to hear from me right now, I set my phone down. I sigh and walk to my desk, flipping open my laptop. "If I'm going to do what she says she needs, I might as well get it over with," I murmur. I log into my email and quickly type a response to the company in Minneapolis offering me the internship opportunity. I inform them I will be happy to come meet with them to further discuss the internship and request possible dates for me to come. I advise them Fridays are the most convenient for me with my school schedule. I reread my letter, looking for any mistakes. I take a deep breath as my finger hovers over my keyboard before I finally tap send. "Well, I guess we'll see," I mumble.

I kick off my jeans and t-shirt and crawl back into my bed, under the comforter this time. I place the picture of Samantha and me back on my nightstand and give it one last look before I close my eyes. The sooner tomorrow comes, the sooner I can see Samantha again and begin straightening out this mess.

Chapter 24

Samantha

"Thanks for letting me hang out while you get ready to open," I tell Logan.

"You're welcome, but now that all our business is out of the way, is there a reason you wanted to hang out here?" he asks perceptively.

I grimace, "Well, it just feels kind of weird around Cory. She's being nice and all, but she keeps asking me questions I don't want to answer or giving me these weird looks." I shrug, "I don't even think she realizes she's doing it, but I don't want to think about it either way," I explain.

He nods knowingly, "I get it, but you have to feel comfortable in your own apartment. You should talk to her," he suggests.

I purse my lips and reply, "I will, eventually."

He chuckles and shakes his head in amusement. "Women," he smirks.

I ignore his dig and add, "I just want to focus on other things right now, like this fundraiser."

"Well, at least that helps me out," he jokes.

I smile and simply say, "You're welcome."

"You can hang out at my place anytime you want. You won't have far to go that way," he offers.

I grin appreciatively, "Thank you Logan. Are you sure Seth won't mind?"

He laughs and insists, "He definitely won't mind. Not at all."

"Well, thanks," I repeat. I better go. I'm supposed to be at the restaurant to meet Brady soon. I'll let you know how the meeting goes," I tell him. I slide my laptop and papers back into my bag.

"I'll catch up with you tomorrow morning after I get up. If that works?" he questions, but doesn't wait for my answer. "I'm closing up here tonight," he informs me.

I nod as I sling my bag over my shoulder. "Okay, sounds good. Thanks," I repeat.

"Good luck," he calls. I give him a quick wave as I turn to leave. I walk out the front door of Mae's and into the warm spring air. The door closes behind me and I look up to find my Volvo. Instead I spot Jackie walking towards me with a devilish grin. I hide a grimace and sigh in defeat. I take a deep breath and brace myself the best I can, for anything she might throw at me.

"Nice outfit," she taunts.

I look down at my yellow sundress with scattered white daisy flowers, white sandals and white jean jacket with gold buttons. "It's nice out," I respond with a shrug, attempting to be civil.

"Looks to me like you're trying too hard," she mumbles.

"Excuse me?" I ask with wide eyes, although I shouldn't be surprised.

She arches her eyebrows and asks, "Coming from a date or something? In a bar?" she asks, as if in shock. "That's tacky," she grimaces. "Then again, you are the girl who broke up with a guy as wonderful as Brady. I wouldn't put anything past you."

My stomach lurches and I can't stop my gasp. "What? How do you know?" I rasp.

Her smile becomes huge at my reaction. "I was out with Brady right after it happened. I knew it wouldn't last. He told me all about it," she gloats.

My heart clenches tightly, making it hard to breathe. "He wouldn't do that," I insist with a shake of my head.

She cackles and announces, "Not with everyone, but he will always tell me everything. Luckily I was there to comfort him. I'll always be there for him," she emphasizes.

I open my mouth to respond; but no words come out. I will myself not to cry as I step around her and stride towards my car. I will not let her see me break. "Have a nice day!" she calls cheerfully. I hold up my hand and lift my middle finger in her direction without turning back around. "Bitch," she mumbles. I stop and quickly search for my keys in the side of my bag. I unlock the door and slip inside. She grumbles, "Classy," just before I'm able to close the door.

I grit my teeth and start my car. I buckle my seat belt and quickly pull away from Mae's, heading straight for Brady's family restaurant. "Ugh!" I scream in frustration as soon as I'm far enough away. "I will not let her get to me," I declare, just as a tear slips out of the corner of my eye. "I did this to myself. It doesn't matter if it's true or not," I lie to myself. "I have no right to be upset about anything Brady was doing or saying or even who he was with," I whimper. I take a deep breath and hold it momentarily to try to stop myself from losing it. I slowly release my breath and attempt to slow down my heartbeat by focusing on my breathing and the road.

It feels like a matter of seconds before I'm parked in front of Brady's family restaurant. I flip the visor down and quickly glance at my reflection in the mirror. I flip it up, satisfied, and step out of my car. I reach for my bag and sling it over my shoulder before closing the door. I square my shoulders and take another deep breath before I walk to the front door. "Here it goes," I murmur.

I step inside and nervously clasp my hands, as I take a step forward without looking up. "Holy shit," Brady mumbles. I lift my head in surprise and he quickly strides towards me. He stops in front of me and gives his head a light shake. "Sorry," he apologizes, "but you look beautiful."

I blush and whisper, "Thank you."

"I wasn't expecting you to be so dressed up. I feel a little bit underdressed," he smirks, showing off his dimple and causing my heart to leap with joy.

"It's just the first nice day in a really long time and I'm ready for the warm weather and sunshine and summer for that matter, so I wanted to wear something that was good for the beautiful day," I ramble my explanation.

"Sam," he interrupts with a chuckle, "you're perfect," he insists.

I feel my body heat even more at his compliment. "Thanks," I murmur. He begins to reach for me, but suddenly grimaces and drops his hand before he gets too close. It's like he's not quite sure what to do with himself, which only makes my chest ache more. He's always so confident. I don't want to be the one to take that away from him.

"Do you want to go to the ballroom? We have it set-up for an anniversary celebration, so you can kind of see what it's like for a party. That might help you decide what you want," he suggests.

I nod, "Alright."

He holds his arm out and gestures for me to walk in front of him, "After you."

I give him a stiff smile and step in front of him. I barely take a step before I anxiously turn back. The bottom of my skirt flares and Brady's eyes quickly flash up to mine. I arch my eyebrows and blurt out, "Are you checking out my ass?"

He chuckles and responds, "I won't lie to you Samantha."

He doesn't say anything else and I burst out laughing, lightening the mood. "Cute," I grin.

"Thanks," he grins mischievously. Goosebumps cover my body and I try to suppress a shiver just from having his smile directed at me. How the hell does he still make me melt and feel so much lighter than I did fifteen minutes ago? Then again going toe to toe with Jackie might bring anyone down. He steps up next to me and we walk side by side to the ballroom. "Can I ask you something?" I propose, as he pulls the double doors open.

"Anything," he replies sincerely. I bite my lower lip and release it repeatedly as he guides me to the first large round table in the room. He pulls out a chair for me to sit and encourages, "Ask me Sam. Whatever it is you want to know, ask me."

I sit down and slowly blow out my breath. "Did you go out with Jackie the other night?" I blurt out. His eyebrows draw together in confusion and not knowing what he's thinking, I quickly scramble to explain. "I mean after everything that happened with us, did you meet her out for drinks or something?" His mouth drops open and I quickly try to backtrack. Maybe I shouldn't have said anything. "It's fine if you did. Everyone needs someone to talk to and I don't have a right to care who you talk to about us. I guess I just wish it wasn't her."

"It wasn't! I mean I didn't. No, and you have every right. Ugh," he stutters. He grimaces and insists, "I didn't go out with her or meet her. I went out with Cody and she was there. I wasn't talking to her, but I guess she overheard part of our conversation and obviously spun it to her advantage with you. I'm so sorry Sam."

"Why are you sorry?" I ask and shake my head. "You don't have to be sorry about anything," I insist. "I'm the reason we're in this situation," I declare truthfully.

He sighs as he covers my hand with his and gives it a light squeeze. My heart inflates with hope at his encouragement. "I am sorry though Sam. I don't want you to have to deal with Jackie because of me," he announces.

I grimace and remind him, "I will have to deal with Jackie regardless because of Lincoln." He opens his mouth to argue with me and I cut him off. "She may also give me a hard time because of you, but I don't think she would treat me any better if you weren't a part of my life."

He shrugs and gives my hand another light squeeze before releasing it. "That may be, but being with me definitely gives her more ammo against you."

I resist the urge to reach for his hand again and shrug, "That doesn't matter to me. I should know better than to believe half of what comes out of her mouth." I take a deep breath and change the subject, before I decide I should climb into his lap instead. "Anyway, can we go over some plans for the fundraiser?" I request.

He nods in agreement, "Sure. What do you think of the layout?"

I stand and walk slowly around the room. There are several large round tables with seats for 10 around the room, all layered with what appears to be a silver tablecloth underneath and a white overlay. Only one table has the service in place. I walk a little closer to see how it's set. Each setting includes a white dinner plate with a silver line around the edge, a salad plate, a dessert plate, silverware, a white napkin wrapped with a silver napkin ring, a crystal water glass, and a cup and saucer for coffee or tea. "I don't think we want this many tables. Maybe we can have 5 of these tables along the back, but we'll decorate with white and purple, to enhance the Cystic Fibrosis colors," I tell him. "I also don't want anything set for dinner. I think it's beautiful, but too much for something like this. Maybe just tablecloths and centerpieces for each table," I suggest.

"Okay, are you thinking no food then?" he questions.

I shake my head, "No, I met with Logan earlier and we were thinking appetizers and drinks would be better for something like this. Then maybe we could also have a dessert table over on this side, but all things you could eat standing up if you wanted," I explain.

"That's a great idea," he agrees.

"Do you have any small tables that are tall? Like ones people can stand at?" I ask.

He nods, "Yeah, I just don't have those set up for this. Do you want maybe ten of those near the bar area?"

I grin, "That's perfect."

"The DJ usually goes up against that wall and then the dance floor is here," Brady points out.

"Then we need another table for the raffles along the wall when you walk in. We already have a lot of donations," I inform him, with satisfaction.

"That's great Sam," he encourages. "You're obviously really enjoying planning this event," he states as he takes a step closer to me.

I nod with a small smile upon my lips, "Yeah, I really am."

He grins, "Good." He stares at me as if he wants to kiss me, but then suddenly clears his throat and steps away. "Why don't we put a few things in writing," he suggests. "We can always change something later if you don't like it, but this will get us going. Then we can also come up with some appetizers you definitely want included as well as what we might want on the dessert table. Does that work?" he asks, not looking at me.

"Sure," I murmur. We go back to the table and quickly work out some of the details. He finally drops his pen on the table and tells me, "I think it's going to be a great event Sam."

"I hope so," I mumble.

He sighs and blurts out, "I want to let you know, I'll be going up to Minneapolis on Thursday night. I'm going to be shadowing at that marketing company on Friday and then discuss the internship with them further. They want me to make a decision."

My chest tightens, making it hard to breathe. I nod my head and force a smile, "That's great Brady." This is what I wanted, for him to make a choice that benefits him.

He nods his head as he watches me closely for my reaction. He sighs and continues, "I'm going to stay with a friend who lives up there. I probably won't come back until Saturday morning, so I can catch up with him."

"That's good," I mumble. "Good luck," I tell him honestly.

He exhales harshly and stands, "Yeah, thanks." He runs his hand through his hair and tells me, "I think we got a lot done, but if you need something else right away, call me."

"I will. Thank you," I tell him, confused. I feel like he's suddenly running away from me.

"I have to go study, but maybe we can get together next week. I'll have some food ready for you to taste and we can narrow down the menu," he suggests.

"Okay," I reply timidly.

He stuffs his hands in his pockets and adds, "I'd like to show you some progress on the barn project too."

I feel my shoulders relax and I tell him, "I'd like that. I had thought we were doing that today," I admit.

"Sorry, I can't. I have shit to do," he replies vaguely. He forces a smile, causing my body to tense again. He turns and walks back towards the front of the restaurant with me following behind, feeling a little like a fool. He stops at the front door and pulls it open for me. "I'll see you next week," he declares, dismissing me.

I wince, thinking about how far away next week actually is, but that's my fault. I look up at him and hesitate. I want to say something, but I don't know if I should, or what exactly to say. Should I just forget about trying to do this by myself and ask him for another chance? I'm afraid I'll keep depending on him, though, if I ask for another chance now. I need to be independent, or I might not ever be good for him. I attempt to gulp down the lump in my throat, hoping he'll forgive me some day. "Good luck on Friday," I rasp.

"Thanks," he murmurs.

I grab my things and quickly rush out to my car before I do something stupid like throw myself at him. "What the hell are you doing Samantha?" I question, annoyed with myself for both walking away and for not believing that was the right decision.

Chapter 25

I walk out of Mae's with my bag slung over my shoulder and stroll down the street. I take a deep breath, enjoying the fresh air. I'm grateful the days are finally getting warmer and I don't have to worry about bringing a jacket unless there's a chance of rain. Today I don't see a single cloud in the bright blue sky, but the light breeze brings the scent of trees budding and flowers blooming, dancing across my nose. I love this time of year, when everything starts new again. I pause on the sidewalk and tip my head up slightly, like I can pull the sun's heat towards me if I get just a little bit closer. "Samantha?" a deep voice startles me back onto my heels.

I gasp and search out the owner of the voice. I find Lincoln staring at me with a crooked smile. "Um, hi," I murmur, surprised.

He gestures to his store behind him and informs me, "I was just leaving work for a coffee break. Would you like to join me?"

I glance up at the wooden Hometown sign above the door before meeting his gaze. "Um, I just finished with a meeting and I was just enjoying the sun," I stammer.

He grins widely, "I see that. I'm glad we finally have some nice weather." I nod woodenly. He sighs and tries again, "Listen, if you're busy I understand. I just thought maybe since you're here, if you have a little time, we could talk for a little while. I'm starting to realize Jackie hasn't made things too easy for you," he begins. I flinch before I can stop myself. He heaves a sigh, "Do you have just a few minutes for coffee? Please?"

I nod, feeling unsteady, "Sure."

He smiles with obvious relief, "Great! We can just go across the street to the diner if that's okay with you?"

"Okay," I agree.

We walk in awkward silence across the street. He holds the door open for me and nods, "After you."

"Thank you," I reply, politely.

"Actually, do you want to grab something to go instead? That way you can keep enjoying the sunshine?" he suggests. I nod and walk towards the counter.

I order a medium coffee with extra cream and Lincoln orders a large black coffee, then places a $10 bill on the counter to pay. "Please, allow me to pay for yours as well?" he requests.

Instead of answering I step back and wait for my coffee. The cashier hands both of us our coffee, mine with cream. I reach for the sugar, adding three heaping spoonful's and stirring before covering it with the lid. "Thank you," I mumble, before stiffly turning back towards the door to exit.

I step out onto the sidewalk and Lincoln steps up next to me with a small smile, "You're welcome."

We take a few steps down the sidewalk in silence. I glance across the street at his store and ask, "Do you like owning your own store?"

He smiles, appearing to be happy I asked the question, or maybe he's happy I asked anything. I'm not quite sure. He nods, "I do. At first it was just going to be a hardware store, but then I slowly expanded to all different kinds of things needed in the home. Even with Madison so close, sometimes it's just easier to not have to go into the city to get some of the basic things." He shrugs, "It just kind of made sense."

I nod in understanding, "I get it."

"What have you been up to? Are you working or taking classes now? It feels weird to not know that. Shouldn't that be something I know?" he questions. He shakes it off, "I guess that's part of why we're getting to know each other better."

I huff a laugh, "Yeah, I guess so." I glance over at him, curious if he really wants to know, or if he feels like he has to ask, but I'm not about to ask him that. "I've actually been doing a couple different things," I tell him.

"Oh? What things?" he asks curiously.

"Well, there was a couple looking at the restaurant for their wedding, but they want something really specific. I gave Brady a suggestion for it and he loved it. He proposed it to the couple and they booked with him and hired me," I blush. "Anyway, I guess I'm helping with all the planning now." His eyes widen and I quickly continue, "We've barely gotten started, so I don't know if it will be something I want to do after this." I shrug, "I don't even know if Brady or the couple will like what I do, but they're all trusting me with it," I inform him. "I hope I do a good job for them," I add.

"That's wonderful. I'm sure you'll be great," he encourages. I press my lips together thoughtfully, assessing his reaction. I can't help it. I want to know what he thinks and if his reactions about what I'm saying are genuine. How do I know, when I don't really know him? "Things are going well with you and Brady then?" he asks curiously.

I open my mouth to respond and feel my face turn red. I don't know how to answer that or I don't really want to. "Um…I…He's," I stammer.

He shakes his head and quickly apologizes, "I'm sorry. It's none of my business. You don't need to tell me about your love life if you don't want to," he declares, with a grimace.

I open my mouth again, to tell him that's not what's stopping me, but I can't tell him I'm not with Brady. It doesn't matter that Jackie will probably tell him. I take a deep breath and force myself to move on. "That's okay," I finally stutter. "I actually wanted to call you or come see you soon, anyway," I inform him. He arches his eyebrows, his eyes full of curiosity. "I wanted to tell you about a project I'm working on with Logan from Mae's," I tell him. My stomach suddenly fills with butterflies.

"This is what you left me a message about?" he questions. I nod my head. "I'm sorry I didn't get back to you," he apologizes. "His events have tended to draw a younger crowd, since he usually holds them at Mae's. He has done a lot of great work around here, since he took the place over," he recognizes.

"Yeah, from what I've seen, I believe it," I acknowledge. "I stopped in at the fundraiser he had the other day. I'm going to work with him on one for next month for Cystic Fibrosis," I blurt out. "I just really want to do something to help."

He sighs sadly and nods in understanding. "I get it. I really wish I could've done something to help her."

I clasp my hands anxiously and nod my head. I glance at him out of the corner of my eye, wishing I knew what he was thinking. "I just felt like I should do something," I emphasize. "Plus, I've always been really good at planning parties. There are just a few more moving parts to a party like this," I joke.

He chuckles and looks over at me with what appears to be pride, but that can't be right. He doesn't know me. "It sounds like you're really enjoying it," he concludes.

I smile, realizing he's right. "I am," I admit. "I haven't really thought about it too much, but I've been working hard. Brady offered for us to have this event at the restaurant, so we have more space. I really want it to go well. I guess, I just want to do something for her, even though she's not here. But honestly, even if it wasn't something I wanted to do for her, I think I would like doing this," I concede, thinking of the wedding reception I'm working on with Brady.

He grins, "That's great to hear, Samantha. If there's anything I can do to help, let me know," he offers.

I smile appreciatively, "Thank you! We'd love to put some flyers in your store if that's okay," I request.

He nods in agreement, "Of course."

"And if you want to donate something for the raffles, that would be wonderful," I prod.

He chuckles and quickly agrees, "I'd be happy to."

"I'd um, I'd also really love it, if you'd come," I admit anxiously. I quickly ramble on, nervous for his response. "You don't have to, but if you want to come, I think it would be great to see you there."

He puts his hand up to stop me, "Samantha, I would love to come. I know Ginny would want to be there too," he tells me kindly. My chest aches, but I'm not sure if it's because he makes me miss my mom and dad, or if I'm craving more from him. Maybe it's both, I admit to myself. I look up at him with a furrowed brow. "Would that be okay?" he asks, confused by my expression.

I look down at my lap and gulp down the lump in my throat. I nod and force the words out, "I'd like that."

We approach a dark green wooden park bench at the end of the street. He gestures and asks, "Would you like to sit down?" Instead of answering, I lower myself onto the bench. I try to relax against the back, as much as I can in an uncomfortable seat. He sits down next to me, leaving a comfortable amount of space between us. He glances over at me, his lips pinched together, like he might be trying to read me. At least that's the same look I have, when I'm constantly doing that with him.

He leans back with a sigh and reminds me, "I know I said this before, but I'm really not sure how to do this. I want to get to know you better, Samantha. I want to know my daughter," he insists, "but I don't want to force my way into your life or push you too fast. Jackie seems to really be having a hard time with this," he admits. I flinch at the mention of her name. He sighs, his voice full of regret, "Seems to me, the two of you are having a hard time with each other."

I shake my head and explain as simply as I can. "That started before we knew," I trail off, not wanting to say anymore.

He nods, "I know. Jackie and Brady have a lot of history and she doesn't let go too easy," he concedes, making me wince. "She's had a tough road the last few years," he adds as rationalization. I attempt to hold back my reaction, but I don't think I succeed. "I have to say, I felt like you and I were doing pretty well and now, I feel like we're moving backwards," he admits. "Is there something I can do to make you feel more comfortable?" he asks.

I bite my lower lip, stopping myself from blurting out anything I might regret. Particularly since I want to tell him he should start by controlling Jackie, especially around me. I shrug, "I don't know. I really had fun at Frankie's baseball game. He's really good. I enjoyed going to pizza with all of you too. Ginny has been so nice to me and Frankie is such a great kid," I smile fondly, thinking of him. He already feels like a little brother.

He grins affectionately, lost in thought. "Yeah, he really is. He's been asking about you quite a bit," he announces.

My heart skips a beat and I arch my eyebrows in surprise, "He has?"

He chuckles, "Of course. He has a new big sister and she already came to one of his games. That's a big deal in his book."

I nod thoughtfully, wondering if Jackie ever goes to any of his games, but that's none of my business. Instead, I confess, "I'd love to come watch another game. Ginny gave me the schedule, so if it's okay, I'll let you or Ginny know when I can come."

"You can just show up, if you want. It would always be great to have you there," he insists.

I feel my body warm with his suggestion. I clear my throat, pushing away the prickling sensation. I run my hands over my thighs nervously and exhale slowly. I finally quietly divulge, "It felt good to be there."

Lincoln's smile widens. He opens his mouth to say something else when his phone rings. He pulls it out of his pocket and glances at the screen. "I'm sorry, I have to take this," he announces. He touches the screen to answer, "Hello?" He pauses, "I thought it was in the back." He grimaces and sighs, "Alright, I'll be back in a few minutes." He clicks end on his phone and looks up at me apologetically. "I'm sorry, but I have to get back to the store to take care of something."

I give him a half smile and insist, "That's okay. We can talk another time."

He nods and stares at me momentarily. "Samantha, would you like to do this more often? If you call or come by the store I will always try to make some time for you," he declares.

I quickly inhale in surprise, nearly choking on my breath. I answer, "I'd like that. You can call me too," I add as a reminder. I don't want to be the only one calling. It would feel like I'm pushing something that's not wanted and that's the last thing I need or want with him.

He smiles and agrees, "I will do that." He pauses and repeats himself, as if to remind him or maybe convince me it's true. "I promise, I will be calling you." He stands and asks, "Are you going to be staying here in Chance?"

"For a little while, at least," I decide instantly.

He nods in acknowledgement and mumbles, "Good." He offers me a small wave, "I'll see you later, Samantha."

"Bye," I wave. I watch him walk away, until he disappears inside the front door of Hometown. I pull my phone out of my bag and glance at the screen to check for notifications. I open it, wanting to tell someone about running into Lincoln. I pull up Brady's name, tempted to call him. He's the one I want to talk to. My finger hovers briefly over his name, before I click the side button to turn it off. I bite my bottom lip and quickly slip my phone back in my bag. "He's probably in class anyway," I mumble, rationalizing with myself. I push up from the bench, with an exaggerated sigh and begin walking back to my apartment, trying not to think about Brady.

Chapter 26

I toss the brochures to the side with a frustrated groan and flop back onto the couch. I can't focus on anything because I can't get Brady out of my head. He left for Minneapolis tonight and I have no idea what he's doing with his friend. They're probably out drinking and partying and picking up girls. He could hook up with some girl up there and I couldn't say a damn thing about it because stupid me broke up with him, so I could focus and now I can't focus on anything except him! I reach for my phone, determined to call him. I open my contacts and scroll to his name. I grimace and toss my phone on the couch in annoyance. What would I even say? "Please don't hook up with anyone. I can't handle it?" I roll my eyes at myself and drop my head in my hands in defeat.

A loud knock at the door has me pushing up off the couch and stomping to the door. "I'm coming," I call grumpily.

I pull the door open and Logan grins down at me. "Hi beautiful."

I cross my arms over my chest and glare at him, "Really?"

He laughs and reaches for my ponytail, giving it a small tug. He quickly runs his eyes over me from head to toe, making me blush at the mess he sees. I'm wearing light blue and green, pinstriped shorts with a darker green off the shoulder sweatshirt. He smirks, "Well, sexy is a better word, but I didn't think you wanted to hear that from me."

I feel my body turn an even deeper shade of red, just as Cody steps out of his apartment. He startles the moment he notices us. He looks back and forth between the two of us and grimaces. He focuses on Logan and asks, "Why aren't you at the bar? I was heading down to see you."

"I took a night off," he states. "Sam and I have some things we've gotta' do," he grins mischievously. He glances over at me and I glare at his response.

Cody huffs and gives his head a slight shake. I quickly blurt out, "We're just working on the fundraiser." I don't want him to get the wrong idea and say something to Brady that's not true. That would only make things worse.

Cody narrows his eyes on me and turns for the stairs, without another word. "Don't want anyone to think you'd be into someone like me?" Logan asks.

My head snaps back to him in confusion, "Are you serious right now?" He crosses his arms over his chest and arches his eyebrows in challenge. I roll my eyes and tell him, "You know you're hot, so don't go fishing for compliments.

"You think I'm hot?" he smirks.

I grunt in frustration and try to slam the door in his face. He sticks his foot out to stop the door from closing, laughing at my reaction. "Come on Sam, I took off tonight to cheer you up. I knew you would be in your head with Brady in Minnesota for the next couple days, so I'm here to help," he states.

"Really?" I question. I narrow my eyes at him, as if in warning, before giving in with a reluctant sigh. "Fine, but can we hang out at your place?" I request.

He nods and grins in satisfaction. "Yeah, but Seth is home tonight," he informs me.

"And?" I ask.

He laughs, "He's hanging out with us too."

"Okay, he's allowed," I state sarcastically.

I grab my keys and pull the front door closed behind me, before I follow him across the hall to his apartment. He pushes his door open and we both step inside. Seth instantly greets me with open arms, "Sam!"

I give him a quick hug and then I step back and smile at the broad, 6'3" bearded teddy bear, "Hi Seth."

"Why didn't I get a hug?" Logan complains.

I glance over to see if he's serious, but he's attempting to hide his smile. "Because you tried to make Cody think we were doing things, instead of working," I declare.

He stops hiding his smirk and mischievously proclaims, "Well, we are doing things besides working."

"You know what I mean," I tell him, sounding annoyed.

"I don't, explain it to me," Seth jokes, "Please."

I roll my eyes and turn back towards the door, "I'm going home."

Logan laughs and jumps in front of me, stopping me. "He's kidding, we understand, but I said it because it's good for Brady to hear it," he informs me.

I cross my arms over my chest, defensively. "Why would that be? I broke up with him," I remind him defiantly.

He nods, "Yeah, but you obviously wish you didn't. Seems to me you need him to fight for you a little bit."

I sigh his name, "Logan, that's very sweet, but..." I close my eyes and slowly open them again, meeting his gaze. "That's not what this is. But hearing something like what you said to Cody, that might make him go hook up with someone while he's gone."

"Sam, I know you don't want to hear this, but if he was going to hook up with someone while he was gone, it would happen regardless of what's going on with you, but if he hears I'm hitting on you and asking you out again, he won't be able to stop thinking about you, no matter what he does," he rationalizes.

"Really?" I ask, more anxious than I was before.

Seth laughs, "He's right."

Logan glares at him, "Shut up or I'll kick you out."

"I was agreeing with you asshole and I live here," he declares.

Logan shrugs, "I don't care." Seth shakes his head and Logan smirks before looking back at me. "Sam, I have no idea what's going on inside your head that made you break up with him in the first place," he admits. "But I have to ask, why are you torturing yourself?"

I grimace and flop down in a leather recliner next to Seth. "Sometimes I wonder," I mumble to myself. "I guess I wanted to figure out what I wanted to do with my life. I need to make decisions for me, not anyone else," I state.

"Here, here," Seth grumbles, holding up a beer bottle, as if to toast me.

"I just want to prove that I'm a strong, independent woman who can take care of herself," I announce.

"Well that's obvious," he says. He starts to blow off what I said, but he sees something in me and hesitates. "Did Brady say something to make you feel like you have something to prove?" he questions, his body suddenly tense.

"No!" I yell and shake my head vehemently. "Of course not!" He doesn't need to know it was my ex who said it.

He grimaces and insists, "You have to know that's exactly who you are. At least that's how I've seen you since the day I met you. You came to me and pushed your way in to work on this cystic fibrosis event. In fact, I didn't even know if I was going to do a fundraising event next month, I was thinking of either skipping it or doing something really easy, since I've been so busy lately. Then you come along and that changed. You can do anything you put your mind to," he declares.

"Yeah, but working on this has seemed easy. It hasn't felt like work for me," I admit.

He huffs a laugh, "That statement could offend a lot of people."

"That's not what I meant. I just mean I've been having a lot of fun doing it, so that makes it easy. That's why it doesn't feel like work," I explain.

He nods, "I get it, but that just means you found a job you love. Isn't that the goal?"

I shrug, "I guess, but it's not just about me, it's also about him. He has that internship opportunity in Minneapolis. I don't want him to make a decision because of me and regret it later. He'll end up hating me." I cringe at the thought.

He huffs a laugh, "I don't think Brady could ever hate you, but I do think he deserves to be a part of that decision. I know I would want to be, if it were me."

I grimace and sigh, full of regret. "I know, but I don't know what to do now. I don't want to make things worse. Besides he needs all the time he can get to prepare for finals. Plus, he has graduation coming up."

"Are you sure those aren't just excuses?" he questions.

I scowl at him and request, "Can we just not talk about him? Even for a little while?"

He laughs, "I'd be happy to not talk about another guy when I have a beautiful woman in my apartment."

I roll my eyes and both Logan and Seth laugh at my expense. A light knock at their door has Logan spinning around and pulling it open. "Hi!" Cory greets Logan cheerily. My whole body tenses. "Seth invited me over for pizza," Cory announces.

"Yes, he did," Logan agrees. "Come on in."

She steps inside and Logan closes the door behind her. She spots me and freezes, "Oh." She appears to quickly pull herself together and shoots a glare my way. She crosses her arms across her chest and demands, "Where the hell have you been? Have you been avoiding me?"

I flinch and grumble, "Sorry. I just don't know what to say."

She huffs a humorless laugh and insists, "Yes, you do. You just don't want to admit it or you're too scared. Either way, it's bullshit," she asserts. She steps closer to me, until we're eye to eye.

"Cory," I attempt to interrupt, but she's too wound up to let me get a word in.

"I'm pretty sure I'm not the one you're actually mad at, but you're avoiding me. I know I'm close with Brady and my brother is his best friend, but that doesn't mean I'm going to assume everything is your fault. You can't keep avoiding me! You're supposed to be my roommate and my friend!" she shrieks.

"But it is my fault!" I announce, yelling over her.

She falls back on her heels and drops her arms at her sides. "Wait, what?" she asks, her mouth dropping open in surprise.

I grimace, "He didn't tell you?"

She shakes her head, "Cody told me something happened with Jackie. He also told me your ex-boyfriend was there and caused some problems. Then he said you guys broke up."

I sigh and reluctantly admit, "Yeah, that's all true, but I broke up with him."

"She thinks she's holding him back," Logan chimes in.

"Are we doing this girl talk thing all night?" Seth complains.

We all ignore him and Cory looks over at me with wide eyes, "Seriously?" I pinch my lips together and shrug because everything she said is true. "You're the reason he's really opening up again," she states as fact. "It's not that he's closed-off, but after Max died, he was just different." She shrugs, "You're really good for him."

I shake my head, disagreeing with her. "I'm not good for him at all. I have too much I'm trying to figure out. I feel like I'm just dragging him along."

We're interrupted by another knock at the door. I freeze and my heart drops into my stomach, wondering if it might be Brady, even though I know he's in Minnesota. Seth jumps up to answer it, "Pizza," he announces. Then he pulls the door open. He grabs the three pizza boxes and two bottles of Cola from the delivery guy. "Logan, he needs a tip," Seth advises. He grins and walks away from the open door.

Logan sighs and reaches into his pocket, pulling out a few singles. He hands them to the delivery guy and tells him, "Thanks," before shutting the door.

"Are you guys going to have a cat fight or do you want to eat?" Seth asks. He opens the first box of pizza, the scent of garlic, cheese and sauce fills the air.

I ignore him and turn towards Cory. I tell her, "I'm sorry, but I wasn't ready to answer any questions about Brady. It's hard to talk about him. That's why I've been avoiding you. I know how close you guys are and I don't want you to feel uncomfortable around me."

"But it's okay for you to feel uncomfortable in your own apartment?" she questions. I grimace and she insists, "You should've talked to me. I know I've been asking questions, but if you didn't want to talk about Brady yet, I would understand," she insists.

"That's what Logan said. He tried to get me to talk to you," I inform her.

She pauses and looks from Logan, to me, and then back again. She purses her lips and finally exhales slowly before nodding in appreciation. "I guess I should say, thank you."

"You don't have to say anything," he insists. "I like Sam," he begins.

Cory interrupts him, mumbling, "That's obvious."

He glares at her and tells her, "I've known you for a long time, but I've already become better friends with Sam. If you say something bitchy again, this conversation is over," he states firmly.

Her eyes widen in surprise and she mumbles, "Sorry."

"This whole pie will be gone, before you girls stop gossiping," Seth calls, reminding us of our dinner.

Cory's eyes flit back and forth between Logan and me before settling back on me. "Truce?" she asks.

I nod and force a smile, "Yeah, truce."

She grins from ear to ear and throws her arms around me, knocking the wind out of me. "Oops," she smiles apologetically and I quickly hug her back. "Let's eat," she encourages. She reaches for a slice of pizza and flops down in the middle of the couch. I grab a napkin and follow suit, feeling slightly relieved.

I turn towards Logan and say, "I guess I don't have to hide-out at your apartment or work all the time now."

"Hey Cory, did you know you're roommate talks about you behind your back all the time? And Sam, you can hang out with me anytime you need to get away from your bitchy roommate," Logan grins cheekily.

Cory and I both roll our eyes, then burst out laughing. "Nice try," she mumbles. He shrugs and takes a bite of his pizza.

Chapter 27

Brady

I drop my pen on my notebook, the blank pages staring up at me. I lift my head and stare out into the nearly empty restaurant, with the same view I had while growing up. My sister Becca slides into the corner booth across from me, with a smile. "It almost feels like we're kids again, seeing you sitting over here studying and brooding on a Saturday night."

I offer her a sad smile and shrug. I inform her, "I only have 2 weeks left of school and I have a lot to do. Finals start in a few days."

She nods in understanding, "So why are you here looking pissed off at the world, instead of at home studying?" she asks curiously.

I sigh and run a hand through my hair in frustration. "I just can't be at my apartment lately," I grumble.

Her eyebrows draw together in confusion and she asks, "Why not? Did you and Cody have a fight or something?"

I shake my head, feeling completely exhausted and mutter, "No." Becca looks even more confused. I decide to explain, instead of having her pry it out of me. It will go faster this way. "Sam and I broke up last week," I blurt out.

Her eyes widen in shock. She asks with disbelief, "What? Why? What did you do? And why am I just finding out now?"

"Why do you think I did something?" I ask defensively, instead of answering any of her questions.

She shrugs and explains, as if it's a known fact, "It's always the guy's fault, especially when it comes to you," she adds smirking.

I huff a laugh and tell her, "Well, I didn't do anything, but she broke up with me anyway."

She grimaces and glares at me. "Details Brady and maybe I can actually help you."

I exhale slowly and try to tell her with a simple explanation. "The short story is Jackie was being a bitch."

"Tell me something I don't know," Becca mutters.

I continue, knowing she won't stop until she understands. "Jackie thought it was a good idea to invite Sam's ex-boyfriend to the event for Max last weekend." I pause before adding, "The asshole still wants her back, by the way."

"She went back to her ex?" she slaps the table in shock.

My heart drops into my stomach involuntarily at the thought. I shake my head, "No! Do you want to hear this or not?" I ask.

She purses her lips, "Yes, sorry."

"Anyway, so her ex was there and he tried talking to her to get her back. He didn't have any luck, so instead he said some shit to her that made her feel like she depends on me too much. He made her think she can't do anything by herself," I complain.

"Asshole," she mutters.

I nod in agreement, but keep talking. "She told him to leave her alone, again. Then she confronted Jackie and fought with her, again. Lincoln had no clue what was happening, so when he stepped in, he honestly just made things worse just by being there," I ramble.

"What do you mean?" she asks.

"From my perspective, it seems like he's doing what's best for Jackie, but at the same time, he's alienating Samantha every time he tries to calm things between them. Honestly, between my history with Jackie and trying to figure out how all of them fit into her life, nothing has been easy for Sam when it comes to the Scotts. Then, I found out about my internship offer in Minneapolis recently and she pushed me to go. She said she doesn't want my relationship with her to affect my decision. She's afraid I'll regret it if I don't take their offer."

"That's right. Mom told me you were there the last couple days," she informs me. "How did it go?"

I shrug, "It was fine. Everyone was nice, but honestly I think it would be a job I could do for any company around here. I could even do what they would have me doing for the restaurant. I don't need to go to Minnesota to get marketing experience."

She nods in understanding and pauses before she asks, "And that decision has nothing to do with Samantha?"

"No, I want to be here. I need to be close to my family," I tell her honestly. "It's why I moved back here in the first place."

"So that's good. Have you told Samantha yet?" I shake my head and she groans in annoyance, "Why the hell not?"

"I honestly don't know if she'll believe me. I don't want her to think I rushed into a decision I'll regret later," I tell her.

"Is there any chance you would regret it if you don't take it?" she prods.

I shake my head and admit, "No, I don't think so. It's not what I want." She smiles proudly and I pause, thinking about going out the other night with Cody. I need to explain to someone what's been going through my head and Cody isn't the one to talk to about this. I begin talking, knowing my sister will listen. "After Sam broke up with me, I was really pissed off. Cody dragged me down to Mae's. We had a few beers and a few shots. Then I told him what happened with Sam. After that, I tried really fucking hard not to think about her."

"How'd that work out for you?" she asks, sarcastically.

I chuckle humorlessly and shake my head. I mumble, "Impossible. The bar was packed and Cody being Cody, encouraged me to hook up with someone or something to get over her." I sigh in resignation and run my hand through my hair, "But all I could see was her, even though she wasn't fucking there." I take a deep, calming breath and confess, "Honestly Becca, Sam's not someone you ever get over. She's the one you regret losing, not a stupid internship. She's the one you would always ask yourself, 'what if' and she's the one you would give *anything* for, to just go back and do something, anything," I emphasize, "to change the outcome. She will always be the one that got away if I don't get her back...she's just...the *one*," I ramble, my heart aching painfully with every word I utter. "I just don't know what to do to get her back," I rasp. "Fuck," I grumble in frustration. I turn away from my sister as a tear slips out from the corner of my eye. I hate that I'm wiping tears away in front of anyone.

"Don't turn away. I'm your sister and I'm pretty sure Sam would like to see your vulnerable side. You don't always have to be the tough guy Brady," she insists.

I glance up at her with a smirk, "I sure as fuck don't feel tough right now."

She glowers at my response and insists, "You have to let her see this side of you. You have to tell her how you feel."

"She doesn't want to know how I feel. She wants to focus on figuring herself out," I grimace. "She says she depends on me too much, but maybe it's the other way around because it's killing me to be without her."

"Just because you want to be with her, doesn't mean you depend on her too much. You know you can survive without her, you just don't want to," she reminds me.

"Maybe that's what she's trying to prove to herself, but she's been through so much since I've met her. She's probably the toughest and most independent person I know. Everyone needs someone to lean on sometimes. I just want to be that person for her," I explain.

"Then tell her that!" she declares insistently.

A throat clears and Becca and I both look up to find Jackie dressed in a short, sleeveless, red fitted dress with a deep V between her breasts, red high-heeled stilettos and matching red lipstick. "Is that painted on?" Becca asks with disgust.

Jackie glares at her before turning to me without replying to my sister. "Do you have your suit with you? You brought a red tie right?" she asks.

My eyes narrow in confusion and I ask, "What the hell are you talking about? What are you doing here, Jackie?"

"I called here earlier when I couldn't get in touch with you. Your mom said you were here. I thought we were just leaving from here, since it's so late," she explains.

"For what?" I ask.

"For the event for Max. That's tonight, remember?" she reminds me, still maintaining her confidence.

I nod, "Of course I remember, but that doesn't tell me what you're doing here."

She hesitates, her confidence faltering, slightly. I notice my sister smirking at her, not even bothering to hide her amusement. I heave a sigh and wait for her answer. She squares her shoulders and announces, "Because you're my date, Brady."

I laugh before I can stop myself. Jackie narrows her eyes at me. I take a deep breath and bury my amusement. Then I remind her, "I'm not your date for this or anything else."

She grits her teeth and a sudden look of determination washes over her face. "After Samantha broke up with you, I talked to you at Mae's about going with me tonight. Since you don't have to worry about her anymore, you can be my date. We already talked about this and you've never missed a single one of these events since Max died," she whines. "Are you really going to betray him now, just to spite me?"

I flinch at her words. I quickly slip out of the booth and stare down at her. Her high heels bring her up to nearly eye level with me. I clench my fists to keep my anger at bay. I open my mouth, my voice coming out in a low growl. "How dare you. I'm not betraying Max, or his family. Not that it's any of your business, but I went to see them, to tell them I can't be there tonight. I have finals, graduation and a lot of other shit to worry about right now, so I can't make it this year. They understand and Max would've too."

"Okay," she squeaks.

I step closer, my anger practically radiating off me. "I've been the one who has been there for you and helped you, so many fucking times," I emphasize, trying to keep my voice down to a harsh whisper. "It's always been me who has been by your side, telling everyone you're just having a hard time and you have a lot of shit to deal with, but you'll figure it out and be better." I grind my jaw in irritation and question, "But you think it's okay to try to manipulate me, about Sam? And about my dead best friend?"

"Brady, I'm sorry," she stammers, shaking slightly.

I shake my head in refusal. "Sorry doesn't cut it, Jackie, not this time," I declare.

"But, that's not what I meant," she begins.

I give my head a slight shake, "It doesn't matter what you say you meant to do. What you did and what you keep doing, that's what matters. I'm sick of you trying to manipulate a situation for your own benefit. I'm sick of you cutting everyone down, especially Samantha," I stress.

"But," she tries to interject.

I quickly continue, before she has a chance to say anything else. "I may have been drinking a lot the other night at Mae's, but I *know* I never agreed to go anywhere with you. Just because Sam and I are taking a break, and that's all it is, a break," I insist, "that doesn't mean you and I are going to start dating again. I haven't been with you for over four years. Me meeting Sam and falling in love with her," I push, making her cringe, "that's not what kept us apart. Shit like this is why we're not together and why we will *never* be together. I'm done trying to help you. I'm done letting you walk all over me. I'm done feeling guilty. I'm just done," I emphasize.

A tear slips out of the corner of her eye and she tries to apologize, but I'm not ready to hear it. "Brady, I'm sorry," she whimpers.

I shake my head and refuse to look at her. I grab my books, quickly stuffing them into my backpack. I look across the table at my shell-shocked sister and tell her, "I have to get out of here Becca. I'll call you later."

She nods slowly. I swing my backpack over my right shoulder and quickly stride for the door, without looking back.

Chapter 28

Samantha

"Did you see this Sam?" Logan asks from his spot on the couch.

"Hmm?" I ask. I attempt to pull my thoughts away from Brady again. I need to focus on the fundraiser and the walk. It feels like I'm constantly trying to not think about him since we broke up.

"The poster the Cystic Fibrosis Foundation sent out to all of the team captains and sponsors for our event?" he prods.

My eyes widen and I jump up. "No," I exclaim. I sit down right next to him to see his laptop screen better. "When did it go out?" I ask.

He chuckles and informs me, "Today. They'll have the same one posted all over at the walk on Saturday."

"That's great," I declare.

He nods, "Yeah, I've never worked in conjunction with another event, not really. I'm interested to see how this works for us. I could see it going in a couple different directions, but either way I would think the increased advertising could only help," he concedes.

"I think so too," I agree. "I can't believe how much stuff they sent us to give away. I think the pop sockets are my favorite," I admit.

He chuckles, "I thought you didn't really like your phone?" I shrug like it doesn't matter and he lightly tosses a purple stress ball at my head, "Personally I like these."

I laugh and bat it away, "Hey!"

He grins and closes his laptop before leaning back and throwing his arm over the back of the couch. "I have to say I'm really impressed with what you've done. You threw everything together so quickly," he praises me, causing me to blush.

"I'm pretty sure both of us have been working hard to make this happen." He gives me a look and I grin. "Thanks. I'm really having fun," I admit.

He stares into my eyes and quietly confesses, "Me too." My heart begins to speed up, as I feel the shift in the room. "Sam," he starts. Then he stops talking. His hands are suddenly in my hair and his mouth is on mine. I freeze, not sure what to do or how to feel. He pulls back and takes in my wide eyes, his own expression suddenly full of remorse. "Shit, I'm sorry, I just," he sighs and drops his hands to his lap with a groan.

"What just happened?" I mumble.

He winces and repeats, "I'm sorry. After spending the last few weeks with you, I couldn't not kiss you anymore. I think you're amazing. You're smart and sexy. I love how hard you're working to help people by doing this with me. I know it's too soon and you're not over Brady yet, but you're not with him either. I love working with you and hanging out with you and I think we could be really good together if you just give us a chance," he rambles.

"Logan, I don't...I can't...it's just..." I stammer.

He forces a smile and insists, "It's okay. Don't say anything right now. I didn't mean to push you. I promised I wouldn't," he mumbles. He adds, "I should go." He picks up his laptop and stands, quickly striding for the door. He pulls it open and turns towards me, just as I'm stumbling towards him, feeling completely out of sorts. "Let's go back to focusing on the walk for Saturday. Then we can finalize everything for the following weekend. We don't have to think of anything beyond that," he suggests.

I feel my body sigh with relief and I nod my head in agreement. "Okay, that sounds good. Thank you," I murmur.

"You're really doing an amazing job," he reiterates. He reaches for me and wraps his arm around my neck, pulling me in for a quick hug.

"Thanks," I say, awkwardly.

I feel his hot breath on my cheek as he whispers in my ear. "I'm sorry I pushed you Sam, but I'm not sorry I kissed you," he murmurs. "Please, just think about giving us a chance. What could one date hurt?" he smirks. He kisses me on my temple and releases me. He turns away, taking the three steps across the hall to his apartment. He walks inside and closes the door behind him, without looking back. He leaves me standing in the hallway, alone and confused.

I glance at Brady's closed apartment door, my heart aching. I wander over to his door and hold my hand up as if to knock, before dropping it back down to my side. I want to know what happened in Minneapolis with the internship, but I don't think I have a right to know, not now. I heave a sigh and trudge back into my apartment, just as Cory comes out of her bedroom. "Hey. Logan left?" she asks glancing around the empty room.

I grimace, "Yeah." Her head tilts in confusion at my reaction. I shake my head and sigh, "Don't ask."

She shrugs, "Okay, but if you want to talk about anything, I'm here."

"I know. Thanks," I mumble.

"Want to watch a movie or something to get your mind off of everything?" she proposes.

"As long as it's some kind of action or thriller or something like that. I can't take a rom-com tonight." I scrunch up my nose with distaste, causing her to laugh.

"You got it," she agrees.

We both curl up at opposite ends of the couch with a blanket. She presses play on a movie with Vin Diesel, explosions beginning almost immediately. I attempt to relax into the corner, but I can't stop thinking about Logan kissing me, or what Brady would say about it. I have a sick feeling in the pit of my stomach, even though I didn't do anything wrong. I didn't kiss him and besides, Brady and I are broken up. Then why do I feel so guilty?

"Are you okay?" Cory asks interrupting my thoughts. I look up at her and she adds, "You just look a little green or something," she explains.

I nod, "Yeah, I'm okay. I just don't feel like myself," I admit a partial truth.

"Okay," she nods slowly. Then she hesitantly turns back towards the television.

I sigh and reach for my phone. I open my text messages and click on the last text between Brady and me. I begin typing and erasing over and over again, hoping to get my simple message right. I don't want to sound too needy, but I don't want to sound like I'm blowing him off either. "Hope your weekend went well," I finally write and pause, wondering if it's the right thing to say. I don't want him to think I don't care about the internship, but I don't want him to think I'm pushing him to go there or trying to get him to stay here. "No regrets," I mumble the reminder.

"Hmm?" Cory asks.

"Sorry," I respond. "I'm just talking to myself."

She turns back and I look back down at my phone. I hesitate before typing, "I was wondering if you had time for me this week? I'd love to see the barn and finalize more plans for the fundraiser." I read it and reread it, before I finally hit send. I suddenly register the sound on the TV has gone silent. My head snaps up and I meet Cory's questioning gaze.

"Who are you texting?" she asks. "Brady?"

I wince and admit, "Yeah."

She purses her lips in thought and crosses her arms over her chest. "Why don't you just tell me what you're trying to do and I'll do what I can to help," she suggests.

I arch my eyebrow in question, "Are you sure?"

She nods, "Yes. Didn't we just talk about this at Logan's?" I wince at the mention of Logan. Her eyes widen, as she notices my reaction. She sits up straight and points at me, "Okay, that right there. What is going on?"

"I...I don't know," I stammer. She arches her eyebrows in challenge and stares me down.

I exhale harshly, sighing in resignation, "Fine." I squeeze my eyes shut tightly, not wanting to see her reaction. I quickly blurt out, "Logan kissed me." Her gasp has me opening my eyes to assess her. "I didn't kiss him back," I add defensively. "He said he wants a chance, but he knows I'm not over Brady."

"You're not over Brady," she repeats, her lips curving up at the corners of her mouth.

I shake my head, "Not even a little bit. I'm still in love with him," I admit. "And I like Logan, he's cute," I say.

She interrupts, "Logan is hot and sexy. Cute doesn't describe Logan at all."

I pause momentarily to shake off her comment. "Okay, but it's more that I like hanging out with him and working with him. He just took me so off guard. I wasn't prepared and didn't know what to say, but now I feel guilty," I confess.

"Why do you feel guilty?" she asks confused.

I shrug, "I don't know. I guess, if I didn't break up with Brady, it wouldn't have happened. And besides I should have stopped him or told him I couldn't, but I didn't."

"Well, you still can tell him not to do it again. Then you can apologize to Brady and fix it with him," she tells me simply.

I grimace and shake my head, "I can't. I need him to make a decision on his internship and what he wants to do with his future. I don't want him to make any decisions because of me. I don't want him to have regrets."

"That's why you broke up with him?" she asks surprised.

"Well, that and I need to figure out my future. I want to prove to myself and everyone else that I can deal with the Scotts, my future and everything else, on my own," I declare.

"Who's everyone else?" she asks confused.

I flinch, thinking about what Paul said to me. Instead of telling her what happened with Paul, I acknowledge, "It's just something I need to do."

"But why do you need to figure it all out without a boyfriend? It doesn't make sense," she insists. I open my mouth to argue, but she shakes her head and cuts me off. "Look, I get that you want to do things on your own, be an independent woman and all that shit, but if you have a good boyfriend who loves you like Brady obviously does, then you have someone who's going to support your choices. Isn't that what we all want? Someone to be by our side and support us, doing what we want to do with our lives and we do the same for them?"

"Yeah," I admit hesitantly.

"Unless you don't love him," she mumbles.

"That's definitely not it!" I insist, my whole body tensing.

She sighs, "Look, it's none of my business and I'm trying not to let my sisterly love for Brady cloud my judgment, but if you love him, the things you want to do can be done with the two of you together. You're both completely miserable and for what?"

I sigh in exasperation, trying to gather my thoughts. "It's just a lot. Everything happened so fast with us. I just need to know he's making decisions for his future without regrets. I don't want to be the one to hold him back. And I'm just trying to focus on what I need, I guess," I stammer.

She sighs and bites her lower lip as she assesses me. She releases her lip and tells me, "I get it Sam, but pushing him away so you don't hold him back, might have the opposite effect. He could end up making a decision that he doesn't really want because he doesn't clearly understand the circumstances in front of him. Would you be able to live with that regret?" she asks.

A stabbing pain hits my chest as her words sink in. I didn't even think of that. Would I push him to make a decision he doesn't want? My phone vibrates in my hand and I look down. My heart leaps at the site of Brady's name. I open his text and read, "How about tomorrow after my classes? I should be at the restaurant by 4."

I gulp down the lump in my throat and reply with, "Ok. See you then."

He likes my reply, probably to acknowledge he saw it. "Is that Brady?" Cory asks.

I look up at her and admit, "Yeah."

"Please, just think about what I said. I'm sure you don't want any regrets either," she reminds me.

I nod my head slowly in agreement. "I'll think about it. I promise."

She smiles sadly at me and then turns back towards the TV. "Ready for more hot, badass superheroes?" she asks just before pressing play.

I know she's right. I have to figure out the best way to balance it all. I can't help but question if he even wants me back after what I did to him. Plus, I have to tell him about what happened with Logan. I grimace just thinking about it, but that's not something I could keep from him if we got back together. I hope we get back together. My stomach flips nervously, just thinking about seeing him again and finding out what he decided on the internship.

Chapter 29

I park my Volvo in front of the restaurant and get out of my car, shouldering my bag. I glance up to the front of the building and swallow hard at the sight of Brady striding right for me with determined steps. He stops in front of me, leaving barely a foot between us. He smiles broadly, lighting up his whole face and sending chills down my spine. "Hi," he greets me.

I gulp down the lump in my throat and rasp, "Hi."

He stuffs his hands in his pockets and stares at me momentarily, assessing me. His clear blue eyes appear to be attempting to read my mind and at the same time allowing me to read his. I tear my gaze away from his and look down, noticing his khaki shorts, or more specifically his thick calves rolling as he sways back and forth on his loafer covered feet. I tug, self-consciously, on the hem of my white, flowing shirt, so it falls just right over my dark skinny jeans. Then I pull the sleeves down off my shoulders, where they're supposed to be. "You look gorgeous," he tells me appreciatively.

I tip my head up to meet his eyes and see nothing but sincerity. I offer him a small, nervous smile, "Thanks."

He clears his throat and says, "I thought we'd go out to the barn, so you can see the progress. I know it's not going to be ready for your event, but it's coming along," he informs me.

I breathe a sigh of relief, not yet ready to talk about us. "I'd like that," I agree.

"I'm parked right over there," he informs me, tilting his head back towards the right. I hold my breath as I slip by him, afraid of what I might do if I get too close. I exhale slowly, trying to control my breathing, as I walk to his truck with him by my side. He reaches around me to pull the door open for me and I climb in, wishing he were lifting me inside, instead. He closes the door and walks around to the other side. I buckle my seat belt and clasp my hands tightly. I watch him climb behind the wheel out of the corner of my eye. He pauses before he turns the key and the engine roars to life. He buckles his seatbelt, before he drapes his arm over the back of my seat. He looks behind him to back out of the parking spot and away from the restaurant. A pop song blares through the speakers, a girl singing about broken dreams and heartbreak. He grinds his jaw and flips the radio off as he pulls onto a bumpy dirt road. I feel the tension inside the cab of the truck and bite my lip anxiously, as I try to come up with something to say. I dare another glance at him, just as his eyes flick back to the road. I blush, realizing he must've been looking at me.

Brady parks near the barn doors, but he doesn't make a move to get out. I force myself to look over at him, my stomach flip-flopping as I meet his intense gaze. "Um, are we going in?" I ask.

He nods, but announces, "It feels like you're uncomfortable around me. I don't want you to be uncomfortable around me."

I shake my head, "I'm not."

He grimaces and questions, "Then why won't you talk to me?"

"You're not really talking to me either," I point out.

He chuckles, the corners of his lips twitching up. "You got me there." He takes a deep breath and releases it. Then he proposes, "Would you like to take a look?"

I grin and mumble, "That is why you drove me out here, or so you say." Then I open the door, smiling as the sound of his deep laughter follows me outside, bouncing over my skin.

I walk over to the doors and he pulls them open. I step inside, the smell of fresh sawdust immediately tickling my nose. I feel his eyes on me as I take everything in. The now open space where several of the horse stalls used to be draws my attention. I walk to the center of the room and turn slowly in a circle. "Wow," I murmur, "It feels so much bigger."

He chuckles, "It's crazy what knocking down a few walls can do." I nod in agreement. "I know it still has a long way to go, but I think it's going to be pretty amazing. I can picture some of the things you were describing even better now." He steps up to me and reminds me, "This is where the dance floor will go." I look up at him and I can't help but dream of dancing right here, with him. My breath quickens, as he steps as close as he can, without touching me. My heartbeat pounds against my ribcage, like it's trying to break free. He whispers, "Promise me the first dance when it's all done."

I gulp down the growing lump in my throat and rasp my response. "Okay," I agree. I close my eyes and take a step back, breaking our connection. I take a deep breath and begin talking about the couple that jump-started this renovation idea in the first place. "With the dance floor here, the band or DJ can be set up opposite the main doors. That way when you walk in, you see the entertainment right away. Then we can set up tables on both sides, so everyone is closer to the action. If they do a buffet, we can set one up on both sides, depending on how many people are coming. Otherwise we can use half the room and set up a divider," I explain.

Brady nods in acknowledgement. "I think we're going to build a permanent divider behind the stage for both the entertainment and for us to bring the food in, along with the staff. We're changing the doors on that side to make it easier to access and that will keep everything separated," he informs me.

I nod in understanding, "That's a good idea."

He grins, "I do have those from time to time."

I giggle and continue looking around and picturing the barn transformed for a wedding. I can see the rafters draped with white tulle and ribbons, with white daisy-like flowers sparsely scattered throughout. The doorway draped with the same decorations and tiny white lights stretched through all the tulle, causing the whole room to feel like it's sparkling with stars. The tables would be covered with ice blue tablecloths. The centerpieces would hold white, blue and indigo colored flowers, but not too tall, so you can talk to the person across from you. The bridesmaids would be wearing a simple pale blue floor length dress with spaghetti straps, while the groomsmen would wear a dark gray tuxedo with a matching pale blue vest and bow tie. My dress would be simple, but elegant and Brady's tux would be a lighter gray. I would be lost in his eyes, never wanting to leave his embrace, as he leads me across the dance floor.

"You seem to be very lost in thought," Brady whispers from behind me, startling me out of my daydream. I spin towards him, as my whole body heats with embarrassment. "Would you like to share what you were thinking?" he questions innocently.

"Um, I was just thinking about how they might want to decorate. I can wait to talk to them about some more of their ideas though," I quickly blurt out an explanation. Brady nods slowly, his eyes narrowing slightly, as if he's trying to figure out a problem. "Maybe we should head back and we can talk about the fundraiser since that is only a week and a half away," I remind him, trying to change the subject.

He agrees, "Okay. The kitchen should have some samples ready for you to try when we get back."

"You're not trying them with me?" I ask, not wanting to eat alone.

He chuckles and reminds me, "I've already tried everything we make."

I feel my face blush a deep shade of red. "Oh yeah," I mumble.

He laughs louder at my reaction. "I'll eat with you if you'd like me to. I am always hungry," he grins playfully. I smile appreciatively back at him. "Let's go," he encourages. He places his hand on the small of my back, instantly covering my body in goose bumps. "Are you cold?" he asks.

"I'm okay," I murmur. His hand falls away and I quicken my pace towards the doors and his truck.

I climb in and close the door before Brady catches up. He slides in behind the wheel. I feel his eyes on me before he starts the truck. He turns the car around and begins the short drive back to the restaurant. "Do you have a big team for the walk this weekend?" he asks.

I breathe a sigh of relief, grateful for the change of subject. "It's definitely a decent size, but not because of me."

"Logan," he mumbles and I nod uncomfortably. My stomach clenches tightly at the reminder of him. "I recruited some people to walk for your team too. I wanted to do something, since I don't know if I can be there with everything I have to get done for school. I'm going to try, but I won't know until the last minute," he explains.

"That was really nice of you. You didn't have to do that," I insist.

We pull back into the parking lot at the restaurant. He shrugs, "I wanted to." He smiles at me and climbs out of the truck, quickly jogging around to open my door for me.

We walk inside and Brady's mom immediately stops us, "Everything is all ready for you in the banquet room.

"Thanks, Mom," Brady grins.

We walk back to the same room that was set for the anniversary party the last time and sit down at the same table. Except this time, everything else in the room has been cleared out. He pulls my chair out for me and I murmur, "Thanks."

He sits down next to me and announces, "Try anything you want."

I force a smile as I look over the mouth-watering appetizers and desserts spread out around the table. "This looks amazing," I tell him honestly.

I reach for an asparagus wrapped with something golden and take a bite. "Mmm," I moan in satisfaction.

Brady clears his throat and shifts in his seat. I grab a toothpick and reach for a bite size meatball, quickly popping it into my mouth. He clears his throat and asks, "So, should I just text you the list of names I have for you for the walk? I can give you their contact information if you need that too."

"Um, sure. Thank you," I say appreciatively. The meatball feels like it drops into my gut and stays there, completely weighing me down. I need to tell him about Logan, or I'm just going to keep feeling worse. I take a deep breath and turn slightly in my seat to face him. "Brady?" I say to get his attention, as I watch him take a bite of the spinach dip.

He turns towards me and his whole face instantly becomes serious. "What is it?" he asks anxiously.

I take a shaky breath and admit, "There's something I need to tell you." His eyes widen and his hands drop to his lap. "Um, you know I've been working with Logan a lot," I begin.

"Fuck," he grumbles. His face instantly going pale, like he already knows what I'm going to say.

I start talking faster. It's not good, but I don't want him to think the worst. He just deserves to know the truth. "Well, we were working the other day and he kissed me." He cringes and his jaw clenches, while his hands form fists in his lap. "I didn't kiss him back, but he completely took me off guard. I know we're not together right now, but I feel terrible. I feel like you should know it happened. I'm sorry," I insist.

"Don't apologize when you didn't do anything wrong," he spits out through gritted teeth, without looking at me.

My whole body feels like it's tingling from the inside out, as I fight the tears from coming. I open my mouth to say more, but I have no idea what else I could possibly say to make this situation better. I snap my mouth closed and take a deep breath to calm my nerves. I take another deep breath and quickly change the subject instead. "So how did everything go in Minnesota?" I ask, needing to know his answer.

He sighs in defeat and says, "It was great." I attempt to hold back my flinch, but I'm not sure if I succeed. "Everyone was nice, but it wasn't home," he emphasizes and finally meets my gaze. "I may have my issues with my family, but after everything that happened with Max, there was a reason I moved home. I realized how important family is and this is where my family lives. I want to be close to them no matter how great the job opportunity. But things have changed here since I started working with you. I'm honestly starting to like my job here. You and your ideas inspire me. I'm really excited about the whole barn project. I'm having a lot of fun working on the renovations and I think it will be a huge benefit to the restaurant and the community."

"That's great," I whisper, trying to keep hope out of my voice.

"I think I've only been fighting it because it's what I've always known. But then you come along and show me another way to look at things. There's really only one thing that might change my mind about staying," he informs me. He looks at me and bites the inside of his cheek, as if he wants to say something, but he's not sure if he should. I rub my hands on my legs, anxiously waiting for him to continue. "Sam, the only thing I could imagine changing my mind would be if you were to leave. If you were gone, Chance wouldn't feel like home anymore," he admits. He shrugs, as if his statement were obvious.

My breath catches in my throat and I stare at him wide-eyed. "Brady," I rasp breathlessly.

"You are family to me too, Sam. In fact, you've become the most important part of my family. I don't want to be somewhere you're not. I don't know if you're ready to hear this, but I need to tell you. I love you and I'm going to fight for us," he emphasizes. "I want us to be together. I want to be able to talk to you every damn day and not just on the phone or by text or even through Facetime. I want to be able to touch you and kiss you every chance I get. I want us. You are the reason Chance feels like home again. It's not the town, it's not my family or friends or the memories from growing up here, it's *you*. *You* are my home. I won't give up on us," he insists.

Tears stream down my face and my heart pounds like a hammer. Blood is rushing so fast I'm barely able to drown it out to hear my own thoughts. I want to jump into his arms and tell him that's what I want too, but is it? I feel completely overwhelmed and open my mouth to say something, but I can barely speak. "I..."

Brady covers my hand with his, in comfort. He insists, "Don't say anything right now. It's a lot. I know what I want and I need you to believe that first. I also want you to make the decision that's right for you, not the one you think you want."

"Brady," I shake my head, trying to clear it.

He clears his throat and suggests, "Why don't you take your time sampling. Give me a call later with what you like. We can talk about the rest when you're ready."

"What about you?" I ask.

He smiles sadly, "I'm already there. I'm just waiting for you to catch up." I gasp and he stands and places a kiss on my forehead. "I love you," he whispers softly.

I watch as he turns and walks away from me for the second time. I gulp at the realization and wonder if I'll be strong enough to stop him the next time. I know he won't wait for me forever. I just hope I have the courage to not let go, if there is a next time.

Chapter 30

I read Brady's text again, "Hope everything went well at the walk today. I'm sorry I couldn't be there with you."

I smile to myself and text him back, trying to keep it simple, but true. "Thank you. Wish you were here too."

"What are you smiling about?" Logan asks. He saunters up to me in the same purple and white Cystic Fibrosis Walk t-shirt we're all wearing along with black, low slung, net shorts.

I look up, still grinning and shrug. "I guess I just feel really good about today. We had the perfect weather," I observe. "Do you think doing the walk helped for the fundraiser next weekend?" I ask hopefully.

He laughs and reminds me, "Well, we put together another team to walk for the cause, so no matter what it does for next weekend, it definitely helped."

"True," I agree.

"But, I also just took a look on-line and the ticket sales for our event have really been jumping. At this rate we might have a full house," he informs me.

"That's wonderful!" I squeal. I jump up and throw my arms around him in excitement, hugging him tightly.

He groans the instant I crash into him. My body immediately heats in embarrassment. "Sorry," I apologize and quickly move back.

He releases me and huffs a laugh, "I'm all sweaty. I should say I'm sorry to you. You have no reason to apologize," he insists.

"Um, actually I do," I confess.

He puts his hands low on his hips and falls back on his heels with a grimace. "Uh-oh. That doesn't sound good."

I sigh and push myself to tell him the truth. I'd rather be uncomfortable now, than later on. "It's just that I really like you Logan, but I like you as a friend," I explain. He pinches his lips together, but doesn't respond. "I really like working with you and hanging out with you, but we can't be anything together."

He nods slowly as if he's processing my words. He finally mutters softly, "You're in love with Brady."

I shake my head and open my mouth to argue, but no words come out. I can't say I don't love Brady out loud because it isn't true. We both know I can't deny it, even if I can't admit it to him right now.

He puts his hand up to stop me. "You don't have to say anything else. I knew it before I kissed you last week," he says, surprising me. He smirks, "Guess I had to take my shot when I could, since I knew it would most likely be the only one."

I smile appreciatively up at him. "Thank you," I reply. I'm grateful he's letting it go so easily. He really is a good guy. "I should probably let you know, I told him," I confess.

His eyes widen in surprise and he asks, "What?"

I wince, "I told him you kissed me. I had to. Even though we were broken up at the time, I felt guilty," I admit.

He sighs in defeat, "You could've at least kissed me back if you were going to tell the guy. Make our fight seem worth it," he jokes.

"Ha-ha, very funny," I tell him.

He shakes his head and mumbles quietly under his breath, "He really is one lucky asshole." My eyebrows draw together in confusion, not sure I heard him right. He ignores me and laughs humorlessly. "I guess I should get going," he says as he turns and starts to walk away. "I'm heading down to the bar. I'll catch up with you tomorrow," he calls to me over his shoulder.

"Bye Logan," I reply with a wave at his back. I feel a little lighter as I turn towards the parking lot.

"Samantha!" a small voice shouts behind me.

I turn to find Frankie waving wildly to get my attention as he runs towards me. "Frankie!" I yell back. I smile broadly as he approaches. He stops when he reaches me, not at all winded. "What are you doing here?" I ask in surprise.

"We wanted to walk on your team. We signed up this morning with Logan when we got here. We've been looking for you all day, but we couldn't find you until now," he informs me, grinning in satisfaction.

"We?" I ask.

He nods, smiling shyly. "Yeah. Mom, Dad and I wanted to be here," he admits.

I look behind him and notice Lincoln and Ginny approaching us. My breath catches in my throat, as my emotions suddenly overwhelm me. "Thank you for coming," I tell all three of them appreciatively.

"We didn't want to miss it," Lincoln enlightens me.

Ginny nods in agreement. "We hope that was okay?" she asks. I nod, not able to say anything yet. "It was a fun day too. We're looking forward to next weekend. Lincoln was telling us about how hard you've been working," she informs me.

"He was?" I ask perplexed. She nods in confirmation.

Lincoln smiles at me, but begins fidgeting nervously. "We're sorry Jackie couldn't be here today. She had something she had to take care of today," he explains vaguely. My shoulders tense at the mention of Jackie's name and I offer him a tight smile.

"Can you come to my game on Tuesday?" Frankie asks.

I smile down at him, grateful to steer the conversation away from Jackie. "Sure, I'd love to come," I agree.

He smiles brightly and mumbles, "Cool."

"We have to get going. Frankie is meeting up with some friends and I have to run by the store. We'll see you at the game on Tuesday then?" Lincoln clarifies.

My heart does a flip at the hopeful sound in his voice. "I'll be there," I confirm, with a wink at Frankie. He laughs and I repeat, "Thanks for coming today."

The three of them smile and Frankie gives me a quick hug before running in the opposite direction towards their car. "Bye, Sam," he waves.

"Goodbye," I call to him.

Ginny waves and follows after her son, "We'll see you soon."

I nod and focus my gaze on Lincoln. "You know, it's nice to see Frankie so excited to spend time with you. I really hope you feel the same," he states, awkwardly.

My breath catches and I force a deep breath before I respond. "I know you don't really know me that well yet, but I'm very excited to spend time with Frankie and get to know him better. I may not know much about baseball, but he seems really good to me. But even if he weren't, I would want to be there for him as much as I could. I've never had siblings and I'm thrilled to get to know mine," I insist vehemently.

"Even Jackie?" he questions, making me flinch. "Look, Samantha, I'm not trying to offend you. I'd like to get to know you no matter what, but like you said, I don't know you that well. I believe you're a good person, but I don't want Frankie to be hurt because you can't show up for one reason or another. Jackie has done that enough," he unintentionally reveals. My eyes widen in surprise and he grimaces, realizing what he just said. He shakes his head and explains, "She doesn't mean to, but he takes it to heart."

"Ugh," I grunt in quiet disapproval, but I nod at him in understanding. I bite my tongue so hard, trying to force myself to keep my mouth shut. The coppery taste of blood quickly fills my mouth. I concentrate on my breathing and slowly loosen my jaw.

"It's just that Frankie already seems to have an attachment to you. He really seems to like you and I don't want him to be disappointed. I don't remember the last time he hugged Jackie like that. Honestly, he probably hasn't hugged her since he was five," he rambles.

"I'm not like that," I blurt out, cutting him off. I shake my head and attempt to explain without bad mouthing Jackie, which is the furthest thing from easy for me. "I just mean that I really do want to get to know Frankie. I want to be involved with his life, like going to watch him play baseball or whatever else he's into. I meant it when I said I had fun at the other game and going out for pizza with all of you afterwards." I pause before adding, "That is, I want to be around, as long as it's okay with you and Ginny."

He nods his head and smiles down at me. "I wasn't really sure what you wanted when you found me, but I'm glad you did," he tells me.

"I honestly wasn't really sure what I wanted either, but I'm really glad I found you too," I murmur.

He takes a deep breath and changes the subject, without warning. "I'm really looking forward to your fundraiser next week," he states.

"Thank you. Me too," I grin.

"Dad!" Frankie yells. "I'm supposed to be at Dan's in five minutes. We're going to be late," he reminds him.

Lincoln glances at the time on his phone and nods in acknowledgement. "Okay, I'm coming, Frankie," he calls out, before he turns back to me.

"Sounds like you have to go," I say.

He nods in agreement, "Yeah." He pauses as if he's trying to make a decision before he takes a determined step towards me. He wraps his arm awkwardly around me and lightly pats me on the back before he quickly releases me. "Goodbye, Samantha," he says and steps away. He turns around and strides towards his car, joining his waiting family.

I stand on the edge of the parking lot, watching them get into their car and drive away. A feeling of melancholy washes over me, but it doesn't feel as intense as it has in the past. I don't wish I were going home with them. I wish my mom and dad were here. I feel the sun shining down on me as I turn towards my car. My body quickly warms and I can't help but feel like they are watching over me. I close my eyes and inhale deeply, then exhale slowly. I feel a strange sense of calm wash over me. A soft smile touches my lips as I think of my parents guiding me and encouraging me to do what's right for me. I know they would be proud of me for how hard I'm working to make a difference. That knowledge only makes me feel stronger.

I open my eyes and slide in behind the wheel of my car. I stare through the windshield for a moment, thinking about what I want and what's right for me. An image of Brady smiling down at me makes my stomach flip. He's always the first thing that crosses my mind. He's always there supporting me, loving me and just being there for me any way he can. My stomach flips again at the thought of losing him because I'm too scared. "You're being ridiculous Samantha," I mumble to myself. "What the hell am I even waiting for? I need to go talk to Brady," I grumble to myself. I buckle my seatbelt and then I start my car without delay. I pull out of the parking lot and turn my car towards home with a smile on my face.

Chapter 31

Brady

"Are you sure you don't want to come with me to Mae's?" Cody asks. "Just for a little while?" he pleads.

I shake my head, "Sorry man, but I'm sure. I have way too much shit to do. Go, have fun," I encourage him. He turns, but pauses briefly at the door. I wave him away. "Have a beer for me," I suggest.

He grins and gives in, "Will do, my friend. Your loss!" He waves and walks out the door, pulling the door shut behind him.

I turn back to my books and pick up my pen as I try to focus on economics. Studying has been difficult when my thoughts are consumed with Samantha. I keep wondering what she's doing or thinking. I'm going a little crazy having no idea where her head is after my little speech. Then again I think I did lose my mind when I told her not to say anything. I groan, knowing that's not true. I need her to believe I know what I want and I need her to be sure about what she wants. I can't go through this again. It sure as hell doesn't stop me from obsessing over it. I tell myself I need to take every minute I can to study or work on my final term paper or project for my different classes, but that doesn't stop my mind from wandering to her. If I had any free time today, I would've taken it to go support Samantha at the walk. I grimace and tap my pen in annoyance. I hate that I wasn't there with her. I remind myself again that I can't do it all. I can't drop the ball now and risk graduation.

A knock on my front door has my heart skipping a beat, in hopes it might be Samantha. I take a deep breath and shake it off. "Coming," I yell, as I drop my pen and jump up. I pull the door open and my jaw drops at the site of Jackie sitting on the floor in the hallway. She's wearing a black and white dress that appears to be covered in dirt and torn at the bottom, above her knees. Her blonde hair is slightly knotted and covering much of her face, but she peaks up at me through a separation.

"Brady," she whispers, desperately.

"What the fuck?" I blurt out.

She begins to cry. I reach for her and pull her up and into my apartment. I close the door behind her and she wraps her arms around me, clinging to me. "I'm sorry," she whimpers. "I know you said I had to deal with this without you, but I didn't know where to go."

She sobs into my chest and I gently rub her back, hoping to calm her down. "What happened Jackie?" I ask. "Are you hurt?"

She leans back, allowing her hair to fall away from her face. She looks up at me and meets my gaze. I grind my jaw, as I get a good look at her bruised cheek, fat lip and swollen eye that's already beginning to turn black and blue. "A little," she mumbles.

"Shit," I grumble, wide-eyed. "What the hell happened?" I demand.

Her lower lip begins to quiver and tears fall faster. She looks down and stammers, "I…don't…know."

"You don't know? Where were you? Was anyone with you?" I spit out the questions quickly.

She takes a deep breath before she tells me, "I went out with friends. I couldn't go to Samantha's walk with my family. Does she have to take everything away from me?" she asks, bitterly.

"This is about Sam?" I ask in shock.

She shakes her head and sighs in defeat. "Can I just take a shower and clean up first? Then we can talk?" she requests.

"Shouldn't I call the police or something before you do that?" I question.

She shakes her head and looks away, as if embarrassed. "No," She mumbles.

I sigh and run my hand through my hair in frustration. "Fine. Do what you need to do. You know where everything is," I tell her, gesturing wildly towards the hallway.

She turns towards the bathroom without saying another word and closes the door behind her. I grab my phone and text Cody, "Did you see Jackie at all tonight?"

"Fuck, no. Why?" he responds.

I sigh and text him again, "She just showed up here looking like she just got the shit beat out of her."

"What?"

"Tell me if you hear anything," I text and hit send.

"Got it," he agrees. "I don't like her, but..."

"I know," I reply.

I set my phone down on my books and glance at the bathroom door, wondering what the hell happened to her tonight. There's another knock on my door. I quickly spin around and pull the door open. Samantha stands in the doorway with a shy smile, wearing a purple Cystic Fibrosis walk t-shirt and tight black workout pants. "Sam," I groan her name, as my heart drops.

"Hi," she grins. She tries to tuck a few curls behind her ear, but they fall forward almost immediately. "I was hoping we could talk for a few minutes?" she requests.

My heartbeat speeds up, knowing this is exactly what I've been waiting for, but I don't know how this will work out for me with Jackie in the bathroom. "Um, ah, yeah," I stutter.

Her cheeks flush and she takes a nervous step back. "If this isn't a good time Brady, I can come back another time," she insists.

A breath catches in my throat and I force out, "No!" I take a step towards her and wrap my fingers around her wrist to stop her. "Please don't go," I beg.

She breathes a sigh of relief and smiles at me again, taking my breath away. "Okay," she concedes and steps inside.

I close the door behind her and glance towards the bathroom door nervously. "Um, Sam, I should let you know that," I begin.

"Brady," Jackie calls from behind the bathroom door. "I forgot a towel. Can you hand me one?" she asks.

My eyes anxiously stay glued to Sam. Her eyes widen and her face begins to pale. She gasps, "I'm sorry, I shouldn't have come."

I reach for her wrist again, "Yes, you should have!"

"Who's here? Your sister?" she barely squeaks out.

I wince, "It's Jackie."

I see the tears in her eyes before she has a chance to turn around. "Let me go, Brady," she whimpers. "It was a mistake to come," she declares.

"No, I'm glad you're here," I emphasize. "Jackie had a rough night and needed help," I try to explain.

"And you jumped in to help her," she finishes.

I shake my head, "No, she showed up here."

"Brady?" Jackie yells again.

"I'm coming," I snap. I grind my jaw and take a deep breath to calm myself down. "Please don't go anywhere," I plead. "I can explain," I insist. She glances towards the door, as if she wants to escape. "You're coming with me," I demand.

"What?" she asks, confused. I turn and take a step towards the bathroom with her in tow. "What are you doing, Brady?" she asks suddenly sounding exhausted.

I pull the linen closet open and grab a towel then kick the door shut. "I have a towel for you. I won't look," I tell Jackie through the door.

She opens the door and I hear the gasp behind me. "What are you doing here?" Jackie questions.

"Take the fucking towel!" I grit through my teeth.

The towel leaves my hands and I drag Samantha away without looking back, but I don't hear the door close. "Can I borrow some clothes?" she asks.

"Whatever," I grumble.

"You can borrow something of mine," Samantha offers, shocking me.

"What?" Jackie and I both ask in unison.

Samantha shrugs, "It's no big deal."

I stare at her in awe. "Damn, you're beautiful," I murmur.

She blushes and whispers, "I'm a mess."

"A beautiful mess," I mumble.

She offers me a stiff smile and points towards her apartment. "I'll be right back with something comfortable for you to wear," she informs Jackie.

When she leaves, I turn towards Jackie, wrapped in a towel. She has bruises developing on her arms and one on her shoulder. Her face appears a little more swollen and bruised. She grimaces and grumbles, "Well, I must look like shit if she's going out of her way to be nice to me."

I give her a look of warning and she holds her hands up in surrender. The towel starts to slip and I remind her, "Your towel, Jackie."

She slowly reaches for it to hold it in place. The corners of her mouth twitch up, making me shake my head. The door opens and Samantha walks in holding a pile of clothes. She walks up to Jackie and holds them out to her. "I don't know what you'll be comfortable in, so I brought shorts and sweatpants, a t-shirt and a sweatshirt," she explains. "Oh and socks too," she adds.

"Thank you," Jackie whispers. She takes the clothes and spins back towards the bathroom, closing the door behind her.

"Um, I should go," she tells me.

My body tenses again. "Don't go," I beg.

She forces a smile and reminds me, "Brady, it looks like you have enough to deal with tonight."

I nod and emphasize, "Yeah, but I want to talk to you."

"We can talk another time," she says, sadly.

"Sam," I say her name almost desperately.

She shakes her head, "Brady, I don't know what happened to her, but she's more important than me right now."

My heart jumps into my throat, overwhelming me with the love I feel for her. "No one is more important than you, for me," I declare. I need her to understand how I feel, even though we both know she's right at the moment.

She blushes and takes a step towards me. My heart begins racing as she gently places her hand on my chest. "It's okay," she insists. She pushes up on her toes and softly kisses the corner of my mouth, sending a bolt of electricity throughout my whole body. "Do what you need to do," she encourages me.

I search her eyes and pray this decision isn't going to bite me in the ass later on. I could find someone to help her. I nod my head slowly in agreement, "Okay."

She falls back on her heels and drops her hand from my chest just as Jackie steps out of the bathroom again. Samantha takes a step away from me and faces Jackie as she approaches her. Jackie looks Samantha in the eyes and gulps before she repeats, "Thank you."

She drops her eyes to the floor. Samantha opens her mouth and closes it before she opens it again and simply replies, "You're welcome." Then she turns towards my door to leave. "I'll talk to you later, Brady."

"Promise?" I plead.

She nods and walks out the door, taking my heart with her. I sigh, feeling drained, as she closes the door behind her. "You guys are back together?" Jackie asks.

I grimace and ignore her question. I walk to the couch and drop down on the end near my books. "What happened?" I repeat.

She sits down on the other side of the couch. She pulls her legs up to her chest and wraps her arms around them. She stares at her feet and begins talking. "We went to a party near campus. I hadn't really been there long when I ran into this guy I've hung out with before. We were talking and dancing and then he went to go get me something to drink. While he did that, I headed for the bathroom, but I was pushed from behind and fell. I got up, but when I turned around, there were four girls glaring at me. They started yelling at me and telling me I needed to stay away from their men. I tried to defend myself, but," she gulps hard, "I guess I slept with two of their boyfriends and one of them liked the guy I was talking to. One of them punched me and I fell again and hit the wall. Then they were hitting and kicking me and nobody did anything to help me. A couple people finally scared them off and helped me up, but I couldn't even tell you who," she whimpers as tears stream down her face. "I'm sorry, Brady. I'm sorry I'm such a mess," she cries.

I sigh and scoot closer to her. I put my hand on her back and begin rubbing soothing circles. "You have to figure yourself out Jackie. I don't want you to end up like Max," I admit.

"I know," she gasps and leans into me. "I'm so sorry," she repeats.

Chapter 32

Samantha

"Thank you so much for coming up this weekend, Ryan," I tell my cousin. "It really means a lot to me for you to be here for this."

He nods, "The whole family would be here if they could. You know I'm happy to be here. I just can't believe you're making me wear a suit."

I laugh and look him over one more time in his black suit with a white shirt and blue tie. I grin up at him and joke, "I'm just glad you showered."

"Ha-ha," he smirks. "Besides, you know I have to smell good for the ladies."

"You mean Cory? She'll be here soon," I tell him. I watch for a reaction, but he doesn't give me anything.

He glances across the parking lot to the front door of the restaurant and asks, "Are you ready to go in?"

I bite my lower lip and take a deep breath before I agree, "As ready as I'll ever be."

"I'm here if you need me," he reminds me. He offers me his arm and I place my hand in the crook of his elbow. I force myself to walk slowly towards the restaurant, so Ryan doesn't have to pull me inside. "Have you talked to him at all since Saturday night?" he asks.

"Sort of," I grimace. "We've been texting some. I asked how Jackie was doing and we talked about tonight. I asked about his finals, but we haven't talked about us at all. He hasn't had enough time," I explain.

"I'm sure he'd make time for you. You should really talk to him," he insists.

I nod in agreement, "I know."

He pulls the door open for me and I step inside. We walk towards the ballroom, my heart beating faster with every step I take. The moment we step into the room, I spot Brady placing flowers in the middle of one of the large tables in the back. He stands straight and instantly notices me. He begins walking towards me, but stops halfway to direct one of his staff. Then he continues striding for me. I take in his dark navy suit, white shirt and purple tie, making his eyes pop even brighter than they usually do. "Hi, Samantha," he greets me, with his dimpled smile.

My heart skips a beat, before picking up its pace. "Hi, Brady," I rasp. "Everything looks great. Thank you," I praise him.

He doesn't take the time to look around the room, but his eyes do slowly glide over me from my white strappy sandals with a one-inch heel, up to my A-line purple and white dress that falls a few inches above my knees. The one-inch straps clasp neatly at the back of my neck, my hair falling in waves over the silver clasp. I gulp over the growing lump in my throat, as his gaze burns a trail of fire every place it grazes. He clears his own throat and rasps, "You look incredible Sam, so beautiful."

I feel my face heat at his compliment. I murmur, "Thank you."

He gives himself a light shake and tears his eyes away from me. He stiffly turns towards my cousin and grins, "Hi, Ryan. It's good to see you again."

Ryan nods and replies simply, "Hi, Brady."

Brady turns and stands next to me. He gestures towards the room, "So, is this what you pictured?"

I look around the room to take it all in. The whole room is decorated with purple and white. Two tables are placed at the entrance, one on each side, to help with the flow. To our right, tall tables with small round tops are scattered around the space in front of the main bar. Every table has a small fish bowl with a floating purple or white Gerbera Daisy. A DJ is set up in the middle, near the wall, with open space for the dance floor. The larger round tables in the back have a white tablecloth with a purple tablecloth overlay and a larger bouquet of flowers in the center. Then to our left, long tables, covered in the purple and white are filled with raffle baskets. Looking at all of the baskets together makes me realize how much we were able to get donated from individuals, families and businesses. A man and a woman, both dressed in purple dress shirts walk back and forth near the tables, selling additional raffle tickets. "It's perfect," I murmur.

He grins, "I'm glad you like it."

"Do you know if Logan brought in the informational brochures? And what about the gift bags?" I ask.

Brady chuckles, "Yeah, I think all of that is under the front tables. He's around here somewhere," he adds with a grimace.

"Brady," I begin, "I'm sorry we haven't had a chance to talk this week."

"It's okay. Between this and finals, it's been crazy for both of us," he concedes.

"Yeah," I agree hesitantly.

"Sam," Logan calls as he approaches. He leans in and places a kiss at the corner of my mouth in greeting, causing Brady's whole body to stiffen. "You look gorgeous!" he exclaims.

"Um, thanks," I mumble, uncomfortably.

"Can you help me set up the information and tickets?" he requests. "I have the thank you gifts underneath the tables to pull out later."

I glance quickly at Brady. "Is it okay if we talk later?" I question. He responds with a nod and glares at Logan, before spinning on his heel and striding back towards the kitchen. I turn and introduce him to my cousin. "Logan, this is my cousin, Ryan. He came to help," I explain.

"Excellent," he grins and shakes Ryan's hand. "Thanks." His eyes narrow and he asks, "Have we met before?"

Ryan nods, "Yeah, at Mae's. I've been there with Cory."

Logan nods in acknowledgement, as the three of us walk over to the tables and get to work. We barely finish setting up in time, before people start to arrive. The room quickly fills with people and laughter. I wander over towards the raffles, trying to focus on one thing at a time, instead of watching Brady. I feel jittery just being in the same room with him.

"Samantha?" a familiar voice calls to get my attention.

I turn on my heel and smile up at Lincoln and Ginny. His eyes look so much like mine with his yellow tie and black suit. Ginny matches him with a pale yellow cocktail dress and her blonde hair pinned neatly to the top of her head. "Hi," I greet them. Ginny steps towards me and wraps her arms around me in a gentle hug. "Thank you for coming. You look beautiful."

"Thank you," she grins. "You are stunning, my dear," she admires. "And we're happy to come to support you and the cause."

Lincoln smiles and nods in agreement as he steps in and takes Ginny's place. He releases me and steps back to meet my gaze. "Samantha, you look beautiful," he compliments me. He gestures to the room and exclaims, "Everything looks amazing and the place is packed!" I nod, as I feel my face flush. "You did a wonderful job," he praises me.

I turn a deeper shade of red and mumble, "Thank you."

"I mean it, Sam. I'm sure you're going to do well tonight," he insists. "Catherine would be really proud of you." He pauses, before adding, "I'm really proud of you."

Tingles start on my insides and climb up my throat to form a lump. My eyes well, but I don't want them to fall now. I take a deep breath and exhale slowly, attempting to fight back the tears. I can't help but think my mom and dad would be proud of me too and not just for this event. I offer him a shaky smile and tell him, "Thank you, but I can't take all the credit. This is Logan's project, I just jumped in to help."

"I'm not sure if Logan would agree with that assessment," Ginny offers, with a genuine smile.

Jackie sidles up to Lincoln and forces a smile, causing my whole body to go tight. "Hi, Samantha," she murmurs, almost kindly.

"Hi," I mumble, suddenly slightly on edge. She looks beautiful in a silver form-fitting dress. Her blonde hair falls loosely over her shoulders, while her make-up appears flawless, showing no signs of bruising. Both Ginny and Lincoln look back and forth between the two of us, as if trying to figure out what they missed. I clear my throat and ask, "Where's Frankie?"

"He's staying at a friend's house tonight," Lincoln informs me.

"We were due for a night out," Ginny adds.

"Tell him I said, Hi," I request.

"Of course," Ginny grins. "We should probably let you get back to work."

"It's okay," I tell her.

"What she's really saying is, 'I want to go check out the raffle baskets and make sure I get my name in all the good ones,'" Lincoln laughs.

"Of course," she agrees. She glances at Jackie and asks, "Would you like to look with me?"

"Sure, Mom," she agrees.

"We'll talk to you in a little while," Lincoln grins. Then he steps away with Ginny.

Jackie hesitates, before she plants her feet in determination and looks at me. "This doesn't mean we're friends, but I appreciate what you did for me."

I nod uncomfortably and ask, "Are you okay?"

She grimaces, "Not that you really care, but I'll be okay." She gulps and I see a flash of vulnerability, before it rapidly disappears.

"I do care," I utter.

"If you did, you wouldn't be stealing everything away from me," she insists, defiantly.

I gasp and explain, "That's not what I'm doing. I just want to know where I came from and figure out who I am."

"And then you'll disappear?" she asks. My mouth drops open before I snap it closed, not knowing how to respond. "I didn't think so," she grumbles. "Look, I've come to terms with you invading my family, but that doesn't mean I have to like it. It's not like you'll ever live with my family and me. I can be cordial, just like you," she states.

"I wasn't trying to be cordial," I tell her.

"I don't want your pity either," she accuses.

"I...I..." I stammer. I pause; honestly unsure of what I felt when I offered to help her the other night.

She puts her hand up, "Save it. Just, why can't you stay away from *him*? Why does it have to be *him*?" she pleads.

"I didn't choose to fall in love with him. I just did," I admit.

I see a flash of pain in her eyes and she reminds me, "Well, you're not together now. So maybe he doesn't love you the same way and maybe he won't take you back. A girl can hope," she mutters.

I wince as she spins on her heel and strides confidently towards her parents. I take a deep breath and lift my head. I look out at the room and immediately meet Brady's gaze. My chest aches and pulls me towards him. He starts walking towards me, when one of the waitresses carrying a tray of appetizers stops him. He looks down at her and I force myself to turn away.

"Sam," Logan stops in front of me, with an older gentleman by his side.

"Hi Logan," I say.

He gestures towards the older man standing next to him. He's wearing tan pants, white dress shirt and a navy blazer. He has a round face, with salt and pepper hair, and friendly blue eyes. "This gentleman wanted to meet you. He's very active with the cystic fibrosis foundation and found out about this event at the walk last weekend. I just finished telling him how this fundraiser got started," he explains.

I smirk, "It got started because of you."

They both laugh. Logan adds, "Yeah, but you were the one that wanted to focus on this cause. Plus, you're the reason it became this big."

I blush and the gentleman holds out his hand. I reach out and shake it. "Hi, I'm Jeremy Brown. This is really an incredible event. I think it's wonderful what both of you are doing," he states.

"Thank you," I grin.

"I was telling Logan that I lost my wife last year to complications from cystic fibrosis," he informs me.

My stomach churns and I apologize for his loss, "I'm so sorry."

He shakes his head and smiles sadly, "Thank you. I miss her every day, but it helps to be involved. We used to do this kind of thing together. I greatly appreciate anyone who tries to raise money to help those who live with it and maybe one day they'll even find a cure." I nod in agreement. "May I ask, is there a reason you chose this cause in particular?"

I take a deep breath and admit, "Well, I'm adopted. I never met my birth mom because she died from complications due to her cystic fibrosis before I ever had the chance to find out who she was."

The man's face turns pale and he gasps in disbelief, "Oh my God! Your hair, your nose…my wife's name is on your list of 'In Memory Of…' You look just like her! You're Catherine's daughter!"

I instantly feel light-headed. My blood pounds hard in my ears, making it hard to hear anything but the beat and flow of my heart. I begin swaying on my feet and Logan catches me before I hit the floor, "Sam!" he calls from far away. "Are you okay?"

I feel my feet slip out from underneath me and I look to see where I am. I meet Brady's concerned eyes and pull myself back to the present. I frantically search for the stranger, "Where is he? Where did he go?"

"Who?" Brady asks. "You just fainted. I needed to get you out of there. Are you okay?"

"I'm fine. Please put me down. Where's the man I was talking to?" I ask desperately.

"I'm right here," he affirms. Brady reluctantly sets me down, but keeps his arm wrapped around me, to help me keep my balance. I take a deep breath to steady myself. Then I glance at Brady and insist, "I'm okay."

Logan reappears and hands me a glass of water. "Here, this will help." He glances at Brady's arm around me and adds, "You should probably just let her sit down. She kind of had a little shock."

Brady guides me to a chair and grudgingly releases me. He anxiously looks between Logan, Jeremy and me. "Can we have a few minutes to talk?" I ask looking at Mr. Brown.

Logan grabs Brady and prods him in the direction of the door. "Yell if you need me," Brady instructs. "I'll be right outside the door."

I nod and continue staring at the man in front of me. He looks at me with tears in his eyes and mumbles, "I should've known. I should've seen it."

"Seen what?" I ask.

"You look so much like her, except your eyes and hair are a different color. It's strange to see her hair in a different color. Maybe that's what threw me," he contemplates.

"You're her husband?" I question. He nods, forcing a smile. "She talked about you."

He grins, "In her letters."

I nod, "Yeah."

"She always wanted to meet you," he informs me. "She would've loved to meet you. She would be so proud," he says, his voice cracking with emotion.

"I tried...I tried, but I was too late," I whimper. I wipe my fallen tears off my cheeks. "I just got all the papers along with her letters in February," I explain. He nods in understanding. "I came here to find my dad. He lives here with his family."

"Really?" he questions. "I'd love to meet him."

I nod in acknowledgement. I begin fidgeting and ask, "Do you have things of hers you could share with me?"

He grins, his eyes shining brightly. "I do and I know she would want that too."

"Thank you," I mumble. I give him my phone number and he immediately texts me a beautiful picture of her. It's a close up of her laughing. Her head is tilted back and her red hair is blowing in the wind behind her. Looking at this picture, I see more of me, making me smile. "Thank you," I repeat.

Brady knocks at the door and opens it cautiously. He immediately meets my gaze and asks, "Are you okay?"

I nod and force a smile. "This is Jeremy Brown. He was Catherine's husband."

His eyes widen in shock and I nod my head in affirmation, with tears in my eyes. He turns towards Jeremy and holds his hand out. They shake firmly and Brady declares, "It's a pleasure to meet you, Mr. Brown."

"Jeremy, please," he insists.

We both nod. My whole body sags with exhaustion. I feel overwhelmed with everything that happened tonight. I know I have to get out of here for my own sanity. I turn towards Brady and ask, "Can you tell Logan I had to leave?"

Brady looks at me with concern, "He told me to tell you he's got the rest of the night taken care of. It's almost over anyway," he adds.

"Really? I didn't realize it was that late," I mumble.

Jeremy steps forward and informs us, "I have to get going anyway. Samantha, it was truly a pleasure to meet you."

"Thank you. I'm really glad I met you tonight, too," I tell him, sincerely.

We both watch him walk out. Brady steps in front of me. He asks, "Can I give you a ride home?"

"Um, I came with Ryan," I remind him.

"Oh, yeah. Could I stop by after we finish cleaning up?" he requests.

I grimace, "I'm sorry Brady, but I honestly think I'll be asleep long before then. A lot happened tonight, between the event and Jeremy and the Scotts."

"What happened with the Scotts?" he asks.

I shake my head and brush it off, "Nothing, really."

He sighs and stuffs his hands in his pockets. "Are you sure you're alright?"

I nod, "Yeah." I need to feel his arms around me, but I'm afraid he'll reject me if I ask. I step up to him and wrap my arms around his waist before I change my mind. His body instantly tenses before relaxing. He slowly wraps his arms around me and my body warms, giving me the feeling of comfort and safety. I mumble, "Thank you."

I untangle myself from his embrace and swiftly rush out of the room before he says anything else. I hurriedly find Ryan and make my escape home.

Chapter 33

"Thank you for lunch," I tell Ginny and Lincoln, appreciatively.

"We're glad you came and shared the news about Catherine with us," Ginny smiles.

"Well, I wanted to apologize for rushing out last night, without even saying goodbye. I was taken a little off guard meeting Jeremy," I explain.

"Of course you were," Lincoln agrees. "I'm glad you're going to be able to learn more about your mother."

Ginny glances at her watch and her eyes widen in surprise, "Oh! I have to go pick up Frankie from Dan's house. I'm sorry to run out so quickly Sam."

"That's okay," I grin. "Tell Frankie I'm sorry I missed him, but I'll be at his next game."

She grabs her purse and gives Lincoln a kiss on the cheek. "I will. Bye," she calls, before running out the front door.

Lincoln's phone rings and he glances at the screen. "I'm sorry, Samantha, but will you excuse me a minute?" I nod and he explains, "It's the store. I have to see what they need."

"Of course," I insist.

He turns and walks into the next room to take the call. I look up at the family picture in the foyer. Lincoln and Ginny look almost the same, but Frankie must be about 6 or 7 and Jackie about 14 or 15. I know it's just a family portrait, but I see something akin to love and innocence in her eyes. I smile sadly, hating that she's been through so much and I only know a small fraction of it because of Brady.

The front door opens and Jackie fills the space with a glare in my direction. "What the hell are you doing here?" she asks.

"I...I came to see your parents," I tell her softly.

"Why? To tell my mom you're her long lost daughter now?" she rolls her eyes. She steps inside the house and slams the door behind her. "Don't you have something better to do than harass me and try to steal my life?"

"You obviously had a bad day. I was just on my way out anyway, so…" I begin and walk towards the door.

"It's only a bad day because you're here," she remarks, spitefully.

"Jacqueline!" Lincoln scolds, as he steps back into the room.

"Daddy," she pleads, stepping towards her father.

He shakes his head and reminds her, "I didn't raise you to be mean to people." She winces and he continues, "Jacqueline, you will always be my little girl. I obviously don't know how to handle everything either. But I want to have the chance to get to know Samantha and for her to know us. I'm not asking you to be friends, but I am asking you to treat her much better than I've been seeing from you. It's obvious I'm not seeing everything either."

"Why are you choosing her side?" she whines.

"I'm not choosing anyone's side, but this time, it's not just about you," he insists.

"I was nice to her last night. Why didn't you hear me then," she grumbles.

"Jacqueline," he sighs. "I know this isn't easy, but I need you to try, for me," he emphasizes.

She glances over at me and narrows her eyes accusingly, "Fine." Then she shakes her head and apologizes, "I'm sorry. I've had a really bad week," she emphasizes.

He closes his eyes, as if in understanding. Then he opens them and says, "Okay, sweetheart."

"I'm sorry, but I have to go," I interrupt, feeling incredibly uncomfortable.

Lincoln nods sadly, "Okay. Thanks for stopping by."

I nod and force a smile. "Bye, Jackie."

"Bye, Samantha," she responds, overly sweet.

I slip out the front door and remind myself not to run to my car, but I feel like I can't get away fast enough. I pull out and turn towards my apartment, deep in thought. I may not like her, but I can't help but wonder what's going on with her. Following her moods is like being on a roller coaster ride. I wish I knew what was going on with her, but I'll probably never find out. I would never expect Brady to tell me. She obviously went to him in confidence. It's only my curiosity that's pushing me anyway, it's not like I could do anything to help. She hates me.

I park my car and take the elevator up to our floor. I walk in and announce, "Cory, Ryan, I'm back!"

"We'll be out in a minute," Ryan calls. I hear Cory giggle and I walk over to the coffee table to grab the remote. I turn on the TV to tune out any noises I might not want to hear from my cousin. A knock at the door has me breathing a sigh of relief, taking my thoughts away from them.

"Coming," I yell and stride for the door. I pull it open to find Logan standing in my doorway, grinning broadly. "Hey Sam! So I just finished totaling the raffles and ticket sales and rough numbers are saying we made over $250,000!" he exclaims. "That's over a quarter million," he reiterates.

I squeal in excitement, "That's fantastic!" He wraps me up in a hug and spins me around. I laugh as he sets me back on my feet.

He keeps his hands momentarily on my waist and continues animatedly. "I know Brady offered you a job, but maybe we can work something out. I loved working with you. You have such great ideas, Sam. I think we can do so much more if we work together. There are so many different grants out there. We could apply for some to do more work like this."

I hear a throat clear to get our attention. I look over Logan's shoulder to see Brady standing in front of us. His arms are crossed over his chest, his biceps bulging, pulling his navy t-shirt tight. "Sorry to interrupt," he grumbles.

I realize Logan's hands our still on my waist and I quickly step back. I insist, "You're not interrupting. Logan was just telling me we made over $250,000 for Cystic Fibrosis the other night."

He grinds his jaw and nods his head. "That's great," he rasps. He gulps hard and looks at me intently. "I just wanted to let you know, my graduation is on Saturday, if you want to come. I'm having people back to the restaurant to celebrate after the ceremony," he adds.

I smile appreciatively at his invitation, "Thank you." I wasn't sure if he really wanted me there.

"Well, I have to head to campus to study," he informs us.

"Good luck on your finals," I encourage him.

"Thanks," he mumbles. I watch as he spins around and heads for the stairs.

Logan chuckles and asks, "What are you doing, Samantha?"

I turn back towards him and ask, "What do you mean?"

"I don't get what's holding you back. Even I feel the electricity between you two and believe me, I'd love to be able to ignore it," he smirks.

I sigh and turn back inside my apartment. He follows me in and shuts the door. I admit, "I was going to talk to him, then some things happened, like Jeremy and other stuff," I respond vaguely. He arches his eyebrows in challenge and I groan in irritation. "He has finals and I have a lot of other things going on. I don't want to depend on him for everything. I don't want to lose myself," I add softly.

"Is that what you think?" Logan questions. I flop down on the couch, ignoring his question. He stalks over and stands in front of me. "You are probably the most determined and confidant woman I know. The only time I see you hesitate is with Brady, but I don't get it," he says with a shake of his head. "I saw the same strong woman in you when you and Brady were together," he declares. "That's one of the things that makes you so damn sexy!"

I feel myself blush. Then I insist, "I wasn't like that with him. I was vulnerable and weak."

"Did I just hear you say you were vulnerable and weak with Brady?" Cory asks as she strides into the room with Ryan right behind her.

I look down at my lap and mumble, "You guys weren't supposed to hear that."

"You're still letting him get inside your head, aren't you?" Ryan asks, as he leans over the back of the couch.

"I'm not letting anyone get to me," I attempt to defend myself.

"Who?" Cory asks, confused.

Ryan ignores her and addresses me. "So the whole thing that happened with Paul a couple weeks ago has nothing to do with why you still haven't asked Brady for a second chance? Or why you would think you're not a kick-ass woman no matter who you're dating," Ryan asks.

I wince. Cory's eyes widen in realization, while Logan suddenly looks furious. "You are not letting some asshole dictate who you are. Who the fuck is this guy?" Logan asks Ryan.

His eyes narrow when he declares with disgust, "her ex."

"I feel like you guys are ganging up on me," I accuse.

Ryan grins, "We are, but in a good way. You obviously need us to kick your ass, mentally that is."

I roll my eyes at my cousin and Cory crosses her arms over her chest, appearing determined. She asks, "I just want to know, do you want Brady or not?"

"I do, but," I begin.

She shakes her head to stop me from talking. "I don't need to hear anything else. You want to show everyone that you're strong and independent? You already did that by doing this fundraiser with Logan," she states.

"She's right," Logan agrees.

"You also moved up here without knowing anyone and started all over. Brady offered you a job because he thought you were talented," she reminds me.

Logan holds a finger up and adds, "I also offered her a job because she's smart, talented and she works hard to get the job done."

"So you've been offered two jobs," Cory amends. "Honestly with both offers, you kind of made your own way, which is not something someone does if they depend on someone else all the time. Plus, you can go toe to toe with someone like Jackie and come out the other side looking better than when it started." I open my mouth to argue, but she stops me. "I've seen you do that several times, so don't even try to deny it. That kind of confidence definitely doesn't communicate wallflower to me," she emphasizes.

"It's okay to lean on the people you love, Sam. That doesn't make you dependent on them," Ryan whispers, knowing me better than anyone. "I'm here anytime you need the support and you sure as hell better be there for me," he smirks, lightening the mood.

"We all will," Cory grins and Logan nods his head in affirmation.

Ryan leans further over the back of the couch and gives me a hug. He puts his mouth right next to my ear and whispers for only me to hear. "Don't isolate yourself anymore Sam. You can't love afraid you're about to lose it at any moment, but you can love hard, so you don't regret a single moment. Don't regret not fighting for him."

My heart aches for my mom and dad and I hold my cousin a little tighter. He's right. "How do you know me so well," I whisper back. "I didn't even realize," I whimper.

"I miss them too," he declares.

I lean back and wipe the tears off my cheeks. I take a deep, calming breath. I rub the pang in my chest like I can make it go away. I glance towards the wall connecting our apartment to Brady's. I realize he's probably the only one that can fill the hollow ache inside me and I'm pushing him away, instead of running towards him.

"Now what would a kick-ass woman do if she wanted her man back?" Cory asks with a grin. I chuckle, but don't answer right away. She rolls her eyes and adds, "We all know you want him back. So what the hell are you going to do about it?"

I look from Logan to Ryan and finally to Cory before I announce, "I'm going to fight for him." I watch the difference in their reactions to my statement. Cory squeals and claps her hands in excitement, Ryan nods in approval and Logan smiles in acceptance, but all three of them support me. "Thank you for the mental ass-kicking," I smirk.

"Do you guys mind if I have a minute with my cousin?" Ryan requests.

"I have to go anyway, I'll catch you guys later," Logan says and turns for the door.

"I'll come with you. I have a question for you," Cory informs Logan. Logan raises his eyebrows, curious. She waves her hand like it's no big deal. Then she gives me a quick hug and informs us, "I'll be back in a few minutes."

"Okay," Ryan responds for both of us. Then we watch her follow Logan out the door.

"So?" I prompt as soon as the door closes.

He looks at me and admits, "I just want you to know that I want you to do what makes you happy. It seems to me that you're making excuses and denying yourself for so many different reasons. If Brady makes you happy, then fight for him. If it doesn't work out with him, that's okay too. I'll be here. But your excuse that you need to prove you're strong and independent is bullshit and I think you know it too. You are not the same person you were after your parents died. Since you moved here, you have been all the things you want to be, whether you're with Brady or you're not. I'm telling you to fight for him because the difference I see when you're together is not you being dependent on him; it's you being happy again. Your mom and dad would want you to be happy. You deserve to be fucking happy, Sam," he emphasizes.

"So that's all I am?" I ask sassily.

He chuckles, "There she is, looking for compliments."

I grin, "Thanks, Ryan."

He nods and messes up my hair. I laugh and push him away. "So what are we doing about dinner?"

"It's only 3," I laugh.

He shrugs, "So."

Chapter 34

"Relax," Cory encourages, standing by my side.

I force a smile and look towards the stage. I haven't been able to see him all week. We've texted some, but he's been so busy with finals, that we haven't been able to get together to talk. He knows I want to talk, but I didn't want to text him what I was thinking and feeling. That's something I need to do to his face, no matter what he decides after I'm done spilling my guts. So now I'm standing on the bleachers at Camp Randall Stadium, waiting for Brady's name to be called, so he can walk across the stage to receive his Bachelor's degree. "He's not even going to know I'm here," I mumble.

"Then it's time for a selfie," she grins.

I look down at my white sundress. It angles down in a v between my breasts and has an eyelet hem. I glance at the shoulder straps and peek underneath for color. "I think I'm getting sunburned," I mumble.

"You're stalling. You look great," she compliments. I smile and she reaches for me and turns me around, holding her phone up in front of us. "Smile!" She snaps the shot and turns back around. "See, it's perfect," she declares, holding her phone out to me.

I glance at the picture. Cory's light blue and tan striped one-piece pantsuit brightens both our eyes. Our hair is blowing lightly in the wind. The black caps and gowns of the graduates, including some with red scarves and red and white cords, are obvious on the field behind us. She tags me on the picture, as well as Brady. Then she types, "Congratulations! #UWMadison #CollegeGrad." I groan nervously. She grins and taps the post button. "Done."

"Brady Williams," the announcer calls. My eyes flash up to the podium. Cory and I both stand and cheer wildly as he crosses the stage, shakes hands with the Dean and accepts his diploma. He searches the crowd as he walks back to his seat. He seems to pause in our general vicinity, causing my breath to catch, but I'm sure it's too packed for him to spot me. We watch as the commencement ends and the graduates toss their caps up in the air in celebration, the roar of the crowd almost deafening.

Cory takes my hand and gives me a light tug, encouraging me to follow her through the crowd. She's good at weaving through everyone and we reach the bottom easily. She links her arm through mine with a smile. I laugh and tell her, "Thanks. I probably would've still been stuck at the top."

"The benefits of being small and fierce," she grins.

I chuckle, then take a look around at all the people. "We're never going to find him in this crowd," I murmur.

"Yes, we will," she insists. She pulls out her phone and types something. Then she smiles wide as she looks around, before quickly tapping another message.

"Should we just go to the restaurant?" I question anxiously.

Cory shakes her head and holds up her phone, "Just wait. He'll find us. I just told him where we were."

"You're here," his deep voice acknowledges reverently.

Goosebumps spread over my skin and my stomach does a somersault, as the sound of his voice vibrates through my whole body. I turn around to find Brady grinning down at me, causing my heart to skip a beat. His dimple is so deep, I want to lean up and lick it, but instead I smile back. "I'm here," I murmur. "Congratulations!" I tell him.

"Thanks," he says, still smiling. He shifts back and forth on his feet. He sighs and mutters, "Fuck it." He steps forward, embracing me, before I have a chance to react. "I'm really glad you're here," he whispers.

My whole body heats from his words. I press my cheek against his chest and relax into him. I listen to the rapid beat of his heart and it calms my own. "Me too," I rasp.

"Are you coming to the restaurant?" he asks, without releasing me. I nod into his chest.

"Alright guys, this is just getting awkward for me, so I'm joining in," Cory announces. She throws her arms around both of us and squeezes us tightly. I burst out laughing. "Congratulations, Brady," she cheers.

Brady chuckles, "Thanks, Cory."

She lets go and happily announces, “Let’s go! We have a party to get to. Cody is meeting us there,” she informs Brady.

He nods and releases me and I reluctantly let go of him. “Ride with me,” he requests.

My eyes widen at his request. I glance over at Cory, “I came with Cory.”

She grins and insists, “It’s fine, Sam. I’ll meet you guys there. I have a stop to make before I get there anyway.”

“Okay,” I agree. “We’ll see you soon.”

Brady places his hand on the small of my back and guides me through the crowd. He’s stopped a few times on the way to his truck, but he only smiles and mumbles his congratulations, until we reach a tall guy with blonde hair falling into his eyes. “O,” he grins. He pats him on the back with one arm, keeping the other hand lightly touching me. He turns to me and proudly introduces me, “Owen, this is Samantha. Sam, this is a good friend of mine, Owen.”

I smile up at him, “It’s nice to meet you.”

“Damn, you weren’t kidding,” he mumbles.

I raise my eyebrows in question and Brady grins sheepishly. He offers me a shrug, before agreeing with his friend. “You know I wasn’t.”

“It’s really great to finally meet you. I’ve had to listen to him talk about you all semester and I was starting to wonder if his description of you was accurate,” he grins. I feel my face heat in embarrassment. Brady smacks him on the arm and Owen laughs. “I’m kidding.” Owen hears someone call his name and looks in the direction of the voice, before he glances back at us. “Congratulations, Man. I’ll catch you later.”

“Thanks, O, you too,” Brady calls after him. He glances back at me and insists, “Let’s get out of here before anyone else stops us.” He reaches for my hand and twines our fingers together. He smirks and tugs me easily through the crowd. We reach his truck and he drops my hand. He pulls my door open, swiftly lifting me into the truck. I revel in his gentle touch and don’t bother to argue. I bite my lower lip to hold back my moan as he releases me. He shuts the door for me and jogs around the front of the truck. I buckle my seatbelt and relax back into the seat.

He slips in behind the wheel with a quick glance at me. He starts the truck, pausing before he puts it into gear. He backs out slowly and pulls behind another truck before he repeats, "I'm really glad you came." I smile softly and he asks, "Can I ask what made you decide to come?" I open my mouth to respond, but snap it shut when I'm stuck with what to say. "It's going to be a longer ride than normal just getting out of this parking lot," he states. "We might as well talk. We both know we need to."

I nod and exhale slowly, "You're right."

He grins, "I like those words."

I laugh, feeling lighter already. "I came for me," I state.

His eyebrows draw together in confusion, making me laugh again. "Let me start over. I came because I wanted to be here with you for this moment, even if you didn't know I was here," I explain. The corner of his mouth twitches up and I huff another laugh. "I figured I wouldn't get a chance to really talk to you until after your party, so I'm not really ready. I'm messing this up. I'm sorry," I state and shake my head at myself.

"Don't apologize, Sam. You're not messing anything up," Brady encourages. "You're here," he repeats.

I blush and smile to myself. "Today is a big deal. I needed to be here," I reiterate. He smiles like he knows something I don't, but he doesn't say anything. I take a deep breath, hoping to calm my nerves swirling around in my stomach, before I continue. "You're important to me."

I notice him grimace slightly. Then he questions, "What do you mean by that?"

"Maybe if I start from the beginning," I mumble. "After my parents died, I just kind of went through the motions of living without moving forward. In fact, Ryan says I retreated from living at all. When everything happened with Paul and Taylor, I finally realized what I was doing to myself and I decided to do something about it. That's when I ended up here."

He smiles, "And when you met me."

I grin, "Yes, that's when I met you. But honestly Brady, it had been so long since I truly felt anything. I had been trying to keep myself numb for so long. Then you come along and all of a sudden I'm overwhelmed with all these feelings again. It was a lot to handle. Then you add the fact that I was dealing with how I feel about reading letters for the first time from my birth mom and meeting my birth father and his family."

He nods in understanding and grumbles, "And of course, one of them was Jackie."

I nod, "Yes, but beyond all of that, I still needed to figure out who I am and who I want to be. When I ran into Paul," I gulp down the lump in my throat, "he may have pushed my buttons, but he was right." I watch Brady grind his jaw and his fists tightly clench the wheel. "He was right because I needed to get myself straight so I could be as much for you as you are for me."

His head snaps over to me, before going back to the road. "You are more than I could ever want," he insists.

I smile, "I just mean, I needed that same confidence in myself. Plus, I did mean what I said about not wanting you to have any regrets in your decisions." He looks at me and opens his mouth to interrupt me, but I stop him. "I know everything you told me the other night and I believe you," I insist. "I'm glad you are where you want to be and doing what you want to do. Since I left college, I've been watching everyone else find a career path, but I didn't really think about any of that until I came here. You and Logan really helped me figure out what I want to do."

"And what's that?" he questions.

"Well I want to be an event planner and keep working on fundraisers as well as parties and other stuff," I admit, somewhat shyly.

Brady grins and asks playfully, "And does the other stuff include weddings, anniversaries and whatever I may be working on?"

I blush and concede, "It does. I'd love to help you at the restaurant if the offer still stands?" He nods his head and opens his mouth to respond, but I quickly interrupt him. "Before you answer that, I think you need to hear everything else I have to say." He nods in agreement. I take another deep breath and continue. "I realize at this point in my life, I could do something like this anywhere. Plus, I want to take some classes towards a degree in maybe communications, but I want to work while I do it."

"Okay," he says, dragging out the word like he's searching for the rest of it.

"I'm sorry I'm all over the place. I'm just a little nervous," I admit.

He reaches across the truck and places his hand on my bare knee. My breath hitches as he gives me a light squeeze in encouragement. "There's no reason to be nervous. No matter what you want, I'm with you," he states firmly.

He puts his hand back on the wheel and readjusts his grip as he finally pulls out of the parking lot. I watch his Adam's apple bob up and down as he gulps, while staring at the road in front of us. I bounce slightly in my seat, which pulls me back to our conversation. "Um, I guess I need to go back to where I started. I've been pushing everyone away for so long, but you have a way of making me want to pull you close. It's just, that scares the crap out of me," I confess. I take a deep breath to gather the courage to tell him how I really feel. "I'm afraid I'm going to end up losing you just like I lost my parents, or even Paul and Taylor, so sometimes I push you away, instead of doing what I really want. I know I messed up and I don't have it all figured out, but from now on, I'd rather try to figure it all out with you. And it's not just that it sucks when you're not around," I concede, enjoying the smirk that lights up his face, "but it's that you're everything to me Brady."

He suddenly pulls over to the side of the road and throws his truck in park. My eyes widen in shock as he unbuckles his seat belt and turns in his seat to look at me. "What did you just say?" he asks.

I look him in the eyes and sit a little taller, determined to get this right. "I said that you are everything to me. I came here searching for who I was and where I came from, but I ended up finding a home. And to clarify, I don't mean Chance, I mean you Brady. You're my home. Please, just give me another chance," I whisper.

He leans across the seat and weaves his fingers into my hair. He holds my head still and looks into my eyes. His gravelly voice questions, "Is that what you want?"

I offer him a hopeful smile. "I want it so much it hurts. I'm sorry I'm slow, but this is me fighting for you, fighting for us," I emphasize. "I want you. I want a chance to show you I'm not going anywhere, if you'll have me. I want to be able to show you how much I love you because I do love you."

His shoulders sag with relief and he declares, "I love you, Samantha." I begin to smile, but his lips crash into mine without warning. I loop my arms around his neck and he pushes his tongue into my mouth. I gasp with pleasure, my whole body instantly on fire. He attempts to pull me closer, but my seatbelt holds me back. I laugh as his lips fall from mine. "Damn thing," he grumbles.

I laugh louder and place my hand over his, "Brady, we can't miss your whole party," I remind him.

"Yes, we can," he insists.

I laugh and he kisses my neck, turning the sound into a desperate whimper. "We're on the side of the road," I prompt.

He groans in annoyance. "Fuck," he grumbles. He reaches for me and cradles my face in his hands. He looks into my eyes and slowly leans down. He softly presses his lips to mine, holding my gaze. Shivers spread throughout my body, while my heart pounds hard inside my chest. "No more backing down. No more hiding. This is us, fighting for each other. I won't ever stop," he declares. My heart tries to leap out of my chest, as he kisses me tenderly, before begrudgingly releasing me.

He moves back to his side of the truck and buckles his seat belt. "How long do we have to stay at this thing?" he grumbles. I giggle in response. He smiles and holds out his hand. I entwine my fingers through his, warmth filling me. He puts his truck in gear and pulls back onto the road.

Chapter 35

Brady

I follow Samantha into her bedroom and shut the door behind me. She slips off her heels and asks, "Do you want something to drink?" I shake my head and take a slow step towards her, my gaze dragging down her body and back up. "You didn't let go of my hand the whole night. I think my fingers are numb," she teases, wiggling her fingers at me. I shrug like its no big deal, but I didn't want to let her out of my site. "For a minute I thought you were going to follow me into the women's bathroom," she adds with a smirk.

I chuckle, "I would've if I could've gotten away with it. I wasn't about to let go of you, when I just got you back. It's been too damn long," I complain. "I missed you."

"I missed you, too," she whispers. She presses her lips tightly together and I take another step towards her. She looks up at me and I see a flash of worry in her eyes. "Is it really this simple?" she asks.

"What do you mean?" I ask for clarification.

"I mean, do you really forgive me, Brady?" she questions so softly I almost don't hear her.

I take the last step towards her and cradle her face in my hands. I press my lips to hers because I can't help myself, but I quickly pull back and look into her eyes. I need to push all her doubts away. "I have no reason to forgive you because you didn't do anything wrong." I notice the skepticism in her look and I place another kiss on her lips and let my hands slide down her arms to her hands. I give her hands an encouraging squeeze. I request, "Let me hold you while we talk?"

She smiles and agrees, "Okay, but first I have something for you."

"You do?" I ask surprised.

She grins, "Yeah. I had to get you a graduation gift." I nod and grudgingly let go of her hands. I watch as she pulls a flat red and white wrapped package out of her nightstand and hands it to me. "This is the first one."

"The first?" I question.

"Just open it," she encourages.

I tear into it and smile at the black frame holding a picture of us. It's a close up of us looking at each other, but the love between us is obvious and it makes my breath catch. "Where did you get this? I've never even seen it," I tell her.

She shrugs, "I guess Cory took it one time when we were all hanging out, but I really love it."

"So do I," I murmur. "Thank you." I lean towards her, intending to kiss her, but she jumps out of my reach and practically bounces over to her closet.

"I couldn't wrap this one, so close your eyes," she instructs.

I chuckle and do as she says. I hear her moving around for a minute, before she finally says, "Okay, you can open them."

I open my eyes and my jaw drops. Leaning against Sam's legs, sits a large framed colored drawing of our barn, with the tree house off to the side. "This is amazing," I tell her and step forward to admire it.

"I know it doesn't look exactly like the reality, but I wanted the tree house to be in it too," she explains. "I asked Logan to do it for me," she divulges.

I huff a laugh, wondering if this is his apology for kissing Sam, but I don't care. "I love that you thought of something like this. We'll have to come up with the perfect place to hang it. Thank you," I say, grateful. I set the picture against the wall and take both of her hands in mine. "Thank you," I repeat and gently press my lips to her.

I let go of one of her hands and she sits down on her bed. I kick off my shoes and let go of her hand as I crawl over her, urging her to lie down. I smirk, holding my body over hers, her hair spread out in waves behind her. I lean down and brush my lips over hers. If I do anything more, I'll never get through this conversation. I groan and drop myself to her side. She scoots herself all the way up on her bed and I move myself to eye level. I lie on my side and let my hand fall onto her hip, rolling her slightly towards me. "Perfect," I mumble. She blushes, reminding me I need to start talking.

"So," she prompts. "You were going to tell me why you don't have to forgive me. This all seems so easy to be back in your arms."

I tuck a lock of hair behind her ear and explain. "That's because it is easy," I insist. "Honestly, I hated that you weren't there with me when I was ready for all of it, but I didn't blame you for it. You've been through so much in the last couple years and if you think about it, it's been a whirlwind since we met." I remind her, "New town, new apartment, new roommate, new friends," I trail off and begin playing with her hair as I let my head drop to my bicep. "I count myself lucky that I got to know your birth mom with you through the letters. Even the first time you read them, I was happy just to be there, but I can only imagine how much that put on you," I tell her honestly. "Then finding your birth father, meeting his family that you knew nothing about and trying to figure out where you fit in. Besides the fact that you're also deciding what you want to do with your life. I tried not to push you, but I fucking loved your ideas about the barn and for the wedding. I would've lost that couple as clients if it weren't for you," I insist. "Let alone, you expanded my family business and made it better without any effort on your part. You did it by just being you," I emphasize.

She blushes again, making me smile. "Damn you're beautiful," I mumble.

"Brady," she admonishes.

I chuckle as her face turns a deeper shade of red. I remind myself what I was saying, hoping to quickly finish this conversation. "Then when you took on the cystic fibrosis fundraiser with Logan, you got this look of determination in your eyes. I knew you would do an incredible job. I was just jealous that Logan got to spend so much time with you. Plus, he was doing something with you that obviously meant a lot to you. I just wished it were me, instead of Logan," I divulge. "I don't even know where to begin with your ex. That guy is such an asshole," I grumble. I shake my head in annoyance just thinking about him.

She giggles, "I think we can both agree that he's an asshole. You don't have to remind me."

I chuckle and continue running my fingers through her hair. "My point is, you've been dealing with more shit than most people do over their lifetime." She arches her eyebrows with doubt, but I push forward. "You had all of this happen in a matter of a few months. Maybe it's because of all of that, but I feel like I've known you for years when I think about everything. I don't know if I can really remember my life before you. I can tell you that it was nothing compared to having you in it."

"Brady," she says reverently.

My heart skips a beat and I clear my throat, forging ahead. "I can't be mad at you because you had more shit thrown at you than any one person should have to handle in such a short time. Maybe I had to remind myself of that from time to time, but I've known what I want and that's you. I don't have any doubts. I've just been impatiently waiting for you to get there too," I smirk.

She laughs, "Impatiently, huh?"

I grin and nod my head, "Yeah. I want to go through everything with you Sam; the good, the bad, and the bullshit. It is that simple," I emphasize.

She scoots closer, her sweet breath mixing with mine. "I want that too, Brady," she whispers. "Thank you for waiting for me."

My breath catches and I rasp, "I'd wait as long as I needed to, but I don't want to wait anymore."

Her breath comes faster and she declares, "I love you, so much."

I exhale slowly, feeling as if a weight is falling the rest of the way off my shoulders. "I love you too, Sam."

I pull her to me, not able to stay away from her for another second. My whole body ignites as I cover her soft lips with mine. She sighs into my mouth and my tongue pushes in, tangling with hers. "I missed how sweet you taste," I mumble between kisses. She moans in response, tangling her fingers into my hair. She bends her leg and hooks it behind me, pushing my hard length against her warm center. "Fuck," I grumble. I reach back and grab her leg, pulling it back down. "I'll be done for, slow down," I plead. "I want to make love to you," I declare desperately.

She whimpers, "Please." She sits up and pulls her dress over her head.

My eyes dilate at the view of her in a white, lacy bra and pantie set. I try to control my breathing. I feel myself becoming painfully rock hard, as I take her all in. "How did I get so lucky?" I murmur. I reach towards her and let my fingers graze down her side from her shoulder to her panties. My fingers instinctively move towards her center, when she begins to unbutton my shirt. I lean back and swiftly unbutton the rest of the shirt and toss it on the floor, before I pull my undershirt over my head with one hand and toss it onto the floor as well.

She smiles, taking my breath away, as her fingers start tracing the lines in my stomach. "I'm the lucky one she murmurs.

I laugh and flip her onto the bed. I kiss her, loving the feel of her bare skin on mine, but it's not enough. My whole body ignites as I slowly press kisses from her mouth, along her jawline, and down her neck, loving the goose bumps trailing behind each kiss. I push her bra strap off her shoulder and continue my trail of kisses. She arches into me with a soft moan. My hand grazes over her breast as I reach for the front clasp of her bra, flicking it open. I push her bra aside, replacing the material with my hand and then my mouth, as I release the other side. I gently suck her breast into my mouth. Her nipple instantly hardens and I flick it with my tongue, torturing us both. I release it with a pop, moving to the other side to do the same thing.

She pulls my hair gently and then runs her hands along my shoulders, tugging me upwards. I lift my head to find her eyes hooded and filled with an intense desire that I know matches my own. I slide up and tilt my head, molding our mouths perfectly together and let them move in a rhythm all their own. I kiss, lick and suck, letting myself be consumed by her. I groan as my hand trails back down her side to her inner thigh. I run my knuckles over her core, feeling her heat pulling me in. I slip a finger underneath, her wetness coating my finger with a quick pass over her folds. She gasps, "Brady, I need you."

I push away in an attempt to control myself. I kick off my black pants. Then I curl my fingers in the sides of her panties and easily tug them off. I crawl back over her and she looks at me in confusion. "You forgot something," she insists.

I shake my head, my lips twitching upwards. "No, I didn't. I need a minute to make you come first."

"I want to come with you inside me," she tells me softly, her cheeks flushed beautifully.

My heart thunders in my chest at her words. I rasp, "You will." I drop my forehead to hers and express, "I need to show you just a little bit of how much I cherish you."

Her eyes sparkle and turn a little more golden, just before I kiss her. My tongue pushes in, searching playfully, until her head falls back, as she gasps for breath. My mouth moves to her breasts as my fingers slide over her entrance. I feel her taut nipple against my tongue and suck gently as I easily push two fingers inside. She gasps and clings to me, letting me know she's already close. I move my thumb to circle her clit and slide my fingers in and out, curling them in. I nibble lightly on her nipple as I continue to work her body and push her over the edge. She arches into me, her insides throbbing around my fingers as she whimpers my name, "Brady."

I lift my head to watch her face as I help her through her orgasm. She sighs and opens her eyes, meeting my gaze with a shy smile. "Damn, you're gorgeous," I tell her, needing her to know.

She blushes and reaches down, running her hand firmly against my hard length. I groan and push up. I kick off my boxer-briefs and smile as her eyes widen. I pull a condom wrapper out of my pants and tear it open, quickly rolling it on. I crawl over her and hover at her entrance. "Are you okay?" I ask her.

She grins, "I'm fantastic!"

I chuckle and rephrase my question. "Are you ready for me?"

Instead of directly answering she prods, "Make love to me, Brady."

I feel like a shot of adrenaline shoots through me and I can't wait another second. I push inside of her to the hilt, in one swift movement. She gasps and I groan enjoying the feel of her hot wet walls encompassing me. I hold her tightly as our bodies adjust to one another. I look into her eyes and hold her gaze, opening myself up to her. "Sam," I rasp, as I slowly begin to move. Her hands slide up and down my arms and back as I move in and out of her, never taking my eyes away from her for a second. As our breathing picks up, I slip my hand between us to find her clit, and begin rubbing circles there. We pick up our pace and her hands stop exploring, stopping on my biceps and holding on tightly. I hold her gaze until her head falls back in ecstasy. Her insides clamp on to me over and over again. White-hot electricity shoots through me, clouding my vision, as my own orgasm takes me over. I pump into her hard and stop with my release. I exhale and slow, before I collapse partially on top of her with a groan.

We slowly catch our breaths and I open my eyes to look at her. She gives me a smile that tugs at my heart, pulling the corners of my own mouth up. I lean in and press my lips to hers. "I love you. Don't move," I demand.

She giggles as I push off the bed. I remove the condom and tie it off before I toss it in the garbage can. Then I pull on my underwear and my black pants, since her roommate is here somewhere. I walk out the door and into the bathroom. I turn on the water to let it warm up, while I pull out a clean washcloth. I wet the cloth with the warm water and turn the water off before returning to Samantha's room and quickly closing the door behind me. "Thanks," she says as she reaches for the cloth.

"Let me," I insist. I gently wipe the cloth along the insides of her legs and over her folds. She gulps hard, making me smirk.

"I'm good. Thank you," she says, as she backs away, making me chuckle.

I toss the cloth towards her laundry basket, but keep my eyes pinned to her. "You're not getting away from me this time," I tell her.

"I don't want to," she claims, filling my chest.

"I was lost without you, you know," I mumble, tucking a lock of hair behind her ear. I lie down, facing her, and pull her close to me. "It's like I didn't have a home."

"I know what you mean. I felt that way too," she discloses.

"You're my home, Samantha," I whisper and kiss her tenderly.

She smiles, making my heart skip a beat, "And you're mine, Brady. You're the home I didn't realize I was even looking for. I love you."

"I love you," I declare, my heartbeat erratic. I kiss her again, never wanting to let her go.

Epilogue

Samantha

One month later…

I stand outside in the gravel parking lot and stare up at the large red and white, freshly painted barn. It looks exactly the same from the outside, except for the larger gravel parking lot to accommodate guests. Brady steps up next to me and entwines his fingers with mine. "It looks wonderful," I declare.

He steps in front of me and grins, "You look wonderful, but you're right. This place does look good."

I giggle, "Such a charmer."

"With you," he smirks. Then he tilts his head down towards me and gently brushes his lips across mine. I sigh, as he reluctantly pulls away. "Are you ready to check it out?" he asks.

I pinch my lips together, feigning nonchalance. "Do I have to?" I grumble.

He chuckles and plays along. "If you don't want to see the new barn, we can just go out to dinner now," he suggests.

"We're here, we might as well check it out," I propose, grinning.

He chuckles and gives my hand a slight tug, pulling me close. He wraps his arm around me, the gesture causing me to feel safe and warm. "This project is because of you, you know," he reminds me. "You should at least see it." He kisses the top of my head and insists, "In fact, I should be thanking you."

"You're welcome," I smile up at him. "Okay, let's go," I concede.

"This way," he says, guiding me to the left of the large, sliding barn doors.

I notice a normal sized door with a smaller black iron handle. "I didn't even see that!" I exclaim.

"It's so we don't have to open the huge barn doors, unless we want to," he explains.

He pulls the door open with his free hand and we walk inside together. I barely take in the sealed oak, chestnut and pine wood floors before shouts come from all around the room. "Happy Birthday, Samantha!"

I startle and laugh at myself, "Oh my God, that scared me." Brady chuckles and I smack him playfully in the stomach. "What did you do?" I ask in awe.

He shrugs, "You have a lot of people that want you to know how special you are. What better way to do that than to throw you a surprise birthday party?"

I feel my face heat and my eyes well with tears, causing his face to become blurry. He reaches up and quickly wipes my tears away. I look into his eyes, my heart aching with love for him. "I love you," I rasp.

He smiles and whispers, "I love you too, Samantha." Then he leans down and lightly brushes his lips across mine in a soft kiss.

"You guys can do that later. I want to give her a hug," Cory calls, from right behind me.

I laugh as Brady pulls away. I turn towards my roommate and I'm instantly wrapped in her arms. "Happy Birthday!"

I laugh, "Thank you."

She releases me and looks at Brady. "You did good," she compliments. He smiles in acknowledgement.

I take a moment to scan the small crowd. Cody stands just behind Cory talking with Olive. Brady's parents wave, before they disappear behind a newly erected wall, directly across from where we entered. Becca is talking to the DJ, set-up right in front of the wall, just before a song by The Fray blasts through the speakers. In front of the DJ in the middle of the barn is a large, slightly raised dance floor. "I knew you were going to take out the back door, but what all did you put back there?" I ask in amazement.

"I'll show it to you later, but we put in a small galley for last minute food prep, another open area for other kinds of prep, like flower deliveries, a couple dressing rooms, a small locker room for staff, a bathroom and a small storage area," he informs me.

"Wow!" I exclaim, suddenly wrapped in Cody's arms.

"Happy Birthday!" he says.

I peer over his shoulder to the rest of the room and can't help but notice the large round tables scattered to my right, each with a fishbowl vase of colorful daisy-like flowers. "You can put her down now," Brady grumbles.

I giggle as Cody sets me down. He clasps Brady on the shoulder and grins broadly. "You better get used to it brother, everyone is going to want a piece of her tonight." Brady glares at Cody and he responds by clapping him on the back. "You know what I mean," he laughs. "Relax. Have fun. It's your girlfriend's birthday," he jokes.

Brady chuckles and shakes his head at Cody. I notice Ryan striding for us and turn from my friends to meet him halfway. He hugs me and whispers in my ear, "Happy Birthday, Cuz."

I fall back on my heels and gasp as Uncle Tim and Aunt Bea pop up behind him. I throw my arms around them both at the same time, both of them hugging me back. "Happy Birthday," they say in unison.

"I'm so happy to see you!" I exclaim.

"We're happy to see you too, kid," Uncle Tim replies. I release them and take a step back, grinning wide.

"You look beautiful, Samantha," Aunt Bea compliments me. I glance down at my simple violet dress, with spaghetti straps. I love the way it flares out at the bottom. "Your mom always said this was one of your colors and she was right," she recalls.

I smile, knowing it's the same reason I wanted to wear this dress. It's a small way of feeling like she's close for my birthday. Warmth spreads quickly in my chest. "I remember," I murmur.

"They'd be really proud of you," Uncle Tim says and Aunt Bea nods in agreement.

Lincoln steps up to all of us. He requests, "Excuse me, do you mind if we say Happy Birthday to Samantha?"

"Of course," Uncle Tim mumbles, staring at Lincoln.

I give him and Ginny a quick hug. Then I clear my throat and introduce them, "Um, Uncle Tim, Aunt Bea, Ryan, this is Lincoln and his wife Ginny."

"Your family?" Lincoln questions. He smiles wide and holds out his hand, "It's an honor to meet all of you. I'm sorry I can't say this to Samantha's parents, but thank you," he states, his voice catching.

They continue their introductions and I resume searching the room. "Is Frankie here?" I ask, wanting to step away.

Ginny smiles, "Yes, he was eyeing the food a little while ago. Jackie is with him," she informs me.

My eyes widen in surprise. "Thanks," I mumble. Brady's arm falls onto my shoulders and I smile to myself. He always knows when I need a little more. He kisses me on the top of my head and slides his arm down, clasping my hand.

We weave through a couple tables and find Logan and Seth sitting down near the picture I gave Brady for graduation. "There she is," Seth grins and stands. He reaches me in two steps and wraps his arms around me. He lifts me up and immediately sets me back on my feet. "Happy Birthday," he grins.

"Thanks. Looks like you guys have the best table," I nod towards the picture.

Seth smirks, "Yeah, far away from the dance floor."

Brady and I both laugh, just as Logan stands and approaches us. He gives himself a slight shake before he hugs me, lifting my feet off the ground. "Happy Birthday," he rasps. Brady clears his throat behind us. Logan chuckles and sets me back on my feet. "It feels like my birthday seeing that on the wall," he admits.

"You've seen your work at different places before," I reply, confused.

He nods slowly, "Not like that. Sure, flyers or posters I've made, but never a framed picture on anyone's wall except my family's," he concedes. He looks at Brady, "Thanks."

He nods, "It's where it should be." Then he smirks and mumbles under his breath, "Just like Sam." Logan chuckles and I elbow Brady in the stomach. "Oof," he groans.

"What he meant to say," I grin, "is he loves it. You're really talented."

Brady chuckles, "What she said." I roll my eyes.

"Anyway," Logan begins, changing the subject, "I got you a little something as both a birthday present and a thank you."

"You didn't have to do that," I respond honestly.

He smiles appreciatively, "I wanted to. Deal with it." I feel myself blush and he adds, "Besides, I'm not the only one. He gestures to a table in the corner filled with colorfully wrapped gifts and my eyes widen in surprise.

"Sam?" Brady prods, giving my hand a light squeeze. "Look who just walked in."

I glance towards the front of the room and immediately spot the now familiar older man with salt and pepper hair, looking quite anxious. "Let's go say Hi," I request. "We'll catch up with you guys in a bit," I tell Logan and Seth as I turn for the door.

Jeremy sees us and smiles shyly. "Happy Birthday, Samantha. I put something together for you," he blurts out awkwardly. "I'm sorry, I'm nervous," he explains. I shake my head, indicating it's no big deal, but I can't speak. Instead, I stare at the pink photo album, embossed in gold with my birthday, June 12th. He holds the book out to me and I slowly reach out to take it, with shaky hands. "It's pictures and some memorabilia I think Catherine would want you to have. I guess it's another way of getting to know her and maybe help you know where you came from a little more too." I pull it to my chest and grasp it tightly. I feel Brady's arm wrap around my shoulders and pull me in close. "I'm sorry, maybe this wasn't the right thing to do," he stammers.

"No!" I exclaim, releasing the breath I didn't know I was holding. I look up at him, tears welling in my eyes. "This is perfect. Thank you," I rasp.

I watch his shoulders relax as he exhales slowly. "Good, good," he mumbles. "After you take a look, you're welcome to call me. You can ask me anything you'd like and I'll do my best to answer," he offers.

"Thank you. You will be hearing from me," I tell him softly. I suddenly spin towards Brady and ask, "Can we go put this in your truck? I don't want anything to happen to it."

"Of course. I can do it for you," he suggests.

I shake my head and insist, "No, I'm coming with you."

Brady's hand falls to the small of my back. He guides me out the door and to his truck. I stop in front of his door and he opens it for me. When I don't move he grips my waist and turns me around. He gently cradles my face in his hands and angles my head up until I meet his gaze. "Do you want to go home?" he asks, surprising me.

My eyebrows draw together in confusion and I remind him, "There's a party going on inside, apparently for me."

He chuckles. "Yeah, but it's your birthday. You get to do whatever you want."

"Really?" I smirk.

"Really," he affirms. He kisses me on the lips, punctuating his statement. "Everyone is here for you, if you want to leave, we go. They would understand," he emphasizes.

I nod and take a deep breath, exhaling slowly. I turn and place the book on the seat of his truck before turning back to him. "I want to go inside and dance with you. You promised me the first dance when this was all done," I remind him.

He grins, "Yes, I did."

I shrug and smile up at him, "Well I want to dance." He releases me and slams the door of his truck. We walk back inside, hand in hand and straight to the dance floor. The last few measures of "You Look Wonderful Tonight" by Eric Clapton play as he wraps his hands around my waist and mine curl around his neck.

"Happy Birthday, Samantha," Brady grins between songs.

I smile up at him as the first few notes of Adele's version of "Make You Feel My Love" echoes through the barn. "I can't believe you did all this for me."

"Why not?" he questions, making me giggle.

"I just mean, when I think about everything you've done, everything you do for me," I shake my head in awe, "it just amazes me. You amaze me, Brady," I emphasize.

He drops his forehead to mine and whispers, "It's not hard to do anything for you, Samantha. I love you more than I could ever express, but I'm sure as hell going to keep trying." I gulp over the lump in my throat and he continues. "I'm going to do everything in my power to keep proving how much I love you over and over again."

I exhale a shaky breath. My heart feels so full I think it might burst. "I want to do the same for you, Brady. I love you so much. Thank you for helping me find my home," I rasp. I push up on my toes and press my lips to his. Electricity shoots through my veins, instantly heating me, all the way to my toes. I fall back on my heels, breathless. "How long do we have to stay again?" I rasp.

Brady's head falls back in laughter and I swear I can feel the sound all the way to my soul. He pulls his head back and drops it to my forehead. He whispers, "As long as I'm with you, Samantha, I'm already home."

The End

Acknowledgements

Thank you hardly seems to be adequate. The first thank you has to be to my husband and two kids. I greatly appreciate your constant support and encouragement. I love you all and I'm grateful for all of you! I want to thank my friends and family for being there and sharing my world with me, both fictional and real. Every comment, every question, every text, every post, every review and every share means so much to me. I need each one of you to know how important you are to me. Kelley and Nancy need their own thank you for everything they do. I cherish both of you and count myself lucky to have you in my life. Also, thank you to all my other Beta readers for your input and reviews. I value each and every one of you.

Thank you to Violette Wicik of Violette Wicik Photography for again creating a beautiful cover photo to fit the story. Thank you to your beautiful model on both covers. She's been a perfect portrayal of Samantha. I really enjoyed working with you on both of the covers and I'm looking forward to the next opportunity I will have to work with you. I admire your work and I'm more than thrilled we were able to work together for my Home Duet. https://www.violettewicik.com/

This Duet was tough for me because it hits home in so many ways. As you may have read previously, I'm adopted like my main character Samantha. Due to my own history, many times I feel like I'm going on the numerous ups and downs along with her. I do want to emphasize that every single story is different and my story is nothing like Samantha's. I am grateful for my own story and experiences. Although completely different, my story did help shape Samantha and everything she went through. Most of all thank you to my mom and dad and my sister, as well as my birth family. Without all of you, this story would never have been created.

Connect with Nikki A Lamers

Official Author Website
www.nikkialamers.com

Author Facebook Page
www.facebook.com/pg/NikkiALamersAuthor

Follow Me on Instagram
@NikkialamersAuthor

Author Goodreads Page
www.goodreads.com/author/show/8451774.Nikki_A_Lamers

Amazon Author Page
https://www.amazon.com/Nikki-A.-Lamers/e/B00NU1VU8M

Made in United States
North Haven, CT
22 November 2022

27115030R00164